KAY L. MOODY

CURSE &

CRYSTAL THORNS

FAE AND CRYSTAL THORNS 4

Curse & Crystal Thorns
Fae and Crystal Thorns, #4
By Kay L. Moody

Published by Marten Press
3731 W 10400 S Ste 102, #205
South Jordan, UT 84009

www.MartenPress.com

Cover by Angel Leya
Edited by Deborah Spencer and Justin Greer

ISBN: 978-1-954335-27-1

ALSO BY KAY L. MOODY

Fae and Crystal Thorns

Flame & Crystal Thorns
Shadow & Crystal Thorns
Blade & Crystal Thorns
Curse & Crystal Thorns
Wrath & Crystal Thorns
Standalone: Nutcracker of Crystalfall

The Fae of Bitter Thorn

Heir of Bitter Thorn
Court of Bitter Thorn
Castle of Bitter Thorn
Crown of Bitter Thorn
Queen of Bitter Thorn

The Elements of Kamdaria

The Elements of the Crown
The Elements of the Gate
The Elements of the Storm

Truth Seer Trilogy

Truth Seer
Healer
Truth Changer

Visit **kaylmoody.com/beauty** to download a bonus story,
Bargain of Power and Beauty, for free.

CRYSTALFALL
Amberglow Marshes
Mushroom Patch
Emerald Lake
Diamond Isles
Gilded Labyrinth
Celestine Meadow
Forest of the Wraiths
Gemfields
Rubyrise Mountains
Crystalfall Castle
Goldvein Mountains
Lifespark Tree
Pixie Grove
Mortals Camp
Valley of Beryl
Sapphire Falls
Crystals Caves

1

THE PROTECTIVE ENCHANTMENT HAD BEEN broken through by the enemy mortals. Chloe's muscles seized, locking her shivering limbs tight until she was unable to move. Her mind still whirred, but the rest of her body had been taken over by dread. Stuck inside the stone vault that had once belonged to the king of Crystalfall, she, Quintus, Mishti, and Ludo had no chance of escape.

The room wouldn't allow a Faerie door to be opened. Quintus still didn't have his magic back. They had only just learned that Quintus's father—the king of Crystalfall—was still alive, but they couldn't do anything with that knowledge since the mortals who were breaking in had murder on their minds.

Did they have any chance of escape? Any at all?

With a heart beating as fast as a spinning top, Chloe had difficulty forcing words from her mouth. She managed to eke out a short sentence just as the vault door got pushed open a small fraction more. "Ludo, what do you think we should do?"

Mishti raised her eyebrow at the question. She glanced at Ludo, then at Chloe, probably wondering why she had asked *him*.

Quintus pinched his eyebrows together, dropping his mouth to a frown as he also glanced from her to Ludo. He wasn't talking to her much anyway, so he had no reason to be offended she had asked for Ludo's opinion instead of his. Just then, she noticed he still had the golden and emerald crown of Crystalfall in one hand.

Sucking in a sharp inhale, Chloe gestured toward his pocket. "Hide that."

His expression froze as only his eyes moved, opening wider. In his next breath, the crown got stuffed into his pocket where the enemy mortals wouldn't see it.

She turned to Ludo expectantly.

Mishti appeared confused and Quintus offended that Ludo had been asked for advice first, but Ludo just looked surprised. He opened his mouth slightly, turning his gaze to his hands, as if they might have the answer.

In truth, the Fairfrost fae didn't usually come up with the best suggestions during a crisis, *but* he did have one talent she needed desperately right now. He had a knack for pinpointing the worst-case scenario. If she could identify that early on, then hopefully she could overcome it early on too.

"We should…" His voice faltered when the vault door opened just enough to fit the shoulder and hip of a mortal. The four of them collectively sucked in a breath at the sight.

That same mortal's head would come through the vault door next. Ludo shook his head and then dropped it dramatically into one hand. "We should surrender. Quintus has no magic, and I cannot even open a door to rescue us."

Chloe nodded. "Okay, so the mortals are going to kill us unless we can open a door. Good to know."

The fear shimmering in Ludo's blue-and-red eyes paused long enough for him to narrow his eyes. "I did not say that."

She waved him off. "Yes, you did. You just did it in your grumpy Ludo way. Even more important, it gave me an idea." She pulled the others close and whispered to them just as the enemy mortal forced his way through the vault door.

Soon, a golden-haired mortal stepped into the vault. Julian. One of the enemy mortals' leaders had joined them, and another mortal scrambled in after him. Julian hurled a dagger, which spun toward them. It would have landed right in Quintus's throat, except he snatched it by its hilt mid-air using nothing but his bare hand and his fae reflexes.

"That was foolish," Quintus said pointedly. "Now I have a weapon."

In a flash, the same dagger soared through the air, candlelight glinting off its surface, until it landed with a squelch deep in Julian's chest. If it were any other mortal, Chloe would have written him off as dead. But since it was Julian, she had a feeling even that wouldn't finish him off completely.

Judging by how his knees hit the stone floor and how he dropped in a weak slump, he probably had no strength for the rest of this fight, at least.

More mortals spilled into the room, but it didn't matter, because now Chloe and her friends had a plan. With one last look between the four of them, they all sprinted off toward their different tasks.

Quintus zoomed toward a wall where a large piece of parchment depicting complex formulas and magical symbols covered the stone. He ripped the paper away and rolled it up so tight it nearly had the resilience of a spear.

As he worked, Mishti ran for the opposite end of the room, gathering glass jars and vials into her midnight blue tunic.

Ludo threw barrier enchantments and blasts of magic from his fingertips, hitting anyone who dared get close enough to him up against a wall. Slowly, Chloe and Ludo inched closer and closer to the door.

The opening still only barely fit two people at a time. That made it easier to fend off attacks when only two could enter at once.

But now, Quintus had finished preparing his spear made of parchment. He thrust open the vault door, allowing light and a soft breeze to enter the stone room. When a group of enemy mortals tried to charge into the vault, Quintus lifted his rolled-up parchment.

He swept the spear-like object across the mortals' stomachs, throwing them to the ground. They dropped at once, as if they were nothing more than thin weeds being barreled over by a branch. Another wave of enemy mortals charged toward him. He easily threw them to the ground using the same technique.

Of course, this had been Chloe's plan. She had suggested he do exactly what he did now, but seeing it happen caused her lips to twitch with a smile. Only Quintus would be capable of turning a piece of parchment into a formidable weapon.

By now, Mishti had finished gathering her jars and vials. She darted outside the vault and chucked the glass objects at enemies. Many of the glass objects were delicate enough that they shattered into tiny pieces as soon as they made contact with an enemy's shoulder or stomach.

Hopefully, the attacks from Mishti would seem random to the mortals. In truth, Mishti cleared a very specific path.

Just as Chloe and Ludo reached the door to the vault, a strained grunt caught their attention.

Julian coughed, sending a splatter of blood onto the chest of his cream tunic. A metallic scent filled the air while he caught his breath. He glared at her and Ludo and then glanced down at the dagger buried in his chest.

Chloe could see the thought in his mind. If he tore the dagger from his chest, he could use it against her. Ludo stood nearby, but even a fae like him didn't have the reflexes Quintus had. If Julian used that weapon now, he'd probably succeed at injuring either one of them.

She hoped he would.

Not that she had a death wish. As much as she hoped he'd use his weapon, she also hoped she'd be fast enough to dodge it. But as an apothecary, she knew what she hoped Julian did not know. If he removed that weapon from his chest, he'd bleed out in only a few seconds. If he tried to use his weapon, it would kill him.

Unfortunately, he must have known the same thing because he turned away from the dagger and looked Chloe straight in the eye. "Where is it?" Blood dripped off his chin, staining more of his cream tunic.

Her limbs shook harder than ever. Breathing became impossible, which made speaking even worse. Still, she managed to let out a single word. "What?"

His eyes narrowed. "The piece that was hidden here. Did you find it?"

She swallowed hard as her stomach twisted into a spiky knot. They still weren't sure how much Julian knew about the pieces and the crown of Crystalfall, but his question suggested he knew too much. Maybe he knew everything.

Amidst her silence, his gaze flitted down to her finger. The golden and emerald ring from Quintus had once belonged there, but it was gone now. Quintus had used it to re-create the crown of Crystalfall.

Seeing her finger bare, Julian scowled. "You found all the pieces then?" He coughed, sending another smattering of blood across his shirt. "Where are they?"

"Chloe, now!" Mishti's shout rang out, piercing Chloe right in the chest.

She couldn't afford to get distracted. Not now.

But how could she complete the rest of the plan when Julian knew far too much?

Ludo grabbed her by the shoulders and shoved her toward the vault door. "Get out of here. You can call your dragon to you, right?"

Her knees knocked together as she attempted to move forward. Each step faltered, making it difficult to follow the path Mishti had cleared for her.

Once she stepped into the sunlight, Mishti called out again. "You have to get those pieces out of here, Chloe. We'll hold them back. You just go."

Chloe tried to take normal steps. Well, at least somewhat normal steps. Her voice trembled as she called out weakly. "Shadow?"

She glanced up at the sky, still moving down the path Mishti had cleared for her. Chloe moved slowly, haphazardly. The skies remained clear, showing no sign of her dragon.

The enemy mortals watched her at first, but not for long. Soon, they closed in around her. It didn't even take much effort. Her knees shook too much for her to run away properly. Even if she hadn't been afraid, she'd never been that fast a runner.

Glancing over her shoulder, she noted how most of the mortals came toward her, but some of them continued to focus on Quintus, Mishti, and Ludo.

That changed when Julian crawled on his arms out of the vault and pointed a finger. "Get. Her."

Every mortal immediately changed course until all of them focused on Chloe. Weapons rose and tilted toward her. She tried to keep running, but two enemy mortals jumped out in front of her blocking the path.

Blinking rapidly, she tried to step to the side and start down a new path. At the last moment, she remembered to glance back into the sky. Her eyes narrowed, as if searching. As before, the skies remained clear.

The first arms reached for her now. They grabbed her elbows, her forearms, her wrists. She'd given up on breathing, but even this caused her to gasp.

And all the enemy mortals around her looked so pleased with themselves. Somehow, they all thought they had won.

But it would have been truly foolish of her to hinge an entire operation on *her* being the one to get away. Everyone knew she got too scared and couldn't run properly. She did, however, make the perfect bait.

And every single enemy mortal had fallen for the trick.

"Got it."

Ludo's voice rang out, loud enough for the mortals to hear. They would soon see he had stepped outside the vault, allowing him to open a door. They would know Chloe had tricked them all.

But she'd delay that moment as long as possible.

"Shadow, please." Her voice quivered and whimpered, and she didn't even have to fake it. With all those weapons and enemies surrounding her, terror truly gripped her heart. She hadn't actually called to her dragon though. Through her bond, she could tell Shadow was happily hunting deep in the Court of Fairfrost.

Another mortal gripped her around the stomach, but his arm got ripped away almost as fast. Quintus had reached them. His jaw clenched tight as he used his spear-like parchment to sweep away the mortals surrounding Chloe. When anyone tried to touch her, he used his other hand to forcefully yank that person away.

Soon, he had her in his arms, and he charged toward the door Ludo had opened. The enemy mortals spent more time trying to figure out what had just happened than they did trying to stop him.

When she and Quintus were only a few steps away from the door, Julian produced another small dagger from a belt under his shirt. He threw it with precision and managed to slice through Chloe's sleeve and make a gash in her arm. A long gash. A deep one.

At least the dagger hadn't stuck in her arm.

The wound caused her to gasp, her whole body tensing when the metal sliced her skin. Quintus glanced down at her as he ran.

When he caught sight of the injury, his face twisted into rage. He whipped around, nostrils flaring as his gaze found Julian. His voice turned to a growl. "You will die for that."

"Not now," Ludo shouted at him.

Mishti stood one pace away from the door, ready to step through it. When she saw how Quintus's expression changed, she rolled her eyes and dropped her head in her hands. "We have no time, Quintus. We can deal with him later."

Quintus bared his teeth, staring harder at Julian. With each moment, he pulled Chloe a little closer to his chest. "You two go."

The longer he stared at Julian, the more time it gave for the enemy mortals to scramble closer to him. They only had another breath or two before the mortals would reach them.

Julian let out a wild chuckle, interrupted by flecks of blood shooting from his mouth. "You think you can kill me?"

A challenge lit in his eyes, turning them so wild, they almost looked red. She'd noticed it before, but once again, Chloe was struck with how old he appeared. All of Ansel's mortals were mid-thirties at the most. She had long since given up guessing why they were so young, especially because it probably had to do with all the awful things Ansel had done to them.

But Julian was different. And yet, he also wasn't. He appeared mid-thirties, but he had wrinkles on his forehead like an eighty-year-old man. His skin didn't seem too old at first appearance, but sometimes it would sag like it had lived a century.

"Quintus!" Ludo shouted again, a little more frenzied than before. "Get over here now, or we are leaving without you."

Quintus had begun stomping toward Julian, but at least those words made him falter. He paused for a moment then shrugged. "I can run to the castle. I do not need a door to get there."

Only now did Chloe speak. She held her breath and glanced up at him. He couldn't very well ignore her when he held her in his arms. Still, she spoke in little more than a whisper. "You can run there, but you can't get inside. All the doors are sealed with magic, so you *do* need a door."

His lip curled while her words sank in. Anger twisted his features, but only for a moment. Soon, grief overtook his face, turning her heart to a jumbled mess. Grief and also pain. Pain forced his shoulders into a deep slump. It stole the light from his eyes until they looked more like rocks than eyes. He breathed out hard enough to ruffle her hair.

It hurt to see it. It hurt worse to know she had caused it.

Quintus had no magic. It had been stolen from him when she locked him out of his court. And now, since the crown that should have saved him still belonged to his father, he might never get his magic back.

"Fine." He said the word in a whisper, but not because he wanted to keep others from hearing it. He clearly lacked the energy to speak any louder. The fight had left him completely.

When he stepped toward Ludo's door again, he hardly even noticed the enemy mortals had gotten close enough to attack.

But Chloe noticed. And she saw something even worse too. Their weapons were ready.

QUINTUS COULD STOP FLYING ARROWS and spinning daggers with his bare hands, but only if he saw them coming. Chloe stopped breathing when the first arrow struck his shoulder. She squirmed, trying to get out of his arms and to the ground where hopefully she could shove him toward the Faerie door Ludo still had open.

The mortals were closing in around them, which would soon make it impossible to reach the door. When a second and third arrow struck Quintus in the stomach and leg, he grunted. "Stop moving, I might drop you."

He spoke the words harshly, which would have bothered her if his intention to protect her hadn't been implied. Since she *wanted* to get out of his arms, though, the protective instinct was more an annoyance.

Luckily, he moved toward the door, even faster than before. His fae strength and speed pushed past four mortals who stood trying to block his path. But even he couldn't get past this many people. Not on his own.

Even worse, a mortal had reached the Faerie door, clearly intending to step through it. Strain etched into Chloe's throat as she shouted. "Shut the door. A mortal is trying to come through."

The door vanished in the next breath, leaving the mortal as stranded as she and Quintus were. It had seemed like a brilliant idea when it came to her, but now that Ludo and Mishti were gone, Chloe wondered if she'd made a mistake.

After the arrows, blades came next. Swords and scythes and axes fell down on Quintus, slicing through the emerald vest and jade green shirt that had been left for him by Faerie.

He could withstand great pain, but this had touched even him. Finally, he did drop Chloe. His arms released her just as his knees buckled, and he dropped to the black soil. His short hair that he must have cut after she locked him out of his court shook when he made contact with the ground. When another wave of weapons fell down on him, he finally had both his hands to fend off the attacks.

His spear-like weapon made of a simple piece of parchment swept through the air. Chloe ducked close to the ground to avoid the swings. Quintus threw mortals and weapons alike by simply sweeping and jabbing his parchment spear.

While he moved, Chloe only just barely noticed a strange movement on the skirt of her gown. Daring to sneak a peek, she caught sight of Julian rifling through her skirts, searching for a pocket. When he found no pocket, he used both hands and ripped a gaping hole in the cascading part of her skirt.

Her eyebrows flew to her forehead as she tried to back herself out of his grip. But when she moved, he just followed. His hands found the side seam of her skirt, which he promptly split apart. Cool air brushed across her leg now that the ripped seam left it bare. He'd only torn the seam up to her upper thigh, not all the way to her waist, but even that was more indecent than she'd ever been in her life.

The urge to grab him by the throat overtook her hands. But they couldn't act because he had already started ripping even more of her skirts apart. "Where are they?" He spoke in a frenzied rush, the words spilling over themselves as his fingers searched and tore. "Where are they?"

"Stop it!" she screamed at him, which only served to remind him that a person was sitting inside the dress he currently tore to shreds.

His gaze flicked upward for a split second. Blood dripped from the dagger still buried in his chest. More blood dripped from his chin. His face had turned paler than a sheet. Yet, none of that stopped him from procuring a strange jagged knife-like weapon from under his tunic. He eyed her throat, then plunged the weapon toward it.

She had just enough time to gasp and slam her eyes shut. But when the weapon should have reached her, it didn't. Swallowing hard, she dared to open one eyelid.

Quintus held Julian tight around the wrist, stopping the weapon less than an inch before it touched her skin. Quintus had his jaw clenched. His nostrils flared as he stared straight into Julian's eyes. "Do not touch her."

With a shrug, the look in Julian's eyes turned from desperate to something far wilder. He pulled something else from his pocket but kept it hidden in his palm. The grin on Julian's face kept twitching, nearly as chaotically as his eyes. "Excellent point. Why bother with her when I could kill you?"

He jabbed the strange knife toward Quintus, which he easily stopped by holding Julian's wrist firmly. But then Julian used his free elbow to jab into Quintus's side. He rammed so hard Quintus coughed just to catch his breath.

In that short moment of hesitation, Julian freed his hand and struck the jagged weapon into Quintus's side. Something else happened too. Something Chloe didn't have words to explain.

A strange shimmery light released from the wound. Julian was mortal, but this looked like magic. How could a mortal like him do any sort of magic?

Quintus's cough cut off before it had even finished. His mouth dropped as all color drained from his eyes. His normally bright brown irises turned ashy, as if they were turning to dust. Golden glints usually sparkled inside the brown of his irises, but no glints could be seen now. Nothing but a dull ashy color filled his eyes.

His skin hadn't lost color, but it changed too. It turned tougher, as if callused. Even the soft skin of his neck had turned thick and textured. He had difficulty breathing as he reached for his side.

Julian ripped the dagger away, releasing another burst of color from the wound. A distant memory flickered in Chloe's mind, taking her all the way back to the first time she'd been to Faerie. Back then, Ansel had used gemstones to do magic. She only vaguely remembered how it looked, but this seemed similar. Was that what had just happened? Had Julian somehow saved a gemstone from Ansel and used it to do some sort of magic on Quintus?

She didn't have time to speculate too much because Quintus grunted and pulled his hand away from the wound. Blood covered his entire palm. More of it pooled over the wound in his side.

His eyelashes fluttered as his body swayed to the side. He still had his knees on the ground, which made it a little easier for Chloe to grab him and steady him.

But then a drop of blood fell from his fingertips. Blood had soaked his clothing through, and even his hand, but this was the first drop of blood heavy enough to fall to the ground. When it did, an icy chill spread through her core.

The moment the blood touched the jade grass stems beneath them, a loud hiss erupted, and the jade cracked loudly. The jade that had been touched by blood disintegrated into dust that floated away on the wind. It left behind an ashy pile of soil that looked even deader than Quintus's eyes.

All around them, everyone froze. The mortals immediately forgot to attack at such a frightening sight. Quintus twitched and shifted toward the pile of ash. The movement caused another drop of blood to fall from his wound. Just like the first, this blood fizzled and turned the ground ashy and lifeless. An acrid and foul stench drifted from the spot. It was so strong, many of the mortals coughed.

Chloe's jaw clenched as she turned slowly to Julian. He stared at the ash, as transfixed as the others. No matter. She'd get his attention soon enough. "What did you do to him?"

The question captured Julian's focus immediately. He glanced at her, the ghost of a grin on his tilted mouth.

She felt her lips curl as she glared. "What did you *do* to him?"

Julian's mouth parted like he was preparing to chuckle. She could already hear the strange, spine-tingling laughter that would erupt. It wasn't worse than the foul stench that still lingered, but it was at least as bad. She couldn't take it. She wouldn't.

Before a sound could leave his lips, she lunged forward and used both hands to grip the dagger still buried in his chest.

With her fingers around the hilt, she did her best to twist the blade and wrench it out of his chest at the same time.

Screaming, he jumped to his feet and stumbled backward.

Her strength had never been that impressive, so she had failed to remove the dagger completely. If she had succeeded, he might have bled out in those few seconds he took to stumble back. Sadly, she only got the dagger about halfway out of his chest.

Regardless, blood began pouring from the wound, almost as fast as the blood that poured from Quintus's. With any luck, her failed attempt might still be enough to kill him.

But what were she and Quintus supposed to do now? Without magic, he couldn't open a door. And with a devastating injury in his side, he probably couldn't outrun the mortals either. Since she had just clearly attempted to murder their leader, the other mortals would probably soon remember they wanted Chloe and Quintus dead.

Her mind spun and whirled, trying to think of an escape, but she kept getting distracted by Quintus's eyes. Warmth no longer existed anywhere inside them. They looked as lifeless as a mutilated carcass. That injury had done something to him. Something far worse than simply cutting through his skin.

At least he had pressed his hand against the wound. That prevented dripping blood from destroying the ground and creating more of that awful smell.

In the next moment, Julian lost his footing. He dropped to the ground in a pile of misplaced limbs. He managed to jab a pointer finger toward Chloe and Quintus. This was it. This was the moment the mortals would remember to attack.

Chloe grabbed Quintus's arm and urged him to get to his feet. He did, but she already knew it wouldn't be enough. He couldn't carry her when injured like this, so he couldn't hold her while running away. And even if he ran away without her, which he would never do, he couldn't possibly run fast enough while his side bled.

Dread carved a hole in her gut, but just before it could start on her heart next, a Faerie door opened right behind them. Chloe barely had enough time to glance over her shoulder when a firm hand grabbed her shoulder and pulled her backward. At her side, Quintus got pulled backward too.

Her feet stumbled as the grip forced her through the door. Soon, she and Quintus stood inside a golden castle room. It smelled dank and dusty, but the faintest scent of vanilla wove through the other smells. All sounds of battle faded to a serene quietude.

"I got them," Mishti said from behind them. "Shut the door."

The door vanished a moment later.

Just like that, the mortals and the danger and the attack had all disappeared. They stood in a small room with golden walls and faded threadbare rugs. Several high-backed, ornately carved golden chairs were in the room, along with a low sofa with maroon and silver upholstery.

If she'd been given another moment, Chloe might have collapsed onto the ground and started crying right then. But she couldn't because Mishti stomped around until she stood directly in front of Chloe and Quintus.

Mishti folded her arms over her chest and narrowed her eyes.

At nearly the same moment, Ludo joined them. He stood next to Mishti wearing an expression identical to hers. Dropping his hands onto his hips, he turned his gaze toward Quintus first. "That was stupid. You should have come right away like we planned."

Mishti nodded, her face turning to a darker glare.

They probably expected to get full attention with such angry faces, but Chloe's gaze flicked over to Quintus's side.

Blood continued to seep from the wound, spilling onto his hands.

Her gaze turned back when Ludo stepped forward.

The Fairfrost fae lifted one finger, wagging it right in Quintus's face. "You need to stop losing your mind any time Chloe gets injured. If you had come like we planned, everything would have been fine."

Mishti nodded again.

Quintus stared ahead, his eyes glazing over. They'd probably assume he wanted to disregard their words, but really, he was likely close to fainting.

When Chloe bent down to get a closer look at the wound, both Ludo and Mishti stood a little taller, as if trying to snatch her attention.

"And another thing," Ludo said, his voice rising. "What if we had not been able to open a door close enough to help you escape?"

"What if you'd been killed?" Mishti added with another nod.

Ludo huffed. "You should still be mad at Chloe anyway. Why do you even care that she got injured?"

Mishti didn't nod at this. In fact, she rolled her eyes a little. "You can't stop him from being in love with her. But even in love, he should still be able to keep his head when she gets injured."

By now, Chloe had bent at the waist and brought her face closer to Quintus than to the others.

Ludo threw his hands in the air, which she could see through the side of her eye. His face turned a darker shade of red. "Are you even listening?"

"No." Chloe gave up all pretense of conversation and reached for Quintus's shoulder. "Hush, both of you. Now isn't the time for a lecture."

Pressing against Quintus's shoulder, she forced him to sit in one of the high-backed golden chairs. He blinked, only barely seeming to sense her or the others. When she tugged at his wrist, he released his hand from the wound without argument.

Blood immediately dripped from his clothing. But it couldn't possibly affect the castle floor the same way it had affected the soil and grass. Right? She should have known better than to hope.

The moment Quintus's blood hit the floor, it turned the gold into a pile of ash that released an acrid stench.

Ludo coughed and dramatically covered his nose. "What was *that*?"

Covering her own mouth, Mishti leaned forward just as another two drops of blood fell to the castle floor, also turning the gold to ash.

Chloe acted quickly, ripping a long piece of cloth from her skirt that Julian had already destroyed. She wrapped the fabric around Quintus's waist, taking care to cover the entire injury. She would have preferred to clean it too, but stopping the blood mattered more right now.

And anyway, even without his magic, Quintus still had the incredible healing ability of the fae. The injury would heal itself soon enough. But if she let the blood drip everywhere, it might eat away the entire floor in that room.

The fabric soaked completely through only a few seconds after she wrapped it. She had to rip a longer cloth from her dress, applying it over the first. Knowing the blood would soon soak through that too, she got a third, fourth, and fifth strip from her skirt. Her hands moved deftly, carefully wrapping the wound and applying pressure to it.

"What happened?" Mishti whispered the words after swallowing hard.

Chloe huffed as she finished fastening the last strip of cloth. "Julian did something when he injured Quintus. He used a gemstone or magic or something. I'm not really sure what happened."

The moment her fingers left the strip of cloth, Chloe whirled around. "Is it an enchanted injury? Is it like the enchanted injuries you and the other mortals have from Ansel?"

Mishti's face and body twitched, but then she shook her head. "No, I've never seen an injury that makes blood…"

She trailed off and pointed to the stinking pile of ash on the castle floor. "Why would his blood do that? *How* did it do that?"

Ludo's face contorted as he leaned in close to the destroyed spot in the golden floor. He poked at it with one finger, wrinkling his nose as he did. "Do you think it is because he is heir to Crystalfall? Rulers are connected to their courts in ways the other fae are not."

"I am not ruler of Crystalfall." Quintus finally spoke for the first time since getting injured. His voice scratched through his throat, and he clenched his jaw tight, but he still managed to get the words out.

Chloe knelt at his side, using the back of her hand to test the temperature of his forehead. "You may not be ruler, but you *are* still the heir. I think Ludo might be right. Crystalfall has never reacted like this to your blood before, but maybe it's because it's a magical wound and because you are connected to the court."

Quintus scowled but said nothing in response.

Mishti raised an eyebrow. "Will it heal like usual then?"

Rather than answer, Chloe sat on the low sofa near one wall. It released a small cloud of dust when she dropped onto it, which she coughed and brushed a hand through. Still clearing her throat, she tore another strip of cloth from her gown. Then she dipped it in a jar of alcohol from her leather bag and used it to clean the blood from her hands.

Once clean, she retrieved her magical book and opened it on her lap. It would be much easier for them if the injury did heal like normal, but considering magic, she doubted it would be so simple.

Even with his fae healing abilities, the injury might need extra magic to cure it completely.

Gripping the book with both hands, Chloe stared hard at the blank pages before her. "Will Quintus's injury heal like normal?"

Holding her breath, she turned the page. A single sentence filled the middle of the page in the same scrawling handwriting as contained in the rest of the book.

The ruler of Crystalfall can heal the injury.

She swallowed hard, ignoring how her stomach wound into knots. Snapping the book shut, she shrugged and attempted a carefree expression. "There you have it, then. We can heal the injury and save this court from the attacking mortals."

Quintus tapped his fist against his thigh while his breathing hitched. "How?"

Pressing her lips together, she looked him straight in the eye. "We have to find the king of Crystalfall."

3

FINDING A PERSON DIDN'T SEEM like too difficult a task. Chloe tried to convince herself of that as she tucked her magical book back into the leather bag from her fae brother. They had Ludo, didn't they? And Ludo's greatest magic was in finding things. They also had Quintus, who had already seen his father twice before in his life, though his father may have been wearing a glamour in those instances.

Still, they had a chance.

But after Chloe declared they must find the king of Crystalfall, no one seemed overjoyed by the idea. In fact, Quintus looked sick. What was likely an attempt to distract himself, he suddenly grabbed the jar of alcohol Chloe had used to clean the blood off her hands. He splashed the alcohol liberally onto the other wounds he'd received during the fight. Already, the gashes in him made from the arrows and blades were starting to heal. But even under several strips of cloth, Chloe could tell the wound in his side from Julian continued to bleed as much as ever.

Mishti shifted from one foot to the other, twisting a string from her leather bracer around her fingers. Ludo stared off into space, saying nothing.

When silence continued to sour the space around them, Chloe beckoned the others toward the nearest door. "Come on. We need to go check on the mortals in the library. And we need to find out if the enemy mortals are still attacking this castle."

"Why would they stop attacking?" Ludo scrambled toward Mishti, looking a little too eager to leave Chloe and Quintus behind him.

Mishti kept her gaze ahead as she continued toward the door. From behind, Chloe could see the young woman shrug. "They haven't managed to hurt us yet. What else can they do that they haven't tried yet? They'll have to give up at some point."

Ludo nodded and tapped his chin. He answered, but by now, the two of them had moved just far enough away that Chloe couldn't make out the words.

Gripping his injured side, Quintus glanced toward Chloe.

Their eyes locked for only a split second, but even that lit electricity within Chloe's limbs. Her heart skipped as she bit her bottom lip. His body seemed to react in a similar way. First, his breath quickened and then his pupils dilated. He didn't move, but she could feel how his body seemed eager to lean toward her, to move a little closer.

The moment didn't last long. Soon, anger burned through the desire in his eyes. He jerked his body away from her and began tramping after the others.

The action might have hurt her, except that wound in his side held her attention too completely. When he twisted his body to the side, it must have ripped open the injury just a bit more.

Soon, her torn red fabric that wrapped around him soaked through with blood. A drop of it fell to the ground, which immediately sizzled and ate through the golden floor like vinegar on a pile of baking soda.

He winced, which caused another drop of blood to follow the first.

Quintus kept walking. His head turned the slightest bit, like he intended to turn back and look at Chloe but then thought better of it.

No matter. She didn't need him looking at her in order to help him.

With the leather bag snugly on her shoulder, she jumped to her feet. She ripped more swathes of fabric from her dress as she bounded forward. The skirt of her once-magnificent dress now had so many pieces ripped from it, it looked more like a patchwork of tattered banners from long-forgotten battles.

Air fluttered around her leg, reminding her that one side seam of her dress was ripped all the way up to her mid-thigh. If Quintus hadn't been dripping blood that ate through the castle's floor, she would have found a way to fix that side seam first.

But right now, she had to focus on Quintus.

Her long hair shifted around her shoulders when she caught up to him. She tried to wrap a cloth around his waist to cover the wound, but Quintus just glared and took a step away from her.

With his arms folded over his chest and his face turned markedly in the other direction, he spat out the words he had probably been eager to say ever since she brought up the idea of finding the king of Crystalfall.

"My father is vile."

She didn't attempt to look at him when she responded. Instead, her focus remained fixed on his wound and the now-bunched-up fabric in her hand. She pressed the swathes of red velvet against the wound, just barely catching a drop of blood before it fell to the ground.

He hissed at the contact. When he tried to move away, her feet followed, as if they were in a strange dance. "Yes, I know he's vile, but…"

She gestured toward the bunched-up fabric, which already had blood soaking through it.

Quintus sneered. "My healing abilities can fix this."

Hopefully he was right about that because *she* probably couldn't heal the wound now that she had no magic. So far, she hadn't even been successful in getting the blood to stop.

Still, he needed to accept that finding the king was necessary. Tipping an eyebrow up, she asked, "What about the enemy mortals? What if they manage to get a stronghold on this court, just like they did in Bitter Thorn? Wouldn't we need the king and his power then? We don't have to stay anywhere near him after that."

The last sentence came out offhandedly, but once it left her lips, she wished she could erase it from existence. Quintus's fists shook at his side as he turned away from her.

If he stayed far away from the king of Crystalfall, he might have to leave the court completely. The court that was his home.

He had spent so much of his life trying to find his home, and now his own father would take it away from him. Again.

"Are you sure we have to find him at all?" Mishti had slowed her pace enough that Quintus and Chloe had caught up to her and Ludo.

Using one hand to rip another piece of cloth from her dress, Chloe raised an eyebrow. "What do you mean by that?"

Mishti shrugged. "Don't you think the king will show up on his own? It's not a secret anymore that Crystalfall exists. If he's the king, wouldn't he come to claim his court?"

31

Ludo turned to her, a distant look in his eye as if trying to remember. "Maybe he does not remember."

Quintus scowled again. "Maybe he *does* remember. Maybe he is even more horrid than we think."

Chloe pressed the newly ripped cloth from her skirt against Quintus's wound. Now that it had two bunched-up pieces of fabric against it, the blood finally stayed back. She'd just need one more fabric strip to tie around his waist and hold the other fabric in place.

Holding the crumpled velvet with one hand, she reached for her skirt with the other. While ripping the fabric, Chloe said, "I think Ludo might be right. Ludo has lost memories, and we know at least some of them are related to Crystalfall. And the pixies have lost memories too. They can't remember anything from before Crystalfall got destroyed."

In a flash, Chloe's head tilted to the side. "I wonder if the wraiths remember anything from before. We should ask them." Shaking that idea away, she continued with her earlier thought. "I'm guessing others from Crystalfall lost memories too. Maybe the king doesn't even know who he is, and that's why he hasn't come to claim his court."

Quintus gritted his teeth together and huffed. He also reached out and helped Chloe rip off the strip of fabric from her dress she'd been struggling with, but he seemed eager to do it so quickly everyone would forget he had been involved at all.

Now that she started wrapping the fabric strip around his waist, he lifted his chin high. "If the king of Crystalfall does not remember who he is, then why did he try to kill me? Why did he destroy my home in Bitter Thorn? Clearly, he remembers enough about himself to want me dead, so he cannot have forgotten too much."

After she tied the fabric strip neatly around Quintus's waist, the four of them continued walking toward the library. They'd soon find out if the friendly mortals remained in the castle where they'd been before the vault. A bit more inspection would let them know if the enemy mortals still attacked Crystalfall Castle as well.

They turned down a new hallway, bringing the great hall and its golden table into sight. Even without entering the room, it managed to steal her attention. Every room in the castle had a warm, golden radiance shimmering in the air, but the great hall showcased it twice as much. Sculptures in bronze and silver depicted fae, creatures such as pixies and brownies, and even mortals. Precious gems encrusted each sculpture, bringing attention to unique eye colors, sweeping robes, and glittering wings.

Wooden chests and cabinets dotted the room, though their splendor had not been preserved like the gold and gems. Each piece of wood had a spongy or warped surface, and it smelled dank and stale. Cobwebs adorned large gilded mirrors hanging throughout the room.

Like everything in the castle, the room had a mixture of gorgeous and perfectly preserved pieces sitting amongst decayed items that served as a reminder that this court had once been destroyed.

Just then, Mishti cleared her voice. "Didn't you say Quintus was called to this court? By some magic or something? That same thing should be happening to the king, right? Even if he doesn't know who he is."

The intriguing nature of that statement got completely swallowed up when one of the fabric pieces on Quintus's wound fell free of the strip holding it in place. Chloe tried to catch it from the air so she wouldn't have to bend over to pick it up, which failed.

But once it touched the ground, she realized she should have been eager to catch it for a completely different reason.

The moment the bloodied fabric reached the golden floor of the hallway, sparks and fizzles hissed out from around it. A gray powdery residue spread through the gold at their feet until it ate a hole the size of a large bowl straight through the ground. Staring through it, she found a storage room full of collapsed barrels, dusty brooms, and rolls of faded cloth.

This was escalating. The blood hadn't just left a pile of ash on the floor; now it corroded completely through it.

Gasping, she snatched the bloodied fabric off the ground and held it against her stomach. She never considered how the blood would stain her gown. She'd only been eager to get the blood off the golden floor before that hole grew any bigger. Her fingers clenched around the wet rag. She pressed it tighter against her stomach as if that might help.

Mishti and Ludo watched in horror and then turned to glance at each other. Mishti nodded at him like they had just decided something, even though neither of them had opened their mouths.

Now Mishti tilted her head toward the great hall. She gestured toward Chloe and Quintus. "You two get in there and figure out a way to contain that wound. If enough of that blood touches the castle, it could affect the integrity of the architecture."

When Chloe stared at her blankly, Mishti clarified. "The whole castle could collapse if the blood eats away at it like that. Take care of the wound."

She shoved them both into the great hall, then she and Ludo disappeared down a corner in less than two breaths.

Chloe didn't mind the forced time with Quintus, but she had a guess he wouldn't feel the same way.

Turning toward him, she prepared herself for the scowl he'd be wearing. When she met his eyes, though, no scowl adorned his features. Instead, a gentle concern tweaked at his brow. He stared at the gash down her arm, given to her by Julian's *delightful* blade.

She had nearly forgotten about that injury until now. With Quintus staring at it, she suddenly couldn't think of anything else. Her flesh stung and tingled with needle-like pain. Throbbing pulsed through it, aching more each time. It took considerable concentration to turn her attention away from it.

Waving one hand at the ground, she stared at Quintus pointedly. "Sit down. Actually, it would be better if you could lay on your side, the uninjured side."

Now came the scowl she'd been expecting. "What about your wound? You should deal with that first and let me deal with my injury on my own."

If she'd been less sleep deprived, she probably could have stopped herself from rolling her eyes. Instead, Quintus saw the motion, which only deepened his scowl.

She dropped her hands onto his shoulders. The moment she made contact with him, something in his eyes changed. A few glints of gold appeared in his dull eyes, giving them a life they hadn't had since she locked him out of his court. His body reacted too. It didn't only *seem* as if he wanted to move closer to her. He actually moved closer. His head dropped and his gaze found her lips.

It only lasted a moment before he scowled his hardest yet. After pushing her hands off him, he took several steps back. "The wound in your arm needs treatment."

She pressed her lips together and shoved her hands onto her hips. "Forget that. Your wound is worse."

His nostrils flared. "And my healing abilities will fix it."

Ignoring him, she bent to rip a few more strips of fabric off her ragged gown. Normally, his attention toward her and his desire to have her healed was endearing. Now though, it seemed more like a thinly veiled ruse to prevent her from touching him. To prevent her from being near him and helping him.

He clearly felt as warmly toward her as he did toward his own father.

That thought sent a small shiver down her spine.

When she moved toward him, he took a step back. "Becoming selfless again, are you? And what happens when your wound becomes infected and you die because you neglected it? Will it be worth it to you then that you focused on my wound instead of your own?"

He had taken two more steps back while speaking, which might have annoyed her, except now he was about to back into the wall. At least then she'd be able to reach him, and he'd have nowhere to go.

She hated to admit it, but the wound in her arm did burn a little worse than expected. It hadn't come in contact with any contaminants, except for the air, though, so it had little chance of being infected. As long as she looked at it immediately after taking care of his wound, it would be fine.

With one more step, Quintus finally backed into the wall. Terror flashed in his eyes when he realized he no longer had a way of getting away from her.

It probably wouldn't help the situation if she released the smug smile that wanted to curl up her lips. Instead, she took the final steps toward him and reached for his wound. "I know you're just trying to push me away. You don't care about my injury, and you don't care if it gets infected. Now, be quiet and let me work on *your* wound."

She started by arranging bundles of fabric directly under his wound to hopefully catch all the blood and prevent it from touching the ground. Then, she carefully peeled back layer after layer of fabric. Soon, she'd get a look at the wound itself, though she still had several layers to go until then.

It had only been a moment since she started touching Quintus. Only a moment of being in his space, but already, his entire body had gone rigid. He bent down just enough to whisper in her ear.

Her skin tingled at the familiar sensation of his breath in her hair, but her heart squeezed at the words.

"Stop this now. I do not need you destroying my life any more than you already have."

Her fingers stopped as the words bludgeoned her chest. Destroyed. Did he really think she had *destroyed* his life? Because she had taken away his magic, and now, since the crown of Crystalfall belonged to another, he might never get that magic back?

Maybe his own father had destroyed Quintus's home, but he clearly believed she had done something much worse. Her throat tightened and ached. Tears pricked in her eyes. She desperately tried to swallow and blink them away.

With Quintus filled with such anger, he was sure to only be angrier at the sight of her tears. They would not worry him. They would not soften him. They would only ignite his rage.

Her hand hovered over his wound. She still had bloodied fabric pieces tight in her grip.

He stared at her with eyes filled with loathing as he ripped the fabric away from her. Pressing the pieces against his wound, he pushed her away and stalked across the great hall.

"I am going to find—"

His words cut off at the same moment his steps stopped. Still blinking away a tear before it slipped from her eyes, she managed to glance over her shoulder.

In a flash, she could see what had stopped him.

A wraith stood in the doorway of the great hall. This was the very wraith who had taken a memory away from Mishti. His name was Chandril.

Now that he stood here, Chloe could ask him if he remembered the king of Crystalfall. Since wraiths traded magic for memories, maybe they had kept theirs. And if Chandril remembered the king of Crystalfall, that could bring them one step closer to finding him.

As long as the wraith didn't ask for too much in return.

STILLNESS FILLED THE AIR AS Chloe dared to take a single step forward. Even Quintus had stopped moving, which was saying something, considering his rage. But no matter how angry he'd been, this wraith before them had turned them both to stone.

The wispy, frail frame of the wraith seemed to glide as the creature took a step forward. He had dark skin, but it was so thin it appeared translucent. The creature's fingers, which were twice the length of Quintus's, raised as he pointed one finger and pressed it against his own chest.

"I am hungry." His wispy words filled the air with a chill, like the tendrils of ice that encased plants on a frozen winter morning.

Quintus hadn't moved. Not even his expression changed. That was how completely the wraith had entranced him.

After a shudder that had been impossible to suppress, Chloe gestured toward a darkened corner of the great hall. "No one has touched anything over there, I don't think. There should be plenty of dust for you."

"No." The wraith shook his head, which shuddered through his entire frail frame. "Dust will not satisfy this appetite."

Chandril took a step toward her, his eyebrows lowering over his blood-orange eyes.

For the first time, Quintus moved. His arm shot out, acting as a barrier between the wraith and Chloe. He even took a small step in front of her. That small movement was all it took to change his expression too.

Now he glared at the wraith, threat of attack dancing in his eyes.

But Chandril ignored him. The creature didn't even seem to notice him at all. Instead, his icy gaze stayed pinned on Chloe. "I did not know."

The words were just as frosty as before, but there was something else in them too. Depth? Or maybe that was the word that described what was going on with his eyes.

She hadn't noticed it at first, but his eyes definitely seemed different from when she had met him the first time. They still had the same blood-orange color, but they had a deeper look in them too. Or maybe they just looked more alive.

Now the wraith trembled, sending undulations throughout his lithe and bony body. "I knew creatures like you could die, but…"

A skip pulsed through Chloe's chest then. Fear pricked at her senses, raising the skin on her arms to little bumps. Yet something flickered along with the fear, something that told her the fear was unnecessary.

Quintus's lip curled as he took another protective step in front of her.

In a flash, the wraith's eyes sharpened as he pierced Chloe with an all-new stare. "Before you, I had never felt that pain before. I had never experienced anything like pain."

She just managed to stop herself from shivering as she glanced at the creature. "Are you... okay?"

But it wasn't the wraith who responded. Quintus turned, his glare burning straight through *her*. He scoffed loudly, teeth bared. "You destroyed *his* life too? Are you determined to destroy *everything* in Crystalfall?"

Anger twitched at his shoulders, turning his face a deep crimson. He let out a huff that caught even Chandril's attention. Without another word, Quintus stomped out of the room, one hand tight over his side to keep blood from dripping out.

Chloe immediately went to follow him, but the wraith stopped her. Had he grown taller? She could have sworn Chandril used to be shorter than her, but he stood at her same height now. He held his long, spindly fingers out wide to keep her from side-stepping him.

The proximity and aggressive position probably should have sent fear through her heart, but sadness gripped it instead. Her lips had rounded, ready to say Quintus's name. But grief sliced through her throat, so only a small whimper escaped.

When the wraith wrapped his bony fingers around her shoulders, she jumped, having nearly forgotten he was there.

The creature's eyes definitely had more depth compared to the first time she'd met him. They were more... more somehow, but exactly how, she couldn't say.

His thin mouth parted just enough to speak. "The pain of death is profound." His shoulders shook, and since he held her by the arms, her body shook too.

But then the lightest smile appeared, first in his eyes and then on his lips. "But now that I know that pain, my joy is profound too."

It took everything in her to let out a sigh without rolling her eyes. The wraith had seemed so frightening a moment ago, but realization dawned that he was no more threatening to her than a small toddler who had just had his first negative emotion.

She pulled out of his grip and pinned him with her own stare. She had no time for this, but she needed to ask him a question anyway. "Do you remember the king of Crystalfall?"

The smile on Chandril's face disappeared as he raised a single eyebrow. He glanced quickly out the doorway Quintus had just exited but brought his gaze back to Chloe before he could even blink.

Was he trying to make her forget he had just looked at the doorway? Did it mean something? He was definitely tenser now, though he attempted a casual expression to hide it.

Ignoring that, Chloe placed her hands on her hips. The movement widened her injury, causing it to release a small drip of blood down her arm. Maybe she *did* need to take care of it sooner rather than later.

Shaking her head, she stared at the wraith more pointedly. "Do you remember what the king of Crystalfall looks like? Or his name or anything? Do you know where he is?"

He flinched at the mention of the Crystalfall king, but then a devious smile worked across Chandril's mouth. "You wish to know what I remember?"

Chloe rolled her eyes.

But the wraith continued, his blood-orange eyes practically glowing. "I will tell you for a memory."

She had already started walking away from him. "No. No more memories. Everyone has already lost enough as it is, and we are suffering because of it. Unless you know a wraith who can restore memories instead of taking them, don't expect any help from me."

Her feet flew over the golden castle hallway in search of Quintus. She found him easily thanks to the piles of ash his dripping blood left behind.

By the time she caught up to him, the fabric around his waist had completely soaked through. She had seen some ghastly injuries mended from fae's healing ability, but this particular injury hadn't shown any improvement at all.

It hadn't been long since Julian stabbed Quintus, but she still expected at least some improvement. With a twinge in her gut, she darted forward and grabbed a handful of her skirt to press against the wound.

Quintus, who was deep in conversation with Ludo, hadn't noticed her coming. Mishti was nowhere to be found, but she was probably off somewhere trying to find out if the enemy mortals were still attacking the castle, and if so, what danger they posed.

The moment Chloe pushed her skirt against Quintus, his entire body recoiled. He scowled at her and tried to turn away.

Luckily, she had been anticipating it and managed to turn with him. At least this time she had enough fabric to cover the wound to ensure no more blood dripped onto the ground.

Now she just had to remove this bunch of fabric from the rest of her dress. It would have been easier with scissors. Instead, she bent at the strangest angle she had probably ever put her body into and used her teeth to cut through the fabric. Once she got a rip started, she could tear it the rest of the way without her teeth.

As she worked, a warm and sticky substance slid down her arm. She would have ignored it, except Ludo pointed right at it and spoke loudly. "Um, you have blood dripping from that gash in your arm. You should probably take care of it."

Quintus let out a hard sniff just then and managed to use the distraction of Ludo's voice to step away from her. The wad of her skirt that had been pressed against his wound fell away, along with several heavy drops of blood.

The moment they fell to the ground, huge billows of smoke erupted as the gold turned to a gray powdery ash. Gritting her teeth, she turned to Ludo and glared. "I'm a little busy with more important things at the moment."

But when she tried to step closer to Quintus, he took another step away. "Ludo is right. Deal with your own injury and stop fussing over me."

Obviously, she ignored him. Gathering one section of her skirt back into a wad, she jumped forward and pressed it against his wound. "I'm pretty sure no one wants Crystalfall Castle turned to decay from the inside out because you were too stubborn to let me treat your wound."

His teeth bared as he tried to take the fabric of her skirt away from her. "Let me deal with it myself."

At the end of his sentence, he finally realized the fabric was still attached to the rest of her dress. It may have been her imagination, but the pointed tips of his ears seemed to turn bright red as his eyebrows raised high on his forehead.

Holding back her snicker, she took her skirt back into her own arms and pressed it against the wound. "Oh, you've done a *wonderful* job of dealing with it yourself so far. Wouldn't you agree, Ludo?"

Ludo had his face twisted into a knot with his eyes narrowed. "You said *wonderful*, but you meant the opposite, I assume? I am still learning how you mortals speak."

As he spoke, Chloe bent into the strange angle again and used her teeth to rip the fabric. Since Quintus was still stunned into silence by the revelation that he'd tried to yank away her dress, he stood still enough that she managed to get a little tear started.

Once the shock wore off, he tipped his nose into the air. "I have not been able to take care of the wound yet since you keep following me."

She raised an eyebrow. "Stop trying to avoid me, and we wouldn't have this issue."

"Didn't we send you two into the great hall to take care of this already?" Mishti had just turned a corner and trekked toward them. She wore an annoyed expression that didn't quite hide the hint of a smile underneath it.

Turning away from her, Chloe caught sight of Ludo next. He wore a wide grin and seemed to share some great joke with Mishti that was completely unknown to Chloe.

With the fabric still in her arms, and still attached to her dress, Chloe glanced between the pair of them. Their grins grew wider. Now her eyes narrowed. "What?"

To her great dismay, Quintus said *what* at the same moment as her. As soon as he spoke, he looked at her wearing an incredulous stare.

For some reason, this made Mishti and Ludo grin even harder than ever. Quintus huffed and stepped away from Chloe. He even moved slightly behind Ludo just to get farther away from her.

Since she never managed to rip any more fabric from her dress, the skirt fell heavily to her ankles. The torn and scratched fabric was now soaked through with blood in the front. She didn't dare let herself remember how much of her legs would show each time she took a step because of how many rips and tears had tattered the fabric. Blood would probably stain her legs when she walked too. Considering how she'd fallen to the ground a few times back by the vault, she'd probably soon have a grimy mixture of blood and dirt covering her legs.

At least Ludo provided a distraction by conjuring a thick wad of fabric. It wasn't pretty or special, but it would be absorbent.

Ignoring the pitiful state of her once lovely dress, Chloe grabbed the fabric from out of his hands. "Perfect."

Quintus tried to step away from her, but Mishti had come up behind him. She grabbed him by the shoulders and pushed him closer to Chloe. "Hold still."

At his side, Ludo grabbed his arm and also forced him to stay in place.

Quintus wore a deep scowl, but at least he couldn't move. Chloe pressed the conjured wad of fabric against him. When finished, she requested more fabric, this time strips of it. Ludo conjured exactly what she needed.

For good measure, she repeated the entire process a second time with another large wad of fabric tied on with strips.

If it were any other injury, she'd be confident the fabric was thick enough and tight enough to stop the bleeding. But this injury had been different, more destructive, from the start. She knew better than to hope too much.

At least for now it wouldn't drip onto the ground.

Eventually, she might have to do stitches, if Quintus would allow it.

Just as she finished, Mishti gestured down the hallway behind her.

"The enemy mortals have started retreating into the trees across from the castle. I don't know if they're giving up though. They've all been gathering around a specific spot, but I couldn't see what they were doing because the trees and bushes obscured my view."

With the dressing finally finished, Quintus shoved everyone away and took several steps down the hallway in the opposite direction. "What can they do to us while we are inside the castle? Nothing. We have the golden table in the great hall, so they cannot stop us from eating. We have an endless source of food."

For the first time since the vault, Chloe dared to glance at the injury in her arm. It wasn't pretty. The long gash went deep and would likely scar. She hated the thought of a scar, which would have been considered a huge detriment to getting a husband back in the mortal realm.

She shouldn't have cared. She had already decided to stay here in Faerie. But with Quintus hating her so much, it occurred to her that he might never forgive her. Did it still make sense for her to stay if it wasn't for him?

But how could she return to the mortal realm now that she had a wooden foot and would soon have an unsightly scar down one arm? Her thoughts spun as she used the alcohol-covered cloth from her leather bag to clean the blood off her hands.

Her contemplation cut off short when a scream pierced the air. Suddenly, someone shouted, "Get down!"

The next thing she knew, someone jumped on top of her and slammed her body to the ground. Just as her cheek met the cool golden surface of the castle floor, a huge explosion erupted in the hallway around them.

She squeezed her eyes shut, but just before closing them, she caught sight of a flying, flaming piece of metal headed straight for her face.

5

Holding her breath, Chloe pulled her arms up just in time to bury her face in them. The hot piece of metal soon flew against her arm, singeing through the sleeve of her dress. It burned, but it only took a small shake to remove it from her skin. From how fast it had been flying, she thought it surely would have broken a bone or two. But maybe the velocity of it had been slowed down somehow.

"Get up. Everyone to the great hall before another one… Hurry!" Mishti shouted the words with increasing intensity. By the time she finished, someone had pulled Chloe to her feet. She hadn't even had time to notice who had jumped on top of her.

Judging by the scorch marks on the castle walls, whoever tackled her had certainly saved her life. It was probably Quintus, but that didn't make her heart flutter like it once had. How could he work so hard to protect her and then turn around and scowl at her in the next moment?

Did it really mean anything that he saved her when he clearly hated her too?

By now, Chloe's feet had finally started moving. She took in her surroundings in a flash. Mishti—not Quintus—held her by the wrist and forced her to keep running toward the great hall. Quintus ran at her side, making great efforts to avoid her eye. Ludo ran just behind them, shouting directions at the mortals coming from different parts of the castle.

Even as they ran, explosions erupted throughout the castle. At least the golden walls never suffered more than a few scorch marks. The explosions were clearly deadly to mortals, but they hadn't damaged the castle, just like Quintus had guessed.

When everyone made it to the great hall, Mishti dropped Chloe's wrist. Her long black braid swung as she whirled around to examine the room. "Sofia, Batu, and Hilda's division are here. We're just waiting for Jansher."

Ludo poked his head out the door and shouted for Jansher. Even before he finished, loud footsteps could be heard pounding closer.

Once the final group of mortals entered the great hall, Ludo turned around and leaned against the nearest wall.

Mishti let out a heavy sigh and bent forward at the waist. Her hands gripped her knees as she took deep inhales, trying to steady her breath.

A few of the mortals had collapsed onto the ground, but that looked more to do with exhaustion than injury. Even so, Chloe took a step toward them and raised her voice. "Does anyone have a wound that needs to be treated?"

Before any of the mortals could answer, Quintus spoke under his breath. "You do."

She turned toward him, but he only stared pointedly at her gash before turning his face away from her entirely.

After falling to the ground and having a flaming piece of metal touch the gash in her arm, it did have a higher chance of infection now. And it would be harder to clean the longer she waited since the blood had started to dry.

But she had to help others first if any of them had even greater injuries than her.

It turned out, though, everyone had gotten away mostly unscathed. She soon had everyone cleaned up and bandaged, except for herself.

To do that, she needed more fabric, which meant she needed Ludo. Most of the mortals stood scattered throughout the room in small clusters. Near one wall, Mishti, Ludo, and Quintus all huddled together.

As soon as Chloe joined them, Ludo let out a small sigh of relief, and said, "Oh, good."

He then stared between her and Quintus expectantly. It caused a small lurch in her gut to see that Mishti did the same thing. They both stared between Chloe and Quintus, waiting. But for what, she didn't know.

"What?" Once again, Chloe spoke the word at the same exact moment as Quintus said the same thing. Their gazes darted toward each other in surprise, but then Quintus scoffed and looked away.

At least Chloe didn't have to respond because Ludo chimed in with a question. "What do we do now?"

His blue-and-red eyes seemed to bore into her skin, or maybe the question itself did that. She tried to laugh, but it came out as little more than a tiny breath. "I don't know. Why are you looking at me?"

"And me," Quintus added.

Ludo shrugged, nonchalantly. "You always come up with the plans."

Mishti gestured toward Quintus. "And you're the heir to Crystalfall."

Quintus's voice wavered when he answered. "Stop saying that." Slamming his eyes shut, his chin fell to his chest. "I am nothing without my magic."

Aches spread through Chloe's heart like a crack splitting through glass. He wasn't *nothing* without magic. He was still strong and heroic and—though he was fae—honorable. Maybe the honor existed deep down in his core, so deep that it hadn't made an appearance since she locked him out of his court and took his magic, but it still existed. Somewhere.

"Excuse me." Batu, a mortal man with blue pants and a sword hanging on his belt had stepped right up to their group without Chloe noticing. He was the leader of one of their divisions. His black hair had dust and bits of debris spilling out of it. His hands were callused and even cracked at the end of his right thumb. He looked toward them with even more expectancy than Mishti and Ludo had worn.

"Is there something specific we're waiting for?" He glanced back at the other mortals and then toward the entryway to the great hall.

The mortals needed a leader, that much was clear. Well, not the enemy mortals. They already had Portia, and maybe Julian, if he had survived. But these mortals in this room needed one. And maybe they needed a name other than friendly mortals and enemy mortals. Differentiating between them had gotten confusing inside Chloe's head.

Since Quintus, Ludo, and Mishti all stayed completely, unhelpfully silent, Chloe did what she had to do. Rolling her shoulders back and smiling slightly, she spoke to the man. "We're just finalizing our plan now." Gesturing toward the magical golden table at the center of the room, she continued.

"Why don't you have everyone get some food while you're waiting?"

He nodded and soon directed the other mortals to the table, where they conjured dishes onto the golden plates using the table's magic.

It wasn't much, but that had bought them some time. She certainly had no idea what to do, but neither did anyone else, so maybe she needed to think of solutions.

Her gaze darted between each of the three people before her, hoping they could answer her next question. "Are we safe here? In the castle?"

Mishti stopped adjusting the leather bracer on her arm just long enough to stare out into the hall. Ludo narrowed one eye and tapped his chin. Quintus stayed completely still, offering no reply and no body language to interpret.

Since no one had answered yet, Chloe expanded on her question. "If we stay away from windows while the enemy mortals attack, can they even hurt us? Like Quintus said, they can't do an actual siege on the castle when we have an endless supply of food. Not to mention Ludo can open a door for us to leave if we want to temporarily, or permanently, go to another part of Crystalfall."

She shrugged. "Maybe we do nothing. Maybe we just make a life in the castle and ignore the other mortals."

Still standing as immovable as stone, Quintus spoke in a low voice. "I thought about it more, and…" He paused for a beat before continuing. "If the castle gets too damaged, the rest of the court will suffer."

Mishti pulled out a dagger and used it to trim a loose thread from her midnight blue tunic. "Why?"

Ludo answered, pulling an empty vial from his pocket as he did. "A castle is the heart of a court. You remember how High King Brannick and Queen Elora could not do anything until they had repaired their castle? If Crystalfall Castle gets too damaged, we cannot let it stay that way."

With her dagger pointing out like she was about to attack, Mishti pinched her eyebrows together. She nodded slowly, then, rather suddenly, turned her dagger toward her leather bracer to wedge out a piece of metal that had gotten lodged there. "That makes sense. And if the king of Crystalfall has forgotten who he is and isn't compelled to return to the court, then *he* can't repair the castle either."

Her gaze slid toward Quintus, whose shoulders slumped forward. Looking away from him again, Mishti finished. "Maybe no one can."

With an uncharacteristically bright smile, Ludo plucked a pink gem from the ground and dropped it into his empty vial. "Yes, but that explosion did not damage the castle much. It really only damaged people and some of the drapes and things. It takes a lot to destroy a Faerie castle. Without iron, I doubt the mortals will be able to do enough damage to the castle that it affects the rest of the court."

His eyes focused as he shook the vial directly in front of his face. The sight of the pink gem tumbling around lifted his smile even more.

But then Mishti spoke in a terse whisper. "Not every mortal is trying to hurt the castle."

Ludo shook the vial again before he realized Mishti had been talking to him. "What?" he asked, turning toward her.

Her face turned a slightly pinker shade of brown as she swallowed. "You said you doubt the *mortals* would be able to do enough damage, but not all the mortals are trying to do damage."

She used her chin to point toward the people getting food, but her hands trembled at her sides while she did.

It was strange seeing Mishti uncomfortable like this. She could threaten with her knives and sword and instill fear into anyone who crossed her, but this was different. She didn't threaten now, she was correcting. And not correcting just anyone, either. She corrected someone she clearly considered a friend. When killing someone, threatening came easily to her since that person's opinion meant nothing. But she did seem to care what Ludo thought of her. At least that was how it seemed when she swallowed again.

"Oh." The word fell heavily from Ludo's mouth, but then he shook his head. "Right. The… What did you call them, Chloe? The *bad* mortals. No, that was not it."

"I've been thinking about that." Chloe glanced around the room, not exactly sure what she searched for. "We really need names other than mortals and fae because it's not mortals against fae anymore. It's those who are trying to destroy and force their will on others, and…" She shrugged. "Us."

Quintus raised an eyebrow, his entire demeanor as warm as ice. "And what are *we* trying to do?"

His question felt like an axe to the chest. It was fair to ask, but the way he asked it reminded her all over again everything she had taken from him. Apparently, it would never matter to him that she hadn't meant to take his magic away. Whether intentional or not, she had done it. And that was all he'd ever remember.

Trying to shove those thoughts to the farthest recesses of her mind, she turned away from him. "I guess that should be our plan then. We need to turn us," she gestured to their small group and then to the other mortals, "into something. We need a purpose."

Silence met that declaration. Ludo, and especially Mishti, wore expressions of contemplation. Quintus still glared too hard to tell his true thoughts. At least they were considering her words, but she would have preferred for one of them to agree right away.

Just as Chloe's heartbeat turned to a hurried thump, Mishti finally responded.

"So… what *is* our purpose? Peace?"

"No, not peace." Chloe reached for a strand of her hair to twist, only to find the one she grabbed had blood dried to it. Flicking it away, she continued. "There will always be disputes among people, fights and arguments we can't control. What we want is…"

Just then her gaze snagged on an object she had seen a few times before, but that had never been important enough to really think about. But now? Now she had found exactly the thing she'd been searching for, even though she hadn't known it until that moment.

Her lips curled upward as she looked even closer at the object. A large golden shield with a carving of a dragon in the front leaned against a wall. Just behind it, a tunic of golden chain mail lay on the ground. Since so many things were made of gold in Crystalfall, the shield and chain mail never stood out much, but they were still grand. Grand enough for her needs.

That shield would be perfect.

With her gaze trained on it, she quickly said to the others, "I have an idea."

6

Glints of light reflected off the golden surfaces of the great hall as Chloe darted toward the large golden shield she had spotted. She had long since given up trying to figure out where the light came from. The room had no glowing green sprites flying above the way the other courts in Faerie did. But the room didn't have candles to light it either. No discernible light source existed in Crystalfall, except the sun, but the great hall had no windows, so the sun couldn't provide light there.

And yet, light glinted off the golden walls as if the sun shone above them. Perhaps the golden ceiling above provided light in some magical way.

In any case, Chloe reached the shield and chain mail, and now she'd have to put her idea to the test. It all seemed fine until she held the shield in her hands, with the chain mail draped across her arms, and turned around. Suddenly, the room seemed smaller, and the crowd of mortals seemed bigger.

Her feet moved her toward the center of the room, but her wooden foot kept clunking against the ground harder than her real foot. Tension shivered in her fingers, causing her to grip the shield tighter than necessary. Even worse, her breaths had turned uneven, causing her inhales to sound like gasps.

She moved toward the crowd of people, but each step felt more awkward than the last. She'd really gotten used to having one wooden foot and one real one, but now, it felt as clunky as her first few days with the crafted foot.

The loud pound of her boot must have been the reason more than a dozen mortals turned to look at her. Their stares felt heavier with each step she took.

What was she thinking? Why had she gone and gotten the shield herself? She should have explained her plan and made Quintus do it. He was heir of Crystalfall, after all. People would listen to him.

Just when she reached the center of the room, a mortal with a thick strand of white in her chestnut hair pointed directly at Chloe. "What happened to your dress?"

The words stopped Chloe in her tracks, which didn't help at all because she had just stepped in such a way that the long tear Julian had made in her dress caused her leg, from her thigh down, to be completely exposed.

Another mortal, this one with a scrape on one knee, pointed toward her too. "I can see both your legs through the tattered fabric."

She couldn't gulp. She couldn't even breathe. Only moments earlier, she'd been so excited about her plan, so certain it would make the difference they needed.

And now she stood in the middle of the great hall, with every eye on her, and she couldn't even move. Heat filled her cheeks, burning away any belief she'd had in herself. The tingling blush even crawled down into her neck.

But then a loud, confident voice filled the entire great hall. "What do you think happened?" Quintus stared hard at the two mortals, daring them to defy him. "Julian happened."

In only a few words, he had effectively turned all attention away from her. Her fingers still gripped the shield too tight, and her knees knocked together, but at least now she could take another step so the slit in her skirt didn't expose her leg.

She needed a new idea. It didn't matter if she knew exactly what to do. It was clear she wouldn't be able to do it herself. When all those gazes latched onto her, she'd frozen. She couldn't think. She had to stop thinking of herself as capable of being a leader. She was just the mastermind. She could think of plans, but someone else always had to carry them out for her.

Movement spread through the room, but she'd been so deep in her thoughts, she hadn't noticed until Ludo came and stood at her side.

He gestured inconspicuously at a golden chair with ornate carvings of jeweled birds on its legs. "Stand up on that chair so everyone can hear you," he said.

She blinked twice before responding. "What?"

This time, he tilted his head toward the chair. "Stand up on there. It will help you feel and look more authoritative."

Just as he finished speaking, Mishti began marching along the outer edge of the crowd. "Gather around everyone. Chloe will explain everything. Just come up close so you can all hear."

To Chloe's immense surprise, the mortals started moving. They had seen her blush, and it must have been an unsightly shade of bright red. They had seen her legs through a tattered and bloodied dress. They had seen her freeze in fear, and yet… Would they really listen to her still?

Ludo stepped toward her and managed to shove her closer to the chair while making it look like she had taken the steps herself.

Her feet still moved awkwardly, but once she got to the chair, she managed to climb on top of it without trouble. And now she had the great golden shield in front her. It commanded more attention than her, but the mortals still looked more interested in her than ever.

Their expressions served as a reminder that she had to get this right. They needed it.

With a few deep breaths, Chloe spoke the words in her heart. "A mortal in Faerie knows his or her name, thoughts, even personality will always be lesser than one thing. Above all, we will be known as what we all are. *Mortal*." She spoke the word like a curse, the way the fae had so often done when speaking to her.

As she expected, the mortals before her flinched. They had all experienced the same, which would make these next words that much more powerful. "We are so much more than just mortals. And we have good reason to want to separate ourselves from the mortals out there." She gestured out with her hand, indicating the mortals outside the castle. "Perhaps it has never mattered to the other inhabitants of Faerie before, but now, *finally*, our purpose will be greater than our designation as mortals."

She had them. Every mortal in the room had gone from glancing toward her to hanging on her every word. Clearly, they felt as deeply as her how much it stung to always be seen as lesser. To always be thought of as *mortal* when there was so much more to who she was.

Standing a little taller on the chair, she continued. "For the first time, we will have a name so great that high fae, pixies, brownies, all the fae will whisper about it. A name so tied to purpose that we will become more than just mortals."

With a long, deep breath, she lifted the shield until it was right under her chin. "From now on, we will be known as the Order of the Golden Shield. We will protect this castle, protect this court. We will ensure this land offers safety to all in need of a home."

Lowering the shield slightly, she turned her head downward and gazed more carefully at the crowd. "Our job is not to *destroy*. Our job is not to kill or to lock people out." She ignored the guilt that came with that last part and lumbered on. "Our job is to *protect*. To *defend*. We are driven by honor. We are driven by integrity. We now have a purpose so great that it will be whispered about, sung about, and maybe even immortalized in epic poems. And that purpose is this."

By now, even Quintus had stopped scowling and stared up at her with eagerness shining in his eyes. She allowed a smile to lift her lips as she filled her lungs with one last great breath. Now for the words they all waited for. "We will offer a sense of belonging to all those who seek it."

Her hands raised until she had lifted the shield high up above her head. She spoke again, and her voice rang out strong, loud, and determined. "We are the Order of the Golden Shield."

Unprompted, the mortals in the room cheered. Their faces changed from plain to purposed. Their cheers spoke of more than just agreement. The cheers spoke of belief in a cause greater than any the mortals had never known.

Setting the golden shield onto the chair, Chloe then lifted the tunic of golden chain mail. "For all who wish to be counted as a Golden Shield, take a piece or several pieces of this chain mail and attach it to your clothing or wear it as jewelry. The chain mail will be our mark that we are now part of something greater, that we are something more than just mortals."

They all cheered again, sending a surge of energy into the room. It filled the space and then it bloomed in her chest, growing and warming her until a powerful feeling buzzed through her every pore.

With that feeling resonant in her heart, she scrambled off the chair and held the chain mail out toward them. The mortals used forks and candlesticks and anything else they could find to pry apart small pieces from the chain mail to attach to their clothing.

It was one small step toward making the mortals feel like they belonged.

Chloe helped at first, attaching chain mail pieces to collars and buttonholes and hats. At one point, someone—it had happened too fast for her to see who—handed her a row of chain mail pieces that she could turn into a bracelet for herself.

Sofia, the mortal with soft eyes and a strand of white in her chestnut hair, helped Chloe use a fork to bend the end pieces of the chain mail row until they attached to each other. Chloe kept the fork, in case she needed it to help someone else.

By the time she turned her attention back to the crowd, Quintus had the tunic of chain mail in his lap. He had crafting tools from his pocket, which he used to expertly pry apart the chain mail circlets. When mortals requested certain objects, bracelets or pendants or earrings, he used his tools to craft them for the mortals surrounding him.

Butterflies fluttered in her stomach at the sight. Maybe he claimed to be unworthy to lead since he was only *heir* to Crystalfall and not king of it, but he certainly had found favor with this crowd. She barely had enough time to appreciate the moment when something new caught her attention.

Mishti came to Chloe's side and then pointed toward the exit. "Come on."

Chloe raised one eyebrow, hopefully showing a question.

Using one hand to push her forward, Mishti spoke again. "You need a bath. You've got blood in your hair, dirt and grime all over your legs, and you still have that gash in your arm you haven't cleaned yet. Let's go."

Chloe allowed herself to be pushed forward, but she still retorted. "We don't even know where to find a bath."

Mishti shrugged. "We know where the king's living quarters are. I'm guessing that's a good place to start."

Glancing over her shoulder, Chloe caught sight of a man who struggled to attach a strand of golden chain mail to his shoes. If she just lent him the fork she still had, he'd probably be able to do it.

Her feet had turned to go help the man, but Mishti simply resorted to shoving harder. "Come on."

Chloe looked down at the fork.

Mishti grabbed it and threw it without looking into the great hall. "Bath."

With a resigned sigh, Chloe stepped into the hallway.

At least the explosions had stopped. The enemy mortals must have realized they'd done nothing. Or maybe they just ran out of things to explode.

As they traipsed down the hallway, Mishti plucked small pieces of metal and other remnants from the explosions off the ground.

As they turned a corner taking them closer to the king's living quarters, Mishti brought one of the metal pieces closer to her face. "I think Julian is from a more advanced time than us. Or maybe just a different place."

Dread seized Chloe's gut as she turned to her friend. "How do you know Julian set off those explosions? He might be dead."

He should have been dead. He'd already suffered multiple injuries that should have killed him, including the dagger in his chest he'd had last time she saw him. But he kept surviving somehow. Still, Chloe wanted to believe that last injury had killed him. Maybe it had finally been the one that would do it.

Mishti rubbed a finger over the metal piece. "Even if he didn't set it off, I'm almost certain he helped build it. He's always had a thing for explosives. And knives. And spears and axes and clubs. I guess he just has a thing for weapons."

"But if Julian only helped build the explosive, then he could have done it before the vault. He couldn't have gotten back to the castle that fast anyway, right? I mean, he had a dagger deep in his chest. He must be dead now, don't you think?"

"Yeah, maybe." Mishti answered half-heartedly, her attention still focused on the metal piece.

Such an answer only served to rile up the fear that Julian had somehow survived yet again.

Finally lowering her arm, Mishti looked toward her now. "Cheer up. Quintus promised he'd make you a new dress if I could get you to take a bath and actually dress your wound."

Cheer had absolutely no place in Chloe's heart at the sound of that. Instead, her heart sank until it felt as low as the deepest abyss.

Even walking felt like too much. Her feet started dragging on the ground with each step.

Mishti raised an eyebrow. "What?"

Chloe had to bite her bottom lip to keep it from trembling. "Quintus told *you* he'd make me a new dress? He's so eager to avoid me that he offered my bribe to you instead of to me."

It was a little ridiculous how whiney her voice came out, but she couldn't do a single thing about it now.

Hoping for some sort of relief, she glanced at her friend.

But that only made her heart sink deeper than ever. Mishti wore a half smile that looked as miserable as Chloe felt. She'd probably been trying to console, but Mishti's look only served to prove what Chloe already knew.

Quintus might never forgive her. Maybe she should just return to the mortal realm now to avoid the heartbreak being around him caused.

CHLOE'S WOODEN FOOT DRAGGED ACROSS the golden floor as she forced herself to take another step forward. Her bottom lip kept trembling, but this time, she made no attempt to stop it. With Mishti at her side and no one else around, Chloe could finally voice the fear that had sprouted inside her.

"Quintus hates me."

"No." Mishti answered quickly but not surely enough.

Throwing her hands over her face, Chloe groaned. "Yes, he does. He *hates* me."

Mishti responded in a voice far too detached to provide any real comfort. "Well, maybe he does right now, but—"

"No, you don't understand." Chloe's voice rose in pitch as an ache stung her throat. "I ruined everything. I never meant to take his magic away, but I did lock him out. It's over. I spent so long pushing him away, and now it's too late to fix things."

Just as they turned another corner, Mishti snorted. The sound was suspect enough, but when Chloe turned toward her friend, it was obvious Mishti was trying to suppress a smile.

"Did you just laugh?" Chloe asked snappishly.

Mishti swallowed, still not quite covering up the smile on her face. "Um…"

Folding her arms over her chest, Chloe pinched her eyebrows together. "This is not funny. I fell in love with him, despite my better judgment, and now, I'm pretty sure I've lost him forever."

This time, it wasn't just a snort that erupted from Mishti's mouth, it was a hearty chuckle.

Chloe punched her friend in the arm for it. Since she had maybe only half the strength of Mishti, the punch had no chance of hurting her, but maybe it would force her think about what she'd done.

Another snort left Mishti's mouth before she raised her hands in defense. "Okay, okay, I'll stop." Despite that promise, one last chuckle left her lips. "It just amuses me that you think it's even possible for him to hate you forever."

"You think he won't? You've seen how he treats me now."

Mishti's eyebrows jumped upward. "Uh, yes. Exactly. I've seen how he stares at you longingly behind your back, and how he never misses an opportunity to keep you safe, and how he supports you when you need it most, even when he *supposedly* hates you."

The thought of Quintus staring at her longingly behind her back did sound nice. But maybe Mishti was making that up so she'd stop whining.

Chloe might have asked for more specifics to see if it was true, except they had just turned into the hallway that led to the king's living quarters. Instead of finding it empty, they found Chandril pacing back and forth right in front of the door.

The wraith's dark skin looked more translucent than ever. He let out a quiet hum that sounded almost like a moan. After pacing one way, he turned to pace the other. That's when he saw them standing in the hallway with him.

His mouth twisted into a grin, showing off his white, pointed teeth. Chloe rolled her eyes. "Not you again."

Even though she had spoken, the wraith seemed completely unaware of her presence. Instead, his gaze fixed onto Mishti. He moved toward her, the look in his eye growing more intense with each step.

A knowing smirk lifted Mishti's lips as she raised an eyebrow at the wraith. "Enjoying my memory?"

"No." Chandril spoke the word in a dry tone, but then his smile grew until an almost-twinkle glinted in his eyes. "Not at all."

The smirk on Mishti's face grew. "I told you." She stepped forward, completely unconcerned by his intensity. In fact, she almost seemed enticed by it. "I told you a bad memory would be better than a good one. Now you know how it feels to be *alive.*"

He had reached them, and now he took one step inside Mishti's personal space. Her breath quickened as he did. His elongated fingers, twice as long as a mortal's, reached out. He moved the finger just over her hair, not quite touching it, from her ear all the way back to her ponytail.

"I want another." He whispered the words, leaning even closer to her with each breath.

"No." Chloe pressed her body in between the two of them until she could shove Chandril away. His lithe frame made it easier to move him.

Now his eyes turned hooded as he frowned. "I want another."

"You should understand by now how precious memories are." Mishti stood tall, somehow leaning toward him the slightest bit. "Would you give me one of *your* memories?"

The wraith's eyes lit up. That was new. His blood-orange eyes had glowed in the past, but with a strange light fitting for an undead creature like him. In contrast, his eyes now looked…alive. Full of wonderment.

"A trade?" he asked. "I give you one of my memories in exchange for one of yours?"

"I said *no.*" Chloe shoved him away again. Then she grabbed Mishti by the wrist and pulled her into the king's living quarters, promptly shutting the door. Mishti managed one last glance over her shoulder at the wraith just before the door closed.

A shiver ran down Chloe's spine while she stomped through the room in search of a bath. "Doesn't that wraith scare you?"

Mishti shrugged. "Not really." A tiny smile quirked at her lips. "I imagine it's life-altering to experience a negative emotion for the first time."

At least she didn't try to leave the room to speak to the wraith again. Instead, they both continued to move through the room, searching for another door that would hopefully lead to a bath. Chloe had already discovered the door that led to the king's secret study, but a few other doors lined the walls as well.

Her feet moved quickly over a holey and worn rug with faded blue and gold designs. It had probably been regal back before Crystalfall got destroyed. A rotting four-poster bed stood at the center of the room adorned with a curtain of cobwebs. The cold, stale air did nothing to make the room more inviting.

Strangely, the silk pillows and blanket on the bed still had an air of opulence, especially with their rich, purple sheen as shiny as gems. A gilded wooden dresser with a lavishly carved mirror sat against one wall. The wood had turned musty and crumbled, but the gilded parts still shined. And the rings and other gems on top looked as new as ever.

At the opposite end of the room, Mishti opened a door and stopped with a start. "Found it."

Chloe joined her in only a few steps.

She stood at Mishti's side and stared into the king of Crystalfall's bathroom. Marble tiles covered the walls and floor. A huge, golden clawfoot tub big enough for three people to fit side by side sat in the middle of the room.

Two golden washing basins sat atop brilliant cabinets carved from obsidian and embedded with emeralds, sapphires, and diamonds. Combs, washing cloths, and grooming tools covered the surfaces.

The scent of fragrant soaps and oils drowned out the dank smell that hung throughout the rest of the castle.

A towel rack displayed a collection of embroidered towels that were so thin and riddled with holes that they'd be as useful for drying skin as a golden plate. Even the opulent robe in a dark purple that hung on the rack looked thinner than parchment. It had probably once been plush and luxurious, but it would be useless now.

The bigger problem was water.

It hadn't occurred to her until now, but staring at the empty tub brought no ideas for how to fill it with water. In other places in Faerie, the fae just conjured water at exactly the temperature they wanted, but neither Chloe nor Mishti could do such a thing here.

Unless…

Mishti touched the tub with her eyes narrowed. "Do you think it's like the golden tables? Maybe it has magic in it to conjure water."

The same thought had just struck Chloe too, but now, it didn't make as much sense. "Why would the king of Crystalfall need a magical tub? A fae like him would be able to conjure water himself."

"True, but this is Crystalfall. Things here are different than they are in other courts. Maybe all the tubs in the castle are magical, whether they belonged to the king or not."

With a nod, Chloe agreed. "I suppose it won't hurt to try."

Mishti closed her eyes and spoke out loud. "Fill the tub with water. Warm water, perfect for a bath."

Right before Chloe's eyes, sparkling blue water filled the tub. The blue had such a brilliant luster, it seemed to have gems floating inside it. Wafts of steam swirled above the water, each with a slight pearlescent sheen.

Reaching behind herself, Chloe untied the knot at the bottom of her corset ties at the back of her dress. "How's the temperature?"

Mishti stuck a few fingers into the glittering water, careful to make sure no water touched the midnight blue of her sleeve or her leather arm bracers. "It's perfect. I wonder if there are any soaps in the cabinet. You'll probably need something to get that blood out of your hair."

"No soaps yet. I need to clean the dirt and blood from my wound first." Chloe had loosened the corset at her back but didn't take the dress off yet. As she bent to remove her wooden foot and her other boot, her gaze darted around the room. "What am I supposed to wear after I'm done?"

Mishti bent at the waist in front of one of the now-open obsidian cabinets. She turned around with a few crystal bottles in her arms. She glanced around the bathroom, and her gaze soon landed on the same robe Chloe had noticed earlier.

But the robe and the towels were nearly transparent and filled with holes. Maybe the castle had lasted through the destruction of Crystalfall, but the robe and towels had certainly not.

After wrinkling her nose, Mishti set the crystal bottles on the little silver and marble table standing next to the tub. Each bottle was filled with a different color of soap or oil. "Maybe the bedsheets are still in decent repair. The bedspread looked nice enough."

She went to leave the bathroom but turned back at the last moment. "Do you need help removing your dress?"

Her question got answered when Chloe threw her dress onto the floor and lowered herself into the tub.

With a chuckle, Mishti left the bathroom. "Never mind."

Steaming water enveloped Chloe's limbs. Even before she sat down completely, the balmy water had already soothed aches she didn't know she had. A contented sigh drifted from her lips as she lowered herself until the water came up to her chin.

The sparkling, glittering quality to the water wasn't even the best thing about it. This magical water seemed to soften and smooth her skin the longer she sat in it. Her legs truly were covered in dirt, blood, and grime, so much more than she had realized. But after only a soft rub with her palm, everything fell away from her skin, leaving it feeling refreshed, clean, and luxurious.

It took a little more prodding to get all the caked blood from the gash in her arm. She'd been ignoring the pain, but poking at it stung and burned as much as ever. Her breath caught in her throat when she rubbed away the blood from a particularly painful spot. Later that evening, she'd have to go conjure some pain herbs from the golden table in the great hall.

Her attention turned to her hair next. The glorious water had already washed away most of the blood and dirt by the time she got to it, but she still had to scrub through some of it. Her fingers worked through the bigger knots in her long blonde hair. It would take a comb, or even better, a brush to work through all the tangles, but the nearest comb sat on a cabinet on the other side of the room, and she wasn't about to get out of the tub to retrieve it.

Just the thought of that caused her to dive a little deeper into the water. It almost seemed alive as it swirled and danced over her skin. Maybe this was why even the king of Crystalfall had a magical tub. It could create a bath far better than any Chloe had had anywhere else in Faerie.

"I don't know if I'll ever be able to leave this bath," Chloe called out.

From the other room, Mishti laughed. "Are the soaps that good?"

With a start, Chloe sat up straight. "I forgot about the soaps. The water itself is that good. But now I need to try the soaps too."

Before she could reach for them, a loud creaking of wood was followed by a heavy thud that shook the ground beneath the claw foot tub. Her arm snapped back into the water as she gasped.

"It's fine," Mishti shouted from the king's bedroom. "I just kicked in the legs of the king's bed, since it looked one sneeze away from breaking anyway. But now the mattress is resting against the floor, so it should be safe to sleep on."

With one fist against her chest, Chloe called back, "Are you hurt?"

Mishti answered without hesitation. "No, just cleaning up the cobwebs and some dust, then I'll bring in the sheet. It's in much better repair than those towels."

Relaxing her hand from the fist she'd formed, Chloe once again reached for the soaps. Each of the crystal bottles held liquids with a shimmering appearance. After lifting the stopper from the first one, the strong scent of lilacs and vanilla filled her nose. Her lips turned upward. It smelled just like Crystalfall. The next bottle had a light oil scented like sandalwood and amber. The final bottle was the largest and also the least full. She could tell why the moment she lifted off the lid.

It had the most luxurious and lively scent of black currant and eucalyptus mint. Without a second thought, she poured the liquid soap into her hand and started rubbing it over her body. She worked methodically, carefully avoiding the gash in her arm, in case the soap had any perfumes that might infect the wound.

The soap that smelled of lilac and vanilla went into her hair, followed by a bit of the sandalwood and amber oil for the ends of her hair. Just as she finished, Mishti walked in with her arms full of a large linen sheet.

She kept losing sections of the beige fabric and would have to rearrange her arms to tuck the pieces back in again. "It's a little big and awkward, but it should work well enough until Quintus finishes your new dress. Do you need help with the soap?"

"No," Chloe answered brightly as she stepped out of the tub. Never before had she felt so rejuvenated. "I highly suggest a bath, by the way. I swear the water itself is magical."

Mishti chuckled as she handed over the sheet.

It took some wrapping and maneuvering, but Chloe managed to cover herself with the linen. Then she bent and rubbed the droplets off the end of her left leg, so she could put her wooden foot back on. Once it and her other boot had been donned, she wrapped the sheet tighter around herself. It dried off the water covering her skin as she and Mishti headed back into the king's bedroom.

Mishti helped to rip away a small strip of the sheet so Chloe could use it to wrap the gash in her arm. She'd need some honey and herbs for it tomorrow, but for tonight, she had a feeling the water from the bath would keep it clean enough.

Soon, they both sat on the bed across from each other.

Mishti fiddled with one of her arm bracers. "I told Quintus we'd sleep here for the night, and he could bring your dress by in the morning. Will the sheet be enough for you until then? We also have the silk blanket."

Chloe wrapped the sheet tighter around herself and snuggled up against the nearest pillow. "It's better than when we slept on the ground on the Crystalfall hills when the enemy mortals were after us. Now we have a feather mattress, and we've had food today."

"True." With that, Mishti stood and began her nightly routine of preparing for bed. She removed her leather arm bracers first, carefully examining them. Apparently, one had been scratched, but she just took a small bottle of oil from her pocket and used a white cloth to rub oil into the spot until nodding to herself.

Her leg bracers came off next.

While she worked, Chloe tucked her knees under her chin and held them tight. "Do you think it's going to work?"

She had meant for the question to stay in her mind, but it slipped out before she could stop it.

Mishti only slightly lifted her gaze from her leg bracers. "You mean the Order of the Golden Shield?"

It helped that Chloe didn't have to explain. She nodded, knowing her face fully showcased the fear coursing through her.

Turning back to her leg bracers, Mishti continued her examination. The leg bracers both got swift brushes with her hand, but neither of them needed oil. She pulled out her first dagger next, along with a bottle of polishing cream and a polishing cloth.

Was she going to answer? Or was this silence the answer? Chloe held her breath while waiting.

8

CHLOE HELD HER LEGS CLOSER to her chest, but Mishti continued to arrange her dagger and polishing items on the bed without saying a word. The speech about the Order of the Golden Shield felt grand when Chloe said it, especially after all the cheers, but maybe her promises would end up being nothing more than empty words.

If Mishti thought the plan would fail but didn't want to say it, silence would be the best option.

But just as she did her first swipe across the dagger with the polishing cream, her mouth finally opened again. "I do think it's going to work."

Her voice came out softer than its usual harsh tone. She swallowed hard before continuing. "I've been in a lot of battles. Even before coming to Faerie. I…"

The timbre of her voice didn't change, but her fingers gripped the polishing cloth a little tighter than before. "I became a soldier when I was eleven."

Chloe's eyes opened wide. "Eleven? Eleven years old?"

Mishti nodded slowly and focused even harder on her dagger.

That revelation seemed nearly impossible. How could anyone put a mere child into a battle? Then again, the mortal realm had all sorts of different places, and each place had its own customs. She'd met enough mortals to know how unique those customs could be. Maybe eleven wasn't so young where Mishti came from.

"Was that normal where you lived?" Chloe asked. "To become a soldier at eleven years old?"

"No." The answer came out tight. Pained. Mishti gulped hard before continuing. "It was a punishment. My brother, he…"

Tears pooled in Mishti's eyes, which she seemed eager to hide considering how she tried to blink them away. Would it be better for Chloe to look away? Or maybe it would be better to say something?

Soon, it didn't matter because Mishti continued. "You know how people who have power or money don't have to live by the same rules as everyone else?"

A twinge of guilt hit Chloe in the belly. Her family always had considerable wealth right up until the last year or so before her parents died. And when she lived with Vesper, they had more than considerable wealth since Vesper could conjure up gold coins whenever they needed anything. Still, she knew exactly what Mishti meant, so she nodded again.

Mishti rubbed her polishing cloth into her dagger with a little more vigor than before. "At my place in the mortal realm, if a woman was found to be with child before marriage, she was killed. Brutally. But at the tender age of eleven, I learned that wealth allows all sorts of exceptions."

Now Chloe had to gulp. She wasn't sure what would come next, but it clearly wouldn't be good.

"Instead of punishing the wealthy woman, she wanted the man punished. But my culture refused to punish a man for what it considered to be his *natural urges*." Mishti wrinkled her nose as she said those last words. "So, they punished the man's younger sister instead."

It took a moment to process the words, but soon understanding dawned inside Chloe's mind. *Mishti* was the younger sister. Her older brother must have bedded a wealthy woman, and when the woman was found with child, Mishti had to pay the price.

Lifting one shoulder in a shrug, Mishti slowed her polishing until her hand barely moved at all. "Oddly enough, my culture respected the life of a child more than the life of a woman. And since my bleeding had not begun, they decided they couldn't kill me. At least not with rods and stones the way they would have done to a woman. That would have been considered murder while I was so young."

Mishti placed a hand over her mouth and swallowed hard. Chloe nearly had to put a hand over her own mouth, but only to stop herself from cursing at the people who made the decision to beat a woman to death just for getting pregnant.

Setting her first dagger aside, Mishti retrieved the second one from one of her arm bracers. "Of course, they still wanted to get rid of me. Someone had to be punished, after all. So, they made me a soldier and sent me to a battle, right on the front line. That way, when I died, it wouldn't be murder but simply a soldier dying for her king."

By now, Chloe had leaned forward enough that she had to readjust the sheet around herself. "How did you survive? Did you run away?"

"No." Mishti scowled at her knife as she polished it. "I went to battle. I had no choice in that. I survived by killing anyone who came near me."

Chloe gasped. She couldn't help herself. When her friend looked up, Chloe asked, "You were that skilled when you were eleven?"

Mishti turned back to her polishing. "I did have some skill. It was common there for children to train with weapons, especially ones as poor as me. But mostly, I didn't want to die. I had the advantage that our army greatly outnumbered the enemy's, and that I was so small every person who attacked me expected me to be an easy kill. I was also young enough that I didn't see the enemies as real people. I saw them as monsters."

Those final words cost her more than any of the others had. Her breath hitched at the end, and the pool of tears returned to her eyes. She focused on her knife but had to stop as a few tears dropped from her eyelashes.

Mishti had been so young when she began killing, of course she didn't see the targets as people. She only wanted to preserve her own life. But Mishti had grown from that little child, and she had learned the value of life. Those early deaths she committed must have weighed heavily on her conscience knowing she hadn't even cared about those people before killing them.

"I never returned home." Mishti pulled several more daggers and knives from pockets and bracers throughout her clothing. She even set her sword onto the bed in front of her. This was not her usual routine at all. She usually worked on exactly one weapon at a time until it was completely polished. But maybe she just needed to keep her hands busier than usual.

"I believe my parents were told I had died in that first battle, though I never found out for sure. One of the soldiers in my company saw how I fought that first time, and she knew

I'd be the greatest asset to our company if given enough training. She protected me from the male soldiers, but only because she didn't want me being found with child once my bleeding began."

Reaching for the nearest knife, Mishti gripped it tight around the hilt. Instead of polishing it, she stabbed it into the bed at her side. "She turned me into a weapon, which brought our company of soldiers glory and money, just like she wanted." Gripping the knife even tighter, she lifted it, which released a small feather into the air. Then she stabbed it into the bed again. "But I never saw any of that money or glory. I was sent from tent to tent to train and practice and drill. I was told over and over again that bringing glory to the king was honor enough for me. That helping him expand his territory was the greatest cause I could have."

Her wrist flicked as she repeatedly stabbed the feather mattress, punctuating each of her new words with a jab. "All I ever did was fight. And kill."

A single tear slid down her cheek as she sank the knife into the bed for the last time. In the next moment, she collapsed forward onto the bed, curling herself into a ball. It took her several heavy breaths until she calmed the shaking of her limbs.

After a final deep exhale, she rolled over onto her back and stared up at the ceiling. The lightest smile tugged at her mouth as she reached up for her ear. She had three golden earrings dangling from her earlobes, each one made from the golden chain mail marking her as a Golden Shield.

Her voice came out lighter, freer than before. "I have fought for power, for glory, for domination. I've fought to claim land, to take over. I have hurt others to force compliance. But..." She let out a sigh. "I have never fought to offer safety. I have never fought to promise freedom and belonging."

Chloe held the linen sheet with one hand as she reached for Mishti's arm. "You don't have to fight at all."

"I know." Mishti sat up straight, her face calmer than ever. "But I think that's part of why I want to help this time. I've never been given a choice before. I've never fought because I wanted to. I've always been used as a tool because my skill was so great. I've never once fought for a cause I actually believe in."

Her fingers trailed upward, touching the golden earrings once again. "I am proud to be a Golden Shield. And for those like me who have always yearned for but never truly known safety or belonging since coming to Faerie, I think they are proud to be Golden Shields too."

Warmth lit like an ember in Chloe's chest. The sensation spread through her while serenity filled her limbs. The story had touched her to her very core. She knew Mishti had always been used as a weapon by her leaders, but to hear how it had all started made it seem so much worse than she'd ever imagined before.

It just made Chloe that much more determined to defeat the enemy mortals. Everyone deserved a place to call home without being turned into a tool or object the way Portia and Julian had done, and the way Ansel had done before them.

More than ever, it was clear that what these mortals needed was safety and freedom. But could they get it when the enemy mortals outside were so focused on attack? And would they truly be safe inside the castle with such determined enemies on the outside?

Only time would tell.

9

THE MOMENT CHLOE HAD HER first conscious thought the next morning, she immediately sat up straight and reached for her leather bag. She had left it next to the bed the night before, even before she'd gone into the bathroom. Now, she just had to get her magical book, hopefully without having to attach her wooden foot.

The sheet around her slipped down from her shoulders and moved off her lower legs, but she didn't bother fixing it. Her arms and lower legs were now bare, but Mishti was the only one in the room anyway, so what did it matter?

And anyway, the information she needed from her book was far more important than modesty.

She bit her bottom lip as she flipped through the pages. Like always, it only took her a few flips of the pages to find the passage she'd been searching for. The book had a way of bringing the right page forward, exactly where she needed it. Now her finger traced the words.

The words had brought her such anguish when she read them the first time. She had begged the book for a way to fix Crystalfall without having to bring Quintus back, but of course, there was no other way.

Then she'd learned that by locking him out of the court and severing their bond, she had also taken away his magic. She never expected to be eager to read these same words again, except now, she looked at them with all-new eyes.

At the end of the bed, Mishti stretched and let out a loud yawn. "What are you doing?"

"Shhh." Chloe leaned closer to her book, which sent the sheet down, uncovering more of her back. At least her front was still covered. But now her finger rested on the one word that could change everything.

May. It didn't say the bond *could* never be repaired again or *would* never be repaired again. It said it *may* never be repaired again. Did that mean they still had a chance?

She mouthed the word *may* and then whispered it into the pages of the book. At the sound of the word, the pages of the book filled with a buzzing energy. Magic seemed to dance across the page as the parchment took on a slight glow.

"Can we repair it?" She whispered these words as softly as possible, almost afraid to have the question answered. "Is it possible to repair the bond between us?"

She leaned forward, which lowered the sheet from her back even more. But soon, the magic in her book increased in energy. She could see that words would soon appear.

Just as the first letter started forming, the door to the room flew open.

"I have your—" Quintus barged in, growling his words. A new green coat with golden accents adorned his upper body. He held a length of fabric in his hand, which was probably her new dress. But he cut off short as soon as he caught sight of Chloe on the bed. She sucked in a breath as she glanced down at the sheet that barely covered her body.

Quintus's eyes opened wide and then they opened wider still. The copper undertone in his face soon became the overtone as his whole face turned red. Through it all, his gaze was fixed on her, as if he couldn't force himself to look away no matter how hard he tried.

Her insides squirmed at the sight of him. Just as he seemed mesmerized, unable to look away, she couldn't seem to move her arms. If only she could slip her legs back under the sheet or pull it up to get at least half her back covered. The only action she managed was to swallow hard.

His eyes had grown twice as wide as before. His mouth dropped open like he intended to say something, his face turning redder by the moment. But he never did speak. He just dropped the dress onto the ground and walked straight out of the room.

The door slammed hard behind him.

Mishti clapped a hand over her mouth, but it didn't stop a snort of laughter from escaping. With a smirk, she raised one eyebrow. "Still think he's going to stay mad at you forever?"

Heat spread through Chloe's cheeks as she dropped the magical book and wrapped the sheet around all the parts of her that had been uncovered when Quintus walked in. It made no difference now since he was gone, but she still felt the need to cover her skin.

Mishti just laughed and jumped off the bed to retrieve the dress. "Stop fussing with that. Just put on your foot, and I'll help you get this new dress on." By now, she had plucked the garment off the worn blue rug. "Oh, what a surprise, it's red."

Just in case, Chloe kept the sheet wrapped around herself as she attached her wooden foot to her leg and put the boot onto her other foot. She even kept the sheet on as she traipsed across the floor toward Mishti and the dress.

But Mishti had undersold this dress. Yes, it was red, but an entirely new shade of red that Chloe hadn't seen before. The brilliant shade of purplish red had the shine of a gem with a touch as smooth as velvet.

The skirts fell in a waterfall-like cascade down the front of the dress with flowery golden embroidery adorning each hem. Small golden flowers shaped like lilacs dotted through the empty spaces of the skirt.

Delicate golden embroidery along the neckline and upper sleeves finished off the magnificent gown. He had outdone himself this time—as he always did—except with this dress, he did it without magic.

Had he stayed up all night crafting this dress? Where had he even found the fabric?

Her questions remained unanswered as Mishti helped her get the gown on and tightened and tied the corset ribbon at the back.

Once clothed, Chloe kept running her hands over her stomach and over her skirts, unable to stop touching the luxurious fabric. During her bath the night before, she had been certain nothing had ever felt so soft and smooth and soothing to her skin as the magical water. But with this gown, she had already been proven wrong.

Mishti snickered as she gathered her weapons and tucked them into her tunic, belt, and bracers. Soon, they were on their way to the great hall.

With her leather bag set on one shoulder and her magical book inside, Chloe finally remembered what she'd been doing when Quintus had barged into the room.

Their bond. She'd never seen if the book supplied an answer. But now she feared more than she hoped. Quintus had accused her of destroying everyone once he learned Chandril had been affected by Mishti's memory. And he had given her bribe to Mishti, since apparently he couldn't stand to even speak to her himself.

To repair the bond, surely, they'd have to rely on each other. Trust each other. With him so adamant about hating her, it probably wasn't possible anyway. She should have known better than to hope.

Once in the great hall, Chloe and Mishti headed to the golden table to conjure themselves some breakfast. Quintus stood near the doorway talking to Ludo, but once he caught sight of Chloe, he clomped across the great hall until he stood in the corner farthest away from her.

She probably would have been more hurt by that if she hadn't noticed a new wad of fabric covering his side. This new wad was just as thick as the fabric she'd used to cover his injury the day before. Did that mean the wound was *still* bleeding?

Her heart lurched at the thought, making it difficult to swallow the honey-vanilla-flavored porridge on her plate. Whether he liked it or not, she needed to look at that wound. She'd have to do stitches if the bleeding hadn't stopped, and some of those stitches might have to be sewn onto internal organs.

When Chloe stuffed the last of the porridge into her mouth, Mishti suddenly grabbed the plate away from her. "Come here. Someone over here needs you."

Chloe barely had time to get her footing as her friend pulled her across the great hall. She certainly didn't have time to think about which direction they moved or who might possibly need help.

She only noticed the feeling of moving fast, and then suddenly slowing down, and then she heard Ludo say to someone nearby, "Yes, you have to stay right here in this exact spot until I get back."

Then suddenly Ludo was right in front of her, whirling on his heel away from the person he'd just been talking to. He smirked at her as he walked away. And Mishti somehow disappeared too.

But now Chloe could see who Ludo had just told to stay right in that exact place, and the ruse became clear.

Quintus stood directly in front of her, and not so surprisingly, no one else stood anywhere nearby.

He gulped hard as his face turned the same color of red as it had been in her room. In a flash, his gaze dropped to the floor.

Chloe would punch Mishti for this, and this time, she might try to punch hard enough to hurt her friend. Not that she possessed the strength for it, but she'd try.

Mishti and Ludo had clearly planned this, so he'd get a punch too. What did they expect to accomplish anyway? Quintus would recognize this was a ruse anyway and would certainly not stay in that exact spot just because Ludo had asked him to.

Then again, he hadn't moved yet. And Chloe *did* have something somewhat important to tell him. She tore her gaze away from his dark hair that was so much shorter than she was used to seeing. Now she took a deep breath before the words would leave her lips.

"I think…"

She swallowed even harder and tried again. "I think maybe it might be possible to repair our bond." Her voice grew smaller. "And hopefully it will bring your magic back."

For the first time since she entered the room, Quintus looked her in the eye. He didn't seem surprised in the least by this declaration. In fact, he almost seemed to expect it. Had he already guessed the bond could be repaired?

His lip curled as he scoffed. "You really think that is possible?"

She tried to stand a little taller. "We might have to touch, since that's how the bond was created in the first place, and we might have to trust each other or something, but I think we should try. If we—"

He cut her off short by stepping forward and glaring hard. "I do not want to try. I want to be around you as little as possible."

Scowling harder than ever, he stomped away.

She reached her arms around her stomach, trying to ease the pain of those words. It would have hurt less if he'd slammed a fist into her gut. Even breathing was a chore while she internalized his incensed declaration.

Tiny gasps escaped her as she forced herself to turn around. She didn't dare try to walk, but it didn't matter. Ludo stood nearby, his blue-and-red eyes glowing.

But the moment he caught sight of her, his face fell. "What happened to your tattoos?"

Her fingers on one hand curled into a fist as the other hand reached up to touch the bone under her right eye where her three star tattoos sat. Those tattoos served as a symbol of the bond between her and Quintus.

She felt nothing when she touched the tattoos, nothing on her face and nothing on her fingers. Sometimes the tattoos themselves tingled, but that hadn't happened in a long time. She had no idea what Ludo could possibly mean when he asked what had happened.

But soon the question got answered for her because Quintus turned around. He'd been stomping away, but he hadn't moved so far away that she couldn't see his face.

When he turned, she could suddenly see exactly what Ludo meant because the same thing had happened to the moon tattoo under Quintus's left eye.

It had faded.

Only a moment ago, when they'd been talking, the moon tattoo was dark and crisp as ever, but now? It had faded to an ashy gray. An ugly, ashy, unsightly gray.

She gasped hard. Quintus had said he didn't want to repair their bond, and now their tattoos were fading. Would her book say the bond *may* never be repaired now? Or would it say *could* never be repaired?

Ludo's face turned pale. His entire demeanor slumped as he looked between the two of them. Mishti had stepped close enough to see the faded tattoos too. Though she wore the same glare and hardened expression as she always did, her eyes had lost their sparkle.

But clearly, not everyone in the room could tell the significance of that moment. Two Golden Shields walked up, as nonchalant as ever.

Sofia stepped into the middle of the four of them and cocked her head to the side. "We have a name for ourselves now, but don't you think we should have a name for the *other* mortals? The ones trying to kill us?"

Batu came to her side, as ignorant as her about the gravity of the ashen tattoo situation. "Some of us Shields were talking, and we think it makes sense for the other mortals to have a name too, mostly so we don't have to keep calling them the *other* mortals."

It took several blinks, but Chloe finally processed what they had just asked. "Um," she said, still trying to get her bearings. "Y-yes. That's a good idea."

Mishti shook her head, seeming to process the words next. Ludo jerked his head toward the nearest Shield, nodding suddenly. Quintus never moved. He'd probably processed everything, but he showed no hint of it with his body language.

Closing her eyes for a moment, Chloe turned to the Shields again. "Yes, they should have a name. Do you have any ideas?"

The two Shields stared at each other, sharing a look that said they obviously didn't have any ideas or they probably would have said them by now.

But Mishti blurted out a word before either of them could speak. "Zeakriesh."

Chloe turned to her in surprise. Had she been trying to say an actual word and got mixed up? But Mishti gave no hint that she'd said anything wrong.

Even more interesting, Sofia and Batu stared at her, as if the word *Zeakriesh* was a word they understood.

After another moment, they both nodded.

Ludo rolled his eyes. "Zeakriesh? Does that even mean anything?"

Mishti glanced at the Shields and then turned back to Ludo. "I don't know. But Julian called us that sometimes."

Quintus raised an eyebrow. "Julian?"

Mishti nodded. "He called us that on very rare occasions. He was so distant most of the time, and then crazy the rest of the time. But every once in a great while, when we'd work together and trick a fae or sneak extra food for ourselves or accomplish something nearly impossible, he'd… that's when he would call us *Zeakriesh*. It made us feel strong. Important. Especially coming from someone who barely even noticed us most of the time."

Sofia and Batu nodded through Mishti's explanation.

Chloe swallowed hard before she responded. "Maybe we shouldn't name them something with such a positive connotation. Positive in their minds, I mean."

Batu shrugged. "It started with only Julian calling the mortals Zeakriesh, but the others started saying it too."

Ludo nodded like understanding had finally struck him. "So, you're saying Portia and Julian's mortals *already* call themselves by that name?"

"Only after major victories," Mishti answered. "But yes. It's the name that makes the most sense. We can ask the other Golden Shields, but they'll probably all agree."

They all turned, ready to gather the Shields again and ask about this name for the *other* mortals. But before anyone could speak or even move, a huge crack sounded through the air.

In a flash, Chloe turned around. The wall at her back split straight down the middle. Shouts and jeers erupted from the crack.

Zeakriesh or not, those *other* mortals were about to make an entrance into Crystalfall Castle.

10

RED HOT LONG RODS PRESSED through the golden crack in the wall. They melted through the gold to create more openings. Chloe took a step backward, holding her breath as she did.

Not another fight. She wasn't ready. She didn't have Shadow to keep her calm. Her feet stumbled over each other, the angle of it nearly forcing her wooden foot off her leg.

It wouldn't do anyone any good for her to be involved in this fight. Sucking in a breath, she stopped moving and covered her ears with her hands.

Sound still drifted through her hands, but at least now the screams and crashes were muffled. She needed to think. The enemy mortals had used some sort of device to create a crack in the castle wall. A huge crack. What sort of device could do something like that?

Mortals built incredible machines in the mortal realm, but this castle was magic. A machine, even the most advanced machine, shouldn't have been powerful enough to crack through the wall of a magical castle. That led to only one thought.

Had they used magic? Had the mortals somehow harnessed magic in some way and used it in their attack?

An object about the size of a book but made of metal brushed across Chloe's arm, reminding her a fight raged around her, even if she did have her ears covered.

"Get down!" Quintus shouted from behind her, but she ignored him.

She'd needed the reminder, but she couldn't stop what she was doing now. It only took another few moments anyway. While everyone else reacted to the attack and tried to fight back, she focused on her best skill, which had nothing to do with fighting.

After another moment, she uncovered her ears and whirled around.

Focus acted like blinders on her eyes, and even her other senses. She vaguely noticed the red-hot rods and flaming arrows flying, but her gaze zeroed in on the only fae with magic in the room.

"Ludo." Her voice came out calm but determined. "Open a door and get us out of this castle. We need to make sure every Golden Shield is safe."

"You want to leave?" Quintus snarled at her as he used a chair to block a barrage of flaming arrows. "But this is—"

"Yes, we have to leave." Her voice came out more than just calm this time. It came out authoritative. Certain. Even Quintus had no argument after hearing her voice.

She continued. "We lost nearly all our weapons already by trying to fight them from inside. We aren't ready for an attack. If we stay, we'll die. Ludo, open the door."

He didn't hesitate to follow her command. His hand whirled through the air and a swirling tunnel appeared before him.

Chloe nodded, already stepping toward the door. "Make it bigger so it can fit more people at a time. Mishti, you gather everyone and make sure all the Golden Shields get through safely. Quintus, you fend off attacks and keep us safe. Come through once everyone else has."

They moved immediately, following every one of Chloe's directions like a well-oiled machine. Maybe it was just because they had no time for questions when their lives were on the line like this. Or maybe—she dared to hope as she rushed toward the Faerie door—maybe they were finally learning to work together.

Perhaps some would have considered it selfish that she jumped through the door first, but for once, Chloe realized it wasn't. She wasn't trying to avoid the fight and make others do the work for her. She knew the Golden Shields would need direction once they stepped through the door, but direction could only be given if someone waited for them on the other side.

Most of her life, she would have shamed herself for stepping through that door so early, but she realized now such shaming has no point. This was purely a strategic decision, one that was desperately needed, she soon found.

The moment she stepped through the door, she realized where Ludo had opened it. It probably would have been smart to give more specific instructions, especially since Ludo's mind was clearly filled with the attack.

Instead of opening his door to somewhere safe, Ludo had opened it to the woods right in front of the castle. An entire squad of enemy mortals stood there protecting a stash of weapons. Those dozen mortals would soon attack her Golden Shields that would step through the door.

Then again…

Her mind whirled, already planning the next step and the next and the next. By the time Golden Shields started jumping through the door and at her side, she knew exactly what direction to give them next.

First, she whispered into the ear of the nearest Shield. She only allowed herself to give a one sentence explanation. Just then, the enemy mortals finally noticed Chloe and the half dozen Golden Shields standing with her. It didn't matter. She was ready.

Their eyes turned hard as they raised swords and spears. But just before they could step forward in an attack, Chloe opened her hands and held them out in front of her.

On each palm sat a mound of black dirt with a white pebble or two inside. She raised both her eyebrows and glanced down at the dirt with what she hoped looked like a sinister smile.

"This dirt has been enchanted to burn and melt your skin. The fae who enchanted it made sure only my own skin is safe from its effects."

She did her best to emulate Chandril's voice, since he had a knack for making his words chilling. One of the enemy mortals stepped back.

But not all of them had been frightened by her threat. One stepped forward, raising a dagger to throw.

Raising her hands, she shouted, "Stay back, Zeakriesh."

That one simple word stopped the mortal in his tracks. He blinked twice and started mouthing the word *Zeakriesh*.

The other mortals glanced between themselves, also mouthing the word.

One of them even whispered, "Did she call us *Zeakriesh?*"

Gritting her teeth together, she took another step forward. "You heard me. All you Zeakriesh, stay back, or I'll throw this enchanted dirt at you."

At that exact moment, her knee bent too fast, causing her to stumble on her wooden foot. She caught herself a moment later, but not before a small pattering of dirt fell from her hand. Most of the dirt pile stayed on her palm, but that small amount drifted away.

It would have reached the ground, except Sofia reached out to help Chloe catch her balance. Just as her hand came out, the small bit of dirt landed on Sofia's hand.

The woman gasped and pulled her hand against her stomach. The gasp turned to a scream, and soon she doubled over, another scream erupting from her lips. "It burns!" In another moment, she fell to the ground and curled tightly in a ball while gasping and screaming and gripping her hand against her body.

Chloe gulped hard, her own eyes stretching open wide. Shaking her head, she forced herself to focus on the Zeakriesh before her. "Get back, or I'll throw this dirt at you."

Now all but two of the Zeakriesh stepped back.

More Golden Shields stepped through the door, which meant they were running out of time. Taking a deep breath, Chloe raised her hands and threw the dirt directly at them.

Each Zeakriesh screamed and turned away.

Once their backs had turned, she shouted to her Golden Shields. "Get them!"

The Golden Shields charged forward, shouting as they moved.

But the attack didn't do much. Only a dozen Zeakriesh had been there in the first place, and they ran away too quickly to catch. But the Golden Shields didn't need to catch them anyway. They just needed the weapons the Zeakriesh had been guarding.

She turned around brightly to face the Golden Shields.

One man stepped carefully over the soil, staring at it like it had fangs. "Will that dirt still work after it's fallen to the ground?"

Chloe smirked. "Oh, it was just regular dirt. I only told them it was enchanted to scare them away." She turned now to Sofia who brushed dirt off her brown dress with both hands.

"Excellent acting, Sofia." Chloe smiled. "You almost had me convinced you were truly injured, even though I told you to pretend to be hurt."

The woman responded with an even wider smile and then took a small bow. "I thought it was a rather remarkable performance as well."

Something changed in the Golden Shields' expressions then. They looked at Chloe with all-new eyes. Maybe the realization finally hit them that just because she was useless in a fight didn't mean she was useless. She stood a little taller at the thought. Perhaps cleverness could be just as effective as a sword.

Gesturing toward the area around them, she spoke again. "Hurry and gather as many weapons as you can. Once the rest of the Golden Shields have joined us, Ludo will have to take us somewhere else that's safe. But we need weapons, so let's grab them while we can."

Nearly all the Golden Shields had come through the door by then, so it didn't take long for them to gather the weapons.

Once Ludo, Mishti, and Quintus finally stepped through the door, Chloe pushed toward them. Ludo had only just waved his hand around to shut the door when Chloe told him to open it again.

"We can't stay here. The Zeakriesh will come back. We could go somewhere far from the castle, but it might be better to stay as close as we can. We just need to go to a place on the other side of it. Somewhere they won't find us easily."

Ludo narrowed his eyes, but soon he nodded. "I know just the place. I saw it through one of the windows last night while I explored the castle."

With another whirl of his hand, he opened a door large enough to fit several people through it at once. Weapons filled every arm as their group stepped into the door once again.

Soon, they arrived in a thick cluster of golden and emerald trees. The air smelled of vanilla as it always did, but it also had a crisp and cool scent added to it, almost like cucumbers and crisp fall apples. At the edge of the trees, a small meadow sat before them. Light blue celestine crystals grew from golden patches in the soil. Each crystal patch had a slight glow and sparkled even more than the glittering gems surrounding them.

Nearly everyone heaved a sigh of relief at stepping into this haven. Chloe would have joined them, except she caught sight of Quintus. His eyes had turned glassy, and his body swayed gently. Was he struggling to keep his balance?

Even worse, the wad of fabric bound to his side had been soaked through with blood. It only took another moment and the first drop of blood fell heavily to the ground. Just like it had inside the castle, the blood reacted to the ground beneath it. The black soil puffed up in a cloud of acrid smoke. A decaying scent filled it, which soon wafted through the area around them.

Chloe held back a gasp. If she didn't take a closer look at that wound soon, there was no telling how it would hurt the land around them, maybe permanently too.

But when another few drops of blood fell, something miraculously different happened. The blood that hit soil still turned ashy with decaying smoke and dust that gave off that horrid stench. But one drop of the blood hit a patch of celestine crystals. Instead of decaying, the crystal glowed brighter and seemed to absorb the blood. The blood didn't make the crystal more brilliant or better in any way, but it also didn't make it any worse. Could those crystals be the key to healing him?

Whether they did or not, she still needed to properly take care of the wound once and for all. But when she marched up to him, he took a step back with a snarl. "I can take care of it myself. You stay away from me."

She rolled her eyes, but then another idea struck her mind. Mishti and Ludo just happened to be standing on either side of Quintus, a fact she planned to exploit. Glancing casually toward them, she soon caught their eyes. Only once they looked at her did she speak again. "Pin him down."

They glanced at each other then. Quintus's eyes grew wide. He even made a valiant effort to run away. But Mishti and Ludo moved too fast. Quintus's injury must have been affecting him much worse than he wanted to admit, because Mishti and Ludo pinned him to the ground with only minimal effort.

They pressed his shoulders into the soil, and any time he tried to lift his legs to wrest himself away, they'd shove his legs down too.

But now the wound sat just above the ground, which meant blood poured onto the soil. Chloe had to work fast.

She knelt at his side and pulled away the many layers of fabric covering his injury. Each time she peeled one off, she carefully placed it on top of a cluster of crystals instead of on the ground. As she hoped, the crystals continued to absorb the blood, instead of turning to ash and decay like everything else Quintus's blood had touched.

Soon, she could finally see the wound itself.

Bits of gnarled skin hung from what was mostly a huge gash. Blood oozed from the wound, faster than would have been possible for a mortal. Her hands immediately went forward, feeling inside the gash itself to see if any organs had been affected.

Quintus thrashed and moaned the moment her fingers started digging through the wound. She knew it would hurt, but by constantly pushing her away he hadn't allowed her to make it less painful. If he'd let her deal with the injury the night before, she could have conjured pain herbs from the golden table and had him chew them before she started.

Now, she had to work with what she had, which was a belligerent patient and no pain herbs.

After a quick examination, she determined no organs had been injured. Unfortunately, she also determined this had to be a magical wound that worked by drawing blood from veins and vessels with only the slightest damage to them.

Quintus's fae healing abilities were clearly working hard, counteracting the constant loss of blood. But even though his healing abilities were keeping him alive, the injury hadn't improved. His incredible healing abilities had only managed to keep death at bay, not actually fix the wound yet.

Her eyes closed while deciding what to do next. Stitches wouldn't help. The magic in the wound would continue to draw blood from his veins. The only real thing stitches would help was keeping his blood from dripping onto the ground and destroying it.

But then the extraneous blood would pool inside his body, which would lead to other problems.

Snapping her eyes open, she reached for the nearest set of blue crystals. It took some strange maneuvering and breaking apart, but soon, she had small crystals placed strategically inside the wound. They wouldn't heal him, but they would absorb the extra blood at least.

If she stitched his skin over the crystals, temporarily, it would keep him from dripping blood everywhere, and it would keep blood from pooling inside him.

After requesting a needle and thread from Ludo, who luckily had some in his pocket, she got to work. Quintus had given up trying to get away, but he continued to snarl and glare at her every chance he got.

When she finally finished, he jumped up and went to turn away.

"Wait." Her voice had just enough strain inside it to stop him. "I didn't heal it. The wound is magical, and even your healing abilities won't be able to fix it. They're only keeping you alive, not making it better."

His face turned ever so slightly green as he stared back at her. And, was his hair a little longer now?

Lifting her right foot, she began rubbing it across the back of her left leg. "I asked my magical book how to heal your injury, and it said…"

Quintus leaned forward. He wouldn't speak to her, wouldn't ask what she knew, wouldn't say he appreciated her stitching up the wound, but he obviously wanted to be healed.

That didn't make it easy to say what she had found. Her gaze turned downward. "The book didn't tell me what to do. It just said the king of Crystalfall can heal it."

His shoulders slumped as he closed his eyes.

"Speaking of that," Ludo said loudly. He glanced over one shoulder at the castle, which they could just barely see through the trees. From this angle, they could all see now that some sort of enormous object had caused the crack in the castle. The object still sat inside it like a knife that had been abandoned halfway through cutting a cake.

Ludo wrinkled his nose. "Apparently the mortals," he shook his head, "the *Zeakriesh were* capable of damaging the castle, even without iron."

Mishti swallowed as she reached for her sword hilt. "That means…"

Quintus dropped his forehead into his hand and let out a heavy sigh. "We have to find the king of Crystalfall. We cannot put it off any longer."

At least he had finally accepted the truth. But Chloe couldn't begin to imagine their next step. How were they supposed to find someone when not one single person remembered him?

11

After touching the magical book inside her leather bag at least three times, Chloe looked out at their little group. They no longer had a castle with an endless supply of food at their disposal. They no longer had rooms and beds and magical clawfoot tubs. At least they had weapons.

And at least they had a strong purpose.

Hopefully it would be enough to get them through whatever lay ahead.

"What about the vault?" Mishti spoke suddenly, right in the middle of cleaning dirt from under her fingernails with her favorite dagger.

Chloe, Quintus, and Ludo all turned to her in surprise.

Moving her dagger away from her nails, she held it out, probably unaware that she looked ready to stab something. "We found the last crown piece inside that vault, which belonged to the king of Crystalfall. Maybe there are clues to his identity in there somewhere."

Ludo grimaced. "You want to go back to the place we almost died? Sounds like a miserable plan to me."

"I think it's worth a try," Chloe said. "And besides, I'm sure there are no Zeakriesh there anymore. Surely, they've all grouped back at the castle by now."

Letting out a grumble, Ludo whirled his hand in the air. "I only joined you so I could find my brother, if you recall. And now we have to find the stupid king of Crystalfall first. I deserve a prize for all I have done to help you."

"Quit complaining. We know you secretly love the adventure." Mishti still had her dagger out and poked it toward him as she spoke. She probably meant it to be no more threatening than a pointed finger, but a dagger in her hands always seemed more frightening than in anyone else's.

Ludo jumped back and wrinkled his nose. "Put that away. Are you trying to kill me?"

Mishti chuckled as she tucked the dagger back into her leather bracer. "Obviously not, otherwise you'd already be dead."

The two of them headed toward the open door. Instead of stepping forward immediately, Chloe turned back toward Batu. "Um."

"I know," Batu said. "We heard. You need to find the king of Crystalfall so he can repair the castle and save the court. Go; we Golden Shields will be safe here until you return."

Sofia nodded at his side. "And we'll offer safety to anyone else who needs it."

Chloe smiled before finally heading toward the Faerie door.

Quintus walked ahead of her. Every few steps, his body would flinch. When he gingerly touched his side, his shoulder twitched. It served as a reminder that just because she had stitched up his wound and stopped him from bleeding, the injury was far from healed.

Once through the door, she stepped onto black soil dotted with pearlescent white pebbles. The area showed obvious signs of their earlier fight with the Zeakriesh. Broken spears and stray arrows scattered across the ground. Blood and ripped clothing sat among the debris.

She had known better than to expect it, but part of her wished to find Julian's dead body lying there. Of course, his body was nowhere to be found.

Maybe there was still a chance he had died. Maybe the Zeakriesh had just taken his body somewhere else to bury it. Her gut turned over on itself. Or maybe he had, yet again, survived an injury that should have killed him.

The stone door creaked as Ludo and Quintus opened the vault door wide. Once inside, all four of them began searching through the shelves and desk for any clues as to who the king of Crystalfall might be.

Did the king live in another Faerie court, completely unaware of his right to rule? Was he sitting around anxious, knowing he needed to do something and go somewhere, but because he had lost his memories, had no idea what or where he needed to go?

Chloe went straight for the hangings on the wall. Quintus had used one of the parchments as a spear so that would be no help, but some drawings of small animals and other creatures still remained. One detailed a pixie with big eyes and lacy wings. The pixie had one hand reaching out, little drops of rain emanated from his fingertips. The water droplets had been drawn in pencil, but the shading made them look extra shiny, as if they were silver water droplets.

It reminded Chloe of the pixie, Plumia, who she and Mishti had met in the hills leading up to Crystalfall Castle. Plumia didn't create silver rain, but she could create golden snowflakes that shimmered and glinted in any light.

If the king had studied these creatures so extensively, maybe he would have felt most at home in a court filled with the most creatures. Was there a court in Faerie that had a larger variety of creatures than the other courts? Other than Crystalfall, of course, since the king obviously couldn't have been there while the court was destroyed.

Quintus stepped close to her. He stared so intensely at the stone wall ahead of him that he was probably unaware of her close proximity. His fingers kept poking and tapping the wall. Maybe he was searching for a hidden compartment of some sort.

Whatever the reason, she'd take advantage of it. Chloe took one side step closer to him and then lowered her voice to a quiet whisper. "The king will know how to heal your wound, and I know we have to find the king so he can repair the castle and help defeat the Zeakriesh, but…"

Quintus stared at her, giving no indication he had even heard her words. The only movement came from the hand at his side that was hovering over the stitches she had just made. Every moment or so, one of his fingers would gingerly touch the stitches, only to pull them away immediately after.

It took a deep breath before Chloe could continue. "If we restored our bond, I think my magic could heal your injury."

He stared without moving for another moment, but then he leaned toward her. It wasn't the sort of thing that looked deliberate. Instead, it seemed like an automatic movement he had little control over. His free hand had come so close, she thought he might place his palm on her cheek. She hadn't known how much she craved that sort of touch from him until his fingers reached for her hair instead.

Though his feet didn't move, the rest of him came closer to her. He breathed in so deeply, she wondered if he was trying to inhale the scent of her. Even his expression had softened. Maybe he could smell the soaps and oils she'd used in the bath the night before.

As he slid his fingers through the strands of hair next to her cheek, heat tingled across her cheeks. It had been so long since he had looked at her properly, and now he didn't just look. He drank up the sight of her like he'd been without water for centuries. He stroked her hair, leaned in close.

It had to mean something.

Flutters filled her stomach as she inched herself a little closer to him. Her cheek moved toward him until his fingers in her hair brushed slightly against her cheek.

His hand froze in place, and his breath hitched. Even as his shoulders pressed toward her ever so slightly more, his gaze fell exactly where she wanted it. On her lips.

This was it. All she had to was grab his tunic, pull him close, and kiss him. This nonsense of pushing her away would stop once he remembered how it felt to kiss her. It had to.

But just before she could move, he touched the bone under her right eye, exactly where her three ashy tattoos sat.

His lip curled in disgust as he leaned back. "It takes two people to restore a bond, and *I am* not willing. I would rather keep the injury."

Pulling his hand from her hair, he jerked his head away. "You need a brush."

He said nothing else as he stalked away, leaving the thinly veiled insult to pin her in place. How was it that he could make her feel so small, so incomplete, with only a handful of words?

All she wanted to do was heal him. And fix her mistake. And bring his magic back.

But she couldn't do any of that while he hated her.

Her arms dropped to her sides, too heavy to lift. It was better than her heart though, which was getting too heavy to beat.

Ludo gasped loudly, filling the entire vault with the sound. If Chloe hadn't been ready to burst into tears, she might have turned a little faster toward him.

By the time she finally saw what had made him gasp, the others had already stepped up to his side. Ludo held a magnificent sword with a golden hilt and a silver blade. Glittery pink gems adorned the cross guard, giving it a dazzling and unique appearance.

"I know this." Ludo kept squeezing and loosening his grip on the hilt as he stared at it. His thumb traced over the pink gems inside the cross guard, then he used his free hand to slide two fingers down the flat side of the blade.

He shook his head several times while one of his eyes narrowed. "I know this sword. I cannot remember what… no, maybe who. I cannot remember who…"

Suddenly he blinked twice then stared off as if he was seeing a whole landscape instead of the vault wall he currently stared at.

With the sword in his hand, he sucked in a breath. "Balalov."

Mishti cocked her head to the side. "Is that the name of the sword?"

"What?" Ludo turned to her in surprise, almost like he had forgotten she was there. "No, Balalov is a city in Fairfrost. It is one of the outer cities."

Raising a single eyebrow, Mishti frowned. "And?"

"We have to go to Balalov." Ludo spoke the words as if they gave him life.

"Why?" Mishti narrowed her eyes in thought. "Do you think the king is there?"

Ludo's mouth dropped slightly. "Uh…" He did a sort of half nod. "Maybe."

Quintus rolled his eyes. "Not the king. He thinks his brother will be there."

"Oh." Mishti nodded, understanding dawning.

With a defensive scoff, Ludo stood taller. "The Crystalfall king might be there too."

Chloe folded her arms over her chest, throwing Ludo a look that hopefully indicated just how likely she thought it was that the king might be in Balalov.

With a sigh, Ludo's shoulders slumped forward. "Okay, maybe the king is not there. But my brother might be, and maybe Revyn remembers the king. Or maybe he will remember something else that leads us to him."

Mishti tilted her head to the side. "Hmmm, yes, that sounds so likely. And by *so* likely, I mean not likely at all."

Gripping the sword tight, Ludo leaned toward her with a glare. "What other clues do we have? We have searched this vault up and down and found no clues. We have nothing else to go off anyway. Should we not at least check Balalov?"

That brought a stunned silence through the vault. As much as Chloe hated to admit it, he did have a point. And besides, maybe his brother, Revyn, *could* help them find the king. He probably wouldn't remember everything, but once he was reunited with his brother, maybe he'd remember just enough to help them. Or maybe Ludo himself would remember something useful.

She would have said as much, except a strong sense of urgency struck through her chest. Her hand flew up, pressing against her ribcage just to temper the feeling. A single emotion filled her mind, which she could only describe with one word. *Hurry.*

Mishti stepped forward, concern pinching her eyebrows together.

"Shadow is here," Chloe said, turning toward the open door of the vault. "I think something is wrong."

12

THE ENORMOUS GOLDEN FORM OF her dragon greeted Chloe once she ran outside the vault. Shadow had her sapphire wings thrown open wide as she released a harrowing call from her open mouth.

"What is it?" Chloe leapt forward until she reached Shadow's side, stroking the creature's golden scales.

But Shadow inched away, only seeming more distressed when Chloe tried to comfort her. The dragon kept turning her great head, using her huge sapphire blue eyes to look behind herself.

It took a moment to understand, but it helped when Chloe's mind was filled with that same intensity as before. *Hurry.*

Finally, she understood. "You want me to climb onto your back? You want to take me somewhere?"

When Chloe said this, the dragon moved her body closer. Now her golden head bounced up and down.

The others had joined Chloe outside by now. Ludo stuffed the sword with the golden hilt and pink gems deep into his pocket. "Where are you going?" he asked, eyeing the dragon warily.

"No idea," Chloe answered as she scrambled up the dragon's back.

"Are you just going to leave us?" Quintus said the question like an accusation, his arms folded over his chest.

"Come with me if you like, but you have to hurry."

He started climbing up the dragon's back before she had even finished her sentence. When Ludo and Mishti rushed over, he helped them get up just moments before Shadow's glittery wings began beating.

Wind rushed through Chloe's hair as she got into place on the dragon's back. She might need more than a brush to untangle her hair after this ride. Each whip of the wind knotted her tresses even more, which felt like a slap in the face after Quintus's insult.

Brilliant emerald leaves covered the golden tree trunks below. Rivers and waterfalls stretched across the landscape, each filled with sparkling liquid that looked like blue gems. They passed over a cluster of deep bronze mountains with thick gold veins running through them.

Jeweled birds chirped, their song sounding more like bells than like birds. Even the buzzing of insects had a melodious quality to it.

From that high up, the air smelled more strongly of vanilla, as if the clouds themselves had vanilla beans growing inside them.

All at once, the crystal caves came into view. Was Shadow taking them outside the court?

But just as that thought entered Chloe's mind, she spotted tiny figures on the ground below. People stood among the trees just outside the crystal caves. They looked around and stared at each other, probably unsure of what to do or where to go.

Even more incredible, Chloe noticed tiny glowing green lights hovering in the air. The lights only came just barely inside Crystalfall, not through the whole court, but it didn't matter. Her heart skipped a beat at the sight of the green glows. Those were sprites. Sprites lived in all the other courts in Faerie, but so far, they had not come to Crystalfall.

It looked like that was changing though. It seemed the sprites had accepted Crystalfall as a true Faerie court.

As Shadow began flying closer to the ground, the pointed ears of the people below came into view. Chloe swallowed as her hand reached up to touch her open mouth.

"Are those fae?" Ludo asked, staring at the group.

"They look like it," Mishti responded.

"I think…" Chloe reached for her bag, ready to dig out the journal that had once belonged to the king of Crystalfall. But then she thought better of it. They'd reach those fae soon, and she had no time to search for the entry she remembered. "I read something in the king's journal once. He said this was known as the court of misfits. Anyone who felt they didn't belong in their own court had always naturally been drawn to Crystalfall. That's probably why Revyn, Ludo's brother, wanted to come here. He didn't like the way he was forced to do things by the king of Fairfrost, so he wanted to move to Crystalfall to have freedom."

Mishti's eyes lit up as she ran her thumb across the three golden earrings in her ears.

But once they flew a little closer, Shadow's sense of urgency suddenly clicked. Mortals jumped out from behind golden trees, brandishing weapons and shouting.

"This is *our* court! You are not welcome here!"

The Zeakriesh may have been fighting against strong and quick-reflexed fae, but they had the benefit of numbers. Nearly fifty Zeakriesh appeared among the trees while only ten or so fae had come out of the crystal caves.

Chloe grabbed onto her dragon's golden reins. "Fly down low, Shadow. And try to stop any weapons from hurting the fae."

The dragon had already started swooping, as if she had already known exactly what Chloe would command long before she said it.

Her golden body dove low. When weapons from the Zeakriesh began flying, she caught them against her scales and sapphire wings, batting each one away before it could cause injury.

Once they were close enough to the fae at the crystal caves, Chloe got to her feet and shouted. "Come with us. We'll take you somewhere safe."

The fae all looked taken aback, too surprised to do what she had asked. When another barrage of weapons came raining down, Chloe had to drop to her knees to keep from getting hit.

"Come on," Ludo said through a grumble. "Do you want to be attacked by mortals with iron weapons?"

The threat of iron was all the fae needed to be spurred into action. Soon, they jumped onto Shadow's back, and the dragon flapped her wings to carry them high into the air.

Only once they were safe did everyone sigh in relief. Then Mishti moved to the front of the dragon. She stretched high on her knees so everyone would be able to see her. "Those mortals," she pointed down toward the trees, "are the Zeakriesh. They want to control Crystalfall and everyone in it. But us?" Now she pointed at herself, Chloe, Ludo, and

Quintus. "We're from the Order of the Golden Shield. You can tell because we all have small golden circlets that we wear."

She reached up, showing off the three golden earrings she had in each ear. Chloe then held up her hand, displaying her bracelet made from a strand of golden chain mail. Ludo tapped his collar, showing the bunch of golden circlets attached to his buttonhole. Quintus showed that his golden circlets were attached to his belt.

By now, all the fae before them had raised their eyebrows and leaned forward.

Mishti continued. "If you want to stay in Crystalfall, we, from the Order of the Golden Shield, promise to offer you safety and freedom."

A Swiftsea fae with dark skin and a necklace made of seashells lifted her chin slightly. "I would like that. I feel at home here."

The fae around her nodded, even though they had all clearly come from different courts.

In only a few moments, Shadow dropped low, landing in the celestine meadow where the rest of the Golden Shields were.

Chloe's bond with the dragon must have grown more powerful than ever. Not only did the creature know exactly where their new camp was now that they'd been displaced from the castle, but she also knew anyone who entered Crystalfall needed protection.

Now if only Chloe could form that strong of a bond with Quintus. Her gaze slid over to him as she climbed off her dragon's back. To her great dismay, his moon tattoo had faded even more. It still looked sickly gray, but much lighter than before. Seeing it sent her stomach into a twist.

The fae slowly climbed off Shadow's back and began to tentatively examine their surroundings. One fae with red roses embroidered into his brocade tunic—probably from Noble Rose—looked at each of the mortals around him. After a moment, he asked, "Are *all* of you from the Order of the Golden Shield?"

Every Golden Shield in the clearing perked up at those words. They stood a little taller before nodding.

Batu took a step forward, his chest broadening as he did. "Yes, we are Golden Shields. We'll make sure you are safe here."

At that declaration, the fae looked nothing but relieved. The Golden Shields around them stepped forward, showing them where they could make a space for themselves and explaining which areas of Crystalfall were safe.

Chloe would have joined in, except someone grabbed her arm just above the elbow and yanked her back behind a cluster of trees. Once she got her balance again, she found Ludo had been the one to grab her. He had grabbed Mishti and Quintus too.

All four of them faced each other as Ludo raised his eyebrows. "This is charming that the Golden Shields are already able to offer protection, but what are we supposed to do with these new people?"

Mishti stood tall, purpose shining in her eyes. "We have to give them a home."

Ludo set his hands on his hips. "But we don't even have a golden table anymore. We have no beds, no shelter. We barely even have enough weapons to defend ourselves."

"Well," Chloe shrugged. "The weather is always nice in Faerie. Maybe no one needs beds or shelter. Maybe they just

111

need conjured sleeping mats and blankets. And you can conjure food too, right?"

He swallowed hard and began wringing his hands. "I do not know if I have enough for this many people."

She cocked her head to the side. "What do you mean *enough*? I thought you could *conjure* food." She lifted her hands and spun them in a circle the way Ludo did when he conjured. "Don't you conjure food? Out of nothing?"

Both Quintus and Ludo turned to her wearing expressions of the utmost confusion.

Now Ludo rolled his eyes. "I know I told you I learned how to conjure meals from the brownies, but I am still high fae. I do not have the magic of brownies."

Now Chloe and Mishti were the ones wearing confusion. They stared at each other, which only made the confusion grow.

"What?" Chloe shook her head, as if that would help. It didn't.

Mishti raised a single eyebrow. "We've seen you conjure food plenty of times. You conjured it from nothing."

Ludo's eyes opened wide for a moment, and then he smacked himself on the forehead. "I never realized you assumed I was conjuring it from *nothing*. No, I have a garden at my house in Bitter Thorn. And I have stores of meat and herbs and spices and plenty of things to make a meal."

Chloe pressed two fingers to her temple, desperate to understand. "So, you weren't conjuring it from nothing? You were preparing it and magically taking it from your home to wherever you happened to be at that moment?"

Could food move like that? It didn't seem right.

"Exactly." Ludo smiled wide. "It is the same as whenever you used your own magic to heal, right? You would use healing herbs and ingredients, but they would be taken from the stores you have in your leather bag.”

He gestured toward her bag as he finished speaking.

But she could only answer by shaking her head. “No. With my magic, I could use any ingredients, not just the ones in my leather bag. And even if I did use the same ingredients that were stored in my bag, it never took any from there. I think I *did* conjure the ingredients from nothing.”

Quintus raised an eyebrow. “That is impossible.”

Ludo waved a hand through the air. “Maybe you just took the ingredients from wherever they grow in Faerie and never realized it.”

Turning to his friend with an even more soured expression, Quintus said, “That is also impossible. Things like that can only be used if they are gathered first.”

“Well, maybe she has gathered enough ingredients in her life that she figured out how to do it with her magic. That is more likely than her conjuring herbs from nothing, is it not?”

“I suppose.” Quintus looked thoroughly unconvinced.

Even stranger, Chloe was more unconvinced. She hadn’t magically gathered anything, especially because some of the herbs and tinctures she used had ingredients that only grew in the mortal realm. She didn’t care if they believed it or not: she was almost certain her magic had allowed her to conjure items from nothing.

That revelation begged the question, how? How had a mortal like her been given a magic even more powerful, more unique, than a fae’s magic?

At least it made one thing clear. With magic as powerful as that, it was certain it could heal Quintus’s magical wound. If only she could convince him to repair their bond.

Mishti leaned against the nearest tree trunk and flipped a dagger out from her arm bracer. "Maybe we'll get lucky, and a brownie will decide to come to Crystalfall."

Chloe nodded. "Maybe so. But until then, you can conjure food for everyone for at least a few days, can't you, Ludo?"

He looked at her, then nodded slowly. "Yes. For at least a few days I can." But then his face shifted into the devious look of a fae. "But only if we go to Balalov."

Since she'd already decided they might as well go, this was an easy thing to agree to. She also noted Ludo made no official bargain. He may have acted grumpy and selfish, but she had a feeling that deep down, he liked being a part of their little group.

"Oh, all right." Chloe gestured toward her dragon, who was busy skipping over the black soil, puffing up huge clouds of dirt each time. "Let's have Shadow fly us there."

As she and the others climbed onto her dragon's back, a new thought flitted through her mind. Yes, this was a slight detour, but maybe, just maybe, it would bring them one step closer to finding the king of Crystalfall.

13

HILLS COVERED IN IRIDESCENT SNOW filled the landscape below. Chloe leaned closer to her dragon's golden scales, hoping they might provide some warmth from the chill in the air. She should have remembered Fairfrost was much colder than the other courts since it had a landscape of frost and snow. But of course, she hadn't remembered until it was too late.

Glancing to the side, Chloe looked in envy at Mishti's long-sleeved, thick tunic made of midnight blue velvet. Even her dark brown pants and high boots probably brought warmth. Chloe wore nothing but some thin underclothes and her dress from Quintus, which had only tiny sleeves and a low neckline.

When Shadow landed on a mound of snow, she considered telling the others to go look for Ludo's brother on their own while she went back to the warmth of Crystalfall. One by one, Ludo, Quintus, and Mishti all slid off the dragon's back.

Chloe only followed because Shadow kept inching toward an untouched mound of snow. Perhaps it was the bond between them, but she had a feeling her dragon wanted to jump and roll around in that snow, and she most definitely did not want to be on her dragon's back when that happened.

But when she slid off the dragon's back, her blue cloak sat on the snow right in front of her. The fur-lined cloak had been made by her fae brother, Vesper, and could block snow and water better than any mortal-made cloak.

She draped it over her shivering shoulders gratefully. The fur lining inside it began warming her at once. After clasping it, she pulled the hood up and over her head.

Quintus had done it. She had forgotten, but after seeing the cloak, she remembered he'd had the cloak in his magical pocket since before she locked him out of his court. He must have seen her shivering on Shadow's back.

It was a kind gesture. One that gave her courage.

Just as she began walking, Shadow leapt forward and pounced directly in the center of the untouched mound of snow, exactly as Chloe guessed she might.

Chloe chuckled as the dragon burrowed her head deep in the snow, only to lift it up suddenly. Snow gathered atop the dragon's head and on the very tops of her sapphire blue horns. A little mound of snow even billowed atop Shadow's nose.

Her eyes went slightly cross-eyed as she stared at the snow. Then, with a great huff, the dragon blew hot air from her nostrils, quickly melting away the snow mound in a burst of steam. Shadow let out a small yip of delight before burrowing her head in the snow once again.

Laughing once more, Chloe skipped forward to join the others. She found Ludo and Mishti walking ahead, each pointing to different parts of the landscape as they spoke to each other. Quintus trekked broodily behind them at a distance that would make it easier to talk to him privately.

She bit her bottom lip, then touched a hand to the cloak clasp at her throat. Maybe this time, he'd finally listen. Taking a deep breath, she hiked forward until she wrapped a hand around his bicep from behind.

His body froze at the touch. But by the time he turned to face her, she could see the cloak had meant nothing. At least not what she had hoped it meant.

He wrested his arm out of her grip and bared his teeth as he stepped away. "Stop touching me." He dug both hands into his hair and shook it hard. "Stop trying to… Just…"

His shoulders and arms tensed as he fixed his gaze on her just so he could glare. "I will not do it. I do not want to be bonded to you."

As he huffed and scowled at her, she could see the ashy edges of his moon tattoo start to fade away. Instead of having crisp, curved lines, the moon now had smudgy, undefined edges. Inside her chest, a physical wedge seemed to dig right into her open heart.

For a moment, she couldn't breathe.

He stared hard enough at her face, where her own star tattoos sat, that he must have seen the same thing happening to them.

Before either could react, Shadow's golden head suddenly poked forward, completely filling the space between them.

Instead of the delighted expression she'd been wearing while playing in the snow, the dragon now had eyes filled with distress. She whimpered deep in her throat, which shook the ground beneath Chloe's feet.

"What is it, girl?" Chloe immediately rubbed a hand over Shadow's head from between her eyes and down to her nose. Her gaze raked over the dragon's body, searching for any sign of injury. She found none, but Shadow whimpered again, seemingly even more distressed now.

Chloe rubbed harder on Shadow's nose, hoping it might comfort the creature in some way. With her eyes focused on that part of the dragon, she barely caught sight of Quintus, who stood on the other side of Shadow's head.

His eyebrows had been driven together so tightly that a crease formed between them. Concern shimmered in his dark eyes as he too stroked a hand over the golden scales. It surprised her to see it. She'd never known Quintus to care much about Shadow's well-being, but here he stood getting just as distressed over the creature's sad whimpers.

She couldn't help it, but her heart skipped at the sight. For him to care about her dragon just as much as she did, it touched her. It took hold of the wedge in her heart and ripped it away while little stitches seemed to sew up the break.

And his hair was definitely getting longer. Before it had been so short there was no hint of the curls he once had. But now, a few tendrils were just long enough to form the beginnings of curls.

Right then, he looked up. Their eyes locked, and considering how he'd acted a moment ago, she expected him to scowl. But he didn't. He kept one hand on Shadow and stared at Chloe like he used to. Like he did when he still loved her.

She bit into her bottom lip while he continued to stare. The sight of it caused a flash of golden glints in his eyes. Despite herself, the corner of her mouth lifted in a smile.

If he reacted to her smile, she couldn't tell, because Shadow lifted her head high and let out an even more delighted yip than before. She sauntered off and soon happily pranced across the snow until jumping into a new pile.

Now came the scowl. Quintus whirled away from her and raced forward to catch up to Ludo and Mishti. Chloe's heart thumped inside her chest, but it didn't hurt as much as it had earlier.

Just then, Ludo called out. "This is it. This is where we found Revyn's dragon."

Mishti turned to him with one eyebrow raised. "You told us you couldn't remember if he ever trained the dragon. You remembered waking up that morning, but you couldn't remember if you ever used his scarf to bond with a dragon."

Ludo's grin only grew as he stepped closer to the icy cavern he approached. "I remember now. I do not remember what happened after Revyn attached his scarf to the dragon, but perhaps I will remember if I catch a glance of the—"

His words got cut off short when a dragon with rocky, earth-toned scales and immense, clawed wings burst out from inside the cavern. It had grass green eyes and horns that sparkled like gems. Ludo's mouth dropped open wide as the dragon shifted, showing off light blue knit reins attached to its neck.

"Get it," he whispered, too full of emotion to speak like usual. "Grab its reins before it gets away."

Mishti lunged forward. But just before she could snatch the reins made from a light blue scarf, the dragon reared its head toward her and growled. A moment later, a crackling noise sounded at the back of the creature's throat.

Chloe stumbled backward. "It's about to breathe fire, get back."

"No." Ludo darted forward. "We just have to grab hold of the reins and then we can control it."

His feet moved haphazardly over the crunchy snow, but determination fueled him.

The dragon roared again, even more ferocious than before. It opened its mouth wide, showcasing rows of serrated teeth, and began to exhale. The first stream of flames shot from its mouth.

In a panic, Chloe dropped to her stomach. Mishti and Quintus did the same. Blue and orange fire erupted from the dragon's mouth. But it only lasted a moment before an even louder growl filled the air.

Shadow had flown forward, using one leg to smack the other dragon across its jaw.

The earth-toned dragon's fire stopped short. A ghastly snarling sound came from its mouth as it turned toward Shadow.

Shadow responded by flapping her wings out wide and opening her mouth, as if ready to clamp her fangs around the other dragon's neck.

"Almost there." Ludo had to stretch his arms as high as they could go, and even still he couldn't quite reach the reins now that the dragon stood taller.

Growling again, Shadow swooped in closer, ready to smack her leg against the other dragon again.

Mishti jumped forward in an attempt to reach the reins on the other side of the dragon's head. When that failed, Shadow hissed and pressed her claws against the dragon's rocky shoulders, pinning him against the icy cave wall.

She may have injured the dragon if given another moment, but then a voice stopped them all.

"Hey! That is *my* dragon. Get that golden beast away from him." From inside the cave, a tall fae with broad shoulders and light brown hair came bounding forward. He shoved Mishti aside and easily caught hold of the scarf reins dangling from the dragon's neck.

Through a gasp, Chloe managed to speak to her own dragon. "Shadow, let him go." She carefully reached for her wooden foot, which had fallen off in her haste to drop to the ground. While re-attaching it, she stared without blinking at the fae before her.

"Get your stupid dragon away…"

Shadow had already moved back, releasing her claws from the other dragon's shoulders.

But now the fae had stepped out in front of his dragon, and he seemed to realize the rest of them were staring at him with widened eyes.

"What?" He patted his light blue brocade overcoat, glancing down at it before speaking again. "Do I look strange or something?"

"Revyn." Ludo managed to say the name, but he failed to speak otherwise. He had stumbled away from the earth-toned dragon, doing nothing but stare at the fae before them.

Revyn whirled around, anger filling his features. "Are you the one who planned this? Thought you could steal a trained dragon since mine is the only one left besides King Severin's? Well, I—"

He stopped short as soon as he caught sight of Ludo. Color drained from his fair skin, but confusion crinkled his eyes. "I…" He shook his head before staring harder at Ludo. "Do I know you?"

A puff of air escaped Ludo's mouth while his lips formed the lightest smile. Tears swam in his eyes before one single drop slid down his cheek. "I found you."

Revyn stepped back, blinking several times. "Found me? How do you even know me?" His head cocked to the side as he lowered his voice. "How do I know you?"

With a laugh, Ludo clapped his hands together. "Can you believe it? He remembers me."

The fae lifted an eyebrow. "I do not *remember* you."

Ludo shrugged. "Sort of. It does not matter. I am certain the memories will start to return now that we are together. Now, where is Clara?"

The confusion on Revyn's face fell away as his expression turned neutral. He narrowed one eye for a very long time before slowly repeating the name. "Clara?"

Frowning, Ludo dug into his pocket and pulled out the sword with the golden hilt and pink gems. He held it out toward his brother. "Clara."

Revyn stared at the sword, his eyes narrowing to slits. Every once in a while he looked like he'd almost catch onto a memory, but then he'd shake his head as if it had slipped away.

As he stared, Chloe finished re-attaching her foot and finally stood. She stepped closer as Revyn continued to think.

But he never gave any sort of answer. Instead, he finally just looked at Ludo and shrugged.

Pain sent creases through Ludo's forehead. "You have no idea where she is?"

Revyn lifted one hand in front of himself. "I have no idea *who* she is, but…" Now his hand pressed against his chest as his breathing turned heavy. His voice went gravelly before he spoke again. "My heart aches without her."

Grinning, Ludo clapped a hand on his brother's shoulder. "Do not worry. We will help you find her."

Chloe's eyes flew open wide as a twinge went through her heart. She glanced at Mishti and Quintus, but both of them stayed silent. Knowing it was up to her to say something, she grimaced. No one would like what she had to say.

As gently as she could, she stepped forward and placed a hand on Ludo's arm. Her voice came out as a whisper. "Ludo, she's probably dead."

Her words froze in the air, sending a cold silence between them. Knots curled in her belly, anxious to see how Ludo would respond.

14

Silence stretched as wide as the ice in Fairfrost. Everyone stared at Chloe. Mishti was sad, Quintus forlorn, and Revyn looked like his heart had just been torn out. But Ludo was aghast.

He jerked his head toward Chloe. "No." His head shook fervently, bouncing his hair. "Clara is definitely not dead."

She raised both her eyebrows, trying to speak even more gently than before. "Didn't you say she was mortal?"

"Yes." Ludo clearly didn't understand why this mattered.

Looking carefully into his eyes, she continued. "Mortals still age and die at the same rate as they do in the mortal realm, even here in Faerie. Elora told me this long ago."

Revyn started, looking at Chloe like she had grown a second head. "Why did you not call her *Queen* Elora?"

Chloe rolled her eyes. "She's my sister. I'll call her whatever I want."

He raised an eyebrow. "Your sister is Queen of Bitter Thorn? But you are not fae like her."

Pressing a hand to her forehead, Chloe tried to explain in the simplest way possible. "Elora used a balance shard to turn herself fae, but I can't do that. I wouldn't survive the change, just like anyone else who tries to use a shard. She only survived because... because she's Elora."

Revyn started to nod but stopped halfway through to tilt his head to the side.

Chloe waved a hand through the air. "That's not the point. The point is, Clara met you back when Crystalfall still existed the first time."

He mouthed the word *time* while utter confusion filled his features.

Ignoring that, she continued. "She met you before Crystalfall was destroyed." Now she turned to Ludo. "How long ago do you think that happened?"

"More than a hundred years." To everyone's surprise, Quintus had supplied that answer.

Chloe turned to him, anxious for an explanation.

He lifted one shoulder in a shrug. "At Bitter Thorn Castle, I once worked with Martin, High King Brannick's mortal father. Kaia, a dryad skilled in healing, kept him alive far longer than most mortals live. I watched him age nearly a hundred mortal years. And after he died, I saw other mortals age too. For a mortal, it has surely been more than a hundred years since Crystalfall was first destroyed."

Grimacing, Chloe put her hand back on Ludo's forearm. She had to take a breath and then made sure her tone would come out as tender as possible. "Ludo, mortals don't live that long."

He took a step back, moving away from her grip. "No, Clara is alive." He swallowed and lifted his chin in the air. "She had a magical amulet from the pixies that would make her age slowly. Maybe she is older now, but she is not dead."

"An amulet?" Revyn touched a hand to his forehead while his feet stumbled over the frozen landscape. "I…" Suddenly, he gripped his dragon's reins tighter. "I must find her."

Showing his fae agility and strength, he hopped onto his dragon's back.

"Ride," he shouted.

Ludo's eyes went wide as the dragon's wings stretched outward. "Wait." He stumbled forward and tried to grip the dragon's side. "Do you have any idea how long I have been looking for you?"

Revyn ignored him, focusing only on directing his dragon.

But a moment later, Ludo got a better hold on the rocky scales and managed to force himself up to the dragon's back. As the dragon started rising into the air, he looked down at Mishti. "I will return to the celestine meadow after I talk to Revyn. We will be back soon."

He had no time to say anything else because the dragon had carried them too far away.

Chloe stared open-mouthed as the two brothers and their dragon disappeared from view. When she glanced at the others, she found Quintus staring with a sideways smile. Mishti, however, had both hands on her hips with her lips pressed forward in a strange, deathly-looking pout. When she noticed Chloe staring, Mishti turned to face her.

The young woman used her eyes to point in the direction Ludo had just disappeared. With an almost wistful tone, she said, "Now I want a dragon." She looked down at herself. "Do you think I have anything that would count as a token that I could use as reins?"

She pulled out various daggers and even glanced at her sword. After looking through those, she tugged a dark blue ribbon out from under her left sleeve. She glanced at it for only a moment before starting to put it back. But then she stopped, pulling it out again more slowly. She stared at it longer this time, blinking twice and breathing slowly. After another moment, she carefully tucked it back into her sleeve.

Chloe placed a hand on Shadow's neck, stroking the golden scales. "Do you want to go look for a dragon? I suppose we *are* in Fairfrost."

Mishti's eyes lit up for only a split second before her face turned stoic once again. "No. Although, what are we supposed to do now? We learned nothing about the king, and now Ludo's gone too."

Quintus stepped past them both, keeping his head straight forward with almost no expression at all. "Night is falling. We should go back to Crystalfall and get some rest."

He didn't wait to see if they agreed. He just climbed atop Shadow's back with his face as still as stone.

Despite his eerily calm reaction, he was right. If night was falling, they needed to get back and sleep. Hopefully Ludo would return by morning and conjure some food for everyone. If not, they might have to travel to another court and see if they could find a brownie in search of a home.

On Shadow's back, on the way to Crystalfall, Mishti got out a dagger and flipped it through the air before catching the hilt with her other hand. She flipped it a second time, then glanced quickly at Chloe before throwing it into the air once more. "Do you think we should make a deal with the wraiths?"

"The wraiths?" Chloe touched a hand to her collar bone. "Why would we do that?"

Mishti kept her eye on the dagger as she flipped it. Now, she pulled a second dagger from the arm bracer and started flipping them and catching them one after the other. "Do you think they remember anything? They might know what the king looks like or what court he came from."

Chloe folded her arms over her chest. "Making a deal with the wraiths means giving up a memory. Do *you* want to do that?"

"No." Mishti answered quickly but her facial expression still spoke of hesitation. "But if we can't find answers anywhere else, we might not have a choice."

Those ominous words burrowed under Chloe's skin as they returned to the celestine meadow and found places to sleep for the night. Even while she slept, the truth of that possibility ached inside her.

She didn't want to think about it. So, of course, it was the only thing she could think about. Each time she started drifting off to sleep, the thought of wraiths and lost memories woke her with a start, causing her to get almost no rest the entire night.

She even thought she heard footsteps nearby at one point, but that must have been her mind playing tricks on her, because her eyes found nothing when she searched the area.

When day dawned, she had only just fallen into a deep sleep for the first time. But soon, Golden Shields began moving through the meadow, waking her once again.

"Isn't it wonderful?" Batu said with a bright smile. "Some of the fae who got here yesterday brought food, and now we have just enough breakfast for everyone."

"Wonderful," Chloe said through a tight smile. But as soon as she heard Batu's footsteps saunter away, she groaned and rubbed her eyes.

When she sat up, she found Mishti directly across from her, pressing a pile of berries and a roll toward her.

Chloe wrinkled her nose at the food and grabbed only the roll. "You keep the berries. They make me sick."

Mishti nodded, plopping one into her mouth. "I forgot about that. Will the roll be enough? Ludo isn't back yet."

Pouting, Chloe stood and put on her foot and boot. She then pinched off a piece of the roll. "I suppose it will be fine. I just wish we still had the table."

Mishti nodded and stared a little more carefully. "You look terrible."

"Ha!" Chloe rubbed one eye with her free hand. "I feel it too."

"The feather mattress was a little more comfortable, I guess."

"No, it wasn't that." Just then, Chloe caught sight of Quintus walking nearby. When he caught her gaze, he immediately grimaced and turned away.

His glare made it clear he still hated her as much as ever.

Gulping down a piece of roll that suddenly seemed too heavy, she continued. "I kept thinking about the wraiths, and—"

She stopped short when Shadow poked her nose against the back of Chloe's leg. "Hey." Chloe tried to whirl around, but her dragon's claws snatched her around the waist and lifted her into the air before she even knew what was happening.

In the next moment, wind whipped through Chloe's loose hair as Shadow held her tight and flew her somewhere far away. She closed her eyes and tried to tell the dragon through their bond to put her down, but maybe she was too distracted for the bond to work.

Her hair would need a brush more than ever after this. She might have plaited it into a braid, except braids had a tendency to remind her of when Quintus had braided her hair and tied it off with a harp string.

That had been so very long ago. Before he'd forced her to enter a battle, which caused her to swear she'd never forgive him. And then she vowed she'd never return to Faerie, but of course she had. And now things had tilted on their side, and it was Quintus who would never forgive her.

The thought sent a lump to her throat. Desperate to ignore it, she glanced down at the landscape. Where was Shadow taking her anyway? And why had the dragon grabbed her around the waist with her claws instead of letting Chloe climb onto her back?

Below, she saw a part of Crystalfall she had never seen before. A maze of tall, gilded walls formed a labyrinth. Why had such a structure ever been built?

The question might have captured her attention longer, except Shadow started swooping down toward it. Chloe closed her eyes, working much harder to reach her dragon through their bond.

Fly. Take me away from this place.

Shadow continued to swoop down. She headed straight for the center of the gilded labyrinth.

No, Shadow. Away.

But Shadow did not fly away. The dragon kept beating her glittery wings with even more purpose than before. But Shadow wouldn't leave her there. Maybe the creature just wanted to play. Maybe she just wanted to explore.

Those thoughts might have calmed the beating in Chloe's heart except the dragon had nearly reached the center of the labyrinth and her grip around Chloe's waist started loosening.

Fear seized in Chloe's gut as she slammed her eyes shut.

NO!

Shadow kept flying down.

With a gulp, Chloe ignored how the grip around her waist loosened even more.

Do not leave me here.

But just as she finished the command, her dragon dropped her right into the middle of the gilded labyrinth. The moment

Chloe's feet hit the pearled grass, Shadow flapped her wings, now pulling herself upward toward the sky.

"Shadow!" Chloe screamed out, hitting her fists on the nearest golden wall. It towered high above, which would make the maze a horrendous pain to decipher.

"Shadow, what are you doing? Come back. Why have you left me here?" Her voice broke over the last few words. Her dragon had never done anything like this before. It didn't make any sense why the creature would turn on her now.

But then Chloe turned around and her heart fell to her toes.

Quintus stood in the labyrinth only a few paces away. He looked as confused and frustrated as her. Shadow must have held him around the waist with her other leg.

And now they were stuck in a labyrinth. Together.

Alone.

Chloe gulped, hardly able to believe her dragon had engineered such a precarious situation. But here she and Quintus stood. Alone.

Together.

15

TAKING A DEEP BREATH, CHLOE curled her arms over her stomach. She wanted a closer look at the tall, gilded walls surrounding her, but she couldn't stop staring at Quintus. Dark hair tumbled over his head. One strand that had grown just long enough to curl kept catching in the wind, causing it to bounce and flutter just over his rich, brown eyes.

Even through a deep scowl, he looked as attractive as ever. He suddenly pointed his chin upward at the spot where Shadow had flown away. Raising one eyebrow, he asked, "You did not tell her to do this?"

Chloe scoffed. "Of course not. You heard me yelling at her." She stepped forward, glancing down the labyrinth passageway. Turning in the other direction, she found it stretched even farther in the other direction. The golden walls rose high above them, casting shadows that danced with a delicate glow. Elaborate designs that were etched into the metal glistened.

Pressing her hand against her forehead she shook her head. "I have no idea what she was thinking. We need to find the king. We need to get back to that meadow and help the new fae feel welcome. We need to make sure Portia and Julian and the Zeakriesh aren't up to anything to that will hurt us or the court."

A lump formed in her throat she dropped her hand and examined the area once again. From above, she'd seen how the passages stretched far with intricate twists and turns. Short of solving the maze while inside it, which could take until night fall, she had no idea how to get out of this labyrinth.

The sweet, sultry fragrance of blooming gardenias filled the air. The scent carried with it a sense of wonder and endearment. Grass made of strands of green pearls grew from the ground with black soil only barely peeking through them. As beautiful as the area was, they still needed to get out of it.

Hopefully, she turned to Quintus, who had placed his forearm against the nearest wall. It pulled the fabric in his sleeves until it stretched tight against his biceps. Even more unhelpfully, the fabric around his chest had tightened too, showing off his broad shoulders and muscled chest.

Did he have to posture himself in such a way? She might lose her mind if he kept doing such things while also pushing her away.

She had to jerk her gaze away from him just to speak. "Do you have any idea how to get out of here?"

He huffed and kicked the golden wall with his brown boot. "How should I know? It is not my fault our dragon brought us here. Why do I have to think of a way out?"

Her eyebrows flew upward. "Did you just say *our* dragon?"

His mouth scrunched into a tiny knot. "*Our* dragon? *Pfft.*" He shook his head and turned away. "Why would I say that?"

She settled her hands on her hips, which did no good because he was still turned away from her. "But you did say that."

"Why do I have to think of a way out?" He spoke louder, giving off the distinct impression he wanted her to forget his earlier words. Or probably just that one word. "*You* should think of a way out. She is *your* dragon."

With his back still turned, he didn't see her exaggerated eye roll. "Oh, don't bother blaming me. It's not my fault Shadow brought us here. I have no idea what she was thinking."

"I will find my own way out." He spoke louder than ever and started marching off. His feet tramped down hard on the strands of grassy green pearls. "*Your* dragon can bring *you* back, but I will not wait for that."

"Fine!" Chloe shouted after him, her hands gripping tighter on her hips. "I was hoping for a chance to look through the king's journal again anyway. I wanted to make a list of everything we know about him to see if it helps us figure out where to look next."

Letting out a loud huff, she dropped to the ground, set her back against one wall, and pulled her leather bag off her shoulder. Huffs continued to burst from her lips as she pulled out the journal. She released the biggest huff yet when she grabbed her magical book.

She couldn't hear any footsteps, but his fae abilities probably allowed him to step too quietly for her to hear. She had to huff as loudly as possible to make sure he could hear even from far away. Maybe it was petty, but so was him stomping off to find a way out without her.

With the journal and the magical book on her lap, she quickly opened her Faerie book first. She needed a blank page to take notes. The pages opened directly where she'd been reading the last time she had been looking through her magical book.

That had been the morning in the king's bedroom when she found the sentence that said her bond with Quintus *may* never be repaired. She had then asked the book if that meant it might be possible to repair it.

Tears blurred her vision now that she had stopped huffing so forcefully, but she could see that a short line of script had been added to the page. Faerie had answered.

Instead of trying to read the words, she blinked away her tears and turned the page. She'd go back and look at the answer later. But right now, with Quintus acting the way he was, she didn't particularly want to know the answer.

Luckily, the very next page she found was blank, exactly like she needed. After retrieving a pen from her leather bag, she started writing a list. Every few words, she'd refer to the king's journal, skimming passages she had read before to add new items to her list.

Only after she finished with the sixth item did she finally hear the first footsteps. Except these footsteps padded over the strands of grass green pearls only a few paces away from her.

When she looked up, Quintus stared down at her with an expression much subdued from when he'd threatened to leave her there.

"What *do* we know about the king?"

It should have given her immense pleasure that she found something interesting enough to him to keep him from stomping away. But the fact that he planned to stomp away at all still stung too much for her to feel any sort of pleasure.

Instead, she pointed to the first item on her list.

Obsessed with memories.

She let out a small sigh and then explained. "He wanted the energy from memories, but he never wrote why he wanted or needed that energy. He made a deal with a wraith or maybe multiple wraiths and purposefully lost at least three memories in order to conduct his research. Who knows how many memories he's lost since then."

Quintus nodded, coming one step closer until he could lean his shoulder against the wall at Chloe's back. "What else?"

She pointed and read, "Uses an axe. I learned that from you and from his journal. And he doesn't like mortals."

One of Quintus's eyebrows cocked up at the sound of that.

"Well…" Her mouth twisted slightly. "I guess that's not entirely accurate. He wrote that mortals and fae were treated as equals in Crystalfall and remarked on how that was very different from the other courts. Then he said, and I quote, 'But it is the mortals who do not trust me. I will let them stay as long as necessary, but if they try to turn against me, they will regret it.'"

She glanced up, noting Quintus's eyebrow had now risen even higher as he processed those words.

"That goes along with the next item. Extremely paranoid about losing his crown." She bit her bottom lip, saying the next words softer. "Enough to want his son dead."

Quintus slumped lower against the wall, his mouth dipping to a frown.

Hurrying on to the next item was probably a good idea. "Good at metalworking. I imagine he was good at building other things too based on the way he writes, but he only specifically mentions metalworking."

Quintus leaned a little closer. "Why does *Longs for love* have a question mark after it?"

"Oh." Chloe touched a finger over the last item on the list, which Quintus had just read. "He wrote disdainfully about a woman who rejected him, but the way he wrote it made me wonder if he actually longed for love. Of course, later he did have a lover, Dyani."

She dared a glance upward, finding Quintus's expression unnaturally still at the mention of his mother's name.

Shrugging, Chloe continued. "But the king didn't seem too attached to her, so I thought maybe he longed for love but wasn't sure *how* to love. Since he's fae, that's really not so strange."

She read over each of the six items again, tapping her pen next to each one as she read it. "Is there anything else we know?" she asked.

With his back against the wall, Quintus drummed his fingers on the golden surface at his sides. "He has fair skin."

Her eyebrows scrunched together as she looked up at him. "You know that for sure?"

"I am not certain, but I am almost certain." Quintus stared hard at the wall in front of them. "I still think he wore a glamour both times I saw him, when he tried to kill me as a child and when he destroyed my home in Bitter Thorn. The image of him… flickered, or…"

After staring for another moment, Quintus waved his hand through the air. "Or something. But his skin was always fair, even through the flicker, so I believe that is his true coloring."

She nodded. "He must originally be from Mistmount, Noble Rose, or Fairfrost then."

"And he smelled of open air and trees."

"Trees?" Her head tilted up to look at him. "Bitter Thorn trees?"

"Yes." But then Quintus's eyes narrowed in thought. "But maybe that was just from walking through Bitter Thorn Forest to find me."

Chloe tapped her pen against the side of her book. "Open air too though. That sounds like Mistmount or Fairfrost."

"I agree."

Putting her pen to the page, she added notes about the king's fair skin and his scent. Next to the smells, she wrote that he was probably originally from Mistmount or Fairfrost.

It only took another moment of staring at the list when her eyes opened wide. "Oh! I just thought of another one."

Her pen flew across the page, adding a ninth item.

Scientific mind, curious, eager for knowledge.

She stared at that as thoughts of her adventures in Faerie tumbled through her mind. "Maybe once we find the king, we should let Ludo do the talking."

"Ludo?" Quintus said through a scoff. "Why?"

Pointing to her note about the king, she answered. "He has that same thirst for knowledge. I know Ludo's been studying and collecting items to help him find his brother again, but I doubt he'll stop just because Revyn's been found. He loves learning new things too much."

She scanned the list again, placing her pen next to one of the notes. "And he longs for love too. You've seen how wistful he gets when talking about Clara and Revyn. But then he sometimes acts disgusted when w—" Her breath hitched as she just managed to stop herself from saying *we*. After clearing her throat, she continued. "When *others* show affection. I think he desires a beloved but isn't quite sure how to be in love. He and the king would probably get along."

Feeling a gaze latched onto her, she glanced up. Quintus stared with a very strange look in his eye, enough to make her think back on what she had just said. When his gaze fell away from her and landed on the list, she reread each item slowly.

A few of them stood out a little more intensely than they had before.

Obsessed with memories

Uses an axe

Fair skin

Smelled of open air and trees, probably originally from Mistmount or Fairfrost

Scientific mind, curious, eager for knowledge

Her finger traced over the word *Fairfrost* as a tightness filled her chest. Ludo did seem similar to this unknown king. Maybe a little *too* similar. Puzzle pieces in her mind were beginning to form a picture she didn't want to see. They had a friend from Fairfrost who matched each of those items from the list, a friend with blue-and-red eyes.

It took great effort to keep her mind from spinning too far out of control, but now it had started, she wasn't sure she'd be able to stop it.

16

CHLOE STARED AT THE LIST she'd written in her magical book. They only knew a few things about the king of Crystalfall and many of them were dangerously similar to Ludo. But Ludo had helped them. He'd been with them through the entire search for the crown. If he was king of Crystalfall, why hadn't he taken the crown after Quintus crafted it?

Unless…

Her stomach tightened hard. Unless he didn't remember who he was. Could it be possible the king they'd been searching for had been there all along?

Gulping, she reminded herself the king of Crystalfall also tried to kill Quintus. The king had destroyed Quintus's home. The king was vile. Paranoid. Even if Ludo had lost memories, he couldn't have done all that. He wouldn't have.

She and the others would find the king somewhere else. They'd get him to repair the castle and get rid of Portia and Julian. Nothing more.

He'd be no one to them, and they'd like it that way.

Her thoughts got interrupted when a warm droplet landed on Chloe's arm. She glanced toward it gratefully, eager for a distraction. Any distraction. The glance quickly turned into a gasp when she realized the droplet had been a droplet of blood.

And it had come from Quintus's side.

Both the magical book and the king's journal fell to the grass strands made of pearls as Chloe scrambled to her feet. She noted dark red circles spreading through the fabric of Quintus's new coat.

"How long has this been bleeding?" Her hands reached for his green coat, attempting to lift it so she could see his wound.

Sucking in a sharp breath, he whirled around in a circle and started backing away from her.

Despite his quick movement, she managed to catch part of the hem and get a quick look at the injury. The light blue crystals she had sewn inside him looked glittery and glowed slightly, but they were also much smaller than when she had first placed them there.

They must have absorbed too much blood because she clearly saw blood pooling around the crystals and out of her careful stitching.

The threads on her stitching had worn too. They were scuffed and frayed and in desperate need of being replaced completely.

Gulping, she closed her eyes and hoped against all hope that her dragon would listen to her now.

Come. Quintus needs help.

Urgency enveloped the words as she sent them to her dragon. She could tell in only a moment that Shadow had received her message and would indeed come.

The dragon seemed to realize whatever game she'd been playing at dropping Chloe and Quintus into that labyrinth, it was over now.

But Chloe was far from feeling relief. She needed a better look at that wound. She needed to clean it up as much as she could.

After keeping her hands casually at her side until Quintus relaxed, she then threw them out and grabbed onto his coat more tightly than before.

This time, she managed to expose his entire stomach and side.

"Stop." His voice came out breathless.

She took a step closer to him, holding even tighter to the fabric in case he tried to pull away. "Is it hurting? I'll be gentle, I just need to—"

"No." He stepped backward…right into the wall they'd been across from only moments ago. "Get away from me."

She rolled her eyes, grateful he could see it now. "Stop being so dramatic. If your blood drips onto the ground…"

She didn't have to finish the sentence because a drop of blood fell to the ground. It hissed and burned the moment it hit the jeweled grass. An ashy, powdery hole formed where the blood had touched. Smoke filled with an acrid smell drifted upward from it.

"See?" She shook her head, moving closer and lifting his coat higher. "Now hold still so I can…"

Trailing off, she used her free hand to gently prod the area around her stitching. It didn't look inflamed at all, so at least it hadn't gotten infected. She slid two fingers over his bare skin next, trying to see if any of the organs inside seemed inflamed.

Every muscle in his body went rigid at the light touch. He let out a puff of breath and then he moved.

In one moment, he had his back against the wall, stuck. But then he grabbed her by the waist and spun her around until *she* had her back against that same wall. Soon, he ripped his hands away from her waist, as if her dress burned his skin like fire. Using his forearms, which were covered by the thick sleeves of his dark green coat, he lifted her arms up until he pinned her wrists against the golden wall behind her.

"Chloe." He breathed out hard, rustling her hair. His face had grown hot enough that she could feel its warmth. He stared at her too, stared like she was the first and only thing he'd ever seen. "Do *not* touch me. You *cannot* do it again."

His chest heaved with breaths that grew heavier and heavier. The only place they touched now was through his sleeved forearms, which still pinned her wrists against the wall. He stood dangerously close. So close she'd only have to lean forward slightly before her chest found his.

And his face. His head had dipped, leaving his forehead only a few inches away from hers. Each time he breathed, she could feel it on her mouth.

But he also glared. He glared so hard it looked like his veins might pop right out of his skin. His lips were parted as he stared directly into her eyes, probably hoping he could set her on fire just with his stare.

But then his gaze dropped. With his mouth still parted, he stared at her lips. His face came closer then. He had undeniably leaned in.

But then he swallowed and went back to glaring at her like she was the single source of every problem in his life.

She swallowed, feeling acutely the rustle of his fabric against her wrists. "I can't tell if you want to hurt me or kiss me."

He let out a breathy laugh, pulling his head back only half an inch. "I cannot tell either."

They locked eyes again, and the staring turned more heated than ever. Her own face warmed, tingling across her cheeks. Each time she breathed, he must have been able to feel it on his own lips.

She wanted him to lean in again. It didn't even bother her that he had her arms pinned against the wall. She'd take him any way he wanted her.

But after another moment, his gaze fell to their feet. He spoke in a gravelly tone. "I would never hurt you. Not physically."

"I know." She tried and failed to catch his eye. "But that might not stop you from *wanting* to hurt me, after what I did." She said the last part in a whisper.

When he looked up again, her heart jumped right into her throat. Never before had every inch of her skin felt so hot. If she stared at his lips, could she get him to lean in again?

While staring, she asked, "Why don't you want me to touch you?"

He laughed, a breathy, shaky sound. Pulling back ever so slightly, he shook his head. "Because..." He stared without moving for a moment. And then. Finally. He released one of her wrists, bringing his free hand closer to her.

Breathing out slowly, he carefully placed his hand on her cheek. It had been so long, too long, since he'd done this deliberately.

Skin against skin. His against hers.

"When we touch," he said, closing his eyes. "*This* happens."

He stroked her cheek with his thumb, which sent through her a feeling of pleasure so strong, she had to curl her toes. Still, that didn't answer her question. Did he just mean it made them fall more in love? Because this touch had certainly done that.

But then she felt it. Sharp tingling pricked at the skin just under her right eye. Though she could see nothing, she felt wispy tendrils from her heart reach out, latching onto matching tendrils from his.

The tingles under her right eye turned warm and quivery. Her tattoos were changing. She could feel it. Glancing up at Quintus, the change worked on his moon tattoo too. The smudgy edges sharpened, turning to the crisp edges of a crescent moon he used to have. The tattoo's faded light gray color turned to a dark gray. And then a darker gray. Curls seemed to form at the top of his head too, the strands all growing just a little more.

When the tattoo changed nearly to black, Quintus wrinkled his nose and shoved himself away. He stepped backward until his back had found the wall across from her. His nose continued to twitch as he stretched out both of his hands. After that, he shook out his shoulders.

He continued to breathe heavily, as if he might never catch his breath.

But now anger had taken sprout in Chloe's chest. She clenched her jaw and stared hard at him. "That's all we have to do to repair our bond? Touch each other? I can't believe you've been so stubborn about this when the solution is so simple."

She marched forward until she stood directly across from him. Now she held her hand out to him, waiting for him to take it. "Come on. Don't you *want* your magic back?"

"No." His voice came out low like a growl. "I do not need magic. Being bonded to you is *worse* than living without magic."

He turned away from her, as if looking at her for another moment would cause him to vomit.

Glittery, flapping wings soon appeared above them. Shadow had come to save them, just like Chloe had known she would.

But now Chloe's heart had been shredded. Not broken, but shredded. And stomped on. She held her breath and turned away as tears slipped down her cheeks. Bending down, she quickly gathered her magical book, the king's journal, and her leather bag.

When she scrambled onto Shadow's back, she made no attempt to move closer to Quintus, who had already found a spot as far from her as possible. She dropped the king's journal into her bag as more tears slipped from her eyelashes.

At least now she could check to see the answer Faerie had written for her. Was it possible to repair her bond with Quintus? The magical book had supplied one sentence as an answer.

It takes two to restore a bond.

She sucked in a breath and clenched her jaw tight to keep her chin from trembling.

So that was it then. She just had to touch Quintus to fix the bond and bring back his magic, but it didn't really matter because that would never happen. The bond would never be repaired unless *he* wanted it to be.

17

Tears pooled in Chloe's eyes no matter how much wind blew at them. Even with Shadow's wings beating and the gorgeous, sparkling landscape gleaming below, Chloe still couldn't keep the tears back.

Her throat scratched each time she tried to swallow. When Shadow landed at the edge of the celestine meadow, Chloe slid off her back with shuddering breaths.

Quintus held his hands close to his side, using them to catch the blood from his wound. When he got to the ground, he stalked off somewhere. She turned away from him deliberately, not wanting to know which direction he went. Shadow flew away next, which Chloe mostly ignored.

Her gaze caught sight of Mishti soon after that. Forcing down a scratchy swallow, Chloe walked toward her friend.

The young woman nodded at the sight of her. Mishti didn't seem to wonder at all where Chloe and Quintus had gone off to. Or why. In fact…

Chloe narrowed one eye, slowly so she wouldn't accidentally free a tear. Mishti had a strange look in her eye, almost like she had a mysterious secret of her own.

Once Chloe came close enough, Mishti gestured toward the camp. "We still haven't figured out a solution for food, but the other Golden Shields and the fae have started gathering supplies to make tents."

Sniffing, Chloe nodded. "Good. Where?"

The sniff caught Mishti's attention. For the first time, the young woman looked a little more closely at her friend. She must have seen bright red eyes and a splotchy face, but if she dared to mention it, Chloe would make sure she'd regret it. Luckily, Mishti seemed to realize that and, very conspicuously, turned her gaze away instead.

After only a few paces, they came to a pile of fabrics and ropes. Chloe reached in, searching for anything absorbent. She soon found a nice dark cotton that was already cut in a wide strip.

Gathering the yards of fabric into her arms, she said, "Go find Quintus and wrap this tight around his waist several times. He's bleeding again."

She dropped the fabric into Mishti's arms and went to walk away.

"You want *me*…" Mishti trailed off, staring at the fabric while narrowing her eyes. "Why don't you do it?"

A near-hiss escaped Chloe's clenched jaw. "Don't ask me that." Her pitch was high and her voice too loud, but she didn't care much at the moment. "Just do it, that's why," she snapped.

Whirling around, she darted off into the nearby trees.

"Wait." With her arms still full of the fabric, Mishti bounded forward until she'd reached Chloe's side. "I need to tell you something." She glanced over her shoulder. "You *and* Quintus."

Flipping her head away from her friend, Chloe trudged forward again. "Go tell him and then come back and tell me. But wrap his wound first."

Her feet carried her away quickly, so Mishti wouldn't have time to say anything else. The young woman probably could have followed, but luckily, she did not.

Tears burned in Chloe's eyes, sliding down her cheeks as hot as embers. This particular wooded area had large gems, bronze bushes, and other debris that kept causing her to lose her balance. And yet, she increased her pace with every step.

Her feet stumbled over a golden rock as big as her head. When her palms scraped across a sharp cluster of crystals, she didn't even bother to check if they had caused cuts on her hands. She just got to her feet, moving even faster than before.

She tripped again, this time scraping her leg on a needly bronze bush. The only thing she did differently when she got to her feet was swipe the tears off her cheeks with the back of her hand.

Why would she bother to check her hands or wipe the blood from her leg? What did it matter? What did any of it matter?

Worse. That's what he'd said. Being bonded to her was *worse* than living without magic. The back of her hand caught another sheet of tears from her cheeks.

He'd made mistakes too, hadn't he? He'd messed up, and she eventually forgave him.

But her? She made one tiny mistake, and now he hated her so much it was worth losing his magic forever.

Okay. Maybe it wasn't a tiny mistake. It was a big one. A really big one. But still.

She sniffed and lost her balance so badly, her entire body whirled around until she landed on her back. Something sharp and twisted dug into her shoulder, but that wasn't about to stop her when nothing else had.

Getting to her feet again, she punched the nearest tree with the edge of her hand, hoping it might pull some of the pain from her heart. It did not.

That same hand reached for her chest next, kneading the skin over her heart, as if that would help. It also did not.

How could he say such an awful thing? And right after she'd been trying to help him with his wound too. She should have known better. She always helped and helped so much, always to her own detriment.

She'd been selfless, caring, eager to give him everything, and he'd stabbed her right in the middle of it.

Her hand swiped away more tears. After a quick glance, she realized just how far she'd gone away from the celestine meadow. How close had she gotten to the castle?

Maybe going that far hadn't been smart. Mishti had said she needed to talk. But Chloe didn't want to talk. Not to Mishti. Definitely not to Quintus. Not to anyone.

Even still, Chloe did turn around. She kept stomping and tripping and huffing, but she did it while walking toward the celestine meadow instead of away from it. Her hands wiped at her tears a little more carefully now.

Maybe she couldn't erase the red in her eyes or the splotches on her cheeks, but she could at least make sure her tears had dried by the time she made it back to the others.

And soon enough, too soon really, the meadow came into view. Golden Shields and fae milled about, busy with their different tasks. It took a few sniffs and long deep breaths, but Chloe managed to stop her tears. For now. They'd probably make another appearance later though.

But just before she left the shelter of the trees, her gaze snagged on a curious sight. Just past the trees, right at the edge of camp, a silver rock had a small piece of paper tucked underneath it.

Her eyebrows leapt upward as she realized that rock sat almost directly next to the spot where she'd been sleeping the night before. How had she failed to notice that note the moment she woke up?

Remembering, she scowled slightly. She probably hadn't noticed because she hadn't slept at all the night before. She'd been far too sleepy to be aware of anything unusual in her surroundings.

A memory of those strange footsteps she heard in the night came forward too. Had someone really been there? And left the note?

Creeping forward, she reached down and took the folded paper into her hands. But before she could open it, Mishti appeared in front of her.

"I learned something important from Chandril."

Chloe's head snapped upward as she tucked the paper into her leather bag. "The wraith?" Her nose wrinkled at the thought, but then worry twisted her gut. "Did you give him another memory?"

After a guilty-looking swallow, Mishti glanced off to the side. "We have an arrangement."

Frowning, Chloe shook her head. "You shouldn't have done that. You told me yesterday you didn't want to give away another memory."

Setting her face back into its stone-like expression, Mishti lifted one shoulder. "What's done is done, and anyway, I learned something important."

After glancing around, probably to check that no one else could hear, Mishti stepped forward and lowered her voice to a whisper. "The king is here in Crystalfall."

Chloe clapped a hand to her mouth as she gasped. "Where?"

Mishti let out a short sigh. "I don't know. I think Chandril wants to keep some bargaining power, so he wouldn't tell me everything he knows. Or maybe there's another reason he wouldn't tell me more. But at least that much we now know for certain. The king, whoever he is, has entered Crystalfall."

Internalizing those words, Chloe then turned her gaze to the fae milling around that she'd only barely noticed before. Those same fae had only just entered Crystalfall.

Nodding, Mishti looked at the fae as well. "That's what I was thinking too. Same with Quintus. He wants to line up all the male fae and have them touch the Crystalfall crown. He says the crown will react if any of them are the king. I said we should have male and female line up and even the mortals too. It will be less suspicious that way, and it won't give away all we know in case someone here is trying to figure that out."

"Good idea." Chloe checked her leather bag, confirming the folded paper was still tucked inside. Then, she and Mishti headed toward the front of the meadow to make the announcement.

Quintus ended up climbing a large rock and directing everyone into a long line. Mishti had indeed wrapped the dark cotton fabric around his waist, but she'd done it too loose. It wouldn't hold the blood back for long. Chloe would have to give her more explicit directions later to fix it, since Chloe certainly wouldn't do it herself.

She might never speak to Quintus again if she could help it.

Standing on the opposite side of the line from him, she watched as he took out the crown, and one by one, had everyone in the line touch it. In the end, the experiment went by quickly and led to nothing. None of the fae who had entered their camp were King of Crystalfall.

But once the fae and mortals started dispersing and going back to what they'd been doing before, Chloe turned toward her friend. "What about Ludo? Isn't he back yet?"

Mishti raised a single eyebrow with a laugh in her eyes. "You think Ludo is the king?"

While she spoke, Quintus stepped a little closer, just enough to hear them.

Chloe turned away from him, making sure she faced only Mishti. "No, I don't think Ludo is the king, but I don't want to never find the king just because we were too afraid to check."

The laughter in Mishti's eyes dulled as her mouth straightened to a thin line. "Afraid to check?" She turned to look at Quintus, which dipped her mouth to frown. "So, you *do* think there's a chance Ludo is the king? Didn't the king try to kill you?"

Quintus never had a chance to answer.

And Chloe never had a chance to scowl at him for daring to speak in her presence.

Before anyone could do anything, a loud crash sounded in the trees at the edge of the meadow. A moment later, a figure stood atop a boulder made of ruby. Portia sneered down at them, her hair slicked back in a tight bun. She wore a dress made of tiny emeralds that had been sewn together with golden thread.

It should have frightened Chloe to see the woman. It should have frightened her that two dozen Zeakriesh soldiers jumped out from behind the surrounding trees.

But neither of those revelations could stab fear into her heart like the figure standing just to the right of Portia's boulder. Julian.

A very much alive Julian stood with his chin jutting out, as if proud to show off the mole on his chin as big as a thumbnail. His wild eyes shone bright as the gems around them. And in his hands…

Chloe peered closer. He held several shimmery and long objects that pricked at an old memory at the back of her mind. What were those? And what would they do?

18

CHLOE CONTINUED TO STARE AT the strange objects in Julian's hands, trying to decipher what they could possibly be. The golden shimmery color seemed oddly familiar, especially with its light glow. Although, they didn't seem familiar as if she had seen them before. It was more like they'd been described to her, but she had imagined them slightly different, so she wasn't entirely sure these objects were the same as those.

In any case, she couldn't remember exactly what the items were anyway. She just remembered something about jagged edges that looked like broken glass, which these golden objects in Julian's hands seemed to have.

Portia cleared her throat deliberately, sneering down at everyone, as if they were dull-witted for not immediately realizing she wanted to speak. Once she had everyone's attention, she began. "For all the fae who thought mortals could only defeat them with iron. For the all the fae who called mortals weak."

She laughed and touched a hand to her collarbone. "For all the mortals who left us and thought they'd survive."

The words were meant to be harrowing. Chloe knew that but pushed it all the way to the back of her mind, while she tried and tried to remember what those strange objects were.

Balance shards! The answer came to her suddenly just as Julian's mouth curled into a wildly sinister grin.

That's what he held, balance shards from the Balance Cliffs separating Fairfrost and Dustdune. These golden ones weren't the kind that turned mortals into fae. They were the kind that turned fae into mortals. Although they didn't actually do that either because no one ever survived the change.

Chloe cocked her head to the side. What did Portia and Julian think they could accomplish by gathering an armful of balance shards? To work, a fae would have to first accept the shard and then slam it into his or her own chest. Surely, none of the fae here were stupid enough to do that. Did Portia think she could simply threaten the fae with the shards and hope that would be enough?

A chuckle might have followed Chloe's revelation. For one perfect moment, she believed these Zeakriesh would make fools of themselves with objects that were completely benign to everyone in the meadow.

But then Portia pointed to the shards in Julian's arms, and her mouth turned to a smile as twisted as his. "We have taken a powerful Faerie relic and bent it to *our* will. We learned how to take the magic already present in Faerie…" She turned and stared directly at Mishti. "And use it for ourselves."

The words settled low in Chloe's gut as their meaning became clear. This was so much worse than she ever could have imagined.

With a jerk of the head, Portia turned to Julian, and said, "Do it."

A wild, raucous laughter erupted from his lips as he lifted the first golden balance shard and chucked it straight at Mishti.

With a gasp, Chloe lunged straight for her friend. Maybe she shouldn't have, but she didn't want that shard touching Mishti, if she herself could stop it.

She should have let it go though. She should have dropped the ground and covered her head and trusted Mishti to take care of herself.

Because Mishti knew better than to lunge toward a dangerous object. She had already started jumping to the side almost as soon as Julian reeled his arm back. By the time the balance shard met the air where she'd been standing, Mishti had already jumped far enough away to avoid being hit by the golden shard.

Except now Chloe had lunged close enough to the shard that she'd be near it when it landed. Her shoulder hit the black soil half a breath before the shard did. It still landed an arm's length away, but that was close enough.

The shard hit the ground and exploded in a burst of pink and golden light. Dirt scattered every which way, several clumps of it hitting her skin at a frightening velocity. The entire ground rippled beneath her. When the light and sprays of dirt settled, it left the soil grimy and singed. It almost seemed like the dirt had melted and then had acid poured on top of it.

Chloe gulped. If the shard had done that much damage to the ground, she couldn't begin to imagine how much damage it would have done to her if she'd managed to jump close enough to touch it. Why had she thought Mishti would benefit from Chloe lunging forward?

Julian laughed and plucked another shard from the pile in his arms. He looked directly at Chloe. "Why'd you try to take hers? I already have one just for you."

With his eyes flashing, he threw the shard at her. Maybe it was luck, or maybe Faerie itself had intervened, but Julian's aim faltered at the last moment. The shard slammed against a tree trunk instead of in Chloe's face like she'd been expecting.

It gave Mishti enough time to grab Chloe by the wrist and yank her behind the pile of fabric and ropes that were supposed to make tents.

In a flash, Quintus had joined them. He drew a spear from his pocket and stared hard as Julian threw another shard, this time at a Golden Shield. "Call Shadow." His teeth gritted as he aimed his spear directly at Julian's chest. "We need to get out of here."

But Julian jumped away before Quintus's spear could reach him. His feral laughter followed him as he danced and started throwing shards in every direction.

Closing her eyes, Chloe sent a barrage of urgent thoughts to her dragon.

Come. We are in danger.

Before she had even finished, she could already sense Shadow flying. She was close.

Screams erupted as the Zeakriesh soldiers rushed out from the trees and started attacking. The meadow had turned to a difficult terrain now that shards had filled it with craters of melted and bubbled dirt.

Julian's throwing became even more untamed. He closed his eyes and snickered, calling out. "Who will meet their end next?"

Some of the shards hit Zeakriesh, but Portia didn't seem too concerned. Neither did Julian.

Beating wings flapped above, allowing Chloe to let out a short breath. With a deep growl at the back of her throat, Shadow swooped down. Crackling sounded in her throat next, and a moment later she breathed fire.

Portia had jumped behind a boulder, safe from the flames. Julan still danced about, throwing shards with his eyes closed, but he stood on the opposite end of the meadow and also avoided the flames. Several of the Zeakriesh weren't so lucky.

When Shadow moved closer to where Chloe and the others hid, Mishti grabbed her wrist and dragged her toward the dragon. Chloe's feet wouldn't move properly, but she did make an effort to help propel herself forward. Mishti probably still did most of the work.

"Fae and Golden Shields," Quintus shouted above the roar of the fight. "Now is our chance for escape."

No one needed any more direction than that. Golden Shields and fae darted out from behind trees and bushes and leapt toward Shadow. Whenever one of the Zeakriesh would come forward, Mishti would point and scream, and Shadow would blow fire.

Chloe sat on her dragon's back, her whole body trembling. The fight moved quickly around her, but at least she hadn't passed out yet.

She very nearly did lose consciousness, though, when she considered what was happening. The Zeakriesh were using magic. They had figured out a way to take balance shards and turn them into magical weapons. Did that mean they could harness the magic of the shards in other ways? Could they use the shards to open a door or to conjure things?

This must have been how they formed that crack through Crystalfall Castle. They had used magic, which still seemed impossible.

With Quintus directing the crowd, he finally shouted to Shadow that they could leave. Her flames filled the meadow, causing more screams to cry out.

Soon, Chloe and the Golden Shields flew safely away on Shadow's back, but Chloe still couldn't breathe. Her body trembled so hard that her muscles ached. Panic was setting in. She hated that her body worked like this. They had left the meadow and found safety in the air, and yet her body thought this was the exact moment she needed to lose control and shake and stop breathing.

Shadow let out a pained moan, which somehow, Chloe knew was meant just for her. The dragon never liked it when agitation controlled Chloe's senses the way it did now.

While Shadow swooped in a sharp zigzag, Chloe managed to catch her breath. The strange motion had been so unexpected, it shocked her out of the anxiety-fueled cloud in her mind. Then Shadow zoomed down toward the ground suddenly. Wind blew into Chloe's face, which forced air into her mouth.

That helped with her breathing. Shadow's flying turned gentler as she flew in a swooping circle. Now, Chloe could reach out and stroke the golden scales on her dragon's back. The steady, repetitive motion calmed her heart to a steady beat.

By the time she had come back to herself, Shadow flew low over a rushing, sparkling river.

"Where are we supposed to go now?" Chloe sniffed and pulled her knees up to her chest.

One of the Golden Shields from the back of the dragon looked up at the sound of that question, his eyes as sorrowful as her sniff. Then a growl of hunger erupted from his belly.

She almost chuckled at the familiar sound. Her own stomach had grumbled so many times here in Crystalfall when she and Mishti had been trying to run from the Zeakriesh.

Sucking in a sharp breath, Chloe leaned to the side to get a better look at the landscape below them. "What about the mortals' camp? The old one?"

Everyone turned to her with eyebrows lowered.

"Remember your camp in the hills leading up to the castle? You had a golden table there, right? Do you think any Zeakriesh are still there?"

The man whose stomach had grumbled sat up higher. "I doubt anyone is still there. Judging by how many Zeakriesh attacked when we were still inside the castle, I'm pretty sure no one stayed behind."

Shadow had already turned around and headed for the mortals' old camp. The pixies might have been there with the table now, but hopefully they wouldn't mind the Golden Shields sharing the table with them.

As they guessed, the camp had been completely abandoned, leaving the golden table and even a few tents free for them to use. When a swarm of pixies flew into the area, Chloe asked as kindly as she could if she and the Shields could use the table. Once the pixies heard how they would be allowed into the area to use the table as much as they wanted too, they readily agreed to the Shields using it.

Once the Golden Shields got down and people started conjuring food with the table, Mishti pulled Chloe and Quintus aside. Chloe folded her arms over her chest and made a point to turn away from Quintus and look only at Mishti. For all she knew, Quintus probably did the same, but she wasn't about to check and risk catching his eye.

Since Mishti let out a long sigh as she pinched the bridge of her nose, it seemed likely Quintus behaved much the same as Chloe.

"You two are insufferable." But then Mishti dropped her hand to the side and glanced backward. "How will Ludo find us now that we moved?"

Chloe bit her bottom lip, considering the question. Her gaze darted around the camp and then up at the sky, hoping for an answer. But then she noticed glowing green lights hovering high above their heads.

A grin started forming on her lips. "We could send him a message."

Without waiting for a reaction from her friend, she started plucking a blonde strand of hair from her head. After lifting her hand into the air with the palm flat, she clicked her tongue three times.

In a flash, one of the glowing green lights from above zoomed down until a tiny creature landed on her palm.

Moving slowly, Chloe brought her hand down, closer to her face. A tiny sprite as tall as a thumb stood on her palm. The little creature had a nut shell as a hat and fruit seeds as shoes. She handed the sprite the hair from her head, hoping it would be an acceptable offering.

After a quick examination, the sprite tucked the long hair into his pocket. Then he stood up straight and nodded at Chloe.

She took a deep breath before continuing. "I have a message for Ludo of Fairfrost. Tell him we have moved to the mortals' old camp. We are no longer in the celestine meadow. Oh, and the message is from Chloe of…"

Only now did her words falter. Chloe of the mortal realm? Chloe of Crystalfall? Did she dare claim Crystalfall as her home when she had nearly destroyed it?

With a soft inhale, she shook her head. "The message is from Chloe."

The sprite tilted his head to the side, and he brought his eyebrows down. But then he shrugged and flew off into the air.

By now, the sky had started to darken. They had found a new camp just in time for night to fall. Chloe shivered, though not because of the cool air. Her thoughts had turned to those moments in the meadow just before the shards started flying.

Chloe shook her head. "Portia is so careful with her appearance I sometimes forget how deadly she can be too. I wonder where she learned to instill fear like that."

"I know where." A glare overtook Mishti's face after she spoke.

When Chloe turned toward her friend, Mishti continued. "Portia's story is similar to mine, except she was the one who had money."

Mishti now turned to Quintus to explain further, since he hadn't heard Mishti's own story. "A man and woman made a mistake together, but only the one without money got punished."

Whatever Quintus's reaction to that information was, Chloe would never know. She kept her head firmly turned away from him.

Reaching for her long black braid Mishti said, "Portia learned as surely as I did that those with money or power got to live by a different set of rules. When Ansel found her in the mortal realm and tried to convince her to come to Faerie to live with him, she knew she needed some sort of leverage against him. So she told him she wouldn't go until he married her."

"Married her?" Chloe laughed. "I can hardly imagine Ansel agreeing to such a thing."

Mishti shrugged. "He did. He thought it a silly mortal ceremony that meant nothing, except it would win him a new pet for his collection. But when Portia got to his house and saw how his pets were treated, she convinced him the marriage vows he made in the mortal realm would be binding even in Faerie."

"He still treated her like a pet, but because of their marriage, she was afforded far more power than any other mortal in his household. Her history taught her how fear can lead to greater power."

"What about Julian?" Chloe thought back to his careless throwing that had injured some of his own people. "How did he become a leader in the household?"

Mishti shook her head. "It's not accurate to call him a leader. But he's always been just crazy enough that no one dared cross him, including Portia."

"So, she's the mastermind and he's the henchman?" Quintus asked from behind Chloe's back.

"Portia is the mastermind, yes," Mishti responded. "But Julian never was a henchman. He's more like the wild animal you use to harm enemies, but that you still have to be wary of because he's not intelligent enough to know you're his master."

That seemed frighteningly accurate for how he'd behaved with those shards.

Suddenly remembering the folded paper in her leather bag she had never had a chance to open, Chloe stepped away. "I need to…" She shook her head. "I need to get some food."

She wouldn't have minded opening the note if only Mishti had been there, but she didn't care to open it with Quintus nearby. And she really did intend to get food. She'd just sneak off a little bit afterward so she could read the note.

19

STUFFING A PASTRY OF RICH rice pilaf spiced with saffron into her mouth, Chloe marched past the camp slightly and sat down on a large boulder made of yellow-orange citrine. The last few bites of the deliciously aromatic and earthy pilaf went into her mouth before she plucked the folded paper from her leather bag.

If she'd had any idea what would be written on that paper, she might have prepared herself more. Instead, she had a jarring transition going from casually eating the remnants of her dinner to staring at a note written in Julian's tight, ultra-straight handwriting with the most harrowing words she'd seen all day.

I know where to find the king of Crystalfall.

Her body froze, staring at the words. Thoughts swirled in her mind, trying to make sense and finding none. She knew Julian wrote the note because he had written her a note before. Back before she and Quintus had found the court of Crystalfall,

Julian had explained how to do the unlocking enchantment she used to first discover Crystalfall. When first reading the note, she thought Faerie itself had left it, but she later recognized the handwriting and knew it came from Julian instead.

And this note in her hand now had the same tight, ultra-straight handwriting.

Was he lying? Mortals could lie, unlike the fae, so maybe he used that to his advantage. But why would he write this in a note? Why not say it while he held the shards and stared right at her? And why did he still try to attack her with the shard?

But then she remembered how his aim had gone horribly wrong at the last moment when he tried to throw the shard at her. Had it been on purpose that he missed?

It didn't make any sense. Nothing about it made sense. Maybe he planned to betray Portia, but if so, why? And how did he even know they were looking for the king of Crystalfall?

So many questions filled her mind, she could no longer sort through them. She pressed a hand to her forehead, but that didn't help.

"Um. Excuse me, Miss Chloe?"

Chloe reacted on instinct, closing a fist over the note to hide its message. When she glanced up, she found a young woman with short hair a yellow dress standing before her. Hilda was her name. She wore a necklace made from a strand of golden chain mail. A Golden Shield.

"Yes?" Chloe asked with a smile. At the same time, she tucked the now-crumpled note into her leather bag.

"Mishti is asking everyone to do a chore before we go to sleep for the night. She wanted me to ask if you could help gather some small gems for our slings. They work even better than stones."

Standing up and adjusting the leather strap on her shoulder, Chloe nodded. "Of course. Is there a certain size of gem I should gather?"

"Yes, come this way," the young woman answered. "Mishti said there's a specific clearing that has the perfect size of gems scattered on the ground. You just have to go there and gather a few handfuls. There it is. Mishti said you should go in that clearing there."

"Of course, I'm happy to help." Chloe continued forward, happily ignorant as the young woman darted away.

That ignorance vanished the moment she entered the clearing. Standing right in the middle of the open area was Quintus, with his horribly perfect hair and his obnoxiously toned muscles.

He glanced up, also blissfully ignorant. But once he caught sight of her, his eyes opened wide.

Chloe let out a puff of air as she hit her forehead. "I cannot believe I fell for that. I can't believe Mishti, even Mishti, would try to trick me like this."

She shook her head, her jaw clenching tighter by the moment. "I'm going to smack her for this."

Whirling around, she went to leave the clearing. But a whoosh of wind blew, and suddenly, Quintus stood at her side.

He said nothing. He didn't even look at her directly. He just grabbed a gorgeous, opal encrusted brush from his pocket and handed it to her.

She stared at it without moving. Then her gaze turned to her hair. It was a sorely tangled mess, which she hadn't bothered even running her fingers through since her bath inside Crystalfall Castle.

Sighing, she took the brush. He stepped away, which she appreciated since she had no desire to look at his face. He probably snickered in his mind about how disgusting and tangled her hair had gotten anyway.

It was a testament to his skill with crafting that the brush worked so well. It took two or three passes through her hair what would have taken a dozen with a normal brush. Soon, one side of her hair had already turned smooth and shiny. Shifting her hair over the other shoulder, she began working through the tangles on the other side.

Just as she went through a particularly nasty snarl, a golden stick poked just under her palm. The stick must have come from one of the nearby trees.

"What is that?" Quintus spoke in a low, accusatory tone.

How lovely. He feared touching her so much he had resorted to using a stick to poke her instead.

"It's nothing," she answered.

"Nothing?" His stick slid up her palm, directly next to a large scrape she had been ignoring.

Instead of responding, she turned her shoulders away from him and took several steps to the side. Then she went right back to brushing her hair. She had almost finished anyway, and then she could throw the brush at him and leave this clearing.

"And what is this?" His stick now poked her lightly on the back of her left shoulder.

With her hair all gathering in front of her right shoulder, he must have found the scrape she got when she fell on the forest floor back by the meadow. His stick pulled away, but she still didn't answer.

"And this?" His stick now lifted her skirts enough to point out the long scratch on her leg, which had bled a lot more than she realized.

She huffed, stepping away to free her skirts.

"And what about this injury?" His small stick now poked at the bandage covering the gash in her arm that Julian had put there back by the vault. He pulled the bandage away from her skin slightly, getting just close enough to look inside it. "Have you even checked this since—"

He stopped short and gave a hard swallow. "That is… You need to look at that."

She shifted away from him once again, finally able to pin him with a glare. "It doesn't matter what I do with that wound. It's still going to scar."

He raised an eyebrow. "What is wrong with a scar?"

"It's ugly." She spat the words at him before focusing back on her hair.

"A scar?" He stepped a little closer. When he spoke again, his voice came out low. "A reminder that you are stronger than your enemy. A reminder that you are a survivor. *That* is ugly?" He turned away, his voice turning more gravelly than before. "Not to me."

Her head shot up. "Well, it doesn't really matter what you think, does it?" She took a step toward him while burning him with an even harder glare. "Since you hate me so much."

After those biting words, she threw the brush at his chest and turned to walk away. "You won't even let me repair our bond and bring your magic back, even though all we have to do is touch each other."

She hadn't expected a response. She expected to stomp off back to the mortals' camp where she'd smack Mishti and then find a spot to sleep for the night. But he did respond. He spoke words that stopped her right in her tracks.

"What good would it do to repair our bond? You will just betray me again someday, and I will lose my magic, and you, all over again."

Her heart pounded as she turned around. He didn't deserve the compassionate look she was surely giving him, but she couldn't help it. Her throat ached as she managed a swallow. "Is that what you think? You think I will betray you again?"

His arms hung heavy at his sides as he stared at the ground. "I know you will."

She closed her eyes, and for a moment, just breathed. Slowly. The space between them had changed to something softer, but it still had sharpness around the edges. After one more breath, she opened her eyes. "I never meant to take your magic. You know that, right? I had no idea that would happen when I locked you out."

Her fingers found a shiny blonde lock of hair, which she started twirling around one finger. "And I know I shouldn't have locked you out, but you wouldn't listen to me."

He glanced up, eyebrows pressed down low. "You locked me out because I wouldn't listen to you?"

"No." She huffed and folded her arms over her chest. "You killed someone, Quintus. You killed an innocent woman just because you wanted information. And it was information she didn't even have, if you recall."

Guilt settled into his features, slowly turning his lowered eyebrows to scrunched-up eyes. His lips pulled to a low frown. His muscles twitched as if in pain. "I know."

"You didn't even—"

"Chloe." He said her name with such fervor, it stopped her mid-sentence. And then he stared into her eyes. "I *am* sorry."

She almost nodded until she realized what word he had just used. Her hand clapped over her open mouth. "You just…" She took a step back, still trying to tell if she had imagined it. But she hadn't. "You owe me a favor now. You said—"

"I know what I said. I am. I am sorr—"

"Don't say it again."

But when she blurted out that command, he just took a step forward, gazing even more intensely into her eyes. "I am sorry. I know I should not have killed that woman. I know nothing I do will ever bring her back."

Only then did he turn his gaze to the ground. He stared at his feet while his fingers twitched at his sides.

It had been so long since the woman had been killed and never once had he showed any remorse. But all this time, this whole time, guilt had clearly been eating away at him, clawing its way out until now in this very moment.

"And that is how I know you will betray me again someday." He let out a sad laugh. "If things ever go slightly wrong between us, you will remember that moment, and you will leave me. I thought I'd lose you because of a mortal death, but now I know it is because of this. How could you not leave me after what I did? How could you ever truly forgive me?"

Her arms itched begging to reach around him as tight as they could go. How he must have struggled with this guilt. He had acted like he hated her, but all this time, he only hated himself. He only feared how his actions had torn them apart.

She stepped forward slowly but deliberately. He must have known she came closer, but he kept staring at his feet. When she reached out and hovered one hand just next to his, he still did not react. She wouldn't touch him though. Not without his permission.

"Can you truly forgive me after what I did to you?" she asked.

His gaze went from his feet over to his side where her hand hovered only a breath away from his. "Yes, but that is different."

She kept her hand hovering in that same spot and took another step forward, closing the distance between them even more. "You can forgive me after I locked you out of the court that is your home?"

"Chloe." He said her name in a rush of a breath.

"After I took away your magic?"

"Of course I can forgive you." He shook his head. "I cannot help it."

She leaned in closer, desperate to catch his eye. For a moment, he seemed determined to stare at their not-quite-touching hands for all eternity. But then, he did it. He glanced up, his gaze locking directly onto hers.

The slightest smile tugged at her lips. "Then I can truly forgive you."

He sucked in a breath, leaning closer until their chests had only the width of a thumb between them. He had heard, but clearly, he didn't dare believe.

"I do." She looked up through her eyelashes. "I do forgive you."

That was all the invitation he needed. His arms wrapped around her back, pulling her tight against him. His lips pressed against hers, hot and hungry. Warmth seeped into her where his hands trailed over her back. But then his upper hand lifted up to her head. His fingers dug into her hair while the gentle pressure of his hand brought their lips even closer together.

She couldn't get enough. Her lips, her arms, her neck, every part of her wanted more. And he gave it. He gave as willingly as her.

After fighting for so long, each touch felt ten times more powerful. Her heart beat quickly, furiously, but with a sure and steady rhythm that supplied all the energy she needed. She wanted to drown in this moment. Drown and never wake up.

All too soon, Quintus pulled away ever so slightly. When he did, she used her arms and hips to press against him harder. But then she heard what he must have heard a moment before her.

A light crackling sound filled the air, sending buzzing energy all around them.

Slowly extricating his hands from her hair and corset ties, he sucked in a breath as she looked down at his hands. Sparkling emerald green magic glowed from his fingertips. *Magic.* Not much of it. It was faded and weak compared to some of the magic she'd once seen shoot from his hands, but it was there.

After staring for several long moments, he looked up at her with a galaxy of golden glints in his rich brown eyes. His hair was longer too. Small black curls rested at the top of his head. Maybe he only had a little magic, but he looked ready to put it to the test.

20

Chloe bit her bottom lip, staring at the emerald magic sparkling off Quintus's fingertips. He'd kissed her, and now their bond had started repairing. But how much had it been repaired? Whatever he did with his magic next would answer that question.

As desperately as she wanted to know, she could see apprehension in his eyes. She felt it in herself too.

Clearing his throat, he retrieved a golden stick and three pearlescent pebbles from the ground. His eyebrows pressed down low while his fingers moved over the small items. He focused on one end of the golden stick, hovering a hand over it.

After a few moments, his breathing turned to huffing and his fingers started shaking. The stick had changed too. It had turned thinner and more flexible, almost like a stiff rope. Little by little, he moved down the stick until it had all turned flexible. He then joined the end pieces together until it formed a circle.

Eventually, his magic attached the three pebbles to one side of the circle. They were spaced unevenly from each other, which didn't look intentional, but it was probably best not to mention that.

After a final, exasperated huff. Quintus dropped one hand to his side and lifted the item he had crafted. Once it hung in the air, his intention became a little clearer.

"Is it a necklace?" Chloe worked hard to ask in the most neutral possible voice. If she had guessed correctly, she wanted it to seem like his craftsmanship made it obvious. But she didn't want to offend him by being wrong, so she tried not to be too confident.

He scowled at her question. "I was trying to make a delicate golden chain with three small stars hanging off it, sort of like your tattoos, but it didn't…" He jiggled the stiff circle of gold with the awkwardly spaced pebbles at the end. Shaking his head, he stuffed the necklace into his pocket. "It is worthless."

"No." Chloe stepped close to him again, placing her hand on his arm. "Our bond is only beginning to repair. You should celebrate that you used magic at all. And in the future, your magic will grow stronger. I can feel it."

A smile twitched at his lips, which seemed to have more to do with her hand touching him than with her words. In an instant, he had both his arms settled at the small of her back. It allowed him to draw her in close.

It took great effort to tilt her head downward, since she wanted to keep kissing too. But now that he had tested his magic, she was eager to test her own. After a tiny gulp, she used one hand to lift the hem of his shirt until a sliver of his stomach was exposed.

"Chloe." His voice came out in a low rumble.

Her hand froze in place, as she looked up at him as innocently as she could. "What? Am I allowed to touch you now?"

Since they'd both had their hands all over each other only a few moments ago, it seemed silly that he'd worry about that now. Still, she wouldn't touch him if he didn't want her to.

But once she caught sight of his eyes, it seemed an entirely different thought filled his mind. He raised an eyebrow. "If you are going to heal an injury, heal this one."

One of his hands slipped off her back and trailed up her arm until his fingers reached the bandaged wound from Julian's dagger. "Or this one." His hand now slid across her bare skin and under her hair until he found the gash on her shoulder. "Or—"

"I'll get to those later." Without waiting for him to agree, she yanked his shirt up higher, fulling uncovering his magical wound. "Yours is more important."

He tried to step away. "My body can heal itself. Yours cannot."

She wanted to stomp her food but simply clenched her jaw instead. "But your body *isn't* healing itself. Just let me test if—"

All at once, Quintus jerked his head to the side. His hand at her waist stiffened as he brought her a little closer.

Had he heard a noise?

She followed his gaze and found exactly what he'd heard. Or more accurately, who.

Mishti stood on the path leading to the clearing. She stood on the balls of her feet, clearly trying to sneak. But she'd been found now. And so had they.

Her mouth twitched in an expression suspiciously similar to a suppressed smile. She turned to walk away.

Heat rose into Chloe's cheeks realizing Quintus still had his arm around her, and she had his shirt up. Swallowing hard, she called after her friend. "Don't think you can get away so easily, Mishti. I know you tricked us into this clearing on purpose."

With her back to them, Mishti shrugged. "It looks like it worked."

The heat in Chloe's face burned hotter. She and Quintus glanced at each other and took a step away, as if that would help.

Huffing, Chloe started stomping toward her friend. "You can't just decide these things for us. We can solve these sorts of problems on our own, you know."

Mishti turned around just to roll her eyes dramatically. "You can be mad all you want, but I *will* do it again if you two keep fighting."

Chloe's mouth dropped open as her brain so unhelpfully supplied not one single retort.

And now Mishti snickered at her friend's silence. "Come on," she said beckoning to them. "I have a nice place set up for us all to sleep. We can figure out what we want to do next in the morning."

Quintus stalked toward her, his face showing off a slight tinge of crimson. But his eyes also had large clusters of gold glinting along with the brown. The sight of it reminded Chloe that his magic had already started to return.

Sleeping came more easily that night. Instead of worrying about whether they'd have to make a deal with the wraiths, she dreamt of Quintus holding her safe in his arms.

When day dawned, work began immediately. The Golden Shields had already created a system for everyone to take turns getting food at the table. They even found a nearby stream where people could wash if needed.

But now Chloe really did need to help gather small gems to go inside slings. And Quintus needed to help craft broken sticks and golden branches into arrows and spears. Gems and metal rocks got turned into arrowheads and small daggers.

While Chloe had been focused on finding the king of Crystalfall, the other Golden Shields had clearly been more concerned with defending themselves. She heard more than a few of them contemplating what they'd do if the Zeakriesh attacked them again.

The Zeakriesh had already displaced them twice, first from the castle and then from the celestine meadow. They had more weapons now, and Quintus helped them craft even more. But Chloe wondered along with the other Golden Shields if the new weapons would be enough.

She might have contemplated it more, except a dark shadow passed overhead. Her eyes narrowed, knowing her dragon was currently playing in a huge lake somewhere in Crystalfall. But what else could create such an enormous shadow?

After a quick glance upward, she gasped and jumped to her feet. It was indeed a dragon, but not hers. This was Revyn's dragon. As Chloe stood on her tiptoes, she craned her neck to see if Ludo sat atop the dragon.

Had he finally returned?

The question got answered instantly when Ludo leaned over the side of the dragon and shouted, "I see them. Land right between that cluster of trees and those tents."

Grinning, Chloe went to call for Mishti and Quintus, but both already moved forward.

By the time the dragon landed, they stood right at its edge. Ludo slid down, and Chloe threw her arms around him in a friendly hug. "I was so worried you wouldn't be able to find us after we moved."

Once Chloe released him, Mishti slapped him on the shoulder. "I was worried you'd complain so much your brother would throw you off his dragon's back."

This caused Revyn, who was sliding off his dragon, to let out a hard laugh. "I thought about it."

Ludo scoffed at the assertion. "I only complained that you were so desperate to find your beloved when you should have been at least a little more excited about being reunited with your brother again. And maybe I complained a little about how cold Fairfrost is."

"You also complained that the dragon scales on Estraelos weren't as warm or as smooth as the scales on Shadow." This declaration came from a pretty young woman with dark hair and fair skin, who slid down the rocky, earth-toned scales of Revyn's dragon.

After landing on the ground, she found Revyn's side and slipped her hand into his.

"You found her?" Mishti turned to Ludo with eyes open wide.

A wide grin split Revyn's face as he tugged the young woman closer. "Yes, we found my Clara, and my heart is finally full once again."

Ludo grumbled and said under his breath, "And I got stuck on the *back* of Estraelos where his scales are rougher."

With a laugh, Revyn pulled his brother into a hug with his free arm. "Stop complaining. I needed you for my heart to be full too, Ludo. The memories are returning slowly, but I am starting to remember."

Clara's dark hair had been swept into an elegant bun decorated with pearl strands and dried red berries. She wore a black gown with a wide skirt that must have had double or triple petticoats underneath it. The long, puffed sleeves looked so unlike the clothing Chloe had worn in the mortal realm. Colorful satin ribbons and strands of pearls wrapped around her gown. Tiny bell-like pink flowers hanging from fine stems had been tucked into her bodice, her sleeves, and even parts of her skirt. A few lace bows had also been tacked on.

Perhaps this young woman came from a time and place in the mortal realm where such extravagant outfits were ordinary, but this attire seemed special.

"What an elegant gown," Chloe said. "Is this everyday wear in your part of the mortal realm?"

"Hardly." The young woman released a puffy laugh. "It's my wedding dress."

Chloe's eyebrows jumped up high. "Your wedding dress? Did you two just—"

Shifting on her feet, Clara wrinkled her nose. "No, not to Revyn. But… I didn't actually get married."

As she finished the sentence, a nearby pixie with a gown made of tiny amethysts sewn together flew toward their small group. Chloe remembered this pixie. Her name was Plumia, and she once terrorized Portia and Julian when Chloe and Mishti had needed it most.

Plumia's wings made the sound of chiming bells as she flew down until she hovered directly in front of Revyn and Clara. She said nothing, and instead, simply stared at the two of them.

Lifting her skirt, Clara gave a small curtsy. "Hello, Plumia. It's good to see you again."

The pixie touched a hand to her chest. "Do I know you?" But even as she asked, Plumia shook her head. "I do know you. I can feel it."

Ludo stepped forward, the grumpiness in his face more subdued now. "You will remember. With more reminders of the past, all of us are starting to remember."

Plumia grinned and started to fly away. But when she turned, she came face-to-face with Quintus, who started picking at his wound.

Because of the disturbance, a tiny droplet of blood fell to the ground and erupted in a cloud of acrid smoke.

Plumia gasped at the sight of it.

Quintus rolled his eyes and moved his hands away from the wound so it wouldn't drip blood anymore. "Do not worry about that. The wound is magical, so it is taking my healing abilities longer than usual to heal. But it will be fine."

An ominous shadow passed over Plumia's face. "That is not a magical wound. It is a cursed wound. Whoever gave that to you wants you dead more than you know."

After a hard swallow, he shook his head. "Of course he wants us dead. We are trying to stop him and take over the castle he has control of. We want him dead too."

Raising an eyebrow, Plumia flew away with that same ominous shadow twisting her features.

"Never mind that." Quintus waved a hand through the air and snarled after the retreating pixie. Now he turned toward the new mortal young woman and Ludo's brother. Giving both Clara and Revyn a pointed glance, he said, "We need to know what you remember about the king of Crystalfall."

The two of them glanced at each other, expressions looking a little too sad to hope for good news.

Ludo swallowed hard and gestured toward a cluster of large boulders. "We should probably sit down for this."

An ominous sense of dread hit Chloe's gut. Despair and trepidation drifted into the space between them. All three of the newcomers now wore expressions without a single glimmer of optimism. But was it because they remembered nothing? Or because they remembered something that was worse than forgetting?

21

ONCE EVERYONE GOT SETTLED ONTO the boulders, Mishti went around giving them all assignments to complete while they talked. Chloe got a stack of arrows and a pile of arrowheads placed on either side of her. A spool of thin wire sat in her lap, which she quickly set about using to attach the arrowheads to the arrows.

Quintus got a pile of daggers to sharpen. Ludo got spears, arrowheads, and a spool of wire just like Chloe had.

Mishti had a pile of lustrous red vines on her lap. The garnet-colored plants were the closest thing they'd encountered to fibers in this court of gems. They still had the strength and shine of jewels, but they were formed from thread-like strands that could be untwisted and then woven back together. She unraveled the vines one by one and then braided and wove the glossy filaments into new slings.

Only Revyn and Clara had nothing to do with their hands. Following the lead of the others, Revyn pulled an axe from his pocket and started sharpening it. Clara kept her hands busy by touching the brilliant pink pendant at the end of her golden necklace. The gem seemed to sparkle as bright and magically as the water in Crystalfall. Even stranger, her face looked as young as Chloe's.

Wrapping a wire tight around an arrowhead and arrow, Chloe stared carefully at her work. Ludo had claimed the mortal young woman had received an amulet from the pixies that would slow her aging. Was that pink pendant the amulet?

Even if it was, Chloe still had questions.

She glanced to the side, not quite sure how to phrase the question she wanted to ask. "Excuse me, but…"

Once the young woman looked at her, Chloe had to stop and think again. It was such a strange question, one that wouldn't mean anywhere near the same thing in the mortal realm. She swallowed and tried again. "We think it's been a hundred mortal years or more since Crystalfall was destroyed, but…you don't look like you've aged at all."

Did it sound like an accusation? Chloe had been trying so hard to make it sound light and non-accusatory, but it came out faster than she'd meant it, and now she couldn't read the young woman's face.

Stroking a thumb over the pink gem at the end of her necklace, Clara shrugged. "That's because I haven't." Her hand dropped to her lap, which she then used to fiddle with a purple satin ribbon adorning her black dress. "I've been in the mortal realm all this time."

A lump formed in Chloe's throat as she examined the young woman's elegant gown again. "Did you… fall in love with someone in the mortal realm?"

A sharp laugh rang out from Clara's throat. "No." She laughed again. "Definitely not."

"Do you remember the king of Crystalfall?" Quintus had stopped sharpening the dagger in his hand and stared hard. Once again, he was the one to remember to get them back on track.

But the young woman's face fell. "No. Unfortunately, I do not remember who the king is."

Revyn nodded, sitting forward slightly. "We all lost memory of the king. And I do not mean the three of us." He gestured between himself, Ludo, and Clara. "I mean everyone in Crystalfall. We remember a huge cloud of prickly magic fell down from the sky. Then suddenly, our memories of the king had vanished."

Ludo grumbled as he twisted a wire over the spear and arrowhead in his hand. "Of course the magic had to hit us right when we were talking about the king."

Mishti cocked up a single eyebrow. "How do you know you were talking about him?"

A deeper frown overtook Ludo's face. "Because my brother was in the middle of a sentence when the magic hit us, but after that, it suddenly made no sense."

Revyn nodded. "I said, 'We always knew it would come to this. A king only has so much power.'" He spoke the words slowly, deliberately. His eyes narrowed, as if he still attempted to find meaning hidden somewhere in that phrase. After he finished though, he just released a sigh that indicated he had given up.

Clara sat a little straighter, her hand halfway through removing a strand of pearls from her hair. "We were trying to do something too. Something important. And suddenly, none of us could remember what it was. We remembered it was something to do with the king, but we couldn't remember if the king was a friend or an enemy."

Ludo threw his hands into the air. "He could have been one of us for all we knew."

Quintus's eyebrows jumped high on his forehead at the sound of that. In the next moment, his gaze slid over to Chloe.

Her own gut began churning, which she attempted to ignore. "We know the king isn't Revyn." She swallowed hard, trying to ignore the turbulent energy inside her. "The king had a lover named Dyani, who is also Quintus's mother." The tips of Chloe's ears burned hot as she glanced down at her lap. "I suppose I shouldn't have assumed, but you did not have a lover named Dyani, did you, Revyn?"

His face looked positively aghast when she finally braved a glance upward. "A lover?" A disgusted wince scrunched up his whole face as he dropped his axe, stood, and moved closer to Clara. "I have my beloved. I have never sought affection from anyone else."

Nodding as quickly as she could, Chloe bent to grab another golden stick and sharpened arrowhead from the piles at her side. "That's what I thought, just wanted to double check."

But now Quintus narrowed one of his eyes and looked carefully at his friend. "Have *you* ever had a lover, Ludo?"

The Fairfrost fae's blue-and-red eyes nearly shimmered as he considered the question. His head tilted while he stared off without speaking. His lips parted, but just before saying anything he simply waved off the question. "Forget that. We still have to tell you what happened after we forgot the king."

Revyn pinched his chin and gazed into the distance. "I am not sure if it happened immediately after or if it happened later."

"What happened?" Chloe didn't even realize she had sat forward so far until an arrow fell off her lap. She managed to pluck it off the ground while keeping her gaze on Ludo and Revyn.

But it was Clara who answered. Her hands dropped heavy in her lap while her facial features turned downward. When she spoke, her voice broke over the words. "Crystalfall was destroyed."

Mishti stopped braiding a sling long enough to throw a skeptical glance toward the young woman. "You were there when it was destroyed?" Her eyes raked over the young woman, probably noting she had no injuries indicating her presence at such a catastrophic event.

"It didn't happen all at once," Clara said, tugging at a lace bow on her gown. "It started with the trees, well, with the leaves."

Revyn nodded fast, his light brown hair bouncing as he finally found his seat on the boulder again. "The leaves popped and cracked until they burst into a puff of shattered emerald. We went to check on Lifespark Tree immediately, since the pixies would die if that tree got too damaged."

At his side, Clara lowered her chin to her chest. "But it was already too late when we got there."

"The mountains came down next," Ludo added solemnly.

Revyn lowered his gaze. "While the mountains were collapsing, we went to the trees just outside the crystal caves. We hoped we'd find Faerie itself trying to repair the court, but we only saw more destruction."

Clara grimaced with a nod. "We saw the person causing the destruction too. A mortal, if you can believe it."

After a hard blink, Chloe sat forward. The arrow in her lap dropped to the ground again, but she didn't bother retrieving it this time. "You saw the mortal who destroyed Crystalfall?"

Clara scowled as she ripped a lace bow from her dress. "Yes. He stood just past the crystal caves and in the high court. He shouted as soon as he saw us. He said he was so excited that I would finally meet my end."

Revyn's hand clenched into a tight fist. "That was when I panicked. I opened a door and brought Clara straight back to the mortal realm. We had already lost memories, and I feared we would lose more. With Crystalfall gone, we would have to live in a different court, none of which were as accepting of mortals as Crystalfall. I knew the only place to keep her truly safe was back the mortal realm."

Clara had managed to rip the other lace bows off her gown, along with some of the ribbons. Apparently, her wedding dress, and probably her betrothed, meant very little to her. "And I was safe there. Not even a morning had passed since Revyn left me before he returned again."

"Of course," Revyn continued. "I made a vow that once it was safe in Faerie again, I would return and retrieve my Clara from that exact place in the mortal realm."

Cocking her head to the side, Clara turned to the other two mortals sitting with them. "He says place, but he means the same place and—"

"Time." Both Chloe and Mishti finished the sentence together. The three mortals glanced between each other then, wearing smirks that the fae could only scratch their heads at.

But once the moment passed, Chloe reached into her leather bag and pulled out her magical book. She had read several times about the mortal who had destroyed Crystalfall. He gained magic by finding and touching the creation magic in Faerie. But then he used the power for evil, and eventually, destroyed the Court of Crystalfall.

Opening the book on her lap, Chloe started thumbing through the pages. "Why did that mortal do it, though? Was he enemy to the king or…" She looked more intently, hoping for an answer to appear on its magical pages. "I wish we knew more about the mortal who destroyed Crystalfall."

Clara suddenly stopped in the middle of plucking a flower stem from her dress. Her eyes opened wide as she asked, "You mean Fritz?"

Revyn's nose wrinkled as he glared at his axe, which he had just retrieved from the ground. He whispered the name *Fritz* under his breath.

When she went back to plucking flowers out of her gown, Clara worked a little more forcefully than before. "That's why Revyn had to take me to the mortal realm. He worried Fritz would try to kill me himself, since we were betrothed at one point."

Chloe's hand fell against her magical book as she dropped her jaw. "You were *betrothed* to the mortal who destroyed Crystalfall?"

The scowls the young woman kept sending to her wedding dress started to make a little more sense. Clara tore a ribbon off the gown and flicked it unceremoniously to the ground. "Yes. He's one of the main reasons I asked Revyn to take me to Faerie in the first place. I was trying to avoid our marriage."

Quintus sat up straighter and looked at Revyn. "Good thing you remembered her and got to the mortal realm when you did, or she might be married by now."

A bright smile lit Clara's face as she ripped a strand of pearls from her hair. "It didn't matter much since Fritz is here. Or…" Her hand dropped to her lap as she narrowed one eye. "Or he *was* here."

She glanced at Revyn. "You said a great deal of time has passed. Well, I guess you technically said, 'Many events have transpired that a mortal would not have lived through.' So, he's probably not here anymore."

"I do not remember Fritz." Ludo announced this loudly while wearing one of his classic grumbling expressions. His eyebrows pinched tighter together while he stared off in thought. "I do not know that name at all."

Clara pressed a hand to her forehead. "Oh, I forgot he started going by a different name. He didn't want to keep the name his father had given him, so he changed his name to…" She turned to Revyn. "What was it?"

He started shrugging, but halfway through his eyes changed. "Josu… or Judu…"

"Julian." Clara pointed at Revyn as she shouted out the name, looking extremely proud of herself.

Of course, in that one small moment, the energy around them changed. A knot twisted in Chloe's belly. She tried to swallow but found her throat too thick for it.

It couldn't be. What were the odds? It had been over a hundred years.

Mishti spoke first. "It has to be a coincidence. It can't be…"

She didn't finish, but she didn't need to. Chloe, Quintus, and Ludo were clearly all thinking the same thing. It couldn't be *Julian* Julian. It couldn't be the mortal who had lived in Ansel's house and currently sat inside Crystalfall Castle, probably planning another attack.

"What," Chloe leaned forward, her voice heavy and thick, "did Julian—Fritz—look like?"

Revyn and Clara glanced toward each other, clearly noting how the energy had changed but not understanding why.

They all held their breaths and watched as Clara used her thumb to stroke the edge of her pink jeweled amulet. "He had blond hair and wild eyes. Blue. Oh, and he grew a mole on his chin. It wasn't there in the mortal realm, but after he touched the creation magic, it started to grow. When he destroyed Crystalfall, it had grown to the size of a thumbnail."

A heavy exhale left Chloe's mouth before she dropped her head into her hands. She wanted to sob, but shock had too strong a hold on her.

It *was* him. Julian had once been betrothed to Clara in the mortal realm, but somehow, he'd gotten to Faerie. He'd found magic and destroyed an entire court, and even though more than a hundred mortal years had passed, he somehow lived.

"How could he have survived?" Ludo's voice came out shaky.

Quintus shook his head before answering. "He has magic inside him from touching the creation magic. That is how he destroyed Crystalfall."

"No." Chloe suddenly turned back to her magical book, remembering something she had read about this mortal. "Faerie blocked that magic from him after he destroyed the court. The magic is inside him, but he cannot access it."

"How did he do it then?" Mishti's voice was cold as ice. "How is he still alive?"

Chloe shrugged, still flipping through the pages of her book. "We saw him use balance shards just the other day. And I've seen him use Ansel's gemstones to do magic. He's been here long enough that he must have figured out a way to use other magic to keep himself healthy."

"It changes nothing." Quintus spoke in a sure voice that still had a bit too much weight to be truly confident. At least he had tried. "Julian is still our enemy, even if he is the one who destroyed Crystalfall."

Mishti nodded, trying to calm herself too. "True. And everyone else has lost their memories about the king, so it's not like Julian knows anything anyway."

But those words sent an even bigger twist through Chloe's gut. She swallowed hard and reached into her leather bag. "I forgot to tell you. Julian left a note near my bed. I thought it was crazy when I first read it, so crazy I forgot about it, but…"

She couldn't say anything else. It would be easier if they read it themselves. So, she held out the piece of paper with his tight, ultra-straight handwriting. And now everyone could read the words she knew by heart.

I know where to find the king of Crystalfall.

The words had seemed preposterous when she first read them. A declaration as insane as Julian. But now? Her fingers shook as the realization became clear.

He was their greatest enemy. And now he might be their only chance of finding the king they so desperately sought.

22

Once everyone read the words, color drained from their faces. Chloe didn't have to state the impossible dilemma inside her head because the same one plagued theirs. Did Julian truly know where to find the king of Crystalfall? And even if he did, how could they ever trust him?

"He must be lying." Mishti shook her head harder and harder with each word she spoke. "He must be."

"Is there any way he could remember? Is it even possible?" Ludo asked.

Revyn sat on his boulder, nearly unaffected by the news that Julian, his beloved's once betrothed, still lived. It was probably because, currently, he gazed deep into her eyes, barely even blinking. "Julian stood just outside the crystal caves in Bitter Thorn when the cloud affecting our memories came down. Perhaps he was unaffected."

Clara stood from her boulder now and stepped closer to Revyn's boulder. He immediately stood and pulled her into his arms.

They clearly didn't understand the gravity of the situation, but maybe it didn't matter. The rest of them understood.

Mishti stared at the pair of them, watching as their heads tilted toward each other. She raised an eyebrow. "But Revyn, you forgot Clara too. You didn't just forget the king of Crystalfall. If that single cloud was the only cause of memory loss, then why did you forget her? Why did you forget Ludo?"

Revyn shrugged, stroking Clara's cheek and not seeming at all bothered to find an answer to Mishti's questions.

Instead, Ludo sat taller. He reached for his chin, tapping it while his eyes narrowed. "I lost many memories, not just my memories of the king. I could not even remember Crystalfall until we went there. Maybe the cloud made us forget the king, but maybe Faerie itself took away our memories of Crystalfall once the court got destroyed. Or maybe the king came and took away memories of anyone close to him so he would not have to worry about his crown being stolen. In any case, I believe it *is* possible Julian knows who the king of Crystalfall is."

Chloe scoffed and closed her magical book. "If that's true, then anyone who was outside of Crystalfall at the time would remember the king."

She started sliding her book into her leather bag when her head tilted to the side. "Dyani might remember him. We should go visit her."

It took one glance at Quintus to see he did not seem so eager about that idea. His light brown skin took on a greenish tinge. He swallowed and stretched different facial muscles in strange ways, as if trying to hide any emotion that might creep onto his face.

Considering his father had tried to kill him and destroyed his home, Quintus probably didn't want to see what his mother might do upon meeting him.

Still, visiting Dyani seemed like a much better plan than making a deal with the wraiths, who were the only other creatures with any chance of knowing the king's location. She could probably convince Mishti to go with her, even if Quintus didn't want to go.

Another dark shadow appeared overhead. Chloe nearly smiled, since she'd just been thinking of taking Shadow to get to Dyani.

But as she turned her head upward, she sensed this still wasn't her dragon. Had some other dragon decided to enter the court? If so, Shadow would probably enjoy the company.

The flying creature above had magnificent pastel scales and purple eyes and horns. The smattering of colors looked brilliant even next to the landscape of Crystalfall. It took a moment of examining, but soon, Chloe sat back.

"I know that dragon." She narrowed her eyes, looking more closely to confirm her suspicion. When certain, she glanced to her side.

Quintus stared upward with the same recognition. They had both worked side by side with the couple now riding atop the dragon. That had been long ago, back before Elora became Queen of Bitter Thorn. But it had been memorable enough to know this dragon on sight.

Quintus turned to her sharply, and said, "King Severin's dragon."

She nodded, not sure what to make of the information now that he'd confirmed it.

Ludo scrunched up his face as he looked upward. "What is *he* doing in Crystalfall?"

Before Chloe could even think to respond, Mishti pointed at the creature. "I have seen that dragon before. I saw it last night, and I saw it while you two," she pointed at Chloe and Quintus, "were off with Shadow."

This new information seemed even more intriguing, but Chloe still had no idea what to make of it. From what they knew of Severin, he seemed more honorable than the average fae. He had even fallen in love with a fae named Tindra, and they had once run away together while his older sister still ruled their court. But now he was King of Fairfrost.

Maybe once he had felt a misfit in his own court, but he couldn't possibly feel that way now that he ruled over it. But if that wasn't why he was in Crystalfall, then why was he?

Still in the middle of an embrace with Revyn, Clara glanced at the rest of them just long enough to ask, "Who is King Severin?"

Ludo's face hadn't un-scrunched. In fact, it scrunched up even more when he caught sight of his brother and Clara. "He is the king of Fairfrost."

After her eyebrows rose, she turned back to the fae holding her, gazing into his eyes. "Oh, is Pavel not the king of Fairfrost anymore?"

Revyn shook his head, speaking low and almost directly in her ear. "No, his son is king now. Well, first his daughter was queen, but now his son is king."

Clara nodded slowly, her hands reaching into his hair so she could fiddle with a piece of it. "What about Winola? Is she still High Queen?"

Surprise sent Chloe's eyebrows upward. High Queen Winola was still alive when Clara was here the first time? A *great* deal of time had passed, then. Yet Revyn stared at her like not a day had passed since they'd been together.

"Uh, no. High Queen Winola…" But Revyn's ability to think had been stolen by the look in his beloved's eyes. He trailed off and leaned closer to her.

"I have an idea," Ludo said in a voice almost as loud as a shout. He tromped over to the pair of them and started pushing them back toward their dragon. "Revyn, you and Clara should take your dragon and travel through all the courts in Faerie. You can tell her how much it has changed since she was here."

Despite the prodding, Revyn looked far less interested in Ludo's suggestion than in holding tight to his beloved.

"Go on," Ludo said a little more insistently. "You remember me now, and you know where to find me. But now you two should enjoy a dragon ride together. That sounds romantic, does it not?"

Clara's eyes lit up at the mention of romance. She nodded and started moving toward the earth-toned Estraelos. Revyn clambered after her eagerly.

"We will be back soon, Ludo," Clara said once atop the dragon.

Ludo waved off those words. "Oh, enjoy yourselves. You do not need to return right away."

It only took another few moments and the dragon flew high into the air. Once they were far above, Ludo let out an exasperated sigh. He pinched the bridge of his nose and shook his head. "I love my brother, and I even love Clara, but sometimes I get tired of all the loving looks between them."

Chloe raised an eyebrow, noting how he made a disdainful comment about love. But once he dropped his hand to his side, every hint of disdain fell from his face. He glanced back up at the retreating dragon, this time wearing a somewhat wistful expression. "Besides, they have missed so much. They need to be together more than they need to be with me."

Chloe's heart thumped at those words. He started off seeming to disdain romance, but now he clearly demonstrated he didn't actually mind it so much. In fact, he maybe even wanted it for himself.

Quintus had turned back to the daggers he was supposed to be sharpening, and his expression gave no hint he'd come to the same conclusion as Chloe.

Glancing toward Quintus, Ludo sat back on his boulder with a spear in one hand and an arrowhead in the other. Holding both pieces, he started wrapping wire around them. "Have you seen the castle since you were driven from the celestine meadow?"

"No." Chloe tried to keep suspicion out of her eye as she grabbed a stick and arrowhead from her own piles to begin assembling. "Have you seen it?"

He nodded so hard, his light-colored hair bounced over his forehead. Worry lines appeared on his forehead and around his eyes. Even his fingers seemed more tense as he wrapped the arrowhead in place. "It is horrifying. The mortals split it completely in half, and part of the walls are ashy and melting."

His fingers grew shaky now. When he dropped the finished spear and reached for a new spear and arrowhead, he had trouble gripping them.

Forgetting his own work, Quintus stared across the clearing. "Are you…*driven* to have the castle repaired?"

"Of course I am." Ludo shook his head, while the worry lines in his face deepened. "Now that Crystalfall has returned, I certainly do not want to lose it again. I have never felt more at home than in Crystalfall."

A visit to Dyani seemed more important than ever. Maybe they could leave Quintus, but it would probably be important to bring Ludo. She dared a glance at Quintus, whose face had turned to a scowl.

Did she dare bring up the idea to visit his mother so soon after he had stopped fighting with her? It probably wasn't the best time to force him into something that might upset him. Maybe she'd let him have the morning. They could spend the morning working on weapons, and then she'd breach the subject again.

While they worked, Sofia and Batu entered the clearing. Each looked at the other expectantly, but neither of them spoke.

When Quintus caught sight of them, his gaze jumped from one to the other. Still, they said nothing. He raised an eyebrow. "Did you need something?"

"Yes," Batu said. And then he gestured toward Sofia.

She stared at him incredulously, but it only lasted a moment. After a short breath, she finally explained. "All the Golden Shields are preparing weapons. Even some of the fae have offered to help. We have worked hard, but…"

She looked at Batu, who nodded expectantly.

After the encouragement, she continued. "Even with all the weapons we stole, and even with all the ones we're making now, we won't be able to defeat the Zeakriesh again." She frowned. "Not as long as they are using the magic of the shards."

Chloe glanced between the two Golden Shields, her lip turning upward slightly. "That *is* a problem. But it seems like you two have thought of a possible solution."

Batu stepped forward, encouraged by Chloe's prodding. "Mishti explained to us last night how you trained your golden dragon. She told us a token is needed, which is formed when an object is imbued with great emotion."

Sofia nodded, taking a step forward too. "And we're mortals. One of the main advantages we have over the fae is our emotions. Since we tend to feel more deeply, it is much easier for us to create tokens. Most of us probably already have something that would work."

The scheme suddenly became clear in Chloe's mind. She let out a small chuckle and said the sentence they'd been speaking around. "You want your own dragons?"

From her boulder, Mishti set her in-progress sling into her lap. "Who wouldn't?"

Ludo scoffed loudly, holding a spear in one hand and mindlessly using it to make his points as he talked. "Do you have any idea how dangerous dragons are? Yes, you can create reins with a token, and once you get them around the dragon's neck, the creature will be trained and answer to you. But doing that is not easy. You will not be able to waltz up to a dragon and slip the reins around its neck while it bats its eyelashes at you. The dragon will try to eat you. And since you are mortals and do not have the speed of fae, the creature will probably succeed."

"We know the risks." Batu stood tall and clasped his hands behind his back. "We still want to do it."

At his side, Sofia reached her arms out with her palms facing upward. "We have no magic. We cannot use iron as a weapon when we're fighting against mortals, and we don't want to hurt the court anyway. The Zeakriesh have already displaced us twice. If they attack, they'll displace us again." She stepped forward, pleading in her eyes. "How else are we supposed to have any chance against them?"

Batu nodded. "An army of dragons is likely our only chance."

The idea was crazy. Insane. Wild. But it was just crazy enough it might work. And though Ludo was right that dragons were dangerous, they had one asset that could help. They had Shadow. She'd helped them when Revyn's dragon tried to attack. Surely she'd help them again.

Best of all, she probably knew exactly where the best dragons would be. They'd get back to the search for the king soon. And they'd still spend the morning gathering weapons. They just weren't at all the kind of weapons Chloe had originally imagined.

Instead, they'd gather dragons.

23

GOLDEN SCALES WARMED CHLOE AS she flew her dragon toward Fairfrost. It took little prodding to convince the creature to find more dragons. Shadow almost seemed to have been hoping for it all along. With Chloe and all the other Golden Shields on her back, Shadow flew with a clear purpose.

On the way, Quintus crafted reins from the tokens the Shields had chosen. Just as Sofia and Batu guessed, none of the mortals had to think very hard before they found an item imbued with enough emotion to be strong enough to train a dragon.

Quintus crafted each one by hand, not using his magic, even though it had returned. Maybe he didn't want the pressure of revealing his magic yet, or maybe he just knew it wasn't strong enough and crafting by hand would be easier.

Despite the lack of magic, he crafted quickly enough that he had nearly finished by the time Shadow flew over the border leading them into Fairfrost.

The sparkling snow and iridescent clouds of the court shimmered beneath them. Quintus retrieved Chloe's cloak from his pocket again, warming her just when she needed it. Eventually, Shadow landed behind a short, snow-covered hill near a partially frozen lake.

Glancing past the hill, Chloe got a perfect view of the area. Glittering icicles and large chunks of ice floated through the water. Trees encased in glossy ice with small ice flowers on the branches grew from the ground. Frosty bushes that smelled of cranberries filled the area as well.

Thick blankets of snow on the ground usually muted the sound in Fairfrost, making it eerily quiet. But that quietude was smashed away by the creatures nearby.

A horde of dragons dotted the landscape around the lake. Low, rumbling sounds filled the air, almost like a cat's purr, except ten times louder. The soft rustling of wings sounded as well. Water splashes and hard breathing came from a few dragons trying to catch fish from the lake.

Other dragons released hisses or guttural growls as their wings and claws crashed into each other during dangerously playful fights. The last few dragons sat quietly or released soft thuds as they jumped into snow piles and flapped their wings until clouds of powdery snow rose up from the ground.

The dragons came in all sizes and colors. Some could fit dozens of people on their backs like Shadow could. Others could fit only two or three people. Their scales came in every color imaginable, and in every imaginable pattern too.

One dragon had scales that resembled faceted crystals in pale pinks and yellows. Its wings were translucent and refracted the light, creating dazzling rainbows across the snow surrounding her.

Another dragon had mossy green scales that turned sky blue whenever it released its wings from its back.

A remarkable dragon with dark scales had glints and sparkles over them that resembled a mortal sky full of stars. Its horns and eyes were a lustrous purple.

Some dragons were multicolored, displaying colors from the entire rainbow. Others had a single color in multiple shades. Others had a few colors with unique color changes or scale shape adding brilliance. Some had muted and pastel colors while others were deeply hued. Others still were bright.

Chloe noted that one dragon with a geometric pattern of silver and teal on its scales watched the lake, seeming to calculate and examine more than it moved. And when it did thrust its clawed foot into the lake, the action seemed more deliberate than when the other dragons did the same. Its crimson eyes and horns glowed slightly whenever it caught a fish.

Since the Golden Shields and Shadow hid behind a low hill, the dragons hadn't noticed them. After watching, Chloe glanced at the others. "It looks like they're trying to hunt fish. I wonder if we could draw the dragons in with some bait."

Quintus stood tall to search past the hill before turning back to her. "How are we supposed to get fish to use as bait when the dragons surround the entire lake?" He spoke gently, not challenging her but noting the plan needed more refining.

She scrunched her mouth to the side before another idea hit. "Maybe Shadow could scare them away? They'll probably leave but not permanently. I imagine they'll return to the lake pretty soon after being scared away."

Mishti nodded. "That would give us enough time to set the bait."

Ludo let out a heavy sigh and folded his arms over his chest. "If they return *pretty soon*, we will not be done catching fish before they come back. And, surely, they will attack as soon as they see us."

"True." Chloe's mind only needed another moment of spinning before she had an answer for that too. "Ludo, do you have any meat you can conjure? Raw meat?"

A light glinted in his eye. "As a matter of fact, I have the perfect thing sitting at my house now."

"Perfect." Chloe turned to her dragon, rubbing her on her golden nose. "I need you to fly in there as loud as you can to scare the dragons away."

Shadow's wings opened wide in a snap.

"But don't scare them too much," Chloe said. "We want them to return."

The dragon released a huff from her nostrils, which Chloe knew indicated the dragon's understanding. Iridescent light glinted off Shadow's golden scales as she shrieked and swooped in low by the lake.

While she made a ruckus, Mishti grabbed the raw meat from Ludo's hands that he had just conjured. Her mouth lifted ever so slightly on one side. "I have an idea."

By then, the dragons had all flown away, and Mishti ran toward the lake. She placed the raw meat onto a small rock, which sat next to a mound of powdery snow. Using the snow to clean the meat residue off her hands, she then called to the nearest mortal.

Batu came to her side, but Chloe still stood behind the hill where the main group hid and couldn't hear whatever direction Mishti gave.

When Mishti came back, Batu stayed behind.

They didn't have to wait long for the dragons to return. Soon the creatures reclaimed their previous positions around the lake. Except the dragon with the silver and teal geometric patterns on its scales hadn't gone back to its spot by the lake. Instead, it crept slowly, deliberately toward the chunk of raw meat sitting on the rock.

The creature nudged the raw meat with its nose a few times. It sniffed the meat, poked it with a crimson claw. After careful inspection, it finally opened its mouth wide and bit into the meat with its sharp, pointed teeth.

That was all it took. Once it started eating, Batu suddenly jumped out of the snow mound that had been directly next to the raw meat.

He held his reins that Quintus had crafted from a tattered orange flag and threw them over the dragon's neck. The silver and teal beast stumbled backward and growled in surprise, but Batu had been close enough that it didn't matter. The reins were set.

Now the dragon blinked and looked down at Batu. The man smiled and held tight to the orange reins as he led the dragon back behind the hill where the others were hidden.

They had done it. Their first dragon had been tamed.

Only one dragon from the horde saw any of it. The others seemed too intent on their fishing or playing to be bothered to notice what another dragon did. But the one dragon who did notice had purple, shimmery flecks on its nose and its wings. The rest of its scales were a creamy white.

It stared as Batu led the dragon away. But before it discovered the others' hiding place, the purple-flecked dragon suddenly turned toward the lake and used two paws to grab a fish it had just seen. The attempt failed, and the dragon lifted its claws to try again. But as it lifted its claws, it suddenly turned its head toward a low cloud passing overhead.

Changing course entirely, the dragon suddenly flew upward and clamped its teeth through the cloud, causing it to wisp away. It prepared for another clamp, but it soon got distracted by an ice flower that fell from a nearby tree. Suddenly, it flew forward, trying to catch the little flower.

Jansher, a tall Shield with a solid frame, stood at Chloe's side. He laughed and pointed directly at the purple-flecked dragon. "I want that one," he said.

It didn't seem likely anyone would be able to choose a specific dragon. They'd have to take whichever one went for the bait near to them.

But when they had Shadow scare the dragons away, and other Shields set more bait, the dragon with the purple flecks did happen to nip at the bait directly next to Jansher.

They set several hunks of bait that second time, allowing half a dozen Shields to get dragons at once. Some had an easier time getting their reins over the dragons' necks than others. Hilda got shoved into the snow and only managed to throw her reins into place because the dragon was distracted by the shrieking of another dragon.

Strangely, Chloe started to notice similarities between the dragons and the Shields who had tamed them. Jansher, for instance, was as easily distracted as his creamy white and purple-flecked dragon.

Another Shield threw reins over a dragon that seemed calmer than the others, but when provoked, it lashed out more fiercely…exactly like the woman now holding its reins.

And when they repeated the process again, Sofia got paired with the dragon whose scales resembled faceted crystals in pale pinks and yellows. From quick observation, it became clear that crystal dragon preferred to stay busy and not sit still. A behavior similar to Sofia herself.

Growls, shouts, and even fire breathing filled the morning, but each mortal had miraculously come away with a dragon that seemed perfect and just for him or her.

Everyone except Mishti.

So far, she had set out bait. Whenever the other Shields hid in the snow, she watched intently, and even nearly hid herself a few times. But whenever she went to hide in a mound of snow, she'd stop a Shield and have that person hide instead.

With the lake area completely empty now, Chloe looked at her friend. "You're the one who wanted a dragon first. Why haven't you claimed one yet?"

The question had no accusation inside it, which Mishti seemed to sense. Her eyes narrowed as she contemplated. After a short shrug she finally responded. "None of them are right."

Her gaze trailed over the horde of dragons that had been claimed. There were clever dragons, fast dragons, careful dragons, every sort of dragon imaginable.

But Mishti seemed even more sure of her response as she looked over them again. She shrugged. "None of them are right for me."

Chloe glanced at Quintus then, hoping he might jump in with some words of wisdom or even just another question.

He did not. He probably hadn't even heard the conversation at all, since he was too busy playing with Shadow. Using one hand, he rubbed up and down her long nose. All the while, he released soft clicking and kissy noises that Shadow was eating up.

That seemed to be the end of the discussion since Mishti turned on her heel and headed away.

Ludo had also stalked off to get a better look at each of the new dragons. He claimed he did not want or need one since he could just open a door to get anywhere he wanted to go. But Chloe wondered if he might have been a little more frightened of dragons than he wanted to admit. Or maybe he just didn't want to admit he had no token to use.

A light smile adorned Quintus's face as he glanced up at Chloe. He still had one hand stroking Shadow's nose while he spoke. "Do you think our dragon will enjoy having all these other dragons around?"

The question brought a happy image to Chloe's mind. Instead of fighting, the dragons played happily at a sparkling waterfall in Crystalfall. But before she could answer, her thoughts snagged on one specific word in Quintus's question.

She smirked and stared directly at him. "*Our* dragon?"

His eyes opened wide. With a hard swallow, he dropped his gaze and went back to stroking Shadow's nose.

But she wouldn't let him avoid the question so easily. She placed her hands on her hips and took a step toward him. "You said it again."

He flinched, focusing even more intently on Shadow's golden scales. Even his shoulders had scrunched up to his ears. But after another moment, he released a long breath that lowered his shoulders.

His gaze still fixated on Shadow's nose, but at least he was ready to answer. "I can sense her sometimes." His gaze flicked up to Chloe for a split second before he looked down again. "I can feel her intentions, and sometimes I know where she is, even when she is not with us."

Chloe's arms immediately fell to her side as her mouth opened wide. After two blinks, she touched a hand to her chest. "That's how it feels for me. I sense her in the same exact way."

Quintus gulped, still stroking Shadow's nose. "I wondered if…" His free hand stretched out, reaching for the harp string reins dangling from the dragon's neck. After running a thumb over them, he finally continued.

"I know the harp string is yours, but the moment it became a token…" He glanced at the ends of her hair, probably remembering when he had used the harp string to tie off a braid in her hair. When it became a token. He swallowed hard. "That moment belongs to both of us. So, I wondered if the token belongs to both of us too."

Taking a slow and very careful step forward, Chloe tilted her head to catch his eye. Once she did, she still had to bite her lip before she could ask the question in her mind. "You do not think it is because of *our* bond?"

Her fingers lifted as she spoke, gently brushing across the star tattoos under her right eye.

He shook his head, but looked away as he did. "I do not think so." His face turned even farther away from her as he gripped the harp string with two hands. "My connection to her continued to grow even when our bond was severed."

That knowledge sent a spark of warmth inside Chloe's belly. Their magical bond had been nearly entirely severed, their tattoos disappearing almost completely. And yet, they still shared a connection through the remarkable golden and sapphire creature between them.

Lifting her hand to stroke Shadow's nose, Chloe smiled. "Well then, I think you're right. I think she is *our* dragon, after all."

His gaze jumped up long enough to be entranced by her expression.

Maybe it was wrong to take advantage of him being entranced like this, but it might be her only chance to do what needed to be done. She held his gaze for a few moments, then spoke in a tone as gentle as possible. "I know our bond is still weak, which means our magic is weak too, but you need to let me try and heal your injury."

He flinched, turning away slightly. "You need to heal your own injuries first."

She would have argued. She would have stood her ground, except the moment shattered when Mishti stepped toward them.

The young woman picked at the sleeve of her midnight blue tunic while she stared intensely at the lake behind the hill. A harried expression covered her face. "That's it."

She darted to the side, moving to the very edge of the hill until she could get the best view of the lake while still remaining hidden. "Where's Ludo?"

Chloe glanced back long enough to see Ludo was already coming. His fae hearing had probably picked up Mishti's question, and he now responded to it.

Only then did Chloe turn toward the lake. At once, she wished she hadn't. Her gut roiled inside her at the sight of an enormous dragon with chipped and bent scales. It had a thick scar over one eye, which probably affected its vision. Stormy blue scales covered its body, which seemed to crackle with electricity each time it moved.

The lone dragon huffed menacingly with each breath. It soon landed next to the partially frozen lake. But when it landed, it did not simply stop beating its clawed and scarred wings. It certainly didn't bring the wings in toward its body.

On the way down, one of its wings accidentally hit a nearby tree. Once its legs hit the ground, the dragon shrieked and whipped its stormy blue head toward the tree. A crackling sound erupted from its throat followed by a blast of blue-and-white fire.

Its silver eyes flashed with rage as it blew flames from its mouth. Chloe hadn't even known it was possible, but the dragon's fire soon melted through the thick layer of magical ice encasing the tree.

Once the ice melted, the dragon only growled harder and released even more flames from its throat. Little by little, the tree changed from wet to dry to nothing but a blackened hull. After burning it to a crisp, the dragon hissed and used one huge leg to smack the blackened bits of the remaining tree into the nearby lake. The charred bark slapped against glittering icicles, breaking several in half.

While the hairs on Chloe's neck bristled and raised, Mishti had an entirely different reaction.

Her eyes lit up. She even grinned a little. "That's the one."

Ludo had reached them now and his jaw hung slack upon hearing her. He shook his head, disbelief still bright in his eyes. "Are you crazy? You want *that* dragon? Even Shadow is scared of that thing."

Unlike Chloe—and apparently, Quintus—Ludo could not sense Shadow's emotions. So he guessed that she feared the frightening creature. But while Shadow was not actually scared, she did pull her wings in and drop her head a little lower, more careful now to keep her body hidden behind the low hill.

After a quick look between the creatures, Chloe realized the scarred and angry dragon with electrifying stormy blue scales was even larger than Shadow. Since Shadow was the largest dragon they'd encountered up to now, that knowledge came as a surprise.

Ludo huffed and shook his head at Mishti. "I think we better find you a different dragon. Shadow will know where to look."

"No." Mishti never took her eyes off the dragon at the lake.

The rest of them glanced toward it in time to see the enormous silver-horned creature smack through the ice chunks on the lake, smashing them all to bits. Overhead, a cloud slowly drifted until it hovered directly above the dragon.

As soon as the beast noticed the cloud, it growled then blew streams of fire at it until the cloud had evaporated into nothing.

Mishti set her jaw, more determined than ever. "Conjure me the meat, Ludo." She leaned forward. "That dragon is mine."

Chloe knew she couldn't change her friend's mind now, but that didn't mean she liked it. Mishti could attempt to train this stormy blue dragon, but if things went even a little bit wrong, Mishti would surely pay for the mistake with her life.

Dread crept inside Chloe as Mishti grabbed a chunk of raw meat from Ludo's hands. Whether Chloe liked or not, this was about to happen.

24

WHEN CHLOE TOLD SHADOW TO swoop in and scare away the dragon with silver eyes and stormy blue scales, Shadow refused. The first inkling of fear appeared in Shadow's mind, which Chloe could feel through their bond. Perhaps she could coax her dragon into scaring the other away, but maybe it was better not to.

The stormy blue dragon clearly had a temper. Did Chloe dare send her cherished dragon into a situation filled with needless danger?

Mishti stood nearby, clasping a hunk of raw meat with both hands. Her gaze jumped expectantly between Chloe and Shadow.

After a short sigh, Chloe turned to her friend and shook her head.

"I *told* you Shadow was afraid of that beast." Ludo had lowered his voice to a whisper. He even ducked his head slightly even though he stood far behind the hill and out of view. "We need to find you a different dragon."

But Mishti just pulled the bait closer to her stomach and peeked out from behind the hill. "Never mind. I can bring the bait in myself."

Before anyone could stop her, Mishti had crept out onto the snowy landscape leading to the dragon with the scar across its eye. She moved slowly and deathly quietly.

With the dragon busy trying to spear a fish with its claws, it didn't notice her moving across the landscape. Soon, she plopped the meat onto a rock, wiped her hands clean, and then burrowed herself under a mound of snow.

She was still getting into position when the dragon turned toward the meat. Its nostrils flared as it sniffed loudly. For a moment its silver eyes flicked toward the snow mound hiding Mishti. But it happened so quickly, it could have been a coincidence.

While huffing, the dragon then stomped over the snow, leaving behind prints as deep as boulders. It didn't sniff or examine the meat once it got to it. Instead, it growled and snapped the entire hunk into its mouth in one bite.

Mishti didn't jump out of the snow. She stood slowly, letting the powdery snow drift off her. The dragon hissed the moment she started moving, already opening its jaw to clamp down again. Despite that, she moved methodically as she tossed reins made from a dark blue ribbon over the creature's neck.

The same method had worked so often before, yet it still seemed impossible for it to work on this dragon. Chloe held her breath as the blue-ribbon reins fluttered down toward the dragon's neck. Only one more moment and the reins would touch its stormy blue scales.

For one split second, it looked like the reins landed. One split second where Chloe knew relief.

But it didn't last. It soon became clear the reins had never landed.

Releasing a blood-curdling screech from its throat, the dragon used one leg to slam against Mishti's body. Electricity seemed to crackle off its scales while it moved, sending a jolt through Mishti once it hit her.

Mishti's body flew through the mound of snow around her like it was nothing more than air. And when she reached air, she soared even faster. In the next moment, her body slammed against a large, frosty boulder.

Breath escaped from her mouth in a hard puff. Judging by how she coughed and sputtered, it was clear the air had been knocked from her lungs. Her body lay helplessly at the foot of the boulder while crumbles of frost drifted onto her face.

She'd been thrown too fast. Too hard. If her spine had hit the boulder just right…

Chloe couldn't bear the thought and had to squeeze her eyes shut, just for a moment. When she opened her eyes again, she wished she hadn't.

Mishti lay completely still on the snow, still coughing. Still not moving. The only part of her that did move were her eyelids when she blinked and her mouth when she coughed.

The bruises from hitting the boulder would be bad enough, but what if something even worse had happened when Mishti hit it?

She needed help.

Taking a short breath, Chloe placed a hand on Shadow's neck and pushed a thought toward her.

Help her. Fly in, grab her, and bring her back here.

But the inkling of fear inside Shadow had grown to a whirlwind rushing through her entire body. Shadow had always been there for Chloe in her most frightened moments. The dragon had always comforted her, protected her. But though she seemed capable of facing anything, it appeared even Shadow felt fear too.

Chloe leaned in closer, wrapping her arm around her dragon's neck. Now she pushed a new thought toward the creature.

You can stay. You are safe.

She did her best to comfort her dragon, but it wasn't easy when her friend still lay helpless on the snow with absolutely no one able to come to her aid. Perhaps Ludo could have opened a door to her if he hadn't been even more afraid than Shadow. And Quintus's magic was still too unpredictable to assume he could open a door. It left Mishti completely alone.

The dragon with a scar over its eye spent those moments snarling and spitting and growling. It stomped its feet on the ground, flattening the snow and brushing it away. Crackles of electricity skittered off its scales, sending pulses into the air around.

But when Mishti didn't move, the beast grew more agitated.

And now it stomped toward her. Each step brought it closer. And closer.

Chloe had to hold her breath. She had to release her arm from Shadow's neck too, because she couldn't possibly offer any more comfort. She needed comfort herself.

When she stepped up against Quintus, he obliged by wrapping his arms around her tight. But fear coursed through him too, which she could feel through his arms and in the short, stunted breaths that left his mouth.

At last, Mishti stood from the ground. It must have cost her greatly because she barely seemed able to breathe. Her hands pressed against her knees as she leaned over, still unable to stand up straight.

The stormy blue dragon growled. Mishti responded by drawing her sword with one hand and drawing a dagger from a leather bracer with the other.

At the sight of the weapons, the dragon growled. It charged forward. The beast moved so fast, it looked like a blur against the landscape.

But half a moment before the dragon reached her, Mishti did possibly the most insane thing she had ever done in her life.

She dropped her weapons.

It wasn't a mistake either. The weapons hadn't fallen from her grip from fear shaking her limbs too much. No. Mishti held both the sword and the dagger tight and looked directly in the dragon's silver eyes. And when the dragon stared back at her, she deliberately dropped the weapons into the snow at her feet.

The dragon had its mouth open, ready to tear into flesh with its teeth. It even tilted its head slightly, probably aiming for Mishti's side. It had moved so close, its heavy breaths fluttered the loose strands of hair in her braid.

But then it stopped. Its body didn't move, but even from her position behind the hill, Chloe could see how its gaze dropped to the weapons on the ground. It let out a sound that could only be described as an angry wail.

At that, Mishti raised both her hands with the palms facing the dragon, showing more clearly that she held no weapons.

If she expected that motion to calm the dragon, it did not. The electricity moving across its scales flashed brighter and flickered more quickly. It flashed its sharp teeth and smacked its clawed tail against the ground. The tail hit so hard, it knocked all the ice off a nearby bush. The dragon howled its loudest ever and pinned its gaze on Mishti.

Opening its mouth wide, a crackling sound began at the back of its throat. That meant fire would come next. The same fire that had melted a magical casing of ice and burned an entire tree to a crisp.

Chloe gasped and pushed herself closer to Quintus's chest. He gulped and pressed his hands tighter around her. Ludo stood nearby with his open mouth covered by one hand. All color had drained from his face.

But Mishti didn't move. She didn't try to run away, although maybe her back was too injured for her to dart away anyway. Why had she done it? Why *that* dragon when she could have had any other?

In the next moment, Mishti did something even more reckless than any of her previous actions.

She lowered her gaze.

Now she wouldn't even be able to see the dragon's next attack. How could she possibly get away when she didn't even look ahead?

With her head pointed downward, she then lifted one hand out. Gently. It was strange to see a young woman who could seem deadly with nothing more than her own fists reach out in such a way. Her arm bent slightly at the elbow. Her fingers spread delicately. Even her wrist appeared relaxed and non-threatening.

The crackling at the back of the dragon's throat cut off suddenly. It stared at her hand then it stared at her eyes, which still gazed at the ground. With a sharp hiss, it used its head to shove Mishti off her feet and into the snow.

Mishti hit hard and released a grunt. But after a quick breath, she got to her feet, brushed the snow off her clothes, and got back into the same exact position as before.

Head down. Hand out. Unafraid.

The dragon snarled, but it didn't have as much bite as its previous actions. It growled at Mishti, but she didn't move. It took another few moments, but slowly, ever so slowly, the dragon's rage seemed to melt away.

Its growling turned to whining, which then turned to silence. Even its scarred wings seemed to relax against its back. After a heavy breath that flared its nostrils, the beast did the unimaginable.

It lowered its own head and poked it forward until the end of its nose sat directly under Mishti's reached out hand.

With her free hand, she slowly, methodically, tossed her ribbon reins onto the dragon's neck. The moment the ribbon touched the dragon, it shot its head upward and released another frightening shout.

Mishti didn't move. Her hand held tight to the reins, and her head stayed lowered.

In another breath, the creature relaxed again. It breathed out hard enough to blow Mishti's long braid up and over her shoulder until it hung behind her back.

Then, the stormy blue dragon with the scar on its eye dropped its gaze and lowered its head until it sat directly in front of Mishti's feet.

Chloe held her breath and had her jaw clenched tight as she watched the scene unfold. It took a moment of seeing the dragon's head at Mishti's feet before the reality of it kicked it.

She'd done it.

Mishti had tamed the dragon.

A relieved chuckle released from Chloe's throat. Quintus and Ludo made similar sounds. A cheer from behind came next. Then another.

Soon, every Golden Shield behind the hill screamed and shouted and proclaimed joy at the impossible task Mishti had just accomplished.

When Mishti finally used the reins to lift the dragon's head, collected her dropped weapons, and then started walking the creature over to the rest of them, a look of immense satisfaction filled her eyes.

She had done what no one else could have. Mishti had seen potential inside a monster.

An army of dragons would give them an edge over the Zeakriesh like nothing else had done before. But they didn't just have an army. They had Mishti, and Mishti had the deadliest, most menacing dragon Faerie had probably ever known.

What chance did the Zeakriesh have against them now?

Once Mishti and her dragon joined the others, Sofia turned to Chloe wearing a wide grin. "What do we do now?"

Chloe responded with the words they'd probably all been waiting to hear. Her lips curled upward as she reached for Shadow's reins.

"Now, we ride."

No one had to be told twice. Each Shield gripped their reins and clambered onto their dragons' backs. Ludo joined Mishti on the back of the dragon he had been so certain she couldn't tame.

And of course, Quintus climbed onto Shadow's back along with Chloe.

Chloe's golden dragon led the way as their horde flew into the air. Her sapphire wings glinted in the light as she flapped higher and higher until she had soared above the iridescent clouds of Fairfrost.

With her at the head, the other dragons formed a V behind her. At the very back, in the middle of the open part of the V, Mishti and her stormy blue dragon flew, bringing up the rear.

Noting that all the dragons had moved into formation without any trouble, Chloe could finally focus on the way ahead. And even more important, she could focus on the ride.

Wind whipped through her hair, blowing it back from her face. The smell of cranberries and wet branches drifted around them. The landscape below went by in a blur as Shadow flew faster and faster through the air. Being atop her dragon brought a feeling Chloe could barely describe.

It felt incredible. She felt on top of everything and bound by nothing. Each time she flew she was reminded that this was one of the best feelings she had ever experienced.

But just as she had that thought, Quintus came in close, straddling his legs on either side of hers and pressing his chest against her back. He reached his arms around her and brought his face close until she could feel his breath on her neck.

In one motion, he had effectively stolen the breath from her lungs. He had a way of reminding her that all the best moments could instantly be improved by his presence. By his touch.

She leaned back into him, hoping his lips might find her skin next. She didn't even particularly care which part of her skin they found. No matter where he kissed, it would always make her shiver in the most glorious way possible.

Instead of his lips, his voice touched her instead. His breath tickled her ear as he held her tight. "I am ready now. I am ready to go see my mother."

25

Finding dyani's home in the forest of Bitter Thorn was easier than Chloe expected. She thought they might have to send the fae a message and wait for her to tell them where she lived. In the end, Ludo used his greatest magic in finding things to easily locate her house.

His magic didn't seem to work on anything in Crystalfall, maybe because of all the memory enchantments or maybe because the court had been destroyed since the first time he lived there.

But on anything outside the court, his magic still worked as effectively as ever. Quintus simply had to pull the crown from his pocket and point out the large emerald that had once been at the top of his mother's gold and emerald ring. Ludo then let magic pour from his fingertips, surrounding the emerald for only a few moments before the magic led them straight to her home.

Chloe noted that Quintus handled the crown carefully with Ludo around, failing to let the Fairfrost fae ever touch the piece. It probably didn't matter anyway. If they were going to see Dyani, she would likely know instantly if Ludo was the king of Crystalfall they sought.

Soon, Chloe, Quintus, Ludo, and Mishti all stood outside the bent and intricately formed trees that formed Dyani's house.

Ludo knocked on the door, and when he did, sparkling blue and silver magic left his hand, drifting straight through the door and into the house.

Only a moment later, a woman fae threw the door open with a spear pointed straight at them. "Stay away. All of you."

Her eyes glared, showing no warmth at all. Dark hair hung freely from her head in gentle curls that ended just past her shoulders. She wore a simple brown dress with beading and fringe at the hem. Her light brown skin had the same copper undertone as Quintus's did, but her eyes were a brilliant turquoise and gold. Just as all the fae, she appeared no older than twenty-one, despite having lived in Crystalfall before it was destroyed.

She jabbed the spear toward them, forcing Ludo to take a step back so he didn't get stabbed. Her jaw clenched tight as she spoke through her teeth. "I want no—"

However she intended to finish that sentence, they'd never know. In a flash, she dropped the spear to her feet, forgetting it completely as she took a step forward. Her mouth opened wide as she reached a hand out.

A moment later, she stood directly in front of Quintus and placed a hand on his cheek.

Words continued to fail her as she blinked at him. Blinked and stared.

When she finally managed to speak, only one word came out in a wispy breath. "Quintus."

He gulped. He kept his body still except for his hands twitching at his sides. He stared into his mother's eyes and asked, "You remember me?"

She laughed then. It was a strangely delicate laugh after she'd greeted them with a spear and threats. "How could any mother forget her own child?"

A wince traveled through her shoulders then, though the cause of it was unclear. She glanced around the area, staring at each of the people before her carefully. Her gaze caught on Ludo a little longer than the rest. Finally, she turned back toward her home. "Do you wish to come in?"

Quintus nodded, his mother's hand still against his cheek.

She beckoned them all inside and soon had them sitting in a circle on chairs woven from brown branches and lush, green leaves. The house smelled like earth and berries with a hint of crisp rain. Even inside, the sounds of fluttering leaves and trickling streams could still be heard.

Her gaze caught on the moment when Quintus put his hand at the small of Chloe's back, helping her into her chair. But though Dyani had clearly seen it, clearly understood at least some of the significance of it, she said nothing about it.

Now that they were seated though, she kept glancing at Ludo and then quickly looking away.

Chloe would have spent more time thinking on the curiousness of it, but Mishti interrupted by getting straight to the point.

"Do you know who the king of Crystalfall is?" Mishti asked, her hands clasped firmly on her lap.

Dyani snapped her head back slightly. "Of course I know who he is. He... is..." When she went to answer the question, her words slowed until she trailed off completely. Her eyes glazed over as she stared at the corner of her home where a bush filled with red berries grew next to the wall.

After a hard blink, she shook her head. "You mean his name?"

"Yes, anything," Chloe answered. She sat forward on her chair and gripped the strap of her leather bag that now sat on the floor. "What does he look like? What court was he originally from? His name would be best of all, then we could send him a message."

The glazed look in Dyani's eyes lifted. "No." She glanced upward at the glowing green lights floating above her. "You cannot send a message to him. The sprites will not deliver it." Her voice lowered. "I have tried."

That information sent Chloe's eyebrows up high. The sprites would not deliver it? She had never known the sprites to refuse delivery for any reason. They were even compelled to deliver messages to Fairfrost back when Alessandra was queen, even though the sprites knew they would immediately be captured and given no sustenance while there.

But maybe the sprites didn't refuse to deliver the message. Maybe they were unable to. Perhaps the tiny creatures had their memories altered too, enough that they could not remember the king of Crystalfall, even with his name.

With her gut sinking, Chloe glanced back at the fae before her. "You cannot remember his name, can you?"

The glassy look returned as Dyani narrowed one eye. After a moment, she waved a hand through the air. "It is hidden from me."

When Chloe turned toward Quintus, he wore a deep frown.

Mishti narrowed her eyes, turning her expression more frightening than she probably intended. "What does he look like? Do you remember that?"

Dyani stood, her hair shining under the light of the sprites. She looked from one end of her home to the other. "When he came to me in my other home, he…" Her head tilted to the side. "He did not look like himself."

Quintus perked up at the sound of that. "He wore a glamour?"

She didn't quite nod as she sat back down again. Her eyes stared off, deep in thought. "Yes." The word came out slowly. "But I still knew it was him. He wanted my ring." Suddenly, she turned her gaze to Quintus. "You had it."

He nodded, though his eyes did not narrow nor did his head tilt. He clearly did not have to reach for this memory but plucked it easily from the front of his mind. "You gave me the ring. I was building a tower with rocks while you read a book. When someone knocked on the door, you went rigid. I did not know why. But I remember I always wanted to play with your golden and emerald ring, and you always told me *no*."

Light danced in Dyani's eyes the longer her son spoke. She nodded and picked up as soon as he stopped. "Yes, I remember. I knew he would want the ring, and even worse, I knew he would want you dead."

Quintus sat a little farther back into his chair and spoke low. "You shoved me into a corner, handed me the ring, and told me to keep quiet."

Her hand splayed out over her left knee, which she then gripped tightly. "I glamoured the chair nearest to you as well. I tried to make it look like the chair was part of the wall so he would not know you sat behind it."

"You did?" Quintus's eyebrows rose, but even more intriguing was how his entire expression opened with the innocence of a child.

Dyani stared down at her lap while her hand gripped her knee even tighter. "It was too much to expect you to keep quiet and to keep still. You were just a child. But if I glamoured you to be invisible, you would have asked too many questions, and he might have barged in right in the middle of it. I know I did not do enough to protect you, but I did try."

This left Quintus open-mouthed. He blinked. Chloe hadn't realized it when Quintus told her this story the first time, but it appeared he had never known his mother went to any effort at all to protect him. He didn't seem sure what to make of it finding out she had.

Since Dyani still had her gaze trained on her lap, she saw none of this in her son's eyes. She let out a weighted sigh and continued. "He did not wait for me to answer the door. He forced his way in and demanded I give his ring back. I told him it was somewhere he would never get to. He grabbed a clay bowl from my table and threw it against a wall, breaking it to bits. He demanded more forcefully that I tell him exactly where the ring was and how to retrieve it. I told him I would rather die."

Her breath hitched as she reached for her heart. "That was my mistake."

Quintus sat up straighter, his eyes blinking hard.

It may have been Chloe's imagination, but the wisp of a memory fluttered at the back of her mind. A memory wasn't an accurate word for it though. As soon as she felt it, it only took another moment to realize it was not hers but Quintus's. Her heart beat harder as the tattoos on her face began to tingle. Was the bond between them repairing more? And with it, was she becoming more in tune with the thoughts and memories in her beloved's mind?

Dyani shook her head, moving it faster with each word she spoke. "He lifted his axe, saying he would happily kill me if that was what I wished." Her face turned to a scowl. "If I had been less attentive, less kind, or maybe more frightening, perhaps he would have killed me, and it would have all been fine."

Fine? How was being less attentive or less kind to the king who drew an axe against her supposed to make a difference? Maybe being more frightening would have helped, but this story hadn't made her sound even remotely kind to the king. Not that he deserved it. But how much less kind could she have been?

All at once, a knot twisted in Chloe's heart. She sensed again that this came from Quintus, and suddenly, she understood. Dyani wasn't talking about how she treated the king. She was talking about how she treated Quintus.

If she'd been less attentive to her son, less kind to him… she thought it might have changed things? Was that it?

A protective urge rushed through Chloe's entire being.

At her side, Quintus clenched his jaw. "I tried to stop him."

Mishti and Ludo gaped at this declaration.

Dyani nodded. "The king brought his axe down, aiming for my heart. But little Quintus, with his cheeks still squishy and his legs so short, came tearing out from behind the chair and screamed. It distracted the king long enough to miss his mark."

Ludo raised an eyebrow, speaking under his breath. "You tried to attack a king? And while you were still a child?"

It didn't surprise Chloe at all. She was starting to feel what Quintus felt, but it was more than that. She understood him like others never seemed to. He'd always been heroic. This only proved he'd been that way since he was born.

Dyani dropped her head into her hands. "But when Quintus ran forward and pounded his fists against the king's legs, the king immediately found the ring on my son's finger. He glared, catching Quintus's hand tight in his wrist. He asked in a scathing voice why I would give his most prized possession to a child. But once the words left his lips, he froze." Dyani stopped for a moment and the air around them froze too. It felt heavier when she spoke again. "He brought Quintus closer, stared at him hard. When he looked at me, he had fire in his eyes. Then he asked why I had a child in my home. Was it mine?"

"I kicked him in the shin." Quintus huffed like he'd do it again if given the chance.

Dyani's youthful face that looked hardly old enough to carry an infant, let alone a grown fae son, suddenly turned motherly. She grinned slightly at the memory of her child kicking her attacker.

But then her face turned gloomy. "It was not enough. When the axe came down again, the king tried to kill my son. *His* son. Quintus stepped away just in time, but the king turned his axe on me again. His wrath left me too injured to walk. I healed eventually, of course, but not soon enough for it to matter. When the king chased my Quintus out the door, I knew I would never see either of them again."

She flinched. "I suppose I only *hoped* I would never see the king again, but I was certain my child would not survive the encounter."

Quintus had gone still in his chair. Turmoil swirled inside Chloe, which could not be anywhere as strong as what her beloved felt. She reached out to him and took his hand.

He intertwined their fingers, holding on tight.

Dyani stared at their clasped hands and then looked up at her son. "How *did* you survive?"

Quintus shrugged, holding onto Chloe a little tighter. "Faerie itself gave me aid when I needed it. And it gave me magic before I was grown."

"Before you were grown?" Ludo said through a sputter. When Mishi turned to him in surprise, he shrugged. "I have never heard of that before."

It was probably cathartic for both Quintus and his mother to relive this horrifying moment in their lives. Chloe was glad they could do it together, but so far, they hadn't learned anything new.

Turning the conversation back where they needed it, Chloe asked, "You said you knew the king, even while he wore a glamour. Could you *sense* it was him, even though he looked different?"

Dyani's head tilted to the side. Her eyes narrowed but her mouth never opened.

Chloe swallowed hard, almost afraid for the next question. "He is not in this room now, for instance, right? If he were, do you think you'd be able to tell?"

It happened quickly, but Dyani's gaze flicked over to Ludo. She stared straight into his blue-and-red eyes while a flinch or scrunch or *something* passed over her expression.

Too quickly, she stared at her lap, making the whole thing feel like something Chloe had imagined.

The Bitter Thorn fae used one thumb to stroke the fabric laying across her knee. "I am tired now. Alone. I thought my son was dead." Her voice broke over the words. She closed her eyes for an extra-long moment. "There is little I know for certain anymore."

Chloe sat forward in her chair, her hand still holding her beloved's. "But you recognized Quintus. You knew him immediately."

Dyani's eyebrow rose. "*He* is not wearing a glamour."

Quintus leaned forward too, looking his mother directly in the eye. "We must find the king. We need to know enough about him to find him."

Screwing up her mouth, Dyani scowled. "He is vermin."

"We know." Quintus scowled too. "We must find him anyway."

Quiet stretched through the air as everyone waited for Dyani to answer. Finally, she stood and turned away from them. "I will not help you."

"Dyani." Chloe said the name softly, which came out with a little more emotion than she intended, although that probably only helped. "Do it for Quintus. Tell us anything you remember, anything that could help us find him."

The turquoise in her eyes nearly disappeared as Dyani narrowed her eyes. "How would that help Quintus?"

Mishti answered. "Crystalfall will be destroyed unless we find the king."

That did nothing to convince the fae before them. But then she glanced down at her son. His eyes pled with her, begged. She swallowed, and her face turned to a resolute expression. But that expression melted away after another moment of looking at her child.

With a great sigh, she flopped back down into her chair. "He liked to build things." She gestured toward Quintus. "Just like you. He had room in the castle for it. He collected things. He could fix nearly anything he touched."

Her gaze lowered and focused on a knot in a branch forming part of her wall. After another beat, she let out a sigh and continued. "If he is in Crystalfall, he is mostly likely to be in the castle. But you may not be able to find him. Only he knows all the secret passages and rooms. Some of his hidden spots were found by others, but I know not all of them were."

They had won a victory. Maybe it was a small one. They hadn't learned much, but Chloe knew deep in her heart it wasn't just about the information they'd gained. A relationship had been born again, one that Quintus had long since assumed was gone forever.

He squeezed Chloe's hand a little tighter and sat forward in his chair. "You could come with us." His voice came out soft. Timid. "You could live in Crystalfall again."

"No." Dyani stood from her chair so fast it clattered the ground.

At the same time, Quintus sat back, his face hurt.

She touched a hand to the wall made of trees at her side. "There is magic in a home." Her gaze then turned sharply to her son's. "Even though he failed to kill you, he still took your home away."

Quintus edged his hand out of Chloe's grip just to slide it miserably down the side of his face. "Twice."

Dyani cocked her head to the side, first turning to Chloe and then back to her son.

Quintus pinched the bridge of his nose before continuing. "After he tried to kill me, and I somehow got away, Faerie helped me build a home here in Bitter Thorn." His face twisted as he glanced to the side. He spat the next words out. "He destroyed that home too."

After a hard swallow, Dyani shook her head. "Then he has power over you that you may never be able to defeat."

Quintus glanced down. His voice came out barely above a whisper. "We might have a better chance if you helped."

"No." She retreated deeper into her home, reaching for the door handle of a room that would lead away from them. She even started pulling the leather strap handle to begin opening the door before she spoke again. "I will not. I have no desire to do any such thing."

With a start, Chloe stood and ushered everyone out of the house. She could see their visit was over and didn't want anyone making things worse. She clearly wasn't fast enough, though, because Quintus's face looked like he'd rather be swallowed up by the ground than go back to Crystalfall and face its problems again.

But even if he wasn't ready for it yet, she could see clearly what they had to do next. They needed to take the castle back from the Zeakriesh.

Perhaps now that they had dragons, the task would be possible. Or maybe the Zeakriesh's magical shards would end that quest before it began.

26

Chloe insisted everyone rest before attempting to steal the castle back from the Zeakriesh. Night began to fall on their way back to Crystalfall from Dyani's home, and it didn't seem right to start an attack right then.

Plus, going back to camp for the night would allow everyone to strategize, and even more important, eat. She enjoyed a huge plate of white beans, sausages, and pork seasoned with garlic, thyme, and bay leaves. With food in her stomach, her mind came to life with all sorts of ideas for attempting to take the castle back.

Her friends and the other Golden Shields offered ideas, and soon, they had a plan that had at least a small chance of succeeding. The odds weren't the best, but it was certainly better than no chance at all, which was what they had before they'd tamed a horde of dragons.

Once dawn began glittering over the jeweled surface of the Crystalfall landscape, they were ready to enact their plan. When their dragons flew toward the castle, the wind still blew in

Chloe's hair like it had after they'd trained all the other dragons. But the feeling of being on top of the world had a little more weight to it now that they needed to defeat some very powerful beings. When the sense of dread in her belly became too much, she glanced back at Quintus, who held her from behind.

"We need to get you another home," she said to him. "It's been too long since you had one. Once we take Crystalfall Castle back, maybe that could be your home."

Even with her neck craned, she could still see how he rolled his eyes. "You think that will go over well once we restore the crown to my father and he reclaims the castle? Can you imagine him being overjoyed about me living under the same roof as him considering how he has taken two homes from me already?"

Though he spoke lightly, his words had a weight to them that hadn't been there before. Was he still upset about their meeting with his mother?

Chloe squirmed in her seat. "Well, once we take back the castle, at least you'll have a proper home until we find the king. That has to be better than nothing."

His eyebrow raise indicated his skepticism about that, and the tension in his arms indicated he ached more than he wanted to let on.

Facing forward, she spoke more deliberately. "After the king reclaims his castle, we won't need it anyway. We'll just make you a new home."

Her body leaned, allowing her back to press against his chest. Back in Dyani's home, she had started to feel Quintus's thoughts and a whisper of his emotions. The bond between them was clearly growing. Maybe if she concentrated, she could get a clearer picture of his thoughts. Could he feel their bond growing too?

She gripped a little more tightly to Shadow's reins. "Your magic will be able to do anything by then."

The only answer he gave was to brush his fingers through her hair. But the castle was still too far in the distance. If he wouldn't speak, pretty soon, they'd both be distracted by what else he could do while sitting so close to her.

Taking a quick breath, she forced out her next sentence as fast as she could. "I noticed you would not let Ludo touch the crown when you showed him the part that used be your mother's ring."

He flinched against her back. Was it because she mentioned Ludo or because she mentioned his mother? When Quintus spoke, his voice came out gruff. "Ludo cannot be the king anyway. Why would he have helped us so often? If he is the king, he would have taken the crown while we were stuck in that vault."

She shrugged, feeling acutely how her shoulder slid across the new coat Quintus had fashioned for himself the night before. "Maybe Ludo does not remember. We know the king purposefully lost memories in pursuit of research. Maybe he lost so many memories he has no idea who he is."

Quintus scoffed. "When my father tried to kill me, I was a child. I can understand if he lost memories after that, but what about when he destroyed my second home in Bitter Thorn? That happened after your sister became Queen and High King Brannick finally claimed his rightful title." His voice went lower. "That happened after you left with Vesper and vowed you'd never return to Faerie again. If the king does not remember who he is, and if the king is Ludo, then why did he attack me so recently?"

It was a valid question and one she'd been pondering since they'd both stared at that list of things they knew about the Crystalfall king. Quintus clearly didn't expect it, but she had an answer ready.

"Maybe something happened that triggered his memory and reminded him of the past. That could be when he destroyed your home in Bitter Thorn. And then maybe he forgot again after sleeping or something." She swallowed and said the next part carefully. "But if Ludo *is* the king, I think maybe…"

She bit her bottom lip, rolling it between her teeth a few times before continuing. "Maybe all this time without those memories has changed him into someone different. Maybe if he learned he is the king he would know you are also his friend, and he would no longer seek to destroy you."

A profound silence greeted her suggestion. After several flaps of Shadow's wings, Quintus finally answered.

"The king is *not* Ludo. That is impossible. He does not need to touch the crown for us to know it."

Chloe might have tried to argue more, except they had gotten too close to the castle. Their discussion would have to continue later. She carefully got to her feet on Shadow's back. She even opened her mouth to shout the words they'd decided on beforehand.

But once she was standing tall on Shadow's back, she caught a glimpse of a totally unexpected sight. King Severin's dragon sat right in the middle of the destroyed celestine meadow where the Golden Shields had once made camp.

The magnificent pastel hues of the creature shone brightly in the sun. But why? Why was the dragon there at all? She had meant to bring it up after seeing the dragon the first time, but she'd gotten distracted by other things and had forgotten all about it. But here was the dragon again. Why?

Quintus stood, placing his hand on Chloe's back as they peered over the meadow. He turned toward her. "Do you think King Severin is exploring Crystalfall?"

She tried to ignore the sense of trepidation inside her as she shrugged. "I just hope the Zeakriesh haven't captured him and his dragon."

Quintus's face twisted with a frightened frown.

Waving off the words, she stood tall again. "Either way, we need to get inside that castle and take it back."

Her arm rose high above her head as she shouted as loudly as she could. A *V* formation of dragons and riders flew behind her. Mishti and her stormy blue dragon flew at the very back. "Okay, everyone. Like we planned."

Taking a deep breath Chloe turned and thrust her arm downward toward the castle. As soon as she did, Shadow changed from flying forward to pivoting into a deep dive. Behind her, every other dragon did the same.

Chloe's heart squeezed at the sight of the castle. It had a huge crack all the way through it, so deep that a small canyon separated the two halves of the castle. The ground around it had lost all its sparkle. The black soil had nearly all color leeched out of it, turning it a sickly white that blended in with the white pebbles inside it.

After talking about the need for Quintus to have a new home, seeing the castle in this state of disrepair was like a punch to the gut.

She had no time to be sad, though, because Shadow had just scrunched up her wings and landed in a hallway inside Crystalfall Castle.

Chloe and Quintus jumped off the creature, sprinting down the hallway ahead. She couldn't move too quickly with her wooden foot, but she managed a reasonable pace.

The other dragons all landed at different spots on different floors and in different hallways of the castle, just like they had planned.

Shadow clambered after Chloe and Quintus, ready to give aid wherever needed. The other dragons had a much easier time fitting inside the castle hallways. But for Shadow, whose body itself was nearly as large as house, she struggled just to force herself through the passages.

At least it was better than Mishti's dragon that had to fly outside the castle, since it couldn't fit anywhere inside.

Suddenly, a Zeakriesh jumped out from behind a golden pillar and raised a sword aimed at Chloe. Before she could even gasp, Shadow opened her jaw and chomped down the entire mortal in only a few bites.

Chloe's stomach surged with the desire to empty its contents, but she managed to pat her dragon on the head instead. "Good girl, Shadow. Now, let's go find some more nasty Zeakriesh for you to eat."

Quintus waved them toward a nearby room. He and Shadow entered it. Judging by the disturbing sounds that soon erupted through the doorway, the room clearly had at least a few Zeakriesh inside.

Desperate to distract herself from the carnage, Chloe glanced down the hallway. She found a perfect distraction only a moment later. They were near the king's quarters, which had been intentional. That was the area of the castle she and Quintus had chosen to clear.

But now that she stood in the hallway, she remembered how a set of stairs, not very far away, led straight outside the castle walls. Her memory of the stairs was hazy given that her head had been greatly injured at the time, but it was something she tucked away. That set of stairs might come in handy later.

A great shout sputtered from the door where Shadow and Quintus were. When Chloe looked that way, she saw two Zeakriesh lunge from the room and sprint down the opposite hall.

Quintus managed to stop one with his spear, but the other got away. With the remaining Zeakriesh dead at his feet, Quintus used his spear to point forward. "We just need to clear two more rooms and then we can meet Mishti and Ludo at the great hall."

Shadow shoved herself through the hall to follow him, Chloe coming up behind them both. The other rooms were empty, so they were able to get to the great hall even sooner than expected.

Once there, they found Mishti and Ludo rushing toward them.

Mishti used a dagger to point over her shoulder behind herself. "We found a locked room. I think the Zeakriesh may have a prisoner there."

Chloe gasped. "The king?"

Ludo grumbled. "Maybe, but I could not open the door with my magic."

They had reached each other now, slowing to a walk as they all turned to go in the direction Mishti had just pointed.

She tucked the dagger back into her leather arm bracer. "We thought maybe Quintus could craft a key." Her head tilted as she glanced at him. "But maybe you cannot without your magic."

She said it like a question. It hadn't occurred to Chloe until that moment, but she remembered now that while Mishti and Ludo had probably noticed Chloe's and Quintus's tattoos were back to normal, they had not seen Quintus's magic return.

He glanced directly into Chloe's eyes, probably knowing she was thinking back on the same moment as him. "I will try to craft a key. I think I can do it."

The walls blurred past them as they rushed to the locked door Mishti and Ludo had found. A dragon growled in the distance, followed by people screaming. They had no time to go check on the sounds.

Chloe could only hope the screams all came from Zeakriesh and not from Golden Shields.

When they got to the locked door, Quintus immediately dropped to his knees before it and peered into the keyhole. He tilted and craned his neck every which way with his gaze still pinned on the keyhole and then, he lifted his hand.

After staring at his hand for a moment, a brilliant emerald glow appeared at his fingertips. His gaze turned back to the doorknob. The magic then trailed off his fingertips and into the keyhole.

Ludo jumped forward slapping both hands against his face. "Your magic is back?"

Mishti punched him in the arm. Hard. "Not now."

He glared at her and started rubbing the spot she punched, but he also kept his mouth shut after that.

Quintus continued to peer into the keyhole, but his expression looked more frustrated than anything. He stuffed a hand into his pocket and pulled out the awkward stiff necklace he had attempted to craft back in that clearing with Chloe.

At least the gold molded and changed a little more easily when he hovered his hand over it now. The muscles in his fingers and face strained while he worked, but the gold formed something much more similar to a key shape than what he'd been attempting when he crafted the necklace.

Each time he let out a breath, it came out a little heavier than before.

After a bit, he stopped crafting and examined the key, which was mostly flat along the side that needed to fit into the lock. That part would need more refining.

While he stared, two figures appeared in the hallway with bows armed with arrows.

Chloe screamed just as a Zeakriesh released an arrow from her bow. Chloe blinked, watching as it flew directly at her.

27

THE UNFINISHED KEY CLATTERED TO the ground as Quintus yanked Chloe down into his lap. He moved her just in time to escape the deadly point of the arrowhead.

Shadow roared at the two Zeakriesh, sending them bolting in the opposite direction before they could release any more arrows.

A rush of breath filled Chloe's lungs as she became acutely aware of her position. She was settled in Quintus's lap, deep in his arms, and looking up into his eyes. Her cheeks warmed at feeling the strength of his arms around her.

Ludo coughed loudly, which served as the perfect reminder that Quintus was in the middle of crafting a key.

He helped Chloe back to her feet and snatched the key off the ground to work on it again. Her cheeks continued to prickle with warmth as she shifted her weight from one foot to the other.

The muscles around Mishti's eyes had grown so tight, she was probably trying to keep herself from rolling them. "Try not to scream again. It's a very distinctive sound that the other Zeakriesh might recognize." She leaned forward slightly. "Which could give away our position."

Chloe reached for a strand of blonde hair, turning it over her finger as she nodded.

Only a moment later, Quintus stuck his key in the lock and gave it a turn. It failed to unlock the door, but he pulled it out and kept working right away. His magic slowly molded the metal, slightly changing the pattern that sat at the edge.

When he stuck it into the lock again, another group of Zeakriesh raced toward them. Chaos filled the hallway while Chloe tried to tell who was who and where they were going. After a few moments, she could finally distinguish Mishti and Ludo chasing after at least four Zeakriesh. And in the opposite direction, Shadow shoved herself through the hallway to go after another seven Zeakriesh.

When Quintus stuck the key in the lock again, it made a clicking sound but not quite an unlocking sound. Even if he hadn't done it yet, he was clearly getting close.

He yanked it out, examining it carefully once again. He even sent more magic into the lock, presumably to determine what shape the key needed to be to unlock the door. But then a Zeakriesh wearing a bright orange ballgown with satin bows adorning the bottom edge jumped into the hallway with them. Portia herself stood before them, her hair pulled tight in its signature bun.

She laughed. "My lucky day. Two of the exact people I was hoping to torture, and you're both right here."

Quintus stuffed a hand in his pocket, probably trying to retrieve a weapon. Before his hand ever came out of the pocket though, Portia revealed a shimmery golden balance shard sitting in her palm. She chucked it forward, aiming for Chloe. But Quintus jumped in front of her, and the shard slammed directly into his chest.

A hard puff escaped his mouth as he fell onto his back with his eyes open wide.

Portia pouted. "Ahh, too bad. I like it better when it makes people turn to a pile of dust, but these shards are so inconsistent."

Even if Quintus hadn't turned to dust, his body still writhed on the ground, unable to direct any of his movements.

Portia threw a second shard. If anyone else had been in the hallway, they might have been able to duck in time to avoid the shard completely. But while Chloe was gifted with strategy, she did not have a gift for quick movements.

The shard hit like splintered glass against the edge of Chloe's shoulder, knocking her onto her back at Quintus's side. It burned. And felt like claws scraping at her skin. Her limbs shook, but… She'd been through pain before, pain worse than this. She might be able to sit up soon.

Maybe she'd gotten hit with a weaker shard than Quintus, or maybe the indirect hit had weakened its effects, but either way, she could soon tell she'd likely have to be the one who got them out of this mess.

Stepping between them with her nose wrinkled, Portia used her shoe to lift Quintus's thick coat. Chloe craned her neck to see the injury in his side, which Portia now examined too.

The threads from Chloe's stitching had frayed significantly. The celestine crystals inside him had shrunk so much, they barely peeked out. Even with the crystals so small, though, no blood dripped from the wound. The skin looked pink and tender but not inflamed. Maybe Quintus's healing abilities had finally started to heal the wound instead of just keeping it at bay.

Portia clapped her hands together in delight at the sight of the wound. "Julian told me about this."

Grinning, she used the point of her shiny black shoes to kick straight through the fraying threads of Quintus's stitching.

His body flinched hard as he curled into a ball and let out a hard breath. But he didn't breathe back in again. Second after second passed and he did nothing except pull his legs to his chest while his body shook and trembled.

Portia giggled at the sight. "Wasn't that fun? I didn't believe it possible for a fae to stay injured for so long without iron, but Julian was right."

She kicked her pointed shoe into the wound again. Harder.

Chloe's chest burned with a white-hot rage as she forced herself to start sitting up.

Blood began pouring from the wound while Quintus continued to writhe and shake. Once the blood hit the golden floor of the castle, it bubbled and turned the gold to ash like it had done so many times before. A pungent scent of decay drifted upward from the ash in a cloud of gray smoke.

Portia raised an eyebrow. "Interesting."

By now, Chloe had managed to force herself halfway up, nearly sitting up fully.

But Portia just slammed her shoe into Chloe's chest and pushed her back to the ground. Light gleamed off her tight bun as the woman tapped her chin. "And what can I do to you that would be more fun than chopping off your foot? I have to admit, that's a hard one to beat."

The words caused an ache to stretch through Chloe's throat until it squeezed tight around her heart.

It stopped her heart completely when Portia's eyebrows rose up high.

"I know," Portia said happily. "I'll take this lovely fake foot you like to wear."

Without another word, the woman yanked the wooden foot off Chloe's leg.

No pain could stop Chloe from sitting up now. She shoved herself upward and used her last remaining strength to scream. "No!"

But the women before her just smiled.

Chloe shouted again, with new purpose now. "Shadow!" Taking a deep breath, she shouted even louder. "Shadow!"

Every muscle in her body was on fire, but adrenaline must have been kicking in because the pain dulled to an ache she could ignore. Lunging forward onto her stomach, Chloe used her arms to crawl toward Portia.

The woman took a step back, startled.

That only added fuel to Chloe's rage. Her knees propelled her forward faster. Soon she'd be close enough to shove Portia's legs, hopefully hard enough to knock her off her feet.

Portia took another stumbling step backward and pulled a knife from her waistband. She threw it at Chloe and turned away without bothering to see where it landed.

Directly in the gash in Chloe's arm was where it landed. Blood dripped from the wound as she pulled the knife out. She tried to throw it at the back of Portia's legs but failed to throw it hard enough.

Once it landed near the woman, Portia stopped long enough to turn and pluck the knife off the ground. She threw it expertly toward Quintus. It landed with a thunk directly in the center of his magical wound. He let out a blood-curdling shriek that shook the castle walls.

Chloe tried to go after Portia. She crawled on her hands and knees with as much speed as possible, but the woman had two feet. Of course she easily got away.

But Shadow appeared just as Portia was disappearing around a corner.

"You have to get my foot," Chloe said pointing toward Portia's orange skirts. "You have to get it back, Shadow."

The dragon needed no more instruction as she bounded down the hallway. Tears burned down Chloe's cheeks as she turned and started crawling toward Quintus. If it were only for her, the foot wouldn't have mattered so much, but…

She shook her head, brushing the back of her hand across her face and nose. The wood from her foot had been crafted from the last piece of Quintus's home in Bitter Thorn. It was literally the last thing even remotely resembling a home he had left.

It couldn't be lost to Portia. Chloe would not rest until it was recovered.

Her eyes slammed shut as she pushed a command to her dragon's mind.

Hurry. Do whatever it takes, just get my foot back.

She had moved to Quintus's side now. Tears continued to slip from her eyelashes, but she had given up on trying to wipe them away.

Her hands reached straight for Quintus. His coat was still lifted, which made it easier for Chloe's hands to find his skin. He refused to let her heal the injury before, but she pushed the memory away. Now he was too delirious to stop her from attempting to use her healing magic, so of course she did.

It only took a few moments to tell why Quintus's key had failed to open the lock. Her magic was not what it once was. She thought through stopping the blood with thick bandages, but only pitiful strips of thin bandages appeared. She carefully thought through stitching up the wound so it wouldn't bleed, but the stitching was lopsided and the threads too thick.

With her own wound re-opened by Portia's knife, blood trailed down her arm. Damage control was the best she could do. She'd have to give up on the magic for now and do things manually. Grabbing the knife off the floor—the one Portia had thrown both at her and at Quintus—Chloe used it to cut off Quintus's coat. Once free from his body, she wrapped it tight around the wound until it stopped the bleeding. It would need far more attention than that, and soon, but that was good enough for now.

Gripping his arm with maybe a little too much force, she closed her eyes and attempted to use her magic once again. She conjured pain herbs into her free hand. They were sickly and pathetic, but hopefully they'd still work better than nothing.

She stuffed a few leaves into his mouth, hoping his jaw would remember how to chew even while he was in such pain.

Just as she got the herbs into his mouth, Shadow yipped and appeared at the end of the hallway.

Chloe held her breath as she looked at her dragon. But it only took one look to bring a sigh of relief to her lips.

The dragon sauntered forward, Chloe's boot hanging from her teeth by the laces. And her wooden foot sat inside.

She wanted to sigh in relief again. She wanted to carefully help Quintus sit up and take some time to just breathe.

But she couldn't because Misht's voice rang through the halls. "Retreat!"

It came from several hallways away. She screamed again a second time, even louder than the first. "Retreat!"

Subtlety left the equation completely as Chloe forced her hand behind Quintus's back and forced him to sit up. He breathed out hard, his jaw suddenly chewing. Perhaps the pain herbs were already starting to kick in.

His eyes had a glassy, far-off look, but when she tried to pull him to his feet, he managed to stand. She had to keep one hand on the wall as she hopped toward her dragon. He stumbled beside her, but because of his arm over her shoulders, and probably the pain herbs too, they made it to Shadow soon enough.

Chloe balanced herself on one foot as she helped Quintus climb the dragon. Once he got to the top, she grabbed the boot and wooden foot from her dragon's teeth.

But just as she started using her knees and arms to scramble up Shadow's back, one last figure entered the hallway.

His blond hair and large mole stood out in the light. Julian lifted one corner of his mouth in a crazed grin. "Ready for my help yet?"

Wild delight danced in his eyes as he stared at Chloe.

He knew she had found the note. It probably would have been better if she pretended she had no idea what he was talking about, but her reaction gave everything away.

His note claimed he knew where to find the king of Crystalfall. After this defeat in trying to take back the castle, they needed the king more than ever.

But had they really sunk so low as to accept help from the mortal who had destroyed the entire Court of Crystalfall?

Chloe finally reached the top of Shadow's back, grabbing her reins tight in her hands. In her mind, she told her dragon to fly.

She glared at Julian, gritting her teeth together tight. "Never!"

His grin suggested he was not worried in the slightest by her declaration.

It took a deep breath just to settle her thumping heart after seeing his crazed look. She reached for Quintus, pulling him closer to herself.

They had Shadow, and they had each other, but would that be enough? Would that be enough to actually get away?

ONCE SHADOW LANDED NEAR THEIR camp in the hills and with the other dragons in the horde landing all around her, Chloe tried to reach for Quintus's side. He jerked away, his body mostly done with shaking after the dragon ride away from the castle.

"My healing abilities can take care of this." He placed both his hands over his side, where blood was already seeping through the fabric of his coat.

Chloe huffed as she slid off her dragon's back. "Just let me look at it."

"No." He sounded almost like a child with how he snapped back at her.

She gestured toward the middle of their camp. "I can conjure herbs from the golden table now. I do not need my healing magic to take care of your wound."

His eyebrows rose high on his forehead until they disappeared behind the dark curls dangling over his forehead. His hair had grown back fully now. "*Before,* you said this was a magical wound and that only magic could heal it. *Now*, you say you can heal it with herbs?"

The anger in his tone worried her. This wasn't just some banter to make sure she took care of herself. Quintus was truly angry. Maybe it wasn't at her exactly, but he certainly seemed to blame her whether she deserved it or not. They'd only gone through a single battle, and somehow, things between them were reverting back to how they'd been before his magic had returned.

She wanted to grab his face with both hands and remind him about their moment in the forest, but she couldn't. Her attention got completely captured by how his face had drained of color after all the blood loss he'd sustained. She swallowed hard. "Maybe I can't heal it *completely* with herbs, but I am certain they will help."

His nose wrinkled as he lifted his chin into the air. "You only say that because you can lie. It is not certain. With an injury like this, nothing is certain. And you need to fix up your own wound before you worry about anyone else's."

He jabbed his finger toward the blood dripping from the wound in her arm. The gash had never healed properly after Julian stabbed her with a dagger. And now Portia had thrown a knife directly in the center of the wound, making it worse than ever.

"Let me worry about that." Chloe jerked her head back toward Quintus, ready to throw another scathing retort back at him.

But before she could, Ludo stomped between them and threw his hands into the air. "Ughhhh. These two." He turned back to throw an exaggerated eye roll toward Mishti. "First, we have to force them to be together so they will stop fighting. And now…" His gaze turned away from Mishti and went back and forth between Chloe and Quintus, pinning them each with a glare as he continued. "It appears we need to force them apart just so they will deal with their bleeding injuries."

Mishti nodded once at Ludo, then grabbed Chloe forcefully by the wrist. She glanced at her friend, and asked, "Any instructions for Ludo?"

Chloe stumbled on her feet as Mishti started tugging her away. "What?"

Mishti used her head to point toward the other two. "What should Ludo do for Quintus's wound?"

"Oh!" But Mishti kept pulling Chloe, putting Ludo and Quintus farther away with each step. "He needs celestine crystals to absorb the extra blood. And the skin needs to be re-stitched over the wound, but you have to let me do that part at least."

Ludo nodded, about to turn away.

But Chloe piped up, a little louder now since Mishti kept pulling her away. "And more pain herbs will help, especially since the ones I conjured in the castle probably didn't even help much. I can use the table to conjure—"

"They'll be fine." Mishti kept walking, even more quickly than before. "Ludo can open a door to the celestine meadow and Quintus—a *master* craftsman—can probably stitch up the wound himself."

By now they had moved too far away for Chloe to see Quintus or Ludo. She couldn't bear to imagine Quintus trying to deal with the wound on his own, but somehow, thinking of Ludo trying to stitch it up seemed even worse.

Mishti had forced Chloe all the way to the golden table by now. She used it to conjure a bowl of water. Then, she used a dagger from her arm bracer to cut away the leftover linen around the wound. One of the other Golden Shields found a swath of clean fabric they could rip into strips to use as fresh bandages.

Soaking one of the small strips of cloth in the bowl of water, Chloe then squeezed the water out over the gash in her arm. The water stung once it touched the wound. Probably nothing would ever feel as luxurious on a wound as the water in that Crystalfall bath, but this seemed to sting more than necessary.

Or maybe she'd just ignored the injury for so long that paying attention to it now brought all the pain to her mind in a rush. Chloe had to squeeze several more slops of water to clean away the lines of blood down her arm.

When she got it clear enough to dab at the gash with a clean cloth, she winced each time the fabric touched her skin. It had become inflamed and tender around the original wound, proving that ignoring it had only led to infection…much like Quintus guessed it would.

She shoved that thought away as she conjured a tincture from the table next. She had to bite down on a clean bandage as she poured the tincture over the gash. If she hadn't, she probably would have screamed.

Pain needled through her skin, burning at the edges and deep inside the injury. She conjured honey and a few crushed herbs next. After using a finger to mix them together, she smeared the concoction over the gash.

Mishti helped wrap the wound with a clean bandage. It would still take several days for the tincture and herbs to counteract the infection, but at least she'd finally taken care of it. Quintus couldn't complain anymore.

With that finished, she also cleaned up and dressed the other small wounds she had gotten when she stomped through the forest near the celestine meadow. For the injury on the back of her shoulder, she had to give step-by-step directions to Mishti.

The young woman may have been expert with weapons and with frightening dragons, but she was *not* gentle when dealing with wounds. Chloe kept gasping through her instructions, but they managed to get through it eventually.

When everything had finally been properly taken care of, a few Shields came to the table to have their own injuries cleaned and dressed. Despite their decided and horrible defeat, very few of the Shields had been injured, and none of them had been killed.

They may have had to retreat and get out of the castle without accomplishing anything, but it appeared their horde of dragons had still given them an advantage they'd never had before.

Chloe didn't know how many, but several of the Zeakriesh had been injured worse, and many of them had lost their lives.

With every treated injury, besides Quintus's, meeting Chloe's apothecary approval, she wandered through camp, searching for a way to keep herself busy.

It only took a handful of steps and a few idle glances to somehow find her way to Quintus. He wore a sleeveless brown tunic now, which he had probably borrowed from one of the Shields. It looked a little strange to see him wear a color other than green, but the rugged attire managed to show off his toned muscles more than the coat he'd been wearing.

It appeared he'd also been wandering through camp, idly finding her at nearly the same moment she found him. They shared a quick glance. She couldn't see under his tunic, but Ludo must have helped him with his wound. And Quintus could see the fresh bandages on her injuries, so he knew hers were taken care of now too.

Tension filled the space between them. His anger continued to simmer under the surface, making her afraid to approach him too quickly. Did he still blame her for something? Did he still want to fight?

His expression gave her no answer, but since he hadn't said anything yet, she tried to assume he had calmed. Hopefully, as long as she was extra gentle with him, the strain between them would dwindle away.

Only a few steps away from Quintus, Ludo sat on a boulder with Sofia standing over his shoulder. Ludo used a pencil to draw on a piece of paper and then pointed to it. "This is where the locked room was."

Chloe stepped close enough to see what he drew.

"And what's this?" Sofia asked, pointing at his crude map.

"That is the great hall. Here." He touched the pencil to paper and wrote *Great Hall*. When finished, he wrote *Locked Door* on another part of the sketched map.

Sofia tilted her head and then nodded. "Okay, I remember it now. That hallway leads to the front of the castle if you go to the right, but if you go to the left instead, you can get to the hallway with the locked door."

"Exactly." Ludo stood and the paper fluttered to the black soil. "Mishti said you might have a way to force the door open."

"Yes, Batu is working on it over here." Sofia wandered off with Ludo, leaving Chloe and Quintus in a small clearing with no one else around.

But Quintus's gaze held fast to the small paper Ludo had dropped. He plucked it off the ground and stared at it with his eyes narrowing. After a long moment, he flicked his gaze to Chloe. "Do you still have the king's journal?"

He spoke to her, that had to be a good sign. The frown tugging at his lips proved things weren't completely normal, but at least he hadn't picked a fight.

"Of course, I do," she said with a tentative smile. Pulling the journal from her leather bag, her mind spun, trying to guess why he might have asked.

The question got answered when he opened the journal and stared at the pages. It only took a breath, and a smile appeared on his lips. Her heart skipped at the sight of it.

"See, Ludo cannot be the king." He pointed first at the words written in the journal and then he pointed to Ludo's map, which he'd placed on top of the next page. Quintus tapped the words on the map. "The handwriting does not match."

Understanding lit in Chloe's mind all at once. She leaned forward onto the balls of her feet and confirmed the handwriting was indeed different.

When she leaned back onto her heels, she wanted to let out a sigh of relief, but it didn't come. She even said, "Good," but that didn't bring relief either.

Of course she was glad to prove Ludo wasn't the king of Crystalfall, especially knowing everything the king had done to Quintus. Except if Ludo wasn't the king, they were now even farther away from finding him.

While contemplating that woeful dilemma, Quintus brought the journal closer to his nose. He ran a hand over the pages, sniffed them even. After a moment, his nose wrinkled.

She tilted her head. "What are you doing with that?"

He thrust the journal toward her. "Write something in it."

"What?"

Pushing the journal more insistently into her hands, he then dug a pen from his pocket. "Find a blank page and write something."

She raised an eyebrow at him, but she also turned to the back of the journal where a few blank pages sat. Opening one of them, she wrote: *I do not understand why I am writing this.*

The writing part was simple enough, but what came after caused her mouth to hang open. As she penned the words in her own handwriting, the letters changed right before her very eyes. Each one shifted and stretched until the words perfectly matched the handwriting on all the rest of the pages.

Quintus scowled and brushed a hand over the parchment. "The pages are enchanted. The king probably wanted to conceal his handwriting in case anyone ever found the journal."

Her eyebrows tipped upward. "Clever king."

"Yes, so clever." Quintus huffed and shook his head. "And also expert at keeping himself hidden."

With a start, she realized they still had no idea if Ludo was the king or not. His handwriting proved nothing. Slamming the journal shut, she stuffed it into her bag. "Get the crown."

He jerked toward her, his shoulders stiffening at her command. "What?"

She softened her tone, but still kept it deliberate. "I wrote in the journal like you asked, now you get the crown."

Narrowing his eyes, his hand disappeared inside his pocket. He followed her when she trailed away, but he did not pull the crown out yet.

It only took a moment of wandering to reach her destination. Standing casually behind a tent, she waved a beckoning hand. "Ludo, come here a moment, will you?"

Quintus's eyes bugged out when he finally understood her intention. "I..." He shook his head.

She wanted to glare at him, but simply thinned her lips instead. "You what?"

His voice lowered to a whisper even a fae could not hear. "I do not want to know if it is him."

Compassion filled her when she spoke again. Hopefully her gentleness could convince him. "No more of this. We need to know. Once and for all."

He still looked like he'd rather meet Portia's pointed shoe again, but he did pull the crown out. When Ludo joined them, Quintus held it out to him without saying a word.

But Ludo made no attempt to touch it. He just stared at it and narrowed one eye. "Why are you trying to hand that to me?"

Bells rang out in Chloe's mind, calling attention to how suspicious it was that he refused to touch the crown.

She did her best to ignore them as she gestured toward the golden and emerald piece in Quintus's hand. "How does that feel to you? Does the weight seem off?"

Ludo's eyebrows popped up, and finally, he reached for the crown. He brought it easily into his hands and slipped it from one hand to the other. "Feels fine to me."

Absolutely nothing happened.

The crown moved between his palms, against his fingers, and it gave no reaction at all. Chloe breathed out hard and then tried to cover it up by pretending it was a laugh.

"That's what I said too, but Quintus keeps complaining it feels off."

Shrugging, Ludo handed the crown back to Quintus and went back to Sofia and Batu where they were trying to figure out how they might break through the locked door in the castle.

"Satisfied?" Quintus asked. But though his tone was arrogant, it held a great deal of relief. He was clearly more relieved than even Chloe to finally know for certain his friend was not the father who had once tried to kill him.

Chloe *was* satisfied by this revelation. She was glad, truly. But just as she had realized before, they were now even farther from finding the mysterious and vile king of Crystalfall.

Suddenly, Quintus stuffed the crown back into his pocket. "I…"

He blinked and stared ahead without really seeing. In that one tiny action, tremors of anger, or maybe fear, filled the air around him. He glanced toward her, and his eyes suddenly appeared duller than usual. His eye even twitched at the sight of her, but he tried to hide it. When he spoke, the words came out casually, but she could still feel an upheaval within him. "I have an idea." He turned away from her. "Go find Mishti and help her with whatever she is doing."

Speaking in the most careful voice she could manage, Chloe asked, "What's this idea of yours?"

He waved off the question, gesturing toward camp and away from himself. "I will explain later." Then he darted away in the opposite direction.

"Where are you going?" she called after him.

"I have to do something," he shouted back. And then he was gone.

Swallowing, she put a hand over her heart, wishing she could calm its rapid beat. Quintus had been acting strange ever since they went to visit his mother. Before that, back in the forest clearing, Chloe had forgiven him, and he'd said sorry, something she thought he'd never say.

But now? She didn't even know what to think about how he acted now. Did he just need more time to process the visit with his mother? Or would things only get worse?

That line of thinking only set Chloe's heart beating faster, so she trudged off to find her friend. Mishti was probably doing something interesting anyway, and Chloe needed the distraction.

In fact, Mishti was mending a tent. After stitching up so many injuries, Chloe had gotten rather good at sewing and stepped in to finish the job.

When night fell, Quintus returned. She tried to get a look at his wound, which prompted him to avoid her. Tension continued to roil between them. He could keep trying to avoid her, but she might have to force him to let her look at the wound in the morning.

But when morning came, she found his sleeping mat empty. It might have worried her more, except everyone else was already up and training and strategizing too. The battle the day before must have tired her out more than she realized. At least she had slept well.

That little thought was the last bit of cheer that graced her mind because soon, her entire being was filled with a dread so deep, it rooted her in place.

Quintus came and found her. He led her away from everyone else, right to the edge of camp. His face stayed oddly straight, and he never once looked her in the eyes.

At last, with the rest of camp a distance away, he turned to her, and she could see exactly why he had worked so hard to avoid her gaze.

His moon tattoo, the black tattoo that should have been under his left eye...was *gone*.

Completely gone.

Her shoulders shivered at the implication.

29

THE GLITTERING TREES AND SCENT of vanilla and lilacs surrounding Chloe did nothing to calm the beating of her heart. They did nothing to lift her spirits or stop her limbs from shivering. She and Quintus had come so far, made great efforts in repairing both their bond and their love for each other. But something must have happened, because…

Quintus's tattoo was gone.

Her heart stammered, waiting for an explanation. She prepared herself for a frightening tale full of monsters and weapons. Perhaps Julian had done it. Maybe he had used the magic of the shards and found some way to ruin their lives even more.

It soon became clear, though, that it was not monsters or weapons or even her greatest enemy that she should have feared. It was her own beloved.

Quintus let out a heavy breath and spoke in a sharp tone. "I figured out how to sever our bond forever."

"Forev…" Unable to finish the word, Chloe clapped a hand over her mouth. She couldn't even begin to think why he would say that. Why he would *do* that.

He supplied an explanation much sooner than she wanted. "You kept trying to heal my wound instead of taking care of yourself. You would not leave it alone."

His jaw clenched through the words. Frustration kept the muscles in his face rigid. After a quick shake of the head, he held his arm out to her. "But look what happens when you try and heal now."

The simple brown tunic he wore had no sleeves, which left his arm completely bare for her to touch. She could not access her magic without touching his skin. He'd avoided her touch so much recently, but now he held his bare arm out to her expectantly.

Trembling filled her fingers as she stretched them toward him. She kept looking at his face. At his eyes. At the spot where his tattoo should have been.

She'd known him before he got that tattoo. They had spent plenty of days together then. Maybe it was just because of what the tattoo represented, but seeing it gone? Seeing his face without it? She could not understand why it looked so strange.

Her fingers wrapped around his forearm. His skin felt drier than usual, almost papery. Was it because of the magical wound in his side? Was it because he had severed their bond?

Silence filled the space between them, but she wasn't about to change that. What was she supposed to say anyway? All she could do was close her eyes and attempt to access the magic, she already knew would be gone.

She reached out with her mind. She concentrated as deeply as she ever had. She tried to feel for the magic from Faerie.

But it was gone.

It was gone, and she knew it. No matter how she tried to use her magic, to call it forth, she felt nothing.

The missing tattoo had been incriminating enough, but a part of her dared to believe it wasn't true. But this? He had no tattoo, and she had no magic.

Somehow, he'd done it. He'd severed their bond forever.

She ripped her hand away from his arm, ignoring the tears that stung in her eyes. Her voice was too quiet for a shout, but her words were just as scathing. "You took your own magic away again just to stop me from trying to heal your magical injury?"

"No." Quintus took a step back, his facial expression evened to a maddeningly neutral expression that told her absolutely nothing about what was going on in his head.

He lifted one hand, holding it in front of his chest. After staring at it carefully for a moment, magic appeared at his fingertips. In a flash, he sent a blast of bright red sparkles straight into the sky.

"How?" Chloe said the word through a breath. She narrowed her eyes, shook her head. None of it helped. "You…kept your own magic but took away mine?"

The only answer he gave was a smirk.

That was worse than the neutral expression. Much worse.

She wanted to throw something at him. She wanted it to hurt.

"How could you?"

Just after she spoke, Batu stepped up to Quintus. The man's mind was clearly so busy with thoughts that he saw none of the contention between Chloe and Quintus. "We are ready," was all Batu said.

Quintus nodded.

Ready? Ready for what? As far as Chloe knew, no one had made any more plans. What were Quintus and Batu going to do?

But when she craned her neck and glanced toward the rest of camp, she realized *we* encompassed so many more people than just Quintus and Batu. Every single Golden Shield stood at the center of camp in a tight huddle. They were prepared for something, but why didn't Chloe know what it was?

Her gut twisted when she realized both Mishti and Ludo stood in the circle as well. They knew? What did they know, and why had they failed to tell Chloe?

"Go mount the dragons," Quintus said, gesturing to the other side of camp where the dragons roamed. "I will be right there."

Batu nodded and left without another word.

Chloe folded her arms over her chest, attempting to don an authoritative expression. "Where are we going on the dragons?"

"*You* are not going." Quintus touched a hand to her back, leading her farther behind a tent where no one else could see them.

Heat from his hand spread over her skin, feeling like a cozy fire that could melt the iciest heart. Why did he have to do that? Why did he have to touch her and make her feel so alive, so on fire, when he had just taken away her magic?

Taken hers and kept his own.

And she even thought things were getting better. He'd kissed her. They'd held each other's hands. They still bickered, but not like they had before.

Did that mean nothing to him? Had he only been pretending to care about her? Had he always planned to sever the bond completely if it didn't happen on its own?

By the time they stood across from each other behind the tent, she could barely even breathe. Why?

Why had he done this?

He clearly had no intention to explain further. He just stared at his hand and took a deep breath. His eyes focused, growing more concentrated with each moment.

After a moment, he whirled his hand in a circle.

A swirling black door filled with golden sparkles opened in front of them. She took comfort in the knowledge that his magic was still weak compared to what it once was. Yes, he had opened a door, but it had been difficult for him.

Hopefully he never got the full strength of his magic back. If he could so casually take her own magic away, he didn't deserve his.

Now he tilted his head toward the door.

She scoffed, holding her folded arms even tighter than before. "You better tell me what's going on before you expect me to walk through any door."

"It leads to the mortal realm." His neutral expression had returned. "Some *time*," he said the word carefully, like he hoped he was using it correctly, "has passed since you were there last, but not much."

A hard breath escaped her, as if she'd been physically punched. Why did he keep doing this? He had taken her magic, and now this? He wanted her to *leave*? To go back to her home with Grace and Vesper and Cosette in a village full of mortals who would never understand her?

His hand fell to the side as he watched the door swirl before them. "I have made a door like this for you before. The door will stay open until one person goes through it. Then it will close."

She scowled. "I will be stuck—" There was no use finishing that sentence. Better to ask a question. "Why would I go back to the mortal realm? You think I'm only here for you? What about Mishti?"

His eyebrow rose as he looked down at her. "You have no magic." Now he gestured toward his face, which still looked supremely strange without its tattoo. "*We* have no bond. Mishti and the other Golden Shields cannot leave Faerie without dying due to the tablets Ansel and later Portia forced them to take. But *you* can leave. This war is growing more dangerous, the battles more deadly and more numerous. This is not the life you ever wanted."

He held his hand out, toward the door.

"And now you can leave."

She may have argued more, except he left. Right in the middle of the worst moment of her life, he turned on his heel and walked off to the other Golden Shields.

She would have called after him, except her throat had turned too sticky and thick. Aches stretched through it when she tried to swallow.

Last night they had talked, it had been pleasant. And now he wanted to get rid of her.

Her gaze turned to the swirling Faerie door.

What was she supposed to do?

30

BLACK SWIRLS AND GOLDEN SPARKLES stared at Chloe. The sparkles couldn't see the way she could, but right then, it felt like they saw her. It felt like they twinkled and spun and laughed asking if she'd made her decision yet.

No, she had not.

Digging her hands into her hair, she let out a scream. It helped, but not enough. Taking a deep breath, she did it again. This scream was longer, angrier, louder.

The dragons and Golden Shields had flown too far away to hear her scream, but maybe one of the fae in the camp would hear it. Hopefully one of them would come over and ask why she screamed.

Then she'd be able to explain. Then she'd be able to vomit all the words out describing how Quintus had done the stupidest thing he had ever done and how he deserved vitriol and hate. And hopefully the fae would gasp and agree with everything she said.

Except no one came. When she wanted another person, any other person, just to complain to, of course, she was completely alone.

She stomped through camp, even peeking inside tents, but the fae were not there. Even the pixies had left the area. Why was she surprised? Quintus and the Golden Shields, including Mishti and Ludo, had all planned something behind her back. Quintus must have sent the fae away for the day, or maybe they took the fae with them wherever they went.

Her chest curled into a knot. Maybe they were never coming back.

Huffing, she marched over to the golden table and flopped onto the nearest chair. She hadn't even eaten breakfast yet. Quintus hadn't even had the decency to let her eat before breaking her heart.

And he knew how much she loved to eat.

Apparently, he really didn't care about her at all.

Gripping a golden plate tight between her fingers, she stared at it, trying to think of a breakfast she could eat without hurling it across the table when she remembered what Quintus had done.

The only acceptable answer was cake.

She spat the word out, glaring at her plate as a frosted cake with strawberries and white frosting formed. An entire cake. And it wasn't even sliced. At least the table knew what she needed.

Snatching the nearest fork off the table, she dug into the cake without bothering to slice it herself. Tearing away a chunk of it revealed a buttery and rich yellow cake under the white frosting. She shoveled it into her mouth, barely taking time to taste each bite.

The cake made her tastebuds sing. It had the most glorious flavor, especially when combined with the sliced strawberries on top. Despite that, tears still pooled in her eyes.

She ate even faster after that, as if it would help. It didn't help at all. Soon, tears spilled down her cheeks, splashing onto the golden table.

Her fork tore away bigger chunks. Maybe a fuller mouth could slow her tears. But then a sob wracked through her shoulders, followed closely by a second one.

With her mouth stuffed full of the delicious cake, she lifted the plate and hurled the rest of it onto the black soil. While stomping the remaining bits of it with her boots, she spoke over the cake in her mouth. "You were supposed to make me feel better, but you didn't."

She glared at the cake, almost wishing it could respond.

This didn't make any sense. Quintus hadn't even tried to bring his magic back. It was only because she pushed so hard that he had the little of it back he had now.

And now he was just going to get rid of her?

Frosting smeared the bottoms of her boots as she stomped back over to the door. She stared at it through a blur of tears. When she blinked, she didn't try to only blink the tears away. A part of her wished the door might disappear too.

Of course, it never did.

Pain sprouted in her heart. Pain that knew something her mind did not want to acknowledge. But deep in her heart, she already knew the truth.

She didn't want to leave. She wanted to stay and help him find the king. She wanted to help him find a home once the king reclaimed the castle. She wanted to stay with Mishti and Ludo and the Order of the Golden Shield and help protect Crystalfall.

She wanted to be with Quintus.

But now truth ached through her entire chest where she could no longer ignore it.

It was over.

It didn't matter if she wanted it to continue. Love only lasted when both people felt it. If he no longer loved her, she couldn't make him feel the same about her. She couldn't force him to feel what she wanted him to feel.

Whether she liked it not, it was over.

She had to leave.

The door looked different after that. It didn't swirl like an out-of-place addition to the landscape. Now it looked like her destination.

Maybe she could figure out how to help search for the king while she sat helplessly in the mortal realm. Maybe she could send her fae brother, Vesper, back to Faerie to relay any information she found.

Whatever she did, she finally accepted the awful truth.

She had to leave.

And now that she knew it, she had to take care of a few things first. Stomping back over to the golden table, she ripped open her leather bag and dug through its contents.

Surely, she had to have something from Quintus hidden in there. One little item was all she needed. She'd find something she'd kept that reminded her of him.

And then she'd burn it.

She'd watch the flames eat up the object, and maybe that would help the tight squeezing that had taken over her chest. Other girls in the mortal realm had done it before. They said it helped release the sadness and anger from a broken heart and helped them move on.

If Chloe had to leave the magic of Faerie behind, then she definitely needed help moving on. But no matter how she dug through her bag, she couldn't find a single thing from Quintus.

She'd once kept the harp string there, but that had been turned into reins for her dragon. Suddenly, her heart stopped.

Shadow.

Her head whipped to the side, checking the clearing where the dragons normally roamed. She already knew what she'd see even before fully turning. It hadn't hit her at the time because she'd been too focused on the door, but now she remembered Shadow had left with the others.

Quintus had taken her.

Our dragon, he'd said, but now he took her along with Chloe's magic.

Chloe released an angry cry and glanced down at herself.

Then, she shouted up into the sky. "How am I supposed to cathartically remove you from my life when the only thing I have from you is the dress I'm wearing?"

She couldn't very well burn *it* and walk in her underclothing into the mortal realm. But then an even bigger problem struck her. How was she supposed to burn anything when the wood in Crystalfall was actually gold?

Huffing, she kicked away the nearest rock, which was made of a brilliant amethyst. Now she grumbled under her breath. "Stupid court needs a way to make fire."

But after the swing of her foot, she realized she did have something else from Quintus besides her dress.

She had her wooden foot.

"Oh." She stupidly said the word out loud, which crashed into the air as heavy as a boulder.

She wouldn't destroy the foot. She couldn't.

But could she bring it with her?

Of course she *wanted* to bring it with her. She needed it to walk. Another foot could be made for her in the mortal realm, though. It wouldn't be as light, as comfortable, or as well-made, but she didn't need this exact foot.

Quintus needed it. The wood came from his home in Bitter Thorn. It was the last piece of it he had left.

She wanted him to suffer for ending things between them. She really did.

Hopefully it tore him to shreds when he realized she had left him. Hopefully he finally realized all the greatness he had lost by giving *her* up.

But to take away the last piece of home he had left?

He didn't need to suffer that much.

Walking slowly back to the door, she sat down in front of it. At least her tears had stopped now. She would leave the foot, but she'd also have to leave a note with it, so he knew she meant for him to keep it.

After retrieving a blank piece of parchment and pen from her leather bag, her gaze fell on the blank page. What was she supposed to say? What did anyone say when it was the end?

So, she wrote the only thing in her heart.

I love you.

The once-gone tears burned in her eyes, coming back so fast she couldn't stop them.

I don't want to leave. I want us to last forever.

Her finger traced over that last word. *Forever.* She'd been doing a fantastic job of ignoring the very problem they'd had from the start. He was immortal. She was not.

But she didn't want that to be a problem. She wanted to live forever so she could be with him and never have to break his heart when she died. She wanted to be immortal too. Not for vanity because she feared growing old. Not because she feared she'd never be great enough or gain enough power if she only lived the length of a mortal life.

She only wanted it for him. So she could be with him.

Forever.

A balance shard wouldn't work. She'd thought it through over and over again, and no matter how much she wanted to believe, she knew that wasn't her solution. She wouldn't survive the change if she tried to use a balance shard to turn into a fae.

It was probably better then. It was probably better to leave him now and let him move on. Her head cocked to the side as she stared at the note through her tears.

If she was going to leave and let him move on, she couldn't leave *this* note. Instead, she tucked that into her leather bag and got a fresh piece of parchment.

Tears continued to fill her eyes and blur her vision. She had to lean backward slightly just to make sure none of them splashed onto the page. It took several moments of deep thought, and even then, she had nothing profound to write.

In the end, she only wrote two words.

Your home.

Sobs heaved her chest as she took off the foot and then removed it from her boot. She carefully placed the note on top, then grabbed her boot by the laces and stood.

Her right foot carried the weight of her as she hopped forward once. Twice. The reality of it had started to kick in.

Why?

It didn't make any sense to her how it ever came to this.

Why did he want her to leave?

A bird chirped overhead just then. She glanced up to see a jeweled nightingale made of aquamarine, moonstone, and lapis lazuli gems and a gold beak and legs. Back in Vesper's village where she once lived, nightingales had been considered good luck charms.

That brief moment reminded her of happiness just enough to bring clarity to her mind. She'd seen clearly how everything had gone wrong, how everything had fallen apart, but never once had she tried to see the brighter side of any of it.

Could there be a brighter side?

Her mind whirled, bringing her back to the last few moments before Quintus left with the others. He had said, *This war is growing more dangerous, the battles more deadly and more numerous. This is not the life you ever wanted.*

"What if…" Thoughts spun in her mind while the blue-and-white jeweled nightingale continued to chirp.

Maybe Quintus *didn't* want her to leave. Maybe he just feared she would.

As her mouth fell open, her body dropped to the soil. Her hand reached for the wooden foot, which sat on the soil next to her. Trailing a finger over the knots and patterns in the wood, she thought even more.

What if he wasn't trying to get rid of her? What if he was trying to protect her by keeping her away from whatever battle or danger the others were involved in now?

Maybe he only gave her a chance to leave because he assumed it was inevitable. He'd said the same thing when their bond first started to repair. He said he knew she'd betray him and then leave him. *Leave* him.

He'd said it like his heart had physically ripped in two just thinking of it.

Thinking back on it, she was certain now, or at least close to certain.

He didn't want her to leave, he just feared she would. And maybe he feared it so much that it seemed better to make it happen on his own terms than waiting for her to do it on hers.

Still brushing a finger over her wooden foot, more thoughts started spilling in. Maybe this was partially her fault too. She had pushed so hard to get close to him again. She'd had Mishti and Ludo pin Quintus down so she could stitch up his magical wound. She had touched him before he was ready. She had ignored him any time he wanted her to take care of herself.

She really had turned selfless again. But it wasn't even true selflessness. She had ignored her own injuries, pushed to heal his wound and repair their bond, which she had been so certain had been the right thing. She had *known* fixing him was more important than taking care of herself. But maybe those things she *knew* he needed weren't actually the things he needed at all.

Her gut twisted as another realization hit her. Fixing the things *she* wanted fixed wasn't selfless either, even if she did it at the detriment of herself. It was selfish to only focus on what she thought was best.

Maybe what he really needed was for her to trust him to know his own needs. To trust that he'd come to her for help if needed. And maybe, considering what he'd said about the war and dangerous battles, maybe he needed to know she was safe without having to risk his own life in pursuit of her protection.

Maybe he needed to be able to trust that she could, and would, take care of herself too.

These realizations hurt and ached, but in a good way. It been a rude awakening, but an enlightening one. She had areas to improve.

He did too.

He had taken her magic, severed their bond, told her to leave Faerie. He had messed up. But was it enough for her to give up on him?

Her gaze turned toward the door, sparkling as bright as ever. Beckoning her back to the mortal realm where she could leave Quintus and not have to worry about how his fears might cause him to mess up again.

But with that thought, she grabbed her wooden foot and stuffed it back into her boot.

She had to stay.

The nightingale flew down and landed on the soil in front of her as she tightened the laces of her boot back over her wooden foot.

"Hello there," she said to the creature. "I don't suppose you want to go through this door for me and see if you can make it close? If you do go through, just make sure you find my sister, Grace. The other mortals, except for Cosette and her children, won't understand why you're made of jewels."

Light twinkled off the nightingale's aquamarine, moonstone, and lapis lazuli surface as it chirped through its golden beak.

Pretending the chirp had been a question, Chloe continued. "How are you supposed to find Grace? Is that what that little chirp meant? Oh, it's easy. Just listen for the most beautiful harp music the mortal realm has ever known. You can probably fly right into her window and land on her shoulder while she plays. She has red hair and the gentlest heart."

The nightingale chirped again, which Chloe pretended meant the nightingale would very much like to meet the lovely-sounding Grace.

By now, Chloe had her boot and wooden foot fastened on again. When she stood and looked at the door, she took a long, deep breath.

Was she really sure about this? About staying?

The blue nightingale flew upward, until it flew almost directly at her eye level.

Seeing it brought a smile to her lips. Of course she was sure.

She had to stay.

"Go on," she said playfully to the jeweled bird. Then she gestured toward the door. "Fly straight through there."

And then the nightingale did.

Her eyebrows flew upward as the little creature disappeared into the door. And though the bird was not a person exactly, it must have been close enough because the door vanished.

That was it. That was her chance to leave, and now it was gone.

And yet, more than any other time in her life, she knew she'd made the right decision. Staying would be messy. She and Quintus still had their biggest problem, immortality and mortality, to face. But as messy and challenging and painful as it might sometimes be, it would be beautiful too. Beautiful enough to fight for.

Whirling on her heel, she headed back to the golden table. While she waited for the others to return, she'd read the king's journal. She had read it all by now, but it couldn't hurt to read through it again.

Anything in it might help them find the king…as long as she paid close enough attention.

31

SKIMMING EACH PAGE OF THE journal, Chloe tried to remember each unusual quirk or thought from the king. She had read all these pages before and everything seemed just as important, or unimportant, as it had the first time she read it. But then a short phrase stood out to her a little more than it had before.

Not everyone in Faerie understands the full magic of the crowns. Sometimes they work in mysterious ways.

Such a curious statement immediately led to a more curious thought. She dropped the journal back into her leather bag and pulled out her magical book. She flipped through it, trying to find a page of information on Faerie crowns. Instead, she kept turning to blank pages.

Shrugging, she leaned closer to the book and whispered a question. "What if a king rules over two courts? Is the magic in each crown separate or are they tied together?"

It took a few moments of staring at the blank page before an answer started forming. She could see a shadow in the parchment first, but then it darkened and turned into words.

Separate.

Chloe frowned at the word, which disproved the current theory that tried to form in her mind. Although…

She turned back to the book and asked another question. "Are *all* the crowns separate from each other… or is Crystalfall's different?"

Nothing appeared until she'd taken two breaths. Then, the words finally started forming.

Crystalfall is different from all other courts. Different in many ways.

A feeling almost like victory made her stomach leap. The questions came faster now, while her theory turned a little more solid. "What if the king of another court was also the king of Crystalfall? And then Crystalfall got destroyed and everyone forgot it and its king. For a time, the Crystalfall crown was destroyed too, right? It couldn't belong to anyone because it didn't exist until the court was restored."

She stared at the page, waiting for an answer. When it formed, she scoffed at the sentence.

There is no time in Faerie.

Of course it would say that. Maybe it would be better to just continue. "So, if that's what happened, then what was the magic of Crystalfall attached to while the actual crown was destroyed? Was the magic attached to the king's other crown? From the *other* court he ruled? That is, *if* the king of Crystalfall was also king of another court."

She only waited a moment, but then barreled on, still trying to string together the different threads of this theory.

"And then if that king died and his crown was passed to his child, would the magic of the Crystalfall crown also be passed to the king's child who *now* wears the crown?"

She tilted her head to the side at the thought. They'd been looking for a male this whole time, but what if it was a female fae? What if it was someone who hadn't been alive when Crystalfall got destroyed? If this were true, it would probably have to be the child of the original king since a child would share his blood. But Faerie had a few courts with rulers like that.

High Queen Winola had died, and her son ruled now. King Euron of Dustdune was dead, and his daughter ruled now. King Pavel died, and Fairfrost had had two new leaders since then, first his daughter, and now his son.

Once again, she remembered how lucky Fairfrost was to have such an honorable leader in King Severin, since the two rulers before him were anything but.

She glanced down at the now completely blank pages of her magical book. It hadn't given an answer, but she also hadn't been asking direct questions.

Focusing more intensely, she leaned in. "Did the king of Crystalfall also rule another court?"

A moment passed and nothing happened, but slowly, slow enough for her to hold her breath, a shadow formed on the parchment.

Before the words began to darken, a loud shout sounded above. Only then did she become aware of the flapping dragon wings above her. Glancing up, she saw the horde of dragons was returning.

They were close enough that they'd be landing soon. With a gasp, she jumped to her feet. Sofia stood at the edge of her dragon's back, clearly about to lose her balance. But if she lost her balance, she'd fall.

Just as Chloe put that thought together, Sofia did fall. Her back leaned too far, and her foot slipped away just enough to lose grip on her dragon's crystalline scales.

Chloe reacted without much thought. The woman was about to land only a few paces away from where Chloe had been sitting. She grabbed the corner of a nearby tent and ripped it free from the stake.

In only the nick of time, she got the tent out just enough to act as a sort of pillow for Sofia to land. The force of it sent Chloe stepping forward, which probably only softened the landing even more.

Still, Sofia rolled off the tent flap and onto the ground.

"Are you okay?" Chloe asked, stepping closer to the woman.

The tightness in Chloe's chest released when Sofia stood from the ground and wiped the dirt off her skirt. "Yes, but—"

She stopped midsentence and went running off toward the other dragons that were now landing. A great commotion stirred among the dragons and Golden Shields. The fae from their camp were there too, proving they had gone with the Shields…wherever they had just gone.

Several Shields had gathered in one spot, clambering over something Chloe couldn't see. But then Mishti's enormous stormy blue dragon slammed a claw into the ground and the commotion slowed.

Heading back to the table, Chloe bent to grab her magical book from off the ground. It had fallen when she jumped suddenly, and now her page had been lost.

No matter. She could ask it more questions later. Right now, she wanted to find out where everyone else had gone.

Just as she tucked her magical book into her bag and put the leather strap over her shoulder, she heard voices.

"Are you sure he is secure?" Ludo asked.

"We got him." Mishti answered in her hardened tone. "He won't be able to cut the bonds this time."

Ludo breathed a sigh of relief before he spoke again. "Where is Chloe?"

"She is…" Quintus answered in a heavy voice. Then he gulped loud enough for Chloe to hear, even though he and the others stood on the other side of a tent. "She is gone."

"What?" Mishti snapped. "What do you mean *gone*?"

"She went back to the mortal realm." For a moment, it honestly sounded like Quintus held back tears.

"No, she didn't," Sofia said through a laugh. "She's over by the golden table."

The tent in front of Chloe rushed with wind as Quintus ran around it. When he came face to face with Chloe, his entire being lit up. His dark brown eyes sparkled with glints of gold.

It was still strange to see him without his tattoo, but his eyes… They made up for it.

Ludo appeared around the tent next, glancing between the two of them. "Oh, no. This is going to be one of their moments."

Mishti released a small chuckle and sat down at the table. "Probably."

Suddenly, Ludo was pushing Chloe and Quintus into the forest near their camp. "Go fall more in love over there. The rest of us do not need to see it."

Quintus was too busy staring into Chloe's eyes while his demeanor turned as bright as the sun to care that Ludo had shoved them away.

In truth, Chloe experienced a similar feeling by seeing how much more delighted Quintus grew at the sight of her.

Once they were alone among the golden and emerald trees, he glanced back toward the camp, toward the tent. "But the door…it is gone."

Turning her gaze downward, Chloe tucked a strand of hair behind her ear. "A nightingale flew through it. Hopefully, a jeweled bird won't cause too much trouble in the mortal realm."

Sheer delight played on his lips. He stepped forward, his arms lifting. He almost dropped his hands onto her shoulders, but he stopped just before touching her. "You are here." He swallowed hard. "You stayed."

His smile was so sweet, she didn't even want to bring up all the realizations she'd had while staring at his open door. Of course, she did have to bring them up or this same thing would probably happen again.

Turning her eyes up at him, she spoke a little harder. "I know you're fae and aren't used to having strong emotions, but I really need to teach you how to process emotions better."

He brought his arms back to his sides and tilted his head.

She raised both her eyebrows at him. "Like, for instance, maybe don't do idiotic things like tell your beloved to do the exact opposite of what you actually want her to do."

He blinked at her twice. "How did you know I did not really want you leave?"

She sighed. "I think a more important question is, why do you think I'm going to?"

He stared at her longer that time, no answer at the ready. Her stomach flopped, knowing she'd have to prod to get the answers out. He might not like it, but it had to be done.

He'd revealed some already, but once and for all, she'd finally find out why he kept pushing her away.

32

MELODIC BUZZING INSECTS AND BELL-LIKE bird chirps filled the air of the Crystalfall forest. Chloe stared at her beloved, asking a second time the question he did not want to answer.

"Why do keep assuming I'm going to leave you?" She pressed her lips to a thin line, waiting for an answer.

Quintus swallowed and turned toward camp. "We should—"

"Talk about this," Chloe finished. She took a step closer to him, attempting to throw him an even firmer expression than before.

His shoulders squirmed, turning now toward the forest.
"Quintus."
He flinched at the sound of his name.

She moved in front of him, forcing him to look her way. "I won't touch you, but I won't let you walk away until you talk to me."

It took a moment of him shifting on his feet and staring into the distance before he finally released one quiet sentence.

"Everyone who is supposed to care for me never did or does no longer."

"Supposed to?" She narrowed her eyes. "Who is *supposed* to care for you?"

Letting out an exasperated sigh, he threw his hands into the air. "My parents. High King Brannick's mother gave her *life* just so he could live. And his father stayed in Faerie even after his beloved died just so he could be with his son. Kaia and Soren would not even let him see his son that often, but his father still stayed without question just for the few moments he got with him every now and again."

Chloe's thoughts started swirling. "But I thought fae did not love their children the way mortals do."

Quintus's lip curled upward. "They do not hate them either. Not unless they have a reason. Even King Pavel, who never cared for anyone, still came to care for his son."

A stirring started in her heart just then. This pain he'd been feeling, she hadn't even known. He'd locked it deep in his heart, never letting on that he cared.

Frowning, he continued. "If it were only one parent, maybe I would not be so worried, but it is *both* my parents. If both of them hate me, then it must be because of…" He glanced down at his hands, staring at the palms. "Me."

She raised her eyebrows, finally seeing this huge leap he had made that had absolutely no logic behind it. "So, because both your parents hate you, that suddenly means *I* am going to leave you?"

He pulled his head back, as if he'd hide it behind his shoulder if he could. "I cannot blame you since I already know there is something wrong with me, but yes, I am certain you will leave me someday. You will want to get rid of me like my father, or you will no longer want to be a part of my life like my mother."

Chloe shook her head. "I'm pretty sure your mother just wants to avoid the king and would love to be in your life otherwise."

His head snapped upward, looking her straight in the eye. "You are guessing. I asked twice, and she refused to come with us. It is because she does not want to be around me."

Letting out a slow breath, Chloe then pinched the bridge of her nose. "Fine, maybe you're right, which I strongly doubt, but it doesn't matter. Maybe your *fae* mother, who hardly even knows emotion, doesn't care about you, and maybe your *paranoid* father wants you dead. That only proves *they're* messed up, not you."

He dropped his chin to his chest and let out a huff.

She wanted to step toward him, to comfort him, but he might not want that right now. Instead, she spoke in her gentlest voice possible. "There's nothing wrong with you, and I'm not going to leave you."

"You might," he said in a whisper. "You probably will. Something may happen someday that... that..."

Her hand reached out, almost of its own accord, and carefully touched his forearm. It was enough to stop his stammering. But then he stared at her hand, and she could already tell he'd find some way to be angry about it if she kept it there a moment longer.

So, she pulled away. She took a step back. With the golden and emerald trees surrounding them both, she said the words that might drive a stake between them forever.

"I can't force you to trust me. If you expect me to leave, you will always find evidence that I want to or am trying to leave, even when I'm not."

He responded with a glare, which was characteristic of his current emotions, but not what she'd been hoping for. At that moment, she noticed his side. Blood droplets had started to seep into the fabric. Fresh blood.

She sighed and gestured toward it. "If you want me to help with your wound, I can stop it from bleeding. And I may be able to help with the pain and some other things now that we have a golden table. But it's your choice."

His eyebrows rose at that, probably too stunned to respond.

She shrugged and took a step toward camp. "I'm going to find Mishti."

And she did. She turned her back on him and took two entire steps away. She finally understood she could never get him to open up by forcing it. She could only wait and hope he would come to her when ready.

But just before she took her third step, he said her name. Softly. Like a dove landing on a ray of light.

"Chloe."

She turned to glance over her shoulder.

His chest rose and fell as he breathed. As he stared. He looked into her eyes deeply. Slowly, his face twisted in pain. When he swallowed, his throat bulged. "How do I…"

He trailed off, staring. Thinking. The strained muscles in his face relaxed ever so slightly. Not much, but enough to notice it. Then he spoke again. "Will you stay with me while I learn *how* to trust? Will you be patient with me?"

The corner of her mouth tugged upward. "Always." He didn't expect her to solve his problem for him. He just wanted her to stay and offer guidance while he learned. That's how it should have been. True love didn't mean fixing every problem for her beloved. It meant standing at his side and offering a hand while he fixed it for himself.

Parting her lips, she added, "And I'll take better care of myself too, so you don't have to worry so much about me."

His lips curled up on one side. He'd turned to her before, when they'd kissed in the clearing Mishti had tricked them into. He'd first admitted his fears about her leaving then, but he'd still been filled with so much fear. Now, he had actually faced those fears. Now, he seemed to see a challenge before him, but one that did not frighten him so much.

Lifting his arm slowly, he reached out, stretching his fingers toward her. She still had her back to him, her neck craned to look over her shoulder. His hand beckoned, not just allowing her to touch him, but asking for it.

Her own fingers twitched, eager to make contact with his. Turning again until she faced him, she stretched her own hand out until her skin met his.

The moment they touched, Quintus pulled her back into the trees where he stood. He'd done it fast too. In a single breath, he had her chest pressed up against his while his hands slipped around her waist. The yank hadn't strained her muscles or caused any sort of pain, but it made it clear just how desperately he wanted, *needed* her.

He kissed her fiercely and without an ounce of fear. He kissed her like the sun might never rise again if he didn't cover every inch of her mouth with his. His arms tightened around her waist, pulling her closer. Closer. So close she had difficulty telling whose limbs were whose.

She lifted herself up on her tiptoes, which wasn't very easy since one of her feet was made of wood. But she couldn't just stand flat-footed when she needed to get closer. To feel more of him.

Her mind, her arms, her entire body was so completely entranced by this passion Quintus had filled her with, she didn't even feel at first the tingling under her right eye.

When Quintus slid his hand down her side, she had to pull back an inch just to catch her breath. In that short moment, her skin finally tingled and sparked enough that she noticed it. Just under her right eye.

It had happened the last time they kissed, but this was different. Stronger. More powerful than ever. With a gasp, she touched the skin under her right eye. Her star tattoos. They had magic in them. *She* had magic in her.

Her gaze tipped up enough to check Quintus's face too. His moon tattoo had returned. Seeing it made her heart sing.

But it didn't look exactly the same as before. It had turned more magnificent. The edges were crisp and the inside of it black, but outlining the crescent moon there was now a glittery golden border.

"Our bond," she said through a breath. "It has returned."

He nodded with a light smile, running his hand over the small of her back. "I know." A flinch overtook his features for a moment. "Or, well, I never actually did anything to sever it. I only glamoured my face to make it look like my tattoo was gone."

Instead of pulling away after finding out he'd deceived her, she moved in a little closer. She still twisted her expression into one that hopefully looked accusatory, though. "But you said you figured out how to sever our bond forever."

With his arms still around her, he shrugged. "I did. If one of us dies, the bond will be gone permanently."

Her head cocked to the side. "But my magic. You took away my magic."

"No." He flinched harder and looked away. "I covered my arm with a material that felt close enough to skin that I knew you would not question it. Then I glamoured it to look like my arm. The only reason your magic did not work is because you never touched my skin."

Once again, she was compelled to move closer instead of pulling away. "That was very tricky of you. Where did you and the other Shields go anyway?"

"Oh!" His eyebrows flew upward. But then he used one hand to brush a strand of hair out of her face. "Back to the castle. We captured Julian."

Her hands dropped to her sides, and she stood up straight. "What? *Julian?*"

Quintus frowned, tugging her closer until she was back to where she'd been a moment ago. "He is over with the dragons trapped under Mishti's ferocious dragon's claws. And he is tied up tight."

Chloe kept her hands at her sides, shaking her head and trying to grasp this reality. "I can't believe you *captured* him."

"Yes, but…" Quintus reached up a hand and slid his fingers along her jaw. When he got to her chin, he tipped it up slightly, closer to his face. "There are other things I want to focus on right now."

She bit her bottom lip, finally looking back into his eyes. A roguish grin overtook his face. Instead of simply kissing her again, he spun them both around until her back was against the nearest golden tree trunk.

The roots came higher where she was now, forcing her to stand with her feet slightly apart. Quintus pressed up against her and found her lips with his.

She'd thought about him kissing while in that labyrinth with her back against the wall, and it seemed nice then. But with her back against this trunk, his breath hot on her mouth, and his fingers trailing lightly up her arm? Nothing had ever felt so good.

Why had she been so concerned about Julian anyway? They could deal with him later. *Much* later.

33

Breath from Mishti's dragon rustled through Chloe's hair. Everyone had agreed that questioning Julian would have to take place as near to the dragon as possible to ensure he had absolutely no chance of getting away.

The stormy blue creature used its belly and its front legs and hind legs to form a half circle around him. A wall of Golden Shields with weapons at the ready completed the circle. They even had Julian tied to a high-backed chair with bonds so tight, it may have been cutting off his circulation a little.

It still didn't seem like enough. Chloe stood before Julian, her arms folded and her back a little straighter than usual. Quintus stood at her side with a spear pointed straight at Julian's throat. Mishti stood next to Julian's chair with a weapon in each hand. Ludo stood on the other side of Julian's chair with deadly magic sparkling at his fingertips.

Despite all their precautions, Julian sat in the chair like he owned the space. His body relaxed in his seat. His mouth tilted into a grin. Crazed delight danced in his eyes, as if he were more excited to see what might happen next than worried about how it might hurt him.

Yes, he claimed to know where to find the king of Crystalfall, but that didn't mean much. They had a lot of questions for him before that claim would hold any weight. But before they got to the questions, she needed him to know where they stood.

"We know who you are." She raised one eyebrow, staring down her nose at him. "*Fritz.*"

The slightest flinch passed through his shoulders at the sound of that name, but it quickly left when he turned to Ludo. "Ah, so you found your brother and his little mortal girl, did you?"

Ludo raised both his eyebrows and took a step back. His hands wavered, the magic disappearing for a moment.

He'd only said two sentences, and already, Julian had surprised Ludo with how much he knew. The mole on his chin stretched as Julian smirked. He enjoyed surprising people, that much was clear. He turned back to Chloe now, his chin a little higher. "She was supposed to marry me once, you know?"

Hopefully, Chloe's expression showed just how unimpressed and unsurprised she was. "We did know that actually."

His nose wrinkled. "Well, did you also know she can't read?" He laughed, a wicked sound. "Such a simpleton. I'm glad I found Faerie instead, because her mind never would have been intelligent enough to keep up with mine."

He made it seem like breaking off their marriage had been solely his choice, but his betrothed had already told Chloe and the others that she had come to Faerie just to avoid *him*.

It was a little odd that she couldn't read. Maybe she'd never been taught. Or maybe Julian lied about that too, though it seemed like a strange thing to lie about. In any case, the young woman clearly was intelligent whether she could read or not. She had demonstrated that easily during her conversation with them.

And anyway, Chloe didn't want to give Julian the satisfaction of knowing he'd surprised her. Attempting to settle her face into a neutral expression, she continued. "That's not all we know. We also know you gained magic by touching the creation magic, and we know you used it to destroy this entire court."

Julian sat back casually, glancing off to the side. "You have seen me wield magic. Were you surprised to find out I have my own?"

Mishti brought her dagger a little closer to his neck. "You can't use your magic. Faerie blocked you from it."

His eyebrow tipped up in surprise.

Chloe nodded. "Maybe you've been able to use Ansel's old gemstones and the balance shards, but we know you can only wield other magic. You cannot use the magic inside yourself."

He flashed his teeth at no one in particular. When he did, a feral look passed through his eyes.

Continuing, Chloe said, "At the vault, we know you were desperately trying to find the pieces of the Crystalfall crown."

She took a tiny step toward him now. Quintus's spear moved forward until the tip rested against Julian's throat. Mishti's dagger and sword came precariously close to his temple and his heart. Ludo leaned his hands toward Julian, the deadly magic at his fingertips once again.

Now Chloe lifted one eyebrow. "You want to help us because you think it will help you find the crown. You think if you touch the crown, it will give you access to your magic once again."

Even with the weapons grazing his skin, Julian shrugged leisurely. "Yes, it's true. I believe touching the crown will restore the magic I have inside me, the magic Faerie has blocked from me."

A short chuckle left Ludo's mouth. "The crown will not give you magic just because you touch it."

They knew that all too well after they'd been stuck in the vault. Quintus had touched the crown, yet it never restored his magic.

Julian rolled his eyes, completely ignoring the weapons around him. "I *know*. The crown will not give anyone else magic unless the current king dies. I'd have to kill him, and then I'd have to wear the crown before anyone else. It's the only way to get my magic back."

Quintus moved the tip of his spear a little deeper into Julian's skin. Not enough to puncture it but enough to make him squirm. "How do you know that about the crown?"

Julian shifted to the side as much as he could to get away from Quintus's spear. Judging by how he kept swallowing, it probably hadn't worked as well as he liked.

He glared a little at Quintus before continuing. "I lived in Ansel's house while Queen Alessandra sought to kill each leader and claim each crown of every Faerie court. Portia and I learned many things about how Faerie crowns work."

Chloe wanted to throw her hands into the air but managed to drop them to her sides instead. "Then why would you tell us where the king is? Even if you know, why would tell us? Why do you think it will help you get closer to getting your magic back?"

The frightening grin reappeared on Julian's face. "You already know I want the Crystalfall crown for myself. I see no sense in hiding that. But the simple fact is, you will never find the king without my help, and *I* will never get close enough to the crown to steal it unless I am with you when you find him."

Quintus laughed. "You think we would let you come with us when we go and find the king?"

Julian countered immediately. "You think I would tell you where to find him without forcing you to bring me along? I'm not going to give you a map; I will take you there myself."

"Take us?" Chloe scoffed. "How could we ever trust you enough to do that?"

His head tilted, as if the answer were obvious. "You do not have to trust me. You already know I won't get my chance at the crown unless I help you, and you know I am desperate for that chance. You also know I'll turn on you since I want to kill the king, and you want to give him the crown, but at least you know exactly *when* I'll turn on you. Doesn't that give you enough of an advantage?"

Mishti shook her head and spoke under her breath. "We don't even know if he's lying."

"Yes." Ludo's eyebrows shot upward. "Yes, mortals can lie. He must be lying."

Julian rolled his eyes. "Just because mortals can lie doesn't mean they always do."

"But how?" Chloe pushed her eyebrows down over her eyes. "How do you know who the king is?"

Julian's eyes flashed with delight. "I remember him. If you spoke to Clara and Revyn, then you know I was here when Crystalfall existed the first time."

"You *remember*. Just as simple as that?" Quintus shook his head. "No one else remembers, but somehow *you* do? You are the only one who remembers?"

"I was not in Crystalfall when everyone else lost their memories," Julian responded easily. "I saw a cloud come down, and I later learned that's how the memories were lost, but the cloud never came down on me because I was not in the court."

"Where were you then?" Ludo asked with a scoff. "If you were close enough to see the cloud but not be touched by it, where were you?"

Julian sat back, as comfortable as ever. "I stood just outside the crystal caves, preparing to destroy the court entirely." A wide, toothy grin spread through his cheeks. "Imagine my luck that my plan just happened to protect me from the memory cloud too."

"No." Chloe shook her head. "Other people forgot too. Dyani, Quintus's mother, also forgot. She was not in Crystalfall when the memory cloud came down either, but she still has no memory of the king. At least not enough to help us find him."

For once, the calm, casual, crazed demeanor in Julian's expression fell away. He looked at her, then at Quintus, then turned back to her again. Intrigue filled his eyes. "How do you know she, whatever her name was, wasn't in Crystalfall?"

It should have felt like a victory that Chloe had information that had so clearly piqued his interest, but it didn't. Something about his curiosity pricked at her nerves. Standing under his gaze like this made her want to shudder.

She only knew because of the king's journal. The king had written that Dyani disappeared from Crystalfall before the end. The king even guessed correctly that she had returned to her original court of Bitter Thorn. She wasn't about to tell that to Julian though. He didn't need to know where they'd gotten their information.

Her back straightened, just so she could stare down her nose at him once again. "We just know. Now answer the question. How did others forget even though they were not in Crystalfall when the memory cloud came down?"

"Everyone forgot eventually, but that is because of Faerie." He shrugged. "It tried to erase the king from everyone's minds, but that magic never worked on a mortal like me. Clara and I are probably the only mortals who survived the destruction of Crystalfall. And even if other mortals did survive, they are all dead now, so their memories wouldn't help you."

That explanation fit, but it only begged another question. "Speaking of that," Chloe said. "How are you still alive?"

He raised an eyebrow. "Just because I have told you some of my secrets doesn't mean I will give away all of them. Now, do you want to find the king of Crystalfall or not?"

They did. They were desperate enough to capture Julian and to consider working with him. But were they desperate enough to actually listen to him?

He had a logical answer for every question they threw at him. His reasoning explained why he was the only one in all of Faerie who remembered the king of Crystalfall. If what he said was true, then they really did need him to find the king.

But what if it wasn't true? A person as conniving as him had to be lying about some of it. But how much? What they really needed was a way to know for sure if he actually knew where to find the king.

Was such a thing even possible?

34

LEAVING JULIAN TIED TO THE chair with Mishti's dragon's claws now pinning him down, Chloe and the others met around the golden table at the center of their camp. Now that they'd questioned him, they needed to decide what to do with the information.

"We all know we cannot trust him, right?" Ludo huffed as he settled into his seat. "Why did we even bother asking him anything?"

Mishti tapped the table with the edge of her leather arm bracer. "He's probably telling the truth about some things. He might even be telling the truth about everything."

Quintus raised an eyebrow. "Why would he tell the truth when he can lie?"

"He already told us why," Mishti said. "He tried getting the crown and hasn't been able to. He knows he'll never have a chance of seeing it unless he takes us to the king. He might even know the king will be too powerful to beat once he wears the crown again."

Chloe frowned, going deeper into her chair. "Even if he is telling the truth, he's still going to turn on us. And yes, maybe we know exactly when, but is that enough of an advantage?"

"We captured him, did we not?" Quintus said, sitting a little taller. "We have dragons and an army of Golden Shields ready to protect us. Julian is only one person. We can keep the king safe from Julian long enough to restore the crown to the king."

Sighing, Mishti clasped her hands together on the table in front of her. "There might be another way. We can still make a deal with the wraiths." She bit her bottom lip while the smallest twinkle seemed to appear in her eye. "Chandril told me where I can find him."

Chloe sucked in a sharp inhale and turned to her friend. "But—"

"I know what I'll have to give up," Mishti said, already guessing what Chloe intended to say. Then Mishti shrugged. "I'd prefer not to lose another memory, but I realize it might be better than working with Julian."

As much as they hated to admit it, she was right. If they ever worked with their enemy, they'd better only do it after exhausting all other options. Even more than that, Mishti didn't just seem willing to work with the wraiths. She seemed *eager*. Or maybe she just wanted to see Chandril again. Instead of being frightened by him, she almost seemed drawn to him, almost like she'd been drawn to her dragon. Maybe Mishti just liked terrifying things.

With Mishti's dragon still holding Julian down, the others took Shadow to a part of Crystalfall Chloe had never seen before.

When they got close enough, Mishti pointed it out and called it the Forest of the Wraiths. Just past the mountains with veins of gold, they found a dense forest so eerie, Shadow got agitated before she even landed.

She flew them to the edge of the forest. But when Chloe tried to get her dragon to enter the trees, Shadow huffed, whimpered, and stepped backward.

"There, there," Chloe said, rubbing her dragon on the nose. "You can stay here until we get back. You don't have to go inside."

Releasing a heavy breath from her nostrils, Shadow plopped onto the ground and pulled her legs in close to her body. Instead of doing the same with her wings, she kept them out ever so slightly, as if she might fly away at any instant. Her sapphire blue eyes shifted quickly, her gaze darting every which way as she carefully watched her surroundings.

Quintus ran his hand down the golden scales of her neck, lending comfort.

Seeing Shadow's reaction to the forest did not make it easier to enter. Only after Quintus wrapped an arm around Chloe's waist did she feel able to step forward into the trees.

They had golden trunks and emerald leaves and sparkling flowers made of jewels just like all the other trees in Crystalfall, but these branches were gnarled and skeletal, clawing at the sky. And there were *so* many of them. It was a challenge just to find a bit of soil to step on that didn't have a large golden root running through it.

A damp, oppressive chill and a sense of foreboding filled the forest air. Layers of powdery dust littered the ground and clung to everything it touched. It smelled stale and lifeless, which only got worse the farther in they moved.

With each step, the twisted branches and leaves seemed to close in, cutting off the sunlight above. Even more disconcerting, the emerald leaves felt more like eyes, making it feel as though someone constantly stared just over Chloe's shoulder.

Quintus's fingers curled tighter around her waist, pulling her closer. That position did not make it easier to walk through such a dense forest, but he clearly cared far more about keeping her safe.

After stepping into a miniscule clearing, they got their first glimpse of a wraith. The creature held an old book with dust caked on the top edge of the pages. His skin seemed translucent, causing him to blend in with the shadows, almost as if they were a part of him. He had a gaunt face and lime green eyes that glowed. A coat and pants that looked like they had been spun from spiderwebs covered his thin frame.

A tongue at least three times the length as Chloe's stuck out of his mouth. He used it to lick off the layer of dust that had settled on the book's pages.

When Mishti stepped into the clearing, the wraith immediately dropped the book. His green eyes glowed as he stood and hungrily eyed all four of them. Now that they had seen him, other wraiths emerged from the shadows all around them.

One with fair skin and a tunic and breeches peeked out from behind a tree. Another with tan skin and a string of pearls in her hair jumped down from a nearby deformed branch. One wraith with a golden belt and dark skin crept toward the clearing from several paces away.

They all had fingers twice as long as a mortal's and eyes as hungry as a dragon's. Their skin came in different shades, but on all of them, it was translucent and thin, making them seem more shadow than form. Each stood no taller than an eleven-year-old child.

Several wraiths came toward them now, but Mishti kept glancing through the trees, as if none of those wraiths would do. "I do not see Chandril," she whispered to the others.

Chloe screwed her mouth into a knot. They didn't need Chandril. Any of these wraiths would give them information…as long as they gave a memory in return. And maybe Chandril only wanted Mishti's memories, but if Chloe offered one of hers instead, any of these other wraiths would take it.

She stepped forward and the wraith with pearls in her hair scurried forward faster than the others.

"I can help you," the wraith said in an airy voice. "Tell me what you wish for."

From behind, Quintus reached both his arms around Chloe's stomach and pulled her back against him. She wouldn't complain about being in his arms, but they wouldn't stop her either.

"There is something I wish to know." She waited a beat. "Who is the king of Crystalfall?"

At the sound of that question, the wraith before her flinched. Disgust tilted her features as she turned away. When she spoke again, it was through her clenched teeth. "I cannot tell you that."

Chloe nodded. "I know. I have to give you a memory first."

The wraiths always asked for a day of life, and they always took the memory of that person's very best day, which worried Chloe to no end. She feared she might lose the moments she'd so recently shared with Quintus just outside their camp. But they needed to find the king, and they didn't have many other options now.

But the wraith just smiled, showing off yellowing teeth that were all sharpened to a point. "Would you not rather know who the first being in Crystalfall was?"

Chloe raised an eyebrow. "Was it the king?"

"No," the wraith answered. Once again, disgust filled her features, but a bit of anger seemed to join.

Chloe pressed her eyebrows down. "Then, no. I only want to know who the king is."

With a frustrated huff, the wraith took a step back. "I cannot tell you that." Her face contorted, agitated by the conversation. After scowling, she stumbled backward, leaving the area completely.

All around the clearing, the other wraiths did the same. They backed away and shivered until all of them had gone out of sight.

In this forest even Shadow had not wanted to enter, Chloe never expected the wraiths to be afraid of her. And why wouldn't they tell her about the king?

Mishti raised an I-told-you-so eyebrow. "We need Chandril." She moved ahead, stepping farther into the dense and unnerving forest. "He will help me."

They discovered two more small clearings before they found another cluster of wraiths. Each one crept toward their group eager with eyes glowing. Leaning against Quintus, Chloe loudly proclaimed they wished to know who the king of Crystalfall was or where he was, and nothing more.

At the sound of that, the wraiths hissed and stumbled away as quickly as the others. But before they had scattered, Mishti raised one hand. "Wait, where is Chandril?"

The nearest wraith wrinkled her nose. "He cannot tell you about the king either."

Another wraith with glowing red eyes, pushed the other away until he stood directly in front of Mishti. He lifted one, enormously long finger. "You wish to know where Chandril is?" He leaned closer, a sickly grin stretching onto his face. "I will tell you for a memory."

Mishti's lip curled at the suggestion, but the wraith in front of her seemed to be encouraged by it. He leaned a little closer, nearly touching his finger to her cheek.

"Get *away* from her." Chandril stomped into the clearing, using his lithe arms to push the other wraith away. His blood-orange eyes flashed. He bared his sharp white teeth at the other wraith, then released a strange and horrifying sound from the depths of his throat.

At the sound of it, the other wraith backed away and ran as fast as he could. Seeing the two stand directly next to each other forced two surprising realizations to Chloe's mind. First, Chandril had definitely grown taller, as she had previously wondered. He stood taller than any other wraith they'd encountered, about the same height as her. And second, while his dark skin still had a translucent quality to it, it seemed more solid, more alive, than any of the other wraiths.

But now the other wraiths had disappeared into the shadows of the forest, and Chandril stood directly in front of Chloe and the others.

When Chandril turned to Mishti, the oddest look filled his frightening face. Instead of an eerie smile, he gave her a…kind smile? Was that even possible for a wraith?

Reaching out, he took her hand in both of his. His translucent, dark-skinned fingers trailed over the back of her wrist before he glanced up at her again. "Mishti." He held out the *sh* in her name a little longer than the other sounds.

Even stranger than any of that was the hint of a smile playing on Mishti's lips. She made no attempt to remove her hand from his. And did she just lean a little closer to him too?

"Can you tell us who the king of Crystalfall is?" Her voice came out lilting, with none of the harshness so characteristic for her.

But just like the other wraiths, Chandril flinched at the mention of the king. He shook out his shoulders, as if trying to get something repulsive off him. Finally, with a sigh, he said, "No."

His expression didn't change until he glanced at Mishti again. When he did, his lips turned down in a frown. He seemed sad about giving that answer, and not just because he'd lose out on getting another one of Mishti's memories. Strangely, he seemed to genuinely want to help her and was now upset that he could not.

The corners of her lips turned downward, but then she asked, "Can you tell us where he is?"

His gaze fell to her hand, which he continued to stroke with his long fingers. "I have already told you everything I can."

Mishti's head angled to the side, turning it even closer to him. "Why *can't* you tell us?"

A shudder passed through his lithe frame. "Faerie itself prevents us." His voice lowered to whisper. "But even then, we do not speak of the king if we can help it."

He lifted his eyebrows significantly and glanced around at the rest of them. Without another word, they all seemed to realize this conversation needed to be quieter.

"Can you take us to him?" Mishti asked in a low whisper.

The wraith shook his head immediately, flinching as he did. "I could, but I will not. Not even a memory or many memories could compel me to do that."

After a huff, Mishti craned her neck back to look at the others. "You're the clever one, Chloe. Think of a loophole."

Chandril's long fingers finally released Mishti's hands. Now he touched her long braid, running a finger and thumb over the plaited hair. "If I give any information that helps you, I require payment."

Mishti nodded, utterly unconcerned with this wraith being in her personal space and intimately stroking her hair. If anything, she was enjoying it. "I will give you another memory, but…under the same arrangement as before."

His eyes lit up as he stared back at her face. "Of course." He paused for a moment, then said her name again, drawing out the *sh* a little longer than before. "Mishti."

When Chandril had first appeared, Chloe thought about insisting that any memory given had to come from her. But judging by his interaction, he didn't seem likely to take a memory except from Mishti. But what was this arrangement they had? Could Chloe really allow her friend to give another memory to this wraith who was more disturbing than he needed to be?

But no matter how she tried to think of all the reasons they shouldn't do what Chandril wanted, Chloe thought of a loophole instead. She almost wished she hadn't.

Frowning, she asked, "You can answer yes or no questions, then? You cannot tell us about the king outright, but if we ask something specific, you can give an answer?"

The wraith narrowed his glowing orange eyes and stroked his chin. But then he said, "That loophole should work. Faerie cannot stop me from answering yes, no, or unknown."

He turned his gaze on Chloe then, raising an eyebrow. "Think carefully on the question before you ask it. I will only answer one more."

The pressure of that declaration sat heavy in Chloe's heart. What was she supposed to ask? What single question answered with yes or no could possibly give them enough information to find the king?

Just as the answer came to her, so did a pounding of dread.

It was the only way. Once they knew the answer to the question at the front of her mind, they could get closer to finding the king. She would have asked something else, anything else, if it would have helped, but this question was the only way.

So, she asked the question she knew she must in the tiniest whisper she could manage.

"Does Julian know where to find the king of Crystalfall?"

Chandril dropped Mishti's braid with a start. He sucked in a breath, which didn't seem to fill his chest at all. He stared at Chloe, then at Mishti, then even at Quintus and Ludo. His mouth opened, but he didn't seem to know what to say.

Did he not know? Maybe he had no idea who Julian was. She assumed he did, since Julian had destroyed the entire Court of Crystalfall, but maybe the wraiths never knew who destroyed their court.

Had she just wasted their one chance to learn more about the king with a question Chandril didn't even know the answer to?

But then the wraith sighed, his arms dropping low at his sides. He glanced over both his shoulders into the forest behind him. Then he leaned close and whispered a single word.

"Yes."

The answer left his mouth and punctured the air. It was only a single word, but it stabbed. They only had one choice now. They would have to cooperate with Julian.

35

THREADS OF CONCERN TWISTED AND soured Chloe's belly. They had an answer, but it hurt to know it. Part of her wished she could still be ignorant, as if that would be any better.

Why did it have to come to this? Why did they have to work with Julian just to find the king of Crystalfall?

While they stood, basking in the weight of what they'd have to do, Chandril conjured a small corked emerald vial. He handed the memory elixir to Mishti, who grabbed it without question.

But she didn't drink it. Instead, she kept staring at him. His hand waved in another circle, conjuring a second emerald vial. Only once he had it ready and waiting in his hands did she pull the cork from her elixir. He did the same with his.

They glanced at each other for a brief moment and then nodded. At the same moment, they both drank from the vials in their hands.

Chloe felt her eyes open wide, stretching her forehead from it. Chandril drank a memory elixir too? Was this their arrangement? That Mishti would give him one of her memories, but he would have to also give her one of his?

Did wraiths even do anything besides wander around licking dust off things? That was the whole reason they took memories from others, wasn't it? To be able to live through other people since their own lives were so empty?

Soon, both their bodies glowed slightly, but Chandril's also changed. In that short moment, his frame became as opaque as Mishti's.

When they had both swallowed the elixirs and tucked the vials into their pockets, Ludo loudly cleared his throat. "Uh," he started.

But before he could get another word out, Mishti grabbed him by the collar and even lifted him off the ground slightly. "Don't say a word about this. Not to anyone. Not ever."

Ludo gulped and stretched his feet, trying to touch them back to the ground. "Okay, got it. I understand."

When she released him, he pulled his collar away from his neck and heaved out a breath. He started walking down the path they had come from and spoke under his breath. "Sometimes I forget how lucky we are that she is on our side."

Chloe very much agreed with that, but mostly just because she appreciated Mishti's friendship. It *was* always fun to see Mishti threaten Ludo into silence though.

By the time they left the Forest of the Wraiths and scrambled onto Shadow's back, Mishti had been overcome, probably with the memory she had just received. She still followed them and sat like she normally did on the dragon scales, but she also stared off into the distance as if her mind was wholly occupied.

It took until they were more than halfway back to their camp before Chloe worked up the courage to ask the question in her mind. "Should we work with—"

"Yes," Quintus and Ludo both said at the same exact moment.

Mishti didn't answer out loud, but she nodded while continuing to stare off into nothing.

They really had no choice, but she appreciated seeing they were all on the same page.

When they got back to camp, they spoke first to the Golden Shields, who agreed to stand at the ready to attack Julian if needed, and to protect the Crystalfall king with their lives once the time came.

Their conviction brought comfort, but it didn't erase all the dread in Chloe's heart when they untied Julian from his chair. Her belly ached as they helped him climb atop Shadow, even though his hands were bound tightly with ropes.

Chloe held Shadow's reins with Quintus close behind. Mishti, Ludo, Sofia, and Batu formed a circle around Julian, each holding a weapon against him. Their dragons flew directly next to and behind Shadow while all the other Golden Shields and their dragons formed a V behind them.

"Where are we going now?" Chloe asked.

Julian sat crosslegged as flippant as ever. "To the castle."

Quintus grimaced. "The castle?"

Chloe gasped and then shook her head. "The king is probably behind that locked door we already found but had to abandon. We didn't even need Julian to find him."

A laugh slipped from Julian's mouth so fast it could be nothing but genuine. "No. I would not leave the king where Portia or any of the others could find him." Then an untamed look appeared in his eye that looked a little more purposed. "Trust me. No one knows where the king is except me."

Such chilling words. They already knew that wasn't exactly true since the wraiths seemed to know as well. But the wraiths' knowledge was worthless to them since Faerie prevented any information from being shared between them.

Quintus scowled, but his face softened when he caught Chloe's eye. "We already checked behind that locked door anyway. We managed to get it open when we went back to the castle. And when we found it empty, we decided we might as well capture Julian while we were there."

A startled look passed through Julian's features, but he hid it quickly. Now, he glanced down at the landscape beneath them.

As Shadow began flying to the castle, Julian lifted his hands. "It will be difficult to show you where the king is while I have these ropes on my wrists. You'd better take them off now."

"No." Mishti didn't even bother looking at him to answer. "We won't take them off at all." She kept her gaze fixed on her sword, which pointed directly at his thigh.

He opened his mouth again with a pleasant expression. But then he closed his mouth and dropped his hands into his lap. He must have lived with Mishti long enough to know it was useless to ask again.

But now they neared the castle, and Julian sat up a little higher. "Tell the dragons to fly low so the Zeakriesh do not see them through the windows. There is a spot on the left side of the castle, right by those mountains, where the dragons should be able to gather and avoid anyone's eye."

The fact that those instructions got them directly next to the castle without any trouble should have been a good sign. It demonstrated Julian really was trying to help them because doing so would help him.

If only they could get his help without giving any in return.

Mishti and Quintus quickly went over the plan with the Golden Shields. Some of them would stay outside the castle to swoop in if needed. Some with smaller dragons would take them inside. Everyone else would surround Chloe and Julian on foot.

Making plans felt a little foolish when they had no idea where they'd be going once inside the castle. But Julian supplied suggestions every once in a while, explaining how parts of their plan would not work because of one reason or another.

He skillfully managed to explain those things without giving any hints as to where they'd be traveling while inside the castle.

Soon, he led them to a small door behind a wall and under a terrace. It wasn't hidden exactly, but it certainly wouldn't have been easy to find without knowing where it was already.

As they crept inside the door, Chloe lifted an eyebrow at Julian. "How did you know about that door?"

He answered with a smirk, which didn't explain anything.

"Were you a servant in the castle?" she asked.

His mouth shifted to a slanted grin. "Maybe. Maybe I was friends with the king. Maybe I got lucky." Bouncing his eyebrows once, he grinned more. "Or maybe I was unwanted and had to get creative in how I entered these walls."

The last one was most likely, but any of them could have been true. Or untrue. Maybe he only knew because the door had once been common knowledge before Crystalfall got destroyed. Whatever it was, it didn't matter now.

They were working with him, whether they liked it or not.

Once inside, they got into the formation they had practiced. Chloe stood at Julian's side. If he tried anything unexpected, she'd alert the others immediately.

Mishti stood in front of them, and Quintus stood behind. Ludo and most of the other Golden Shields surrounded them, forming a circle or lines depending on how wide the hallways were. The Golden Shields who had brought their dragons stayed at the back of the group.

If anything happened that required the dragons, everyone else would drop to their bellies and the dragons would fly over top of them to take care of the danger.

It was funny how being so secure, with such a solid plan, it somehow just left Chloe with a pit in her stomach. Julian supposedly knew the castle and the Zeakriesh enough to be certain the two groups never met. He supposedly had the king hidden somewhere no one but him could ever find.

But those were two more *supposedlies* than Chloe preferred. It didn't make her feel a single bit better after they successfully passed through three hallways without any trouble at all.

As soon as they turned down the fourth hallway, Julian suddenly went rigid. He sucked in a breath, which sounded like genuine fear, not just pretended fear.

When Chloe glanced toward him, he shoved a thumb toward the nearest door. "Everyone in there. Fast! And hide the dragons around the corner."

Was this a trick? It was a good thing she wasn't in charge of making quick decisions in the moment because she would have stood there thinking for far too long. Instead, Mishti and Quintus directed everyone inside the room Julian had indicated.

The Golden Shields with their dragons hid around the corner just like he suggested. Chloe still feared the whole thing would be a trick, but just as the door to the room was closing, she could barely make out the sound of heavy footsteps on the golden floor of the hallway outside.

Mishti silently slipped the door closed just as a small group of Zeakriesh passed by. Through the golden walls, Chloe could barely make out their words.

"Do you think those dragons will come back?" This voice belonged to a young woman.

"I hope not," a man responded. "One of them bit my finger off."

The young woman spoke again, in a lower voice. "Portia says we have to kill them, but they're so beautiful."

"Of course we have to kill them." The man's voice was harsher now "One of them bit my finger off. Stop being so sentimental."

They had passed now, and it occurred to Chloe that if these Zeakriesh continued down the hall and then turned the corner where the dragons hid, their entire group would be found.

But after several bated breaths, no screams or roars erupted. The Zeakriesh must have turned the other corner and never seen the dragons. Or maybe the dragons and Shields had simply hidden in another room.

At the silence, Julian let out a sigh of relief. There were times like this when his guard came down, and his true self shone through. He always looked older then. More tired. The lines on his face deepened, giving a hint to his true age of over a hundred.

But even more interesting, he had been just as relieved as the rest of them that their hiding spots had not been revealed. He was relieved they had not been caught.

He had said he wanted them to find the king. He had explained how doing so would help him. But for the first time, Chloe really felt it was true. He absolutely would turn on them when the time came, but maybe they'd have an easier time navigating the halls if she trusted him more completely.

But just before they could leave the room and resume their search, a sizzling, popping sound burst upward from the ground followed by a cloud of decaying gray smoke.

Her head jerked to the side. Quintus stood hunched over, holding his side with both hands. His injury must have worsened during their scramble inside the room. Maybe he'd twisted it the wrong way or maybe he'd accidentally run into something that poked at it. Whatever it was, it caused a drop of blood to fall to the ground. And a second drop would fall soon.

An almost-smile tugged at Julian's mouth seeing the wound he'd caused, but then his face twisted into a scowl. "Do something about that. The smell will lead them right to us."

Quintus held both his hands over the injury, his posture tense.

Chloe did her best not to look at Quintus. Not to look at the wound. She could not force him to let her heal it, no matter how ridiculous it was. If he stubbornly wanted to deal with it himself, she'd let him.

The agitated look in his eye turned to frustration as he conjured a scratchy wool bandage that would repel the blood more than absorb it. He fumbled, trying to wrap it around his waist. Though she watched him from the side of her eye, she still tried to stop herself from staring directly at him.

If she did, he'd see the eye roll that wanted to draw her gaze upward. This was *his* choice. She couldn't make it for him.

"Are you done yet?" Julian asked through a frustrated whisper.

Quintus had the wool bandage in place, and he had even conjured a second cotton bandage to go over it, which was too thin to do much. At least he was trying.

But he must have recognized his efforts were fruitless. In a huff, he removed both bandages, gathered them into a ball, and tossed them at Ludo.

The Fairfrost fae's blue-and-red eyes bugged out as he just managed to catch the bloodied fabric before it touched the ground.

While he bustled around the room looking for a place to set the rags without allowing them to touch any of the gold, Quintus lifted off his tunic in a flourish. Chloe couldn't help looking at him now. Did he have to remove his shirt with such intensity? This really wasn't the time for such thoughts, but her gaze immediately drifted to the lean muscles in his chest and stomach. Her own stomach flipped at the sight. Heat rose in her cheeks. Pretty soon she'd need a fan. She only barely registered how he held the tunic in his hands directly under the wound, stopping any drops of blood from falling to the ground.

Right, *blood.* This was no time to be focused on how his upper body was bare. She needed to focus on the blood he tried to catch using the tunic bundled in his hands.

That would work for a few minutes, but not for long. He needed a more permanent solution if they were going to go stomping through the castle again. But apparently, he had just the solution.

His head tilted to the side as he looked straight at Chloe. Even with his bare chest to compete with, she couldn't help being pulled into his gaze.

As soon as they locked eyes, he glanced down at the wound. "You can…" He nodded slightly, still staring at the wound. "Will you heal it? For me?"

She wanted to roll her eyes dramatically and say *finally* in the most obnoxious voice possible, but the heat in her cheeks still burned too much for her to speak coherent words. Instead, she gave a short nod and came to his side in only two steps. Using two fingers to gently prod the area around the wound, she got a better idea of what healing it needed. Only then was she able to ignore the magnificence of his appearance because now her apothecary instincts took over. Her mind focused in on the injury until there was nothing else in her mind at all.

Even after the quick examination, one thing was certain. This was still a magical wound. It would need more than a tincture or herbs and honey to heal it. If she'd attempted this after their first kiss in the clearing, when their magic had only started to return, she would have conjured more of the blue crystals that could absorb his blood. Then she would have stitched over the wound with fresh thread.

But so much had changed since then. Quintus's moon tattoo had a golden border around it now, and her stars probably did too. After their more recent kiss, her magic was more powerful than ever. She no longer had to settle for keeping the injury at bay. Now, she could heal it entirely.

Closing her eyes, she touched one hand against his stomach and one against his back. The wound sat directly between both of them. Even before she started, magic pulsed in her palms, crackling and sparking at the ready.

When healing an injury with magic, she usually just had to imagine the process in her mind exactly how it would have happened in real life. She did that now, except many of the thoughts that came to her were nothing like the healing she'd ever done.

She imagined removing the tiny remnants of the original crystals. Then she crushed a new set of blue celestine crystals and combined the dust with a dark purple liquid she couldn't even name. That mixture got poured into the wound. While it sat inside his body, she created a thick paste of crushed ruby berries from a Crystalfall bush, black soil from the ground, and a few drops of sparkling water from the waterfalls near the crystal caves.

In her mind, she used a golden spoon to smooth the mixture over his skin around the outside edges of the open wound. How had she known to use these ingredients? She'd never used any of these things to heal before. She didn't have names for the concoctions or explanations for how they would help.

Faerie itself must have helped her because thoughts continued to drift easily to her mind exactly when she needed them. Now she imagined using a soft green cloth to absorb all the liquid she had previously poured into his wound.

Next, she pressed his skin together. Where she usually would have stitched the wound, she ran her finger over it twice instead. In her mind, golden magic burst from her fingertips, bubbling over the skin she had touched. When she pulled her hand away, no trace of the wound could be found.

Nearly gasping, her eyelids flew open as she examined Quintus's side with her actual eyes. Just like she had seen in her mind, no trace of the wound remained on his skin.

Still, something wasn't quite right about this wound. The blood had stopped, and his skin and organs had no damage to them, that much she could feel. She brushed her hand over him slowly. Something of the poisoned magic still remained. She could feel that too. Maybe it would eventually go away, but he needed something that could keep it healed until then.

With one hand still against Quintus's back, she waved her hand in a circle. Doing so conjured a light blue celestine crystal into her hand. The raw gem was a little smaller than her thumb. It sparkled, giving off a light glow.

"Can you conjure me a leather string?" Her gaze flicked up to Quintus's eyes just long enough to ask, but she turned her attention straight back to the crystal.

She didn't know why or how, but she knew this crystal would keep him healed as long as he kept it close. When he handed her a thin leather string, she tied the ends around the top of the crystal, turning it into a necklace.

Then she draped it over his neck where it hung down his chest, hitting just above the stomach. Placing a hand over it, she looked into his eyes more closely. Really looking at him for the first time since healing the wound.

He stared back with an intense gaze that suggested he wanted to show his thanks with more than just words. And of course, she was reminded like a bucket of water splashing in her face that he still had no shirt on. She enjoyed the view far more than she wanted to admit, though she also enjoyed how it made her insides flip.

Still, they needed to find the king. She could stare longingly at Quintus later. Now it was time to focus on the reason they had entered the castle. The king. When she turned around, they were finally ready to continue their search again.

Except now Julian stared at her. Hard. His eyes had narrowed to tiny slits. "How did you get magic?"

"The same way you did." She shoved him toward the door, reminding him why he was there. "I touched the creation magic. Or, well, my hand was thrown into it. I was unconscious at the time."

"Then why do you have to touch *him* to use your magic." Julian's lip curled as he threw a pointed gaze toward Quintus.

Chloe raised an eyebrow. "That's because of you. After you destroyed Crystalfall, Faerie put a block on your magic. When I touched the creation magic, Faerie immediately put a block on my magic as well. But then I did a ritual, which bonded Quintus and I together." She left out the part about how she had only accidentally bonded herself to Quintus. Julian didn't need to know how she had intended to touch a rock, not Quintus's hand during that ritual. She shrugged. "Now I can access my magic, but only when I'm touching Quintus."

Not quite nodding, Julian stared harder at Quintus, or more specifically, at where his wound had been. Then he turned back to give that same hardened gaze to Chloe.

But the quiet moment didn't last long.

Perhaps they'd been talking too loudly. Or perhaps the Zeakriesh actually had found the dragons around the corner. Whatever the reason, the door to the room soon flew open. Portia stood in front of them with an armful of shards and rage shimmering in her eyes.

36

 caused so much pain to everyone in the room probably should have made Chloe angrier. Instead, seeing Portia with magical shards in her arms just filled Chloe with fear. She took a step back, stumbling over her wooden leg.

Last time she saw the woman, Portia tried to steal that foot. Would she succeed this time? Every hair on Chloe's arms stood on end. Her stomach lurched. Trembling broke out across her limbs.

No one else in the room reacted at all the way Chloe did. None of them screamed. Panic filled none of the eyes she could see.

Mishti drew a dagger, her face hardened and determined. "Now!" she called out.

On that cue, weapons from all around the room flew straight at the woman in her tight bun. Portia flashed her teeth and hurled a handful of balance shards into the room.

Golden Shields ducked and lunged to miss the magical items. Billows of smoke and shrapnel filled the air. Everything moved too fast for Chloe to tell if any of the shards had a target other than items in the room.

At least one of the Shields' weapons hit Portia, though. A shriek tore from her throat as she stumbled back into the hallway and dropped to the ground in a heap.

"I'm injured," she said so pathetically it no longer seemed genuine. "Get them! Kill them all. Look at what they've done to me."

The next voice that rose above the chaos was Quintus's. He lifted a fist and pointed it toward the doorway. "Hall formation."

A flurry of movement filled the room as the Golden Shields formed lines that filed out the door, not with perfect precision but practiced reliability. Dragons roared, soon barreling into the hallway with the others.

Weapons flew through the hallway. Some were shards, some the weapons the Shields had spent several days preparing.

Chloe's knees still knocked together too much to even walk.

Julian ducked when a weapon soared into the room. He scurried off to the wall that also held the doorway, except he moved far enough away from it that he couldn't be seen by anyone in the hall.

"Why are you still standing there?" he whisper-shouted at Chloe. He rolled his eyes when she didn't move. "A person as useless as you would have been cut from my followers long ago."

She couldn't think about what he meant by *cut* because fear gripped her mind too tightly. Closing her eyes, she forced herself to remember what she needed to do next.

Move.

That was it. That was the simple instruction she needed to follow. She needed to move so she wasn't a sitting duck by that open door and hallway full of weapons and enemies.

Move.

She said it to herself again, and this time, her feet began taking steps. It was such a tiny thing, something that would have been so easy for nearly anyone else. But for her, she could hardly believe she'd achieved this victory.

Whenever fear hit her and froze her in place, she always became completely useless. Everyone around her had to keep her safe, to force her to move when she needed to.

But she had promised Quintus she would be safe. She had promised she would take care of herself. So, when fear spread through her limbs and held her in place, she did what she had never been able to manage before.

She moved.

Soon, her back pressed against the wall next to Julian while she tried to catch her breath.

"Pathetic," Julian whispered under his breath.

Too bad for him, she couldn't have cared less what he thought of her. Her friends, Quintus, Mishti, Ludo, and the other Golden Shields who knew her better, would appreciate just how big of a triumph this was for her.

Now she just needed Shadow to come and help calm her racing heart. If Shadow never came, she might pass out soon. Her breathing had gotten too fast. She could tell because her chest ached, and her breaths never filled her lungs enough.

She had to get out there.

Panic whispered around her, forcing her to picture all the grotesque ways she might die. All the horrid ways the Zeakriesh might use their weapons to inflict pain. Even with her eyes open, she still saw awful visions in her mind. Blood. Gore. Broken bones.

Shivers shook through her shoulders. Would Shadow know to come to her when she couldn't even call her? She tried. She'd been able to move, but her thoughts spun too fast now to form any coherent thought.

When two Zeakriesh entered the room, Chloe's vision started funneling. Her breathing grew even shorter. One of them had an axe. One of them had a jagged dagger the length of a forearm.

Those could inflict so much damage. Too much.

She had to get out of there. She had to leave, or she would pass out. The visions in her head were too much to endure along with the sight of the Zeakriesh before her.

Seeing Julian, the two Zeakriesh rushed forward. "Julian! Let's get those ropes off you."

Scowling and checking the doorway, Julian used his foot to kick one of the balance shards on the ground. His kick lifted it high, and it hit the nearest Zeakriesh in the knee. The woman screamed, which got drowned out in all the chaos. She dropped her axe and suddenly stopped breathing. Her body shook and turned gray as she collapsed to the ground. By the time she fell, life had been sucked from her.

"Isabel," the other Zeakriesh said. He blinked at her once and turned to Julian. "What have you done?"

Julian checked the doorway again, then stepped forward just enough to grab the fallen axe with his bound hands. The other Zeakriesh rushed forward now, his eyes filled with rage.

But when he stepped close enough, Julian just slammed the axe into the man's chest, causing him to drop to the ground dead even faster than the woman had.

Taking one last glance at the doorway, Julian dropped the axe and pressed himself closer to the wall. He inched closer to Chloe too.

Maybe Chloe should have been grateful her life was no longer in danger, but how could she think of that when she'd just watched Julian murder two of his own people?

It was a good reminder that though he was on her side now, that would only be true until they found the king. And considering how easily he just killed his own soldiers, she couldn't imagine how much more easily he'd kill the rest of them if given the chance.

Her throat bulged with a swallow as she tried to step away from him. She had to get out of there. Panic still stretched through every muscle in her body. It hurt to breathe. It hurt to stand. Her body shook so much, she had to keep her shoulder against the wall just to keep herself from falling.

Shadow. She needed her dragon to help calm her, even if it was just so she could breathe properly again. But she still couldn't form a clear enough thought to send it to her dragon.

She had to get away. She had to go anywhere that wasn't this fight.

"Who has the crown?" Julian had moved too close, his pungent breath smelling of garlic and mildew filling the space between them.

Shaking her head was the only answer she could manage. Why would she ever tell him *that?* Especially right now.

But then his face turned to one of gentility. It struck her suddenly that he had likely been wealthy in the mortal realm. He had an air about him that spoke of privilege and grace. Something she knew well, since she too had once been part of a wealthy and respected family. When living with Vesper and Cosette, their family were more eccentric than respected. But before her parents died, her father's skill with the sword had won them all kinds of money. And because he could kill anyone who crossed him, it afforded them the highest respect as well.

Julian tilted his head kindly at her. "We can leave." He spoke slowly, soothingly. "I can take you away from here. Just tell me who has the crown, and I'll go get him. Then all of us can climb onto your dragon, and I'll tell you where it should take us."

Chloe shook and shook and folded her arms over her stomach, trying to breathe. Breathe.

"I will take you to safety. Where no one else can hurt you. Just tell me who has the crown."

Quintus had it. Imagining Quintus and Chloe escaping this fight on Shadow's back felt serene. She could imagine nothing better.

It didn't matter how crazy and untrue Julian's offer was, it was still tempting. Of course she knew he was lying. If he found out Quintus had the crown, Julian would surely kill her and go after him.

She knew that.

And yet, her mind kept latching onto his soothing words, begging her to consider them. She *wanted* to give up. She wanted to be taken far away from this fight to safety.

Her resolve kept her from it right then, but how long would it last while fear gripped her muscles so tightly?

The slightest grin crept onto Julian's face, revealing he knew how close she was to her breaking point. "I just need to know that one little thing. Tell me who has the crown, and I can take you away from here. We can leave this battle."

Hugging her arms tighter against her body, she managed to clench her jaw. Through her teeth, she said a single word.

"No."

Just then, Shadow crashed in through the window, shattering glass everywhere. She flew in fast, immediately pinning Julian against the wall with one leg. The creature then nuzzled her head against Chloe's side.

The dragon kept nudging until Chloe pulled her arms away from her stomach. She then wrapped them around Shadow's neck. Feeling the warmth of the golden scales against her cheek, brought her mind away from the fight.

Instead of seeing visions of gore and destruction, she only saw Shadow. Finally, Chloe's breathing started to even. It started to slow.

She managed to take in a breath that properly filled her lungs. She could do this.

Julian whispered again, his voice slightly more on edge from his soothing voice before. "Do *you* have the crown? You and I can get on this dragon right now, and I will take you straight to the king. I won't even try to hurt you."

It took three more beats of her heart. One. Two.

Three.

Finally, she turned to him with a look that was probably halfway between a smirk and a glare. "We have our own plan. Now get on my dragon and keep your mouth shut."

He squirmed, trying to release himself from Shadow's grasp. The attempt was unsuccessful, and soon, the dragon threw him onto her back. When Chloe managed to climb up with him, the ropes on his wrists had started to loosen. They still kept his hands bound in front of himself, but she'd need to have one of the others tighten the ropes as soon as possible.

If she had any skills with knots, she would have done it herself already.

Fear and panic still prickled inside Chloe but ignoring it became so much easier now. She grabbed her dragon's reins and looked at the doorway. "Go into the hallway, Shadow. Destroy anyone who isn't wearing a golden circlet."

Shadow roared and tore into the hallway.

Her wings flapped, sending wind through Chloe's hair. The movement brought Chloe's mind back to life just a bit more. She could do this. Yes, she'd gotten scared and froze in the middle of a fight, but she'd gotten herself out of it too.

And just because she needed a dragon to help her through her anxiety didn't make her less than anyone else. She wasn't useless. She wasn't pathetic.

She was Chloe.

Powerful healer. Clever mastermind. Protector of Crystalfall.

In the hallway, Shadow followed the fight around a corner and to the great hall. This part of the castle had the great split all the way through it, ending in a shallow canyon in the black soil beneath the castle.

The great hall now had walls on three of its sides, but the fourth side had nothing but open air.

Shadow roared and flew into the great hall. As she did, Chloe could see clearly that whatever rooms and hallways had once been beneath the great hall had all been destroyed now. A great distance sat between the floor of the great hall and the bottom floor of the castle. Three stories, four, maybe even five separated the two floors. If anyone fell from the open edge of the great hall, they would surely land too hard on the golden floor below to survive.

And without the support from walls beneath the floor of the great hall, standing on that floor very well could have meant death on its own.

But the Zeakriesh wouldn't stop until they'd won. So, fighting on the precarious floor was the only choice the Golden Shields had.

At least Chloe could do her part by not adding to the weight. She kept Shadow back, watching from the edge of the room. Chloe wasn't useless for failing to join the fight in the great hall. She did an equally important duty of keeping watch on Julian.

He huffed at her and tried to rip his hands free of the ropes holding them, but he did not succeed.

But soon, an even bigger problem appeared. Portia had returned.

Several Zeakriesh helped her hobble through the hallway as she limped. The whole thing seemed like a great ruse since the only injury she'd sustained was an arrow to the arm. And it had been in the fleshy part of her arm, too, so it couldn't have done much damage.

They stood at the end of the hallway, just a few steps outside the great hall. At the sight of her, several Zeakriesh retreated into the hallway with her until only Golden Shields stood on the floor of the great hall.

None of the dragons were there either. They must have been in a different part of the castle.

With all her Zeakriesh around her, Portia dug into her pockets and pulled out handfuls of shimmery balance shards.

Then she shouted in a voice as fierce and piercing as a blade. "I may have attempted to use these shards on you before, but there's no point in that now." She chuckled, her face growing more menacing by the moment. "Now I will use them on…"

Her eyes narrowed as she leaned forward. "The ground."

Chloe gasped, which caused several Golden Shields to glance up at her in surprise. They probably hadn't noticed until then that she sat on Shadow's back flying just outside the open edge of the room.

Portia laughed at the gasp. "The floor beneath you is unstable and the ground below is too far down for you to survive. One little explosion is all it will take to kill you all."

Then she raised her hand, ready to throw the first shards.

37

CHLOE'S GAZE SWEPT OVER THE Golden Shields standing in the great hall. She tried to think of a way to save them, but she already knew it would be impossible. Shadow could swoop in and catch some of them on her back, but there were too many people, and they were too spread out. And the ground, while a deadly distance away, was still too close to have enough time for Shadow to swoop in and catch everyone before they hit the ground.

But just as Portia went to throw the first shard, Mishti raised an eyebrow. "I wouldn't do that if I were you."

"Why not?" Portia looked at her feet, taking another step farther away from the great hall. But just as Portia knew, she stood in a safe area that had solid ground beneath her.

Instead of waiting for an answer, she hurled the first shard at the ground. The second shard came down almost as fast. Then she threw another and another until four shards hit the ground in quick succession, all in slightly different spots on the ground.

"Because," Mishti said over the sound of cracking and splitting gold beneath her feet. "Dragons are very protective of their riders."

By the time she finished speaking, the ground had given out. Each Golden Shield began to fall.

Chloe sent Shadow forward, going to catch Quintus first. But then she could suddenly see why Mishti had been so unconcerned.

A horde of dragons with sparkling and shimmering and electricity-filled scales swooped in from all edges of the castle. The Golden Shields must have called to them. Mishti's retort must have given the dragons just enough time to reach their riders.

Relief sent a breath from Chloe's throat. Shadow still caught Quintus onto her back, and she caught Ludo too, but all the other riders were saved in the next few moments by their own dragons. They flew up high, victorious faces staring back at their enemies.

Portia swallowed hard, shaking her head. "Kill them," she said desperately. "Kill them all!"

Mishti's stormy blue dragon with silver eyes flew up above the rest while Mishti stood tall on its back. "Come on, Shields. You know what to do. It is your sworn duty to protect this castle. Ride!"

Even Chloe was filled with an enormous sense of purpose. Pandemonium filled the castle and her insides. She had nearly lost sight of what they meant to accomplish.

But it wasn't just about finding some vile king who didn't even deserve the crown of Crystalfall. It was about freedom. Safety.

They fought so that Crystalfall could be a haven to all who needed a home.

With that powerful reminder of their purpose, the Shields raised their weapons, and their dragons swooped in.

Each blow delivered deadly retribution for all the wrongs the Zeakriesh had done. Many were cut down, decreasing the Zeakriesh's greatest advantage…numbers. Soon, the remaining Zeakriesh retreated. They stumbled away and trembled and could barely breathe as they attempted to run from the fight.

The Golden Shields ignored anyone who retreated, but any Zeakriesh who tried to kill, who tried to control, those were met with the purposed weapons of the Golden Shields.

At one moment, just when it seemed like the Zeakriesh had nothing left to give, Portia threw a golden goblet up toward Mishti and her dragon. The cunning woman knew exactly where to hit, which was clear once the goblet hit Mishti in the side.

A sharp breath puffed out of her as Mishti dropped to her knees onto her dragon's crackling scales. She tried to breathe but kept clutching her side instead. Mishti's dragon let out a great roar that shook the castle walls so hard, Chloe worried the rest of it might fall to the ground.

"How dare she?" Ludo said through his teeth. "Portia hit Mishti in her magical wound again. When this happened before, it took Mishti nearly a full day just to breathe properly."

Anger burned inside Chloe at the sight of her injured friend. She flew Shadow down, close enough to Portia to let the dragon snap her jaw at the woman.

With the dragon so close, Portia managed to grab onto Chloe's wooden foot. Her face snarled as she ripped the foot off Chloe's leg. Sucking in a breath, Chloe lunged to the side and barely managed to snatch the foot out of the air. Shadow had to do some quick and skillful flying to keep Chloe from falling to the ground.

In the midst of the tense moment, Portia pulled a small dagger from under her belt and threw it at Chloe's good leg. It landed with a hard slice right in the muscled part of Chloe's left leg. Pain sliced through the skin like flame and ice. She grunted and sank lower on Shadow's back.

Quintus jumped off the dragon, using his fae speed and strength to clamber across the ground until he'd come directly in front of Portia. The woman laughed in his face. She pulled a shard from her pocket.

But before she could do anything with it, he had his spear out with the arrowhead pressing against her neck. "You have hurt my beloved too often. I will not allow you to ever do it again."

When he went to drive the spear into her neck, she managed to toss the shard at him. Due to the angle, it only barely grazed his skin, but it dropped him to his knees all the same. He let out a heart-wrenching growl.

Her mouth turned to a grin as she pulled another shard from her pocket.

The blue crystal swinging against his chest glowed as he got to his feet. His spear shot forward again. It was shaky and the aim not quite right, but it still hit Portia.

The force of it caused her to stumble. If just the spear had pierced her, it might not have been enough, but Shadow managed to slam her claws against her chest too. The combined movement of both actions was just enough to make her lose her balance.

Portia's body teetered in the hallway, one side of it nothing more than open air. Her arms flailed, desperate to get her balance.

And then…she fell.

Her feet stumbled right off the edge of the golden floor, until they had nothing but rushing air beneath them.

No dragon swooped in to save her.

No one shouted in protest.

She just fell until her body slammed against the ground below. A crunching thud sounded out, confirming her immediate death.

It had all happened so fast, Chloe's mind processed the result faster than the cause.

She was dead.

Glancing around the side of Shadow, Chloe could see that no gemstone or magic or anything else would help now. She wasn't just badly injured. Life had left the woman completely.

They'd fought her for so long, and she'd survived often enough to seem immortal. She had done dreadful, horrible things. And now, in one short instant, she was gone forever.

The few Zeakriesh left in the castle retreated as fast as they could. They all raced as quickly as their legs could carry them.

Soon, the only one left was Julian.

They hadn't even entered the castle to claim it back. They'd been trying to sneak in, and somehow, they had claimed it anyway. The reality sparked like a tiny ember in Chloe's chest, so small she could barely feel it.

But the more reality started to settle in, the more that ember grew. They had done it.

They had reclaimed the castle and gotten rid of Portia for good.

All that was left now was to find the king and give him his crown.

Julian would still turn on them, but what could he really do now? Purpose burned and warmed Chloe's chest as Shadow and the other dragons congregated in the safest area of the castle.

She climbed off the dragon, yanking Julian along with her. Shadow landed in a golden hallway. She'd wait there until needed again. Before they did anything else, Quintus held his hand out to Chloe and pointed to the wound Portia had just sliced into Chloe's arm. With a nod, Chloe took his hand and healed the wound.

Once finished, she healed the damage Quintus had sustained from the shard and then she healed a few injuries in the other Golden Shields. It only took a few minutes and then they were finally ready to do what they had come to do.

Find the king.

At Quintus's direction, a few Golden Shields stayed with the dragons, at the ready. The other Golden Shields spilled into the hallway back into the formation they'd used before.

Chloe and Julian walked in the center. Quintus stood directly behind them. Golden Shields formed a circle or lines around them. Ludo walked among them. The only difference now was that Mishti still lay on the back of her dragon. Portia had attacked Mishti's magical injury, put there by Ansel. As previously, she refused to let Chloe try and heal it. Mishti would not recover soon.

But she would recover.

And they had enough Shields to protect the king, no matter what Julian tried.

For once, Julian stared at the people surrounding him and no longer adopted his casual body language. The color had drained from his face. He stepped heavily and his gaze kept darting from one Shield to the next. Every few moments, his face looked a little greener.

Chloe turned to him, basking in his discomfort. Then she raised an eyebrow. "Now, Julian, take us to the king."

38

The blood rushing through Chloe's veins pulsed from the victory she and the others had just claimed. Maybe she should have been more worried, but for the first time since realizing they had to work with Julian, she thought maybe they'd have a chance at keeping the upper hand.

His steps had turned shaky. He gulped hard each time she glanced at him.

He still led them through the castle, leading them to where he had the king hidden, but he kept looking at everyone around him. Sizing them up. No amount of surety filled his face. His face wore the expression of someone whose careful planning had now been ruined.

Good. The more worried he was, the better for the rest of them.

He guided everyone through a small hallway, then lifted a holey tapestry, which had a secret staircase hidden behind it. When they got to the bottom, a circular room lay before them.

With his hands still bound in ropes, he tried to push past the Golden Shields to get to the wall. Except, in that entire circular room, the walls were completely smooth. No doors or any other sort of opening lay ahead.

Chloe folded her arms over her chest, glaring at Julian as the Golden Shields easily stopped him from breaking past them. "What do you think you're doing?"

He snarled, his eyes flashing. "I need to find the door."

She glanced skeptically at the smooth walls around them. "I don't see any door."

His shoulders shook, trying to wrest himself out the grips of the Shields holding him. "It's there, but you have to feel for the latch that opens it. You can't see it."

"Tell us what it feels like," Quintus said, stepping up from behind.

Julian scrunched up his mouth, and for a moment, it looked like he intended to spit in Quintus's face. He didn't though. He just spoke again instead. "You think I'm that stupid? I'm not telling you anything. You either let me find the door or you'll never find your precious king."

Perhaps they could have found the door themselves, but they didn't know what the latch felt like. And they didn't know what to do with it once they found it.

Letting Julian do the work would go faster.

At Chloe's direction, the Golden Shields released Julian and allowed him to reach for the wall. They stood close at his sides, weapons at the ready if he tried anything.

After sliding his hand several times over the golden wall in nearly the same spot each time, Julian's eyebrows suddenly jumped upward. His fingers moved over the wall, and a door immediately swung inward, not revealing itself until it had opened.

Once it did, Julian attempted to step through the doorway first. The Golden Shields surrounding him immediately tackled him to the ground. He shook his shoulders and wriggled his body but failed to come anywhere close to freeing himself.

Chloe took a step through the doorway, but she only entered a short passageway that led to a larger room. She'd have to take several more steps to enter the actual room.

From behind her, Quintus spoke to the Golden Shields. "The rest of you stay out here and watch Julian while Chloe and I go in."

That command was followed by a distorted laugh from Julian. "You two are going in alone with no one to offer protection?"

Chloe glanced back to give him her best eyebrow raise. "The king won't need protection since *you* are going to be out here."

"Oh!" Julian said through a laugh. "Do what you want. But don't you think *anyone* else will need protection?"

Chloe immediately remembered how the king had tried to kill Quintus the last time he saw him. He might be slightly more subdued if Quintus gave the king his crown and clearly showed that he meant the king no harm. But maybe not. Maybe the king would want his son dead anyway.

While those thoughts roamed through her mind, Quintus seemed to have similar thoughts, though perhaps ones that involved her being injured. He stared at her carefully and breathed heavily through his nostrils.

When he glanced back at the Golden Shields in the room, he acted like it suddenly seemed much too small a group to help protect them from the king. Clearing his throat, Quintus gave new instruction.

"Tie Julian's ropes to the stair banister. You," he pointed to Jansher, one of the toughest-looking Golden Shields, "stay here with him. The rest of you, come with Chloe and me."

Julian was far too occupied with cowering before Jansher to offer another retort.

Stepping into the passageway again, Chloe now had Quintus close at her side as they moved toward the open room.

They moved slowly, almost on their tiptoes. It might be difficult to face what was in that room, but it had to be done.

But it turned out, the only thing they had to face was a locked door. They may have gone back to get Julian if the room had simply been empty with nothing in it, but a locked door was a challenge they could meet on their own. Especially now that Quintus had his magic back.

He dropped to his knees and stared carefully through the keyhole. Then he sent magic into the keyhole to determine what shape the key needed to be to open it. Pulling a golden stick from his magical pocket, he formed a key as easily as snapping his fingers.

It took a bit of checking and re-checking and a few adjustments, but soon, he fit the key into the lock and turned it easily. The clicking sound of the door unlocking proved his key had been successful.

Once again, they found themselves opening a door and carefully stepping into a room. It only took a moment to see Julian had kept his word and brought them exactly where he had promised.

In the center of the room, a tall fae with pointed ears and fair skin sat in a golden chair. His eyes were glazed over and tired. He had white-blond hair and crooked teeth, and he wore short breeches and a long gray coat over a navy blue vest with silver buttons. On one finger, he wore a ring sporting a polished blue gem.

His head shifted strangely at the sight of them, as if he couldn't quite get his neck to do what he wanted. And he didn't look directly at them, as if his eyes couldn't focus.

What had Julian done to him?

In any case, he wasn't in any state to deliver harm to them, although, that might have changed once he got his crown back.

Quintus gasped at the sight of him, reaching up to put a hand over his chest. He stared.

And stared.

Then he swallowed. Lowering his voice, he moved his head slightly closer to Chloe. "He looks the same as when I saw him last."

She hadn't expected that. Quintus had always assumed his father had been wearing a glamour, and even Dyani suggested the same. Then again, maybe the memories Faerie had tried to take from everyone just made his appearance seem strange, even to those who had once known him.

But now the time had come. Quintus even reached into his pocket. His hand stayed inside it for a few moments while he stared at this fae with white-blond hair and crooked teeth.

His father. The fae who had tried to kill him. They had finally found him.

Reaching for Quintus's arm, she looked straight into his eyes. "Are you ready? We can wait if you need to."

The king had made no sign of recognition toward any of them. His eyes stayed glassy. He acted only vaguely aware of the room around him.

Chloe's encouragement was all Quintus needed. With a deep breath, he pulled the golden and emerald crown from his pocket. When he stepped forward, the Golden Shields came in close behind him, ready to protect.

Finally, he stood in front of the king and held the crown out to him. "For you," he said.

But the king did not move. He did not speak. The only thing he did was blink. Whatever Julian had done to him, it had affected him deeply.

Quintus spoke through the side of his mouth in a whisper. "He cannot even move."

Squeezing Quintus's bicep, Chloe tried to offer encouragement once again. "I'm sure he'll get his strength back, or his mind back, or whatever it is he has lost once he has the crown again.”

Nodding Quintus took a step closer. He went to put the crown on the king’s head but pulled it away at the last moment. Instead, he dropped it slightly lower and lifted the king’s hand. Even at that touch, the king gave no indication he felt anyone’s touch or heard any voices.

But now, Quintus moved the king’s hand and the crown closer together until the king’s finger touched one of the emeralds.

The moment his fingertip touched the crown, a shower of sparks burst between them. The emerald sparks were so large, so spectacular, that they rose nearly as high as the ceiling.

Quintus took a step backward, his eyebrows shooting upward. If they’d had any doubt, it disappeared.

This was most certainly the king of Crystalfall. And now, all that was left was to place the crown on his head.

After only a short moment of recovery, Quintus did just that. He stepped forward, looked his father in the eye, and then dropped the golden and emerald crown onto the king’s head.

Showers of magic burst from the crown, unlike anything Chloe had seen before. She had been there when Brannick was crowned High King of Faerie. She had seen how his crown showered and sparked with magic as it dropped onto his head.

But this was even more spectacular. Crystalfall truly differed from the other courts. This crown seemed to have more power, more magic, more majesty than anything else in Faerie.

With that thought, the glazed look in the king’s eye started to fall away. He blinked, reaching out his arms and stretching his fingers.

And then he started to laugh. A *wild* laugh.

“Yes!” His fingers shook as magic danced around and through them. “Yes, finally!” Another crazed chuckle left his lips before he spoke again. "Faerie can block me from my magic no more."

By then, Chloe recognized his voice, but it was too late now. Too late for anything.

He *had* been wearing a glamour. He had tricked them all. But now he grabbed the ring with the polished blue gem and tore it off his finger.

The glamour fell away, revealing not the pointed ears of a fae but the rounded ones of a mortal. A large mole the size of a thumbnail adorned his chin. His crooked teeth straightened as the rest of his facial features came into view.

The white-blond hair changed to a warmer, golden shade. *Julian.*

Julian stood before them wearing the crown. How he had gotten past Jansher and into this room before the rest of them, she could not guess, but he must have known of a secret passage. He must have had this planned long before they ever got to the castle.

"But…" Quintus stumbled backward, tripping over his feet. "You are mortal."

The savage laugh from Julian's throat grew while the magic around him did too. "Yes. A mortal. You fae are so simple-minded to believe you are the only ones who could wear a crown. I made this one myself after I got my magic. Only Clara ever believed I could do it. But she must die now that I have my magic back. She and Revyn."

His face twisted into the most horrible smile. "And all of you must die too."

The Golden Shields standing behind them were the only reason Chloe and Quintus got out of the room. They yanked them away just as Julian blasted magic toward them. The walls blurred as someone carried Chloe away.

She only barely registered the dead body of Jansher at the foot of the stairs before she got pulled upward. Quintus had come back to himself by then.

He never glanced back as he sprinted far ahead, lifting and helping the others so they could avoid the king coming for them.

Dread hadn't hit yet. Nor fear. Nothing but shock unraveled through her limbs.

And then a strange thing suddenly made sense. This was why Quintus had survived his father as a child. Quintus had outrun him.

Quintus had the speed of a fae, and his father, a mortal, did not.

But though mortal, Julian had frighteningly powerful magic. Magic they had just handed him. And he would do exactly what he had done before. He would immediately wield it for evil.

Somehow, they reached the dragons. Somehow, they flew away.

Emerald magic exploded out from the castle while Julian's wild laugh chased after them. Her heart stammered. Ached. It all hit her then. Hit like a boulder smashing into her chest.

What would Julian do now that he had gotten his magic back?

And what would they ever be able to do to stop him?

ACKNOWLEDGMENTS

Thank you so much for reading this book! Chloe and Quintus have been through quite a journey together, and I am so grateful I get to share it with you. If you enjoyed the book, I would be honored if you left a review for it.

A huge thanks goes to my very close author friends, the Queens of the Quill. All of you have a special place in my heart. Your support and encouragement helped me get through this year, which was definitely not my best year, health-wise. But now that I'm finally feeling better, and thanks to you, I feel like my writing is better than ever.

To everyone who read the book early and provided an editorial review, thank you for reading the book so fast and for providing such amazing reviews!

I'm so grateful to my wonderful editors, Deborah Spencer and Justin Greer. You helped make this book so much stronger and cleaned up some of the plot issues that needed work. You guys are the best!

I can never give enough appreciation to my amazing book cover designer, Angel Leya. You always manage to make the cover so much better than I ever imagine. I was so excited about how this cover turned out!

Thank you to the illustrator @allexandracurte who created the most beautiful art of Chloe and Quintus. Working with you was a dream, and the illustration turned out stunning.

To my husband, who has helped me though so much in this life, thank you for standing by my side and helping me to see where I have room for growth. And thank you for always being willing to accept council from me on your own areas of growth. You make me feel like we are the perfect team, and I am beyond grateful to have you.

ABOUT THE AUTHOR

Kay L. Moody is proud to be an epic fantasy romance author who gets to create worlds for a living. ;) Her books feature strong female characters, court intrigue, royalty, magic, and slow burn romance with men who fall first.

With 17 romantasy books across 4 complete series, she's no stranger to hidden princesses, deadly competitions, or couples who go from enemies to lovers. Her books have sold more than 100,000 copies worldwide and have earned accolades including *Best Fantasy Book* (Many Books, Dec 2023) and *Bestseller: Fantasy* (BookRaid, Apr 2024).

Her favorite non bookish things are pizza, summertime, the color pink, and having pretty nails. She lives in the western USA with her husband and four sons. Follow her on social media to stay in touch (@kaylmoody).

ALSO BY KAY L. MOODY

Fae and Crystal Thorns
Flame & Crystal Thorns
Shadow & Crystal Thorns
Blade & Crystal Thorns
Curse & Crystal Thorns
Wrath & Crystal Thorns
Standalone: Nutcracker of Crystalfall

The Fae of Bitter Thorn
Heir of Bitter Thorn
Court of Bitter Thorn
Castle of Bitter Thorn
Crown of Bitter Thorn
Queen of Bitter Thorn

The Elements of Kamdaria
The Elements of the Crown
The Elements of the Gate
The Elements of the Storm

Truth Seer Trilogy
Truth Seer
Healer
Truth Changer

Visit **kaylmoody.com/beauty** to download a bonus story,
Bargain of Power and Beauty, for free.

BONUS STORY
BARGAIN OF POWER AND BEAUTY

Visit **kaylmoody.com/beauty** to download your copy

To receive special offers, bonus content, and info on new releases, sign up for Kay L. Moody's email list! You'll also get this story for FREE. *Bargain of Power and Beauty* is a romantic standalone story from the Fae and Crystal Thorns series.

Power is dangerous. Beauty is fatal. Love is the only risk worth taking.

WRATH & CRYSTAL THORNS

In a court of chaos, their love is the most powerful weapon.

Quintus must be protected at all costs. The words echo in Chloe's heart, a desperate vow against the encroaching darkness. The newly returned king of Crystalfall plans a terrible ritual, one that requires the blood and sacrifice of his own son. Quintus.

Her beloved Quintus, the true heir, is the king's final key to ultimate power. While Quintus spirals into despair from their defeat, Chloe must find strength for them both.

She must rally her found family of Golden Shields and face an enemy who seems to know their every move before they make it.

This final battle isn't just for a throne; it's for his life. And she cannot, will not, let Quintus fall.